The Mystery Of Chaco Canyon

A Novel of the American Civil War

Doug Hocking

Buckland Abbey, L.L.C.

Buckland Abbey, L.L.C.
Sierra Vista, AZ
Published and Printed in the U.S.A.

This is a work of fiction. Some of the characters, organizations, and events portrayed in this novel are taken from actual history, and some within are products of the author's imagination or are used factiously.

ISBN: 978-0-9907619-2-1
LCCN: 2014920713

Dedication

To my wife Debbie and to Sherrill who helped
And to Mother who never let me forget that
My great-great-grandfather still had books in print

Other Books by Doug Hocking

Massacre at Point of Rocks (2013)

Short Story Anthologies

Outlaws and Lawmen (2012)
"Marshal of Arizona"

Dead or Alive (2013)
"The Bounty"

Broken Promises (2014)
"Echo Amphitheatre"

"It happened in the Canyon of the Gambler in that very place"
Traditional Jicarilla introduction to a legend

Table of Contents

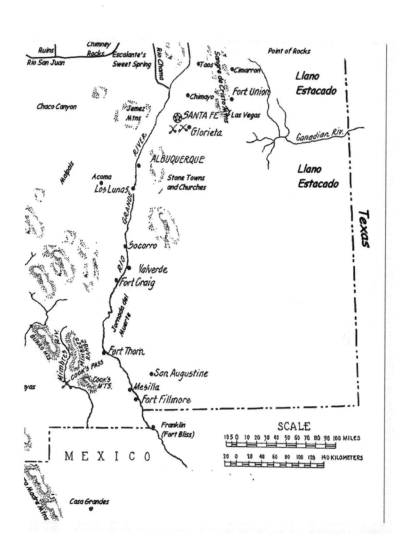

Chapter 1

Knocked on the Head

Alone for the moment, Dan sat with his legs dangling in space and looking down on the pueblo they called Bonito, Suspended over a precipice summed up his feelings about his quest. The trouble had all started when Topper made a dying appeal that sent him on this years-long quest. Now he'd left behind a trail of dead men, his friends had been wounded and were still in mortal danger and Sebriana . . . But she was a different problem which began when a young woman took him by the hand and led him into the dark away from the *baile,* to a fandango of a different kind. Or was it different? She was here, her life at risk, and he didn't feel right about any of it. Maybe it all started with another *baile*, Topper's birthday party and what a merry jig the old man had led him.

The frontiersman stood tall with broad shoulders, his hat nearly touching the *vigas*, blackened roof beams, of the long, low, smoky room. His skin bronzed and his eyes squinted from the sun, he gazed purposefully through the crowd of drinkers and gamblers. A broad leather belt carried a Bowie knife and Colt's cap and ball revolver. He wasn't a man to be trifled with. Spotting his quarry, he strode purposefully across the room.

"Professor, come along," the frontiersman, Dan Trelawney, said quietly. "We should be going. You know there hasn't been an honest *monte* game in Santa Fe since Doña Tules died." Willowy and beautiful even in middle age, Doña Gertrudis Barcelo, La Tules had treated Dan as a special guest in her *sala*, gambling parlor, on notorious Burro Alley in sight of Santa Fe's Palace of the Governors.

"Gertrudis was a beautiful lady, Daniel," said Professor Tristan Ottiwell Pendarvis, known as "Topper" from his initials. "Her body was thin, her skin smooth and unwrinkled, her hair long and black. Her blue eyes were pools a man could drown in. The curve of her naked buttock was round and firm" Topper sighed and closed his eyes. Perhaps he had been one of her lovers. She would have enjoyed his intelligence and wit but not the leathery skin, liver spots, and hunched back of the small man.

Dan wondered if the suggested liaison was possible. It was the last day of March, 1860. Topper had told Dan he could remember the War of Revolution, making him at least 80, maybe 84 since he could "remember." He was still in good shape, wiry and rugged though suffering from a palpitating heart that left him short of breath in Santa Fe's high mountain air. Although his hair was white, it was thick and wavy; he didn't look much over 60. Tonight he was dressed in a long, black coat that had seen better days.

"It's my birthday, Daniel. I will celebrate."

Dan glanced around the low ceilinged, smoky *sala*. The room was filled with the people of the capitol, reveling soldiers back from chasing Utes and Jicarillas, and Mexican women in loose white blouses that left much of their breast exposed as they gambled, drank, and smoked *cigaritos*, Mingling with them were Mexican men of all classes from the poor farmer with a folded *serape* across his shoulders to the bold *ricos* in fine vests decorated in silver and black embroidery. Mountain men in fringed, beaded buckskin rubbed shoulders with merchants from the States in black broadcloth suits. Anglo women, still a rarity in New Mexico, were absent. They were never seen in public drinking, smoking, or gambling, and with blacks and Indians, they were barred from the *salas*. The thick air was a choking mix of *piñon* smoke from the *horno*, tobacco, alcohol, and unwashed bodies.

Dan sensed he and Topper were being watched. Peering through thick smoke that stung the eyes, he saw two men observing him closely. They shied away to a dark corner when they saw Dan looking back at them. He didn't recognize them. Some rough looking *vaqueros*, cattle drovers, debouched themselves in the *sala*. They, too, seemed to be watching. Dan wondered if they were contemplating mayhem. It would not be uncommon on Burro Alley. The professor had been lucky at cards all evening. These nighthawks might be after the elder gentleman's purse. A group of Texans avoided Dan's gaze, turning away suddenly and pointedly.

Uncouth, dressed in a mix of buckskin and Mexican clothing, Texans were not admired. They raided caravans on the Santa Fe Trail, giving in explanation the notion that New Mexico as far west as the Rio Grande was part of Texas. The caravans were trespassing. The territorial dispute should have been settled when Congress made New Mexico a territory, but memories were long on both sides. Texas was hard. The land was hard with harder soil, harsh weather, and hard enemies. Mexicans, Indians, and outlaws vied with each over who was most cruel. Thieves and the unscrupulous were drawn to Texas like flies to a dead buffalo. Often, they were drawn directly from political office in the States. It was a land of ne'er-do-wells and scoundrels, both brave and craven.

"Topper," Dan began, before realizing he'd lost track of the old man. Dan looked for the men in black who hid in the shadows and followed the target of their gaze. He soon found the professor. He was back in a corner being smothered between the breasts of a very young lady wearing a cheap hair comb. Her rouged nipples showed through and above the neckline of her loose blouse. She was busy blowing in Topper's ear.

"Professor," Dan said, "people are watching us…"

"Let them watch," Topper replied. "No one denies an old man his pleasure."

"Topper," Dan continued nervously, "we should go. It isn't safe here."

Dan was no coward, but he was alert to danger.

"Nonsense," Topper replied. "I'm celebrating. It's after midnight, so it's my birthday. Señorita Saturnina has volunteered to help me celebrate." The buxom woman beamed prettily, exposing a gap-toothed smile.

"Happy birthday, Professor," Dan replied. "We should go. You don't want to do this."

"Of course, I do," Topper smirked. "I may not be able, but I want to. Besides, I've already checked, and no one vouched for the girl's father. I'm pretty sure he's not a Mason, so I haven't promised not to violate her chastity." Topper gave a convincing leer.

"Maybe she'll come with us to La Fonda or your rooms." Dan started him toward the door as Saturnina, abandoning the old man for the moment, latched onto Dan.

Saturnina wanted to gamble and drink. She didn't want to leave the *sala* just yet and she didn't want to let the handsome young man go. Dan looked around again as the girl clutched his arm. He'd lost Professor Topper Pendarvis. Rolling his eyes heavenward, Dan viewed the great, smoke-blackened *vigas*. Not as fine, he recalled, as the herringbone pattern of smooth, peeled wood *latillas* that was the ceiling in La Tule's *sala*. Nor was the Saturnina anywhere near so refined or pretty.

Dan thought he'd captured Topper, but he was intercepted by a small troll, small for a troll anyway, average-sized for a man. Its features were a mass of knobs: high knobby cheeks, prominent knobby, cleft chin, knobby ears, and a knobby brow-ridge covered in great tufts of eyebrow. Its deep-set eyes were merry and sparkling; its face was decorated by a giant handlebar mustache framed by sideburns. Its uniform was impeccable. Its breath was deadly and combustible. Dan had noticed the officer as soon as he'd entered the *sala*. Captain Henry Sibley of the 1st Dragoons had been sitting with his back to Dan playing *monte* and drinking *aguardiente* in company with a large man in fine clothes. Dan didn't think Sibley had noticed him, but he had.

"Daniel Trelawney," the captain breathed, "how are you? Does this mean Roque Vigil is somewhere about? I want to talk to you both."

"Henry," Dan replied, "I'm fine. How're you doing? I'm trying to catch Topper. He's got a couple of young ladies in tow and is headed out for adventures too wild for a man his age."

"Daniel," Henry continued despite the plea, "I need to talk to you and Roque. Major Canby is getting up an expedition against the Navajo come spring green-up. I can get you both on as scouts. Good pay."

"I don't know," Dan replied. "We haven't done any scouting since we worked with Major Carleton against the Jicarilla in '54 and '55. I saw things I never want to see again. I don't like working against families."

"We're going out to confront their warriors," said Sibley, "and recapture the sheep and cattle they've stolen. We don't plan to kill families."

"Never do," Dan replied bluntly. "Will the Mexican auxiliary militia be coming along to take slaves?"

"Think it over," Henry said. "It's a prime job."

"I'll think on it," Dan said without conviction.

Dan knew the murder of whole families and the slaving wasn't Captain Sibley's fault. The Utes, who hated the Navajo, as well as Mexican raiders, would show up to "help out." They'd murder and take slaves. They'd been doing it for centuries, and the Navajo returned the favor with equal gusto whenever they could. By and large, the Navajo weren't innocent; they stole more livestock than any other tribe and took more slaves.

Dan studied Sibley's drinking companion. It took Dan a moment to place the big, well-dressed gentleman. He'd been introduced to Albert Pike by Topper. Pike was a brother Master Mason, but Dan didn't care for him. Pike was a Southerner who professed strange ideas about slavery and the nature of God.

Searching the room, Dan worried about Topper. Over the last few months he had been revealing secrets to Dan about a vast lost treasure Topper believed was hidden out in the Navajo country. Since coming West in 1849, Dan had heard many tales of mysteries hiding in desert and mountain. He set most of them aside as tall tales, but Topper showed him that many of these had a basis in truth that had been garbled in the telling. Dan had seen lost cities and magic runes carved into the rock.

Topper's tales seemed less likely than most, but Dan had spent his childhood around sailors who spoke of currents and tides, sea routes, prevailing winds, and strange voyages. Sailors claimed voyages and landfalls no scholar ever put in books. The old man's tales were possible if very unlikely. The Israeli tribe of Dan might have sailed to the Rio Grande just as the Egyptians had. Warrior monks of the Crusades might have come as well. Dan wanted proof and doubted very much that Topper had it.

His secrets raised the hair on the younger man's neck. Men would kill for what Professor Pendarvis knew if it contained even one grain of truth or if they believed it did. Nine days before their night on the town, Dan began to notice men trailing them. He had a sixth sense possessed by men who survived on the frontier; things not seen, heard, felt or smelled consciously provided warning. Men in black suits ducked into shadows when Dan looked behind. Texans seemed to be headed in the same direction as Dan and Topper more often than seemed right. Seven nights before a party of Mexicans had attacked Topper before Dan drove them off.

"Daniel," he had said, "they just wanted to rob me. It happens all the time."

With his poor clothes, the professor didn't seem to Dan a likely target for robbery. But wealth was relative, and more than one *paisano* thought all *gavachos* rich. Unlike the professor who seemed aloof from worldly cares, these brushes made Dan more vigilant. Alerted, he saw more lurking shadows. Furtive figures flitted and worried him. By the evening of Topper's revelry, Dan's skin tingled in anticipation of unseen danger.

Once again, he'd lost sight of Topper. He studied the terrain more carefully with Saturnina still entangled on his arm. Her sweet scent disguised her lack of regular bathing and good hygiene. The stink of tobacco smoke, spilled tequila, and Taos Lightning and the stench of too many unwashed bodies too close together were making Dan nauseous and causing his head to swim. A poorly made *horno*, beehive-shaped fireplace, in the corner leaked smoke and heat into a room already too warm and smoky.

When a young girl moved out of the way, Dan glimpsed a small, white-haired figure. He was entwined with her as the two challenged *monte*. A gloomy Mexican trying hard to look *rico* dealt out four cards face up using the Spanish deck of forty cards. Topper and his new companion each selected one of the four by placing their coins next to the selected card, thereby betting that its suit would be matched by the fifth card dealt. If the fifth did not match any suit previously dealt or if no one had bet on the suit that came up with the fifth card, the pot went to the house, the *sala*, giving it a significant advantage.

Monte referred to the mountain of discards left when all forty cards had been dealt in five-card hands. The Spanish suits were coins, cups, swords, and clubs. The three court cards were Jack, Horse, and King.

Card counting might help at little, and Pendarvis had the mind for it, but *monte* was mostly luck. In time, the house would win.

The professor chose coins, and his companion took swords. The fifth card was the King of Coins, and Topper won. He consoled the girl with a small coin. They bet on the next deal as Dan made his way across the room encumbered by Saturnina. When he finally arrived at the *monte* table, the professor introduced Dan to his new lady friend.

"Daniel, I want you to meet Apolonia. She's as lovely as her name implies."

She was lovely. Dan hoped she wouldn't smile and ruin the effect. Instead, she farted loudly. She was undoubtedly a *refrito* epicure.

Encumbered now with two ladies, Dan could only watch in horror as Topper walked across the room and stepped out of the gambling den into the dark streets of the City of the Holy Faith of Saint Francis, Santa Fe. Two men in black coats stepped out behind him.

It took Dan some minutes and a few coins to satisfy the ladies' greed and vanity, convincing them they were perfectly beautiful. He pled an upset stomach that left him unable to pleasure them both, but he promised to return another night. Finally free, Dan stepped into the darkness of Burro Alley.

He heard voices in the dark.

"Tell us what we want to know," said one voice. It was followed by a slap.

A small man broke free of the dark and hurried past

Dan. It was Topper who was quickly corralled by an arm extended from the murky gloom.

"Give us the book that contains the secrets of the Masons," demanded the voice connected with that arm. The sound of a heavy blow followed. Topper broke free and ran again into the arms of a third villain waiting in the dark. The altercation, thought Dan, sounded like a Masonic initiation.

The second man was unfolding what might have been a hood. Dan realized that they must plan to kidnap Topper. Interrogation required time and privacy. Dan thought Topper safe enough for the moment.

The third man struck Topper with a heavy thud.

"Tell us where it is hidden or die!" the dark man roared.

Dan heard the click of a revolver being cocked. Now he worried. What if they already had most of the information and needed only a simple key, Topper's journal, to unlock them. Just like the three brothers of Masonic legend, these assailants must themselves be Masons to know this much.

"Never," Topper said quietly.

Shocked into action Dan drew his pistol cocking it as he did.

"Unhand him," Dan cried. His words sounded silly in his own ears, but these words were all that came to mind. The entire episode struck him as bizarre.

As his eyes adjusted to the dark, Dan saw Topper grappling with the hand that held his assailant's gun. Blam! A blinding flash stole Dan's vision. The assailant pushed Topper away as the old man crumpled to the ground. Dan heard him fall.

Firing at the sounds the third thug made, Dan heard his bullet strike flesh making a sound like a penny dropped on a drum. The man staggered and Dan guessed the dark-coated villain was hit in the gut. Dan watched transfixed as the wounded man tried to lift his weapon. Failing to raise it high, he fired hitting Dan in the leg, knocking him to his knees. Still game, Dan fired back. Smoke and flashes of shots blinded him. He heard boots strike cobbles and the sound of a body being dragged.

Leg still numb Dan was unable to stand, and so crawled to Topper and cradled his head.

"Daniel," he whispered, "listen."

"You're all right then. You'll be okay," Dan mumbled.

"No, Daniel," he breathed, "listen because I haven't got much time, and there is much still to say." He coughed blood and weakened by the spasm went silent. His chest expanded, and he resumed, "It's in the ritual. They hid it in the ritual."

"What do you mean, Topper?" Dan pleaded. "Stay with me."

"Can't," Topper croaked and coughed again. "I'll soon depart for that undiscovered country. Think. What could be better? Hidden…in the ritual. Not in order. Use what you know. Use your brain." He gasped again. "Let your brothers help you. Find it for me. Quest…" He was fading. "Swear."

"Okay, Topper," Dan sobbed. "I swear. You have my oath, but I need you to help me find it. I'm not ready to go without you."

Topper smiled faintly and said in a voice barely above a whisper, "You can. You must." He coughed blood, shuddered, and lay still. Cradled in Dan's arms, Topper who had been a mentor to Dan was dead. The younger man, a tough frontiersman, sobbed.

"Danito, what has happened?" asked Roque running

to his partner. "I hear pistol shots on a dark night in Santa Fe. Naturally, I think of you and come running." He clutched his pants in one hand holding them up and his pistol in the other at the ready. Roque looked to the blood trail left by the man Dan had gut shot, and then he looked to Topper.

"He's been murdered, Roque," Dan replied. "Topper is dead."

Roque knelt and put his ear to Topper's chest. "His heart still beats. We must get him to his casa."

Dan, visibly shaking with grief, agreed. "Roque, we must get to the Professor's casa immediately! *Andale, amigo*! We must take Topper."

Feeling returning to his wounded leg, Dan rose. The two big men, one limping, cradled the old man's sagging body between them. Dan limped and slowed them. They moved as fast as they were able down streets and alleys to Topper's home. As they turned the last corner, a light shone from Topper's open doorway. Three men in dark clothing, the same, Dan thought, as had shot Topper, were emerging from the professor's casa. The last man cast an oil lamp back into the room clutching his stomach as he did so.

"*Halto!*" ordered Roque, but they fled. Roque drew and fired without effect. Setting Topper gently against a wall, the two turned toward the flames. They found the door stove in, the mattress slashed, trunks turned out, bookshelves turned over, and the books ripped apart. Flames grew, feeding on books and mattress.

Behind them Topper croaked, "The *nicho*. Behind the *nicho*."

Challenging smoke and flame, Dan fought his way to the far side of the room. A *nicho*, a storage place recessed in the wall, lay open with its door torn free, and its shelves swept clean.

"Roque, tell the professor the *nicho* is empty."

"Thank the Great Architect," Topper replied relaying through Roque. "They didn't find it. Pull the shelves out. Look behind."

The thieves hadn't uncovered the secret compartment. Grasping the shelves Dan pulled, and the back of the *nicho* came free to reveal a spacious compartment within the wall. From this compartment, the young man extracted a thick parfleche, a protective rawhide bundle, and fled with it through thickening smoke and flame.

He handed the parfleche to Topper who cradled it to his bloody chest. "It's here. The Master's secrets are not lost."

"Time to leave before we face too many questions," said Roque, helping Dan lift the professor once more. "Fortunately, the *viejo*, he is not yet feeling pain."

Together they carried Professor Pendarvis into the shadows and through dark streets to their rooms.

With no civilian doctors around, the military doctor from Fort Marcy was called, and as Roque bound Dan's bleeding leg, the doctor worked to save Topper.

"If he was a younger man," said the doctor in time, "I would say he didn't have much chance and faced a long recovery. But this is an old man, and he is wounded in the abdomen. I don't think any vital organs are damaged. I have removed the bullet and a bit of his shirt. If the bleeding stops and if there is no infection, he may live but probably not."

In the morning, Kit Carson arrived with a Jicarilla Apache medicine man, *Shitaá Piishíí,* Father Nighthawk, who looked under Topper's bandages, made and added a poultice, and brewed a thick tea for the professor to drink.

The professor was able to speak in whispers, and the old men chatted amiably in Spanish

Kit explained the shaman's presence. "We can't let a valued brother depart early for that undiscovered country from whose borne no traveler returns." A simple man whose speech came from the deep backwoods, Kit loved the big words of the Masonic ritual. It had been he who had vouched for Dan and Roque admitting them for the first time to the Lodge.

"Kit, I need to speak to you privately." Dan led him into the next room. "I thought Topper was dying last night, and I made him a promise."

"Promise is a promise, Dan." He rested his hand on Dan's shoulder.

Dan nodded. "He's been searching here in New Mexico these last 10 years for something as fantastic as unicorns."

Kit smiled. "I've heard of them."

Dan went on. "I don't know how long he was chasing dreams and fantasies before that."

"Are you sure," said Kit softly, "that they're fantasies? I've seen some things I hardly believe. You've seen some of them, too."

"When I was a child in Greenport near the ocean, sailors delighted in telling stories to amaze, that made a boy's eyes large and round. Topper's stories are that strange. How many years should I devote to chasing shadows? My whole life, like he has?"

"Perhaps."

Dan's frustration was obvious. "It'll be dangerous. There are others that believe Topper's stories and are willing to kill for information."

"You haven't been inclined to much fear before," said Kit.

"And it's more than one man can handle alone," insisted Dan. "I haven't the right to ask anyone to follow me on my quest. I haven't the right to risk their lives."

Kit smiled as strangely as the Mona Lisa. "Wait and see who volunteers. It'll be their choice, not yours."

Roque Vigil burst in on them leaving the *curandero*, a folk healer, he had brought at the professor's side. Both the professor and Father Nighthawk greeted the elderly Mexican as an esteemed colleague. Roque was almost as tall as Dan and as broad shouldered. He was dressed Mexican style, wearing moccasins and rawhide leggings tied below the knee. Over these his silver *concho* adorned pantaloons were open to the thigh, the *conchos* serving as great buttons to open and close the seam. A red sash at his waist concealed a pistol and very large, sharp knife. A white shirt was partly concealed by a black, felt vest embroidered in black with silver buttons. Thirty-year-old Roque, always on the lookout for pretty girls, was careful of his appearance and of what he rode.

"I have news," said Dan's Mexican partner. "A dead man was found by the *rillito*. The man Dan shot, I think. I have seen the body and pulled back the shirt to see he was gut-shot. He wore a strange garment under his shirt, white and covered in Masonic symbols."

Both Dan and Kit shook their heads never having heard of a Mason wearing such a garment. From the other room, Topper, whose ears were sharp, called weakly. They went to his side.

"Years ago," began Topper, "Joseph Smith was made a Mason, and I shared my secrets with him. That's why Brigham Young took the Mormons West. The man you killed was a Danite, a secret warrior." Exhausted he fell silent as his two doctors fussed and told the Masonic brothers not to disturb him further.

"Kit, there's more than just these Danites," Dan exploded. "Last night, there were Texians watching us and Mexicans, too."

"Hush and come with me, Dan. You too, Roque." Leaving the house, Kit led them to the Masonic Lodge, and they entered. "We should be safe from cowens and eavesdroppers here. You're both Masons, same as me, entered, passed, and raised. You've been knocked in the head and so has your friend Rojo."

Roque sighed. "The Pope, he is so anti-Mason, I thought you would never take a Catholic."

Kit nodded. "We take all men what fear God, no matter what name they know him by."

Dan looked at Kit. "I never thought the Lodge would accept Rojo. He's Jicarilla Apache."

"He believes in God," said Kit. "As Masons, you three can share Topper's secrets among you and with no one else."

Dan considered this a moment. "What about Albert Pike. Topper has told him things?"

Kit pondered. "I would tell him nothing." He would say no more.

Back at their rooms, they tended to Topper. Age was against him. He got no worse, but no better either. Father Nighthawk and the *curendero*, coming to see him often, just shook their heads.

Father Nighthawk said, "He has lost touch with his *Power*. Somehow he has offended his *Power*."

Dan pondered. What was Topper's *Power*? The way that Nighthawk used *Power*, he meant some natural force that assisted Topper's scholarship. It was hard to imagine what it could be. Dan wondered if Topper knew. He and Father Nighthawk might have discussed it. It must be bound to secret knowledge locked in books, and revealing it to the wrong person might offend such a *Power*.

"That's crazy," thought Dan.

One day when no one else was about, Topper called Dan to his side. "I told Pike too much. Less than you suspect, but enough. I've always been able to sense who to trust, and I did not trust Brother Albert."

Dan feigned surprise. "But he's a Mason sworn to hold your secrets as his own."

"None the less," said Topper weakly and fell silent.

Dan thought about the time he'd spent with Topper. Topper had been coach to Dan, Roque and Rojo, teaching them their Masonic proficiencies, all the things a Mason was required to know and take to heart. But he had done more with Dan, who remembered how easy it was to listen to Topper's stories. They were exciting, and his puzzles worked the mind. Along with Masonic proficiencies and general information about the Lodge and its long history, Topper had taught deeper lessons, such as logic and a method of choosing between competing explanations. He called this a philosophy of science, and along with it went lessons in logic and fallacy. It was after Dan was "raised," that is, made a Master Mason, that the real lessons began. Professor Pendarvis, Dan couldn't think of him as Topper at times like those, called it a secret history and a scientific exploration. The frontiersman from Greenport, Out East, hadn't taken his stories seriously. They were the stuff of legends. Dan thought back to the stories he'd heard Out East, the eastern end of Long Island, a part of New England. Sailors claimed that in Mexico *Indios* raised pyramids same as Egyptians to whom they must be related. Who could believe such wonders? Topper's stories were the same. Now, at least to Dan, it was clear that others besides the professor took his stories to heart.

They were willing to kill for the professor's knowledge and for the treasure buried somewhere out among the canyons, deserts, and mountains. Dark, powerful, ruthless forces were at work.

"Dan," whispered Topper, "I'm in good hands. It is time for you to begin your quest."

Chapter 2

Ancient Kings

> **Deuteronomy 33:**
> [22]And of Dan he said,
> "Dan is a lion's whelp;
> He shall leap from Bashan."

"Topper," said Dan, "I'm not sure I can begin the quest. I wish you had the strength to go over everything with me again, to tell me again all you've learned, but you don't."

"Think back, Dan," Topper replied. "You have a good memory."

Dan reviewed the past year of lessons.

"I should begin at the beginning," Topper had said soon after Dan was "raised." "That's the best place to start. But, which genesis is our beginning? There are at least four. Hmmm? Let's begin with where it started for me as a newly graduated scholar and newly raised Mason." They had worked in Topper's rooms, a casa alongside the Church of San Miguel with a beehive *horno* in the corner of each room. His home smelled pleasantly of *piñon* smoke, mild pipe tobacco, the professor's talc, and the must and mildew of the ancient documents he possessed. The windowless rooms were dark, the only light coming from fireplace and candle. He showed Dan documents one by one, but the greatest revelations were written only in a secret ledger, wrapped in a parfleche, a raw-hide cover, hidden in a place even Dan was not shown, not until the night Topper was wounded.

"In Newport, Rhode Island," the Professor continued, "there is a tower, a sort of stone lighthouse of very ancient origin. You've heard of it, Daniel?"

"I grew up Out East in Greenport. Newport was close by sea."

"Good. Who could have built it? I was fascinated. The people of Newport all said it was there before settlers came from England. Records in the Lodge referred to it as being there when the Lodge was founded. The earliest church records mentioned the tower.

"I tracked down and spoke with a Nipmuc shaman," the Professor went on. "His people had been numerous around Rhode Island before Roger Williams arrived, but sadly, very few remain. At first, he would not speak with me. By habit, I offered a Mason's handshake. Strangely, this loosened his tongue. His people's legends confirmed that the tower was old. During a storm creatures had come from the sea on a floating island topped with tall trees. The island disappeared beneath the waves. Like lobsters the *Glooscap*, demigods, had hard shells on their heads and bodies and were equipped with a single great, sharp claw. The creatures built the tower and dwelt within it.

"Each night they lit a fire in the upper story. The lobster people watched the sea looking for something. They used wooden shutters to make the light blink.

"Lobster people," Professor Pendarvis went on, "hunted in Nipmuc forests and demanded tribute in grain, food, and finished skins. Nipmuc objected, but the *Glooscap* were powerful warriors. The tribute asked was small. Nipmuc watched as *Glooscap* died over the years of sickness, injury, and old age. The last aged lobster was a powerful shaman. Nipmuc accepted him into their village, and he taught them much.

"At this," Topper said, "the old shaman grasped my hand, shifting the grip several times in familiar ways. He said a word that might have been Templar. Demanding paper and pen, the Nipmuc wrote familiar symbols and indicated I would find them at the tower."

Dan had been fascinated. He had heard similar stories about the Newport Tower.

Professor Pendarvis had more information. "I searched the tower carefully and found indications where shutters might have hung. In the upper level, faint and faded with age, I found symbols carved in the rock near the floor where they might pass unnoticed. The square and compass appeared twice on either side of two men in helmets riding a horse. From the horse, a faint line led across the floor to a rose and beside it a short line. Above the two symbols appeared a square and compass containing the letter G. These symbols aligned with two windows west-southwest and nor'-nor' east. Beneath another western window, south of the first, I found the horse and riders repeated and another line across the floor not quite parallel to the first. The line led to a representation of two hills, one with a cross and the other with a building fronted by two columns surmounted by a crown.

"Daniel," the Professor had asked, "can you guess at meaning of these symbols and at ways to test my theory?"

"Two men on a horse is a symbol for the Knights Templar," Dan had replied, "so you have taught me. A line might suggest a journey. The two hills? The cross might indicate Golgotha, the Place of the Skull. The building with two pillars and a crown might be Solomon's Temple, so the whole would be Jerusalem. The rose and line, rose-line? It might mean Rosslin or Roslyn. The square and compass with the letter G, might be a Masonic Lodge or a chapel used by Masons. I have heard of such a place in Scotland, Roslyn Chapel."

Dan hadn't come to this information all at once. It took time for him to work it out even though Topper had taught him the meanings of most of the symbols.

"Aye," Topper said, "that is what I concluded, too, but it took me several years. It was only when I saw a sketch of Roslyn Chapel that everything fell into place. At Roslyn, what appears to be an unfinished wall is a recreation of the Wailing Wall, the last remnant of the Temple. The symbols showed two journeys made by Knights Templar. I thought about the repeated square and compasses beside the knight's horse and realized the symbols must mean they were also or had become Masons. But that's later. I recorded all the symbols and alignments in my ledger. How do we test our conjectures?"

"Well," Dan had speculated, "if the lines ran from window edge to window edge..."

"They did," confirmed Topper.

"I would theorize," Dan responded, "that the bearing of the lines was important and that one should lead from Newport to Roslyn and the other from Newport to Jerusalem. I would take a compass and measure."

"One did point precisely to Roslyn. But," continued Topper, "the other did not point to Jerusalem, or more precisely, not from Newport to Jerusalem. If I ran the azimuth backwards from Jerusalem, parallel to the drawn line, I came up with a point much farther south. It might have pointed from Jerusalem to Taos or somewhat farther north, but there were other possibilities. It puzzled me for a long time. I made copies of all I had found and deposited them with the Lodge at Newport. When I had done all I could, I decided it was time to visit Roslyn.

"Daniel, have you ever traveled?" he asked unexpectedly.

"I have," Dan replied using the ancient formula learned by Masons.

"Whence and whither?" Topper continued.

"From west to east and east to west again," Dan said giving the ritual response.

"You'll travel again, Daniel," he said. "I have an errand to ask of you. Have you still got the compass and sextant your father gave you?" Dan nodded. "Good, be sure you take them...and a good watch, so you can always tell exactly where you are." At the time Dan thought Topper's statement some obscure homily or moral lesson. Only later did the young man learn what the professor had in mind.

Before the last decades of the 18th century, there had been no good way to measure longitude. Latitude, the distance north and south of the poles, could be measured with a sextant, but distance east and west were measured by the difference in the time the sun rose. Before the late 18th century, there was no accurate way to measure time. Even the difference of a few minutes could amount to many miles. So the professor's lines showed direction accurately, but the distance was indeterminate. A line drawn from Newport might lead to Pennsylvania or Missouri or New Mexico or even Siam. They could guess that a line from Newport that passed Roslyn or Jerusalem was meant to end there, but there was no telling where the line west from Newport might end.

While the professor lingered in bed an invalid, he

reviewed lessons with Dan and taught him new ones familiarizing Dan with the book he'd saved from the fire the night Topper was wounded.

In those days, there wasn't a library in New Mexico other than the records kept at the Governor's Palace.

"The Catholic Church may have records," the professor guessed, "but I doubt they'll share them with us." He was still confined to his bed. He would seem to improve for a few days and then lapse into fever. On a day when he was lucid, he again spoke of the quest, encouraging Dan to depart with all haste. He continued talking in a whisper. "Daniel, there were two other ancient sources in the Territory: Penitentes, otherwise known as the Holy Brotherhood of Our Lord Jesus Christ, whose patron was *Jesús Nazareno,* and the Pueblo Indians. Neither is likely to talk to us."

That night a stranger in a hooded cloak appeared at their door and asked for admittance. Dan learned later that Roque had been sent to summon the visitor. Dan seated the dark stranger at the professor's bedside.

"Daniel, you know Padre Martinez." Topper introduced the priest indicating that Dan should bring a chair for himself.

Dan knew Padre Antonio Jose Martinez, the Taos priest, by reputation. Accepting his offered hand, Dan carefully looked over a man of middle height who possessed a long oval face made the longer by a high forehead framed by shoulder-length dark hair. His skin was the alabaster of tombstones, and deep in its surface was carved, large and abysmal eye sockets set with small, dark, glistening orbs. The padre's mouth was an epitaph etched in a frown. Padre Antonio Martinez, a man rendered in black and white, was a liberal reformer who was conservative about *vecino*, New Mexican, traditions and customs. He was a man of wealth who cared for the poor but protected the right of priests to charge huge stole fees for the sacraments, fees so high most New Mexicans went unmarried.

Dan had heard talk of this around Santa Fe and from Roque. The French-born bishop, Lamy, had confronted Padre Martinez concerning his defense of *vecino* traditions. It was difficult for Dan to understand how much power this parish priest wielded. He had started the seminary, and when the bishop arrived almost all of the priests were the Padre's former students. He was a member of the legislature, owned the only printing press in New Mexico, and was reputed to be the head of the Penitentes. Meeting the man Dan had been told was evil, he unwisely wanted to confront him.

Instead, Dan nodded his head politely and took the padre's offered hand. He began rudely winning a reproachful look from Topper. "I understand you favor high stole fees that make it difficult for people to receive the sacraments."

The priest's lips twisted upward away from their perpetual frown. "I do not favor high fees of any kind for ritual services. I favor compassion. The priests are poor since *vecinos* have never paid a mandatory tithe. If the bishop had his way by making them pay before any sacrament can be given, he would soon have more wealth than the legislature and the people would be poorer than they are and still get no sacraments."

Topper sought to intercede. "Padre Martinez loves our American Constitution and has taught it in his schools."

"Yes, indeed," said the priest. "The Constitution allows the people to be protected from the church by the state."

Dan had to think about the paradox of a notion of

freedom of religion that allowed the state to protect the people from the church. It seemed the priest wanted to protect the people from the bishop who was trying to make the tithe mandatory. To Dan the notion of a priest protecting the people from his own bishop seemed crazy.

"And," Topper went on, "Padre Martinez is pressing for statehood in the legislature."

Martinez nodded. "That is correct. But the southern states oppose us. They want New Mexico to be a slaveholding state, and this it can never be."

Dan opened and then closed his mouth. New Mexicans practiced peonage, debt slavery, and they also held *cimarrones*, wild Indians, captive in their homes as slaves until they learned to be good Christians. To Dan this practice was a form of slavery too. But since the state, in both cases, was temporary, New Mexicans did not see it as slavery which they viewed as evil.

Dan shook his head in wonder. "But I understood Padre Martinez does not like *gavachos*."

The priest stood tall. "I do not dislike *Americanos*. I dislike *gavachos* who steal from the *vecinos* and who sell *aquardiente*, your Taos Lightning, to *Indios cimarrones*, who steal from *vecinos* to have something to trade."

Dan knew Topper hoped this man would open church records for him. Martinez was the senior and best educated priest in the territory. He had a depth of understanding of church history unequaled by any of the *vecinos*. It was time for Dan to back off and let Topper charm the man.

Dan made hot chocolate for all of them before taking his seat. It was preferred by *vecinos* over coffee or tea, but it was expensive. It was sweetened with *piloncillos*, little cakes of brown sugar, and made spicy with cinnamon.

The professor mentioned the relationship of the

Masons to the Templars.

"The Templars were evil men," Martinez said. "They stole from the Pope that which rightfully belonged to Mother Church and hid it far away out of reach. It has never been recovered.

Martinez turned and fixed his gaze on Dan. "The chocolate is good, Daniel," he said. "You have the knack. Perhaps you are a *vecino* after all. That woman in Chimayo must be teaching you." He referred to Doña Loca, Roque's *prima*, cousin, who was currently married, her fifth time, to a very jealous man.

Dan felt his heart had been gripped in a cold fist. How did the padre know about his relationship with Sebriana, who was known as *Doña Loca*, Madame Madcap, a resourceful and independent-minded woman? Was she in danger?

"What did the Templars take from the Pope?" asked Topper.

Dan realized that this was a very sensitive discussion, with both men concealing much of what they knew from each other and tempting each other with tidbits to say a bit too much. It was delicate duel of wits, and Dan knew not to intrude. He did his best to remain quiescent and invisible while worrying about his sometime girlfriend, Doña Loca.

"Church furnishings," the padre replied, "things that belong in the cathedral. These were nothing of any great value except to the church." Dan suspected him of sly evasion. "The ignorant monks may have thought them treasure, decorated with gilt as some items were. The Church would like to get them back."

"Can you describe these things?" asked Topper. Dan feared Topper had pressed too hard. "Perhaps I have encountered reference to them in my studies and travels.

I've been through the archive at Roslyn Chapel, you know. There were some references to the Templars." He gave the padre a tidbit. He would surely have heard of Roslyn and be curious about its rumored Templar library.

"Oh," Martinez replied, "a table, a chest, a lampstand and a few things that go with them.

Martinez changed the subject. "But your message said you wanted to know about the Holy Brotherhood of Our Lord Jesus Christ, or as some call them, the Penitentes. They are ancient among us, living up to a tradition of medieval knights. They came with the first conquistadors. They are the *Terciarios de Pentencia*, the Third Order of Penance of the Franciscans. They do much good among the people, performing rituals for the poor in places where there are not enough priests."

Topper raised an eyebrow. "You said that they have a tradition of medieval knights. Are they related to the Templars or the Hospitallers?"

"The Templars?" the padre scoffed. "Certainly, not. They were outlawed and proscribed, excommunicated and cast out. The Knights of the Hospital, the other Knights of Saint John, enemies of the Templars, yes, perhaps the Penitentes are their progeny. Both groups were monks and knights dedicated to protecting God's children as they traveled to the Holy Land."

"Who is their Grand Master?" Topper pressed.

"It is a secret." Dan thought he saw the tombstone face about to crack as the priest tried not to smile as he spoke. "No one is allowed to know except the most senior members."

Topper asked a few innocuous questions about the ritual and services performed, never pressing about the rumored flagellation and crucifixion. Roque and Dan had witnessed a ceremony on a mountainside near Truchas.

They hadn't been trying to spy on brotherhood. They were just in the wrong place at the right time. Flagellation and crucifixion were part of the ceremony. A man was raised on a cross, and he was still suspended though alive when Dan and Roque made their way down the mountain. Dan didn't know if they left the man to die up there. Those who try to "take on the wounds of Christ" seek a deeper understanding of the Lord's suffering, but the path seemed a strange one to Dan. Padre Martinez offered crumbs of knowledge, but he never provided details. Instead, he talked of the skeleton, Doña Sebastiana, riding in her little cart with her bow and arrow to take away those whose time had come or might come all too quickly.

As the professor's responses became less and less coherent, Padre Antonio Martinez took his leave.

The next morning, rested, Topper said to Dan, "That padre knows much more than he is telling. He knows more about the Penitentes than any priest should. After all, Bishop Lamy has forbidden them to worship in this way. It is clear that Martinez knows their ceremonies and ritual quite well."

"What are you telling me?" Dan asked. "I'm confused."

"The Templars and the Hospitallers were rivals in the Holy Land. You know the Templars were called the Knights of Saint John of the Temple because their quarters were in the temple mount. Afterward, when the Templars were excommunicated, they became enemies. The Knights Hospitaller benefited by receiving most of the Templars' property after the Templars were forced underground. I think the Pope may have sent them to recover his property. The Templars had found something hidden beneath King Solomon's Temple. I found records of their excavations but only suspect what they found. The padre told us the truth when he said the Penitentes are the descendants of the Hospitallers. I think they were sent here among the conquistadors with a mission from the Pope, and I think that priest knows what the mission is or was.

"However," Topper went on, "I don't think he'll be much help getting us into church records. He is at war with Bishop Lamy, and the only way a priest could be so bold is if he was the protégé of someone higher than the Bishop."

Two days later, Dan spoke to the professor. "Topper, you know there have been men in black coats, your Danites, following us. I wasn't sure before, but now I am. There are Mexicans following us as well."

Professor Pendarvis nodded absently and mumbled. "It's probably some of the padre's Penitentes."

"Professor, who are these Danites?"

"In the Bible, Dan was one of the Twelve Tribes of Israel. They were known for two things. They were charioteer guardians of all Israel, and they were the only tribe known for seafaring. Indeed, the Greeks claimed a settlement of them, and the Celts claim they took their Queen Tea Tephi all the way to Ireland.

"When Joseph Smith needed a secret police force and palace guard, it was only natural he should call them his Danites. After all he claims the people he is gathering to Zion are the lost tribes of Israel." He coughed and fell silent, exhausted.

Dan thought people seemed to show undue interest in the professor and then turn away swiftly if observed watching. Others seemed to have nothing to do but hang about near Dan and Roque's house. Dan thought he had identified three distinct types. One group was the black-coated Danites who had attacked Topper. Another was made up of Mexicans, and the third were uncouth men, heavily armed and broad-hatted. Texians, Dan thought.

Unexpectedly, Topper said to Dan, "If we find anything in the government records, it's not likely to be direct evidence. We'll see pieces moving in response to the one we are interested in which is apt to remain in shadow." He left the younger man to ponder what else such hidden connections might mean.

The next day, the professor beckoned Dan to him. "Daniel, there are things I would show you in the Bible. Look here:

[22]For the king had at sea a navy of Tharshish with the navy of Hiram: once in three years came the navy of Tharshish, bringing gold, and silver, ivory, and apes, and peacocks. 1 Kings 10:22

[27]And Hiram sent in the navy his servants, shipmen that had knowledge of the sea, with the servants of Solomon.

[28]And they came to Ophir, and fetched from thence gold, four hundred and twenty talents, and brought it to King Solomon. 1 Kings 9:27-28

[17]Gilead abode beyond Jordan: and why did Dan remain in ships? Asher continued on the sea shore, and abode in his breaches. Judges 5:17

"Daniel, Solomon was sending fleets to Ophir, the land of the Queen of Sheba, and to Tharshish, which is the old name for the Iberian Peninsula. The King had ships in the Atlantic and in the Indian Ocean. It's only a few weeks' sail from Israel to the Iberian coast, so why did his ships take three years to make the journey?"

Dan thought about these voyages and came to a stunning conclusion. "They must have gone much farther. Could it have been across the Atlantic? The time is long enough."

"Yes, Daniel, it is long enough," Topper replied. "And it would explain much. Judge Deborah tells us the men of Dan had ships before King Solomon's time. Dan and the men of Tyre sailed together in Solomon's time.

"Daniel," Topper asked, "what was the greatest treasure of all time?"

"There have been many," Dan replied. "Pharaoh's treasures, the treasure of Alexander the Great, Captain Kidd's lost treasure…"

"Think bigger and better," Topper said, "the most important thing ever given to mankind."

"Perhaps the Ark of the Covenant," Dan guessed. "It contains God's commandments written in stone by His own hand. It was so holy that to touch it with bare hands was to die. When it was carried into battle by the armies of Israel, they could not lose."

"Exactly," Topper smiled. "Where was it kept and what became of it?"

"First in the Tabernacle and then in Solomon's Temple," Dan responded. "It is never spoken of again after the Babylonian destruction of Jerusalem about 560 B.C."

"Correct. The Babylonians captured the Table of the Presence that held the showbread, the Menorah, and the Trumpets of Truth and carried them off to Babylon. There is no mention of the Ark, the greatest treasure of all, kept in the same temple as the other treasures. When the people were allowed to return after the Babylonian Captivity, the Table, the Trumpets and the Menorah were returned with them, but not the Ark. What might you surmise from this, Daniel?"

"That the Babylonians never had the Ark," Dan grinned. "I remember stories of the Philistines capturing the Ark. It brought them all sorts of bad luck while they had it. You're going to tell me next that the Babylonians didn't report any bad luck."

"Correct, no bad luck," Topper said. "So perhaps they never had it.

"I found a scroll at Roslyn. If I'm interpreting correctly – there are bits missing, place names make little sense, many words are obscure – the scroll says Danites were put in charge of a delegation of priests and people from all tribes.

"The Danites," Topper continued, "had long been the guardians of Israel. Wandering in the Sinai, they were the rear guard. In the Promised Land, they were given a portion between Israel and the Philistines. Samson, the great slayer of the heathen, was a Danite. They dwelt by the sea and had been sailors since the Captivity in Egypt. They were given the greatest charge of all. They were to protect the Ark until Israel should again call for it.

"The Bible," he went on, "records an interesting relationship between the Ark and the Danites, a reason for entrusting it to them; they made it. Look here." Topper turned in his Bible and began reading from Exodus 31:

[6]"And I, indeed I, have appointed with him Aholiab the son of Ahisamach, of the tribe of Dan; and I have put wisdom in the hearts of all the gifted artisans, that they may make all that I have commanded you:

[7] the tabernacle of meeting, the ark of the Testimony and the mercy seat that is on it, and all the furniture of the tabernacle [8] the table and its utensils, the pure gold lampstand with all its utensils, the altar of incense,[9] the altar of burnt offering with all its utensils, and the laver and its base—[10] the garments of ministry, the holy

garments for Aaron the priest and the garments of
his sons, to minister as priests,

[11] and the anointing oil and sweet incense for
the holy place. According to all that I have
commanded you they shall do."

"They took it by sea to a far Western Land they
named Paradise. How many of the great religions, Daniel,
speak of a Western Paradise? All of them," he answered
himself. "And all references to the Western Paradise date
to after the Ark was hidden there. I believe these
references start with Wandering Jews, people of the
Diaspora, seeking the return of the Ark.

"In the Western Paradise, the Danites conveyed the
Ark of the Covenant up a long river flowing from the
west. Eventually, they housed it in a temple carved by the
Hand of God deep into the heart of the land. The other
Temple treasures were secured in a temple vault that was
captured by the Babylonians.

"The High Priest believed that a land known only to
the priests of Israel would be the ultimate place of safety,"
Topper explained. "The river they described might be the
Rio Grande. It fits all the particulars they gave. I have
them written here." He produced a paper. "But I believe I
may offer a shortcut to confirmation.

"I came to New Mexico to follow the legend of a
stone located near Los Lunas in the *Abajo*, the region
south of Santa Fe. There is an inscription there in what
might be ancient Hebrew. I've taught you some Hebrew,
and I give you this note of what the inscription might look
like. If it is what I think, this is the place, the Western
Paradise. Daniel, go and look for me." The professor
collapsed it seemed into sleep or something deeper.

Dan mumbled, "Western Paradise, Professor
Pendarvis? Is it any wonder I doubt? The Ark of the

Covenant in New Mexico?"

The professor, his eyes still closed, whispered, "Go, Dan. Go and look for me."

Dan Trelawney was embarrassed and humbled. He'd have to go despite his doubts.

"Daniel," Topper went on, "I was going to make this journey myself, but age and this wound have made me infirm. I need you to take Rojo and Roque and travel to Los Lunas."

"What," Dan asked, "if I find this inscription? What if it is in ancient Hebrew?"

"As far as I know," Topper said, "There are only one or two people in the world—besides myself—familiar with that script and neither is in New Mexico Territory. I only learned its characters in the library at Roslyn. It is a largely unknown script."

"And if the inscription is in ancient Hebrew?" Dan persisted.

"Then it will be at the beginning of a trail."

Chapter 3

A Damsel in Distress

Dan still hesitated. When he was alone with Topper, he raised the issue that was torturing him. "Professor, I don't think I have the right to ask my friends to undertake such danger."

The professor raised himself on one elbow. "Roque and Rojo will insist on going with you. They are the kind of men who stand with their friends no matter what."

"If we can find Rojo, he might go." Dan paced the room. "But don't you see, knowing they'll say yes makes it all the harder. Risking their lives becomes my responsibility."

"Daniel, the matter is urgent. Stop dithering. There are other powers moving. I've been waiting ten years, and would like to see my work vindicated before I die." Dan shuddered. He could not tell Topper that despite the known dangers, he still doubted that there was a hidden treasure.

Events overtook Daniel. Pedro Martinez raced into Santa Fe on a lathered horse, bringing it to such an abrupt stop that it nearly fell to its hindquarters. He yelled to Roque and Dan, "I have come from Chimayo with terrible news! You must come quick. Get your guns. *Andale! Arriba! Arriba!*"

"What's up, Pedro?" Dan asked, grasping his horse's bridal to steady the exhausted beast.

"*Que paso?*" echoed Roque.

"Sebriana!" he gasped. "She has killed her husband. His family, they will murder her!" Breathlessly, Pedro told Dan and Roque, "Don Carlos forced Sebriana to marry him with threats to her family, threats she knew he'd carry out.

Pedro gulped air. "Sebriana, she told me she did not want to marry him and would find another way to protect her family. But, he took her by force and carried her to the *iglesia,* the church in Santa Cruz. Only the priest and Don Carlos Baca's family know what happened there, but the priest was Baca's *primo*, his cousin. Sebriana said she was sure he only wanted her money. She feared for her life if she married him. Once he had her property, he wouldn't need her any longer. Doña Loca, with her wild ways and independent mind, would be an embarrassment to him.

One last gasp for air and Pedro went on. "Now, it is he who lies dead, his throat cut with his own blade they say. She killed him yesterday. I heard this morning and thought of you. Don Carlos' family holds Sebriana at their hacienda. The *alcalde* will hear her case tomorrow. The *alcalde* is Carlos' *tio*, his uncle."

Roque, gifted at understatement, nodded. "I think we better go help her."

Dan took only seconds to grasp the situation. "We're going to need help and a fresh horse for Pedro. Peregrino Rojo told me that if I ever need to find him, I should tell the Indians who sell pots and jewelry by the Governor's Palace. The word will reach him very fast."

A man a little taller than average of medium build, Pedro Martinez had dark, flashing eyes of quick intelligence. His handlebar mustache was wider than his face. He dressed like his countrymen in white cotton clothing with a colorful Chimayo serape about his shoulders. Pedro's clothes were cleaner and newer than most, and he wore tooled boots instead of sandals or moccasins. His dark face, hooded eyes, and impish smile told the world he was a born rogue and happy to be so.

As they rode north, Dan thought about his occasional sweetheart. Roque rode in close. "When you gonna marry that girl and keep her out of trouble?"

Dan didn't answer. Between husbands, she was his and that was enough. She wouldn't wait for him to decide. Sebriana was a *prima*, cousin, of Roque. She's probably Pedro's *prima*, too, Dan thought. People were closely related in the Rio Arriba. A year older than Dan, Sebriana had just outlived her fifth husband. Her first three husbands had died in such a state of wedded bliss that the priest insisted, in each case, on a closed casket because he couldn't wipe the smiles off their faces or so the legend said.

They called her *Dona Loca*, Madam Madcap. Dan did not wish to trifle with her for fear of offending Roque and because she was no woman to treat lightly. Her fourth husband, while drunk, made the mistake of beating her. He awoke to the sound of a billet of firewood smacking soft flesh, his. He tried to rise after the first blow, but the second and third followed too quickly, and after the third he was unable to rise. She didn't tire of beating him for a longtime. By then, every muscle in his body was badly bruised. A day later when he was finally able to crawl from the house, Sebriana was long gone and so was most of his property. He yet lived bent and hobbled like an old man.

Dan's heart twisted in his chest. He feared for her and

pictured her as he had last seen her; small and lithe, wonderfully curved, with glossy black hair. When Dan first met her, before he could speak Mexican, they had danced together at *fandango* in Chimayo. She invited him with her eyes and a firm grip on his arm to come away with her into the night. In those days, shortly after the funeral of her second husband, she was nineteen, vivacious, and very attractive. An altercation between Kit Carson and her most recent husband, Don Carlos, interfered with the tryst, giving Dan reason enough to hate the *hidalgo*.

"Why did she marry Don Carlos?" Dan asked. "Surely, she hated him."

Roque replied. "He didn't give her a choice. A woman alone is vulnerable."

"Why did that beast want her? She was a widow. A *don* could have had any woman, a young one, a virgin."

Roque snorted. "He's had lots of those, and he left them ruined. Sebriana inherited from her first three husbands. He wanted her wealth."

Dan knew she had used this property and her own business acumen and made herself a woman of wealth. And wealth made her interesting to Don Carlos Baca y Armijo. He was a big man and broad to the point of obesity. By the others' deference and his demeanor, people recognized him as a man of importance. His shirt, at that long ago *fandango* in Chimayo, was white and shone like silk, and his vest was embroidered with silver thread on black. The *conchos* on his velvet pantaloons glinted like fire. He stood a head taller than the others and carried himself as if he thought he were king. He held a young man at knife point, enraged because Miguel had dared to dance with Maria. Carlos thought he had a claim to Maria; she thought otherwise. Kit Carson had stepped in and separated Carlos from Miguel.

Riding north at a fast trot, Dan thought about his feelings for Sebriana. She was a friend and that was enough to mount an expedition to save her, but there was more. They had been lovers in the interludes between her marriages. He had vacillated about making her his wife, uncertain that he should marry below his station. He was a New Englander, and she was from a poor New Mexico family and a widow several times over. She was never willing to wait for a man who couldn't make up his mind.

As the three rode north to the hacienda at Santa Cruz, they passed the Indian Pueblo called San Ildefanso.

Appearing suddenly on a hill near the pueblo, Rojo rode out to join them. "I heard you needed help."

They explained the situation.

"I think," said Rojo, "you should stop in the *cantina* in Santa Cruz and listen to the talk, that is, after we get fresh horses in Chimayo for ourselves and one for Sebriana to ride."

Adobe structures can be beautiful and comfortable. Adobe is cool by day and warm at night. The packed earth roof is even an excellent place for the kitchen garden up high where livestock can't disturb it. Floors could be treated with ox-blood and polished to a deep russet sheen. With a beehive, *horno,* in the corner reflecting the fire's heat into the room and giant *vigas*, log beams, overhead supporting a *latilla* ceiling of branches laid in a herringbone pattern, the adobe casa is elegant, even beautiful.

Improperly built and poorly maintained, an adobe is no more than a mud hovel. When the soldiers of the *reconquista* fought their way back into *Nuevo Mexico* in 1692, they found the cantina in Santa Cruz already standing and already run down. The Cantina Agua Puerco had been built to be disreputable and allowed to degenerate from there. The *vigas* sagged, and the stucco had fallen off. Dan hesitated to touch the door, a dirty rag that might once have been a Rio Grande blanket. His skin crawled at the thought of vermin it might contain and the stench that moving it might release from within.

They stepped from late evening twilight into darkness. *Vigas* and walls were coated with soot from centuries of fires. A small fire burned in the *horno,* giving feeble light. The floor was pitted and uneven, the result of a leaking roof that periodically turned the surface to a pool of mud.

Spain, and then Mexico had kept the *Rio Arriba*, the Rio Grande country above Santa Fe, poor in tools and metal.   Kings and dictators had decreed that all manufactured goods should come from or through Mexico City. Only raw materials were produced in the provinces. This policy kept the land poor and ensured that there was little furniture, for there were no tools to make it, no glass for windows, and no hinges for doors. A *banco*, an adobe bench, ran around the wall. Patrons sat on it or on the floor.

Rojo and Dan did their best to look like the *vecinos*, local Mexicans, in clothing and manner. Rojo had the jet hair, black eyes, and dark skin for the part. With light brown hair and eyes, Dan fancied he might pass for a Spanish *guero,* blonde, which to Mexicans included light brown. Roque's fine clothing might make him stand out in this environment, but they were claiming to be men of trade. Pedro's mustache was large enough to be memorable anywhere, even among Mexicans and he was close to his Chimayo home and probably known here. They kept to the shadows and spoke little. These little cantinas were very territorial. The local men had grievances with men of surrounding villages. They fought over wood lots, water rights and grazing land as well as over women. They also fought in pure drunken meanness that grew out of oppression and desperation. Being an outsider was dangerous; strangers were beaten and robbed. Roque thought it best, and Pedro agreed, that they should give the impression the four of them were from the *Abajo*, south of Santa Fe, and on their way to Taos to purchase livestock.

The landlord brought their drinks in hollow gourd cups and delivered them with rude disdain. Just as well, Dan thought. They wanted to listen, not to become the subject of conversation.

In twos and threes, patrons came in and found seats. A rough looking *vaquero*, cowboy, in filthy clothes, with a bandana tied over one eye in place of a patch, entertained a group of similar looking men with stories of his exploits. A livid scar ran out from under the dirty cloth down to his chin where a long drooping mustache hid its end. *Don Cicatriz*, scar face, Dan mused, assigning him a name. To his left sat a huge man of dull-witted mien in equally ragged and filthy garments, *Tonto*, the dummy. On his right was an evil looking *vato* with a long pointed nose and equally pointed goatee. He so resembled an old goat that Dan began to think of him as *Señor Cabrón*. A greasy pony-tail hung from under a gypsy bandana tied to his head. Loud and obnoxious, they laughed and joked, casting the occasional insult in the direction of the rescue party, who declined to take notice.

"He held a gun to her head," laughed Cicatriz, "taunting her." The mention of a woman held with a gun to her head caught Dan's attention as well as that of his comrades. "I was there; I saw. Told her she had better start acting like a lady and like a willing *puta*, a whore, in his bed."

"He called her a *puta*?" asked Cabrón.

"Sí, and told her she was *muy fea*, too, most ugly," snickered Scar-face. "He told her he had her land and property and didn't need her anymore. She smiled sweetly through all of this. I was there. I saw."

They all laughed. Cicatriz continued, "He played with his pistole, putting it to her ear and under her chin. Don Carlos told Doña Loca he was like a god with the power of life and death over her. Carlos grabbed her hair and pulled Sebriana to him so tight her head was tilted back. Carlos Baca pressed the gun deep into her cheek by her ear, but she drew his big knife unnoticed by any but me. Don Carlos laughed. And suddenly he backed away, his expression one of surprise. The handle of his knife protruded from under his chin and the tip of the blade from the hair at the top of his head. He died so suddenly he didn't have time to bleed, just fell over and leaked a puddle on the ground. His gun went off, firing uselessly into the air like one who is too excited over a woman losing his load before the fun begins."

"How could a woman," asked the Cabrón, "push a knife so hard to go through his skull not once but twice?"

"Who can say?" replied Cicatriz. "She is Doña Loca and she was very angry. She spat on him, then stood there laughing."

With mention of the name, Doña Loca, Cicatriz gained the full riveted attention of the four rescuers although they tried not to be obvious. The dark cantina concealed them. Cicatriz laughed and his amigos cheered and laughed. They were getting very drunk.

"The Baca family," continued Cicatriz, "took her then and stripped her naked in front of everyone so she could not run away. A *tio viejo*, an old uncle, brought out his Penitente whip and flayed Sebriana till she bled from back and arms. The women kicked Doña Loca until she was bruised all over. Then they got willow switches and worked on her legs and feet. She never cried out. They threw her into that storeroom that has only one door next to the *sala* by the *zaguan*, the front gate, and there she remains until the trial. They will find her guilty and burn her at the stake as a *bruja,* a witch."

"You have seen her since," mumbled the giant. "Tell me about her *chichis*."

"Last night," said Cicatriz, "I grabbed her *chichi,* her breast, and squeezed it so hard you can still see the print of all my fingers in the bruise. Tonight when I am alone guarding her, perhaps I will spread her legs and make her feel like a woman. I hear she is very good."

Cicatriz grinned vilely, exposing black-gapped and crooked teeth. Cabrón returned the smile revealing brown dentures as ugly as his friend's.

Dan's friends grabbed him and held him back. His feelings for the woman were stronger than any he had felt before, but Roque suspected, stronger than Dan was willing to admit.

"It is time," pronounced Cabrón, the Goat, "We all must stand guard tonight."

They staggered out into the night, which was already half spent.

"Let's go where we can talk," said Roque.

Once outside, Rojo spoke. "That's a piece of luck. The guards are drunk and have told us what we need to know."

Rojo, trained since childhood in sly thieving, laid out a simple plan. He and Dan would go, climb to the roof, locate the guards, drop into the plaza, and neutralize them while Roque and Pedro waited out of sight outside the *zaguan* with the horses. It was close to midnight. They didn't have far to go.

"Our plan is simple," Dan mumbled. "We'll make it up as we go."

The night was dark and overcast and the moon had long since set. They located the imposing bulk of the Baca hacienda and rode right up to its windowless outer walls. Rojo and Dan stood in their saddles while Roque and Pedro held the reins of their mounts. They crawled onto the roof, which was flat and no more than eight feet above the ground. Rojo had changed to Apache garb and Dan to his buckskin. The Jicrallia carried knife and bow while Dan clutched knife and revolver. Both of them wore moccasins as they crawled silently, they hoped, across the roof to where they could see the plaza, the inner courtyard.

The *hacienda* was a hollow square that looked inward. The *zaguan*, the great gate, stood at one end. Family quarters rose two stories at the other. The rest of the building was only a single floor. There was a well and *horno* for baking bread in the plaza. Doors opened onto the courtyard. Most of the rooms were connected internally though Dan and Rojo had no way of knowing which. The external wall stretched at least one hundred feet. The rooms were no more than fourteen feet in depth, but some were as much as thirty feet long.

They soon spotted the guards. Tonto and Cabrón stayed at the edge of darkness in the passage by the *zaguan* guarding the front entrance. Cicatriz was directly below Rojo. Dan could see that all three were armed with knives and spears. That the men lacked guns was not surprising. Spears, bows, and knives were still the most common weapons in the *Rio Arriba*. They might even have bow and quiver resting against the wall somewhere. As lancers, these men could be quite imposing. On foot, they were less so. Dan couldn't tell if their sashes concealed pistols.

Cicatriz looked one way and the other. He was alone, he thought. He wouldn't be interrupted or surprised. Feeling safe, he disappeared into the room below the two raiders.

Rojo signaled Dan to wait. A dim glow came from the doorway below. Scarface, Cicatriz, had lit a candle. Dan heard a low moan from within. Rojo grabbed Dan's arm and shook his head. He wanted Dan to wait. The Apache pointed toward the *zaguan* passage. Deal with the other guards first, he mimed. He signaled that he would get one with an arrow while Dan dropped onto the other with his knife.

Dan saw that the guards by the *zaguan* were out of sight in the passage. A groan came from the room below. There was no stopping Dan. He slid down off the roof into the courtyard hoping he wasn't making a sound. Dan landed in a crouch, knife in hand, and looked around. He was alone.

In the candlelight, he saw Cicatriz his pantaloons dropped to his knees. His spear was on the floor beside him. He held a woman's foot in each hand trying drunkenly to force her legs apart. In one smooth motion, Dan stepped across the room and raised his knife. Grasping the vaquero's hair, Dan jerked his head back and carved him a second grin beneath the first. Blood spurted over the wall and the woman, drenching her. Dan lowered the dead Mexican toward the floor. Neither Dan nor his victim had made a sound.

With a whimper, the woman drew her knees to her chest and huddled naked in the corner covered in blood and wounds she had received earlier. Sebriana appeared a pitiful creature. Except for the candle, the room was empty. They'd left her no clothing, no bed or bedding, or any blanket. She cringed on bare earthen floor and shivered.

"Sebriana," Dan whispered.

Her head jerked up, and Dan saw her eyes wide in the candlelight. "*Pobrecito*, depart. Do not taunt me! I know you can only be a wraith, not my true love." *Pobrecito*, she had called him, poor boy. It was a term of affection.

"Sebriana," Dan whispered again. "It's me. *En pelota*, in the flesh."

"Danito, I prayed you'd come," she said. She almost smiled at Dan's jest. *En pelota* means "in the skin," naked.

Sebriana rose stiffly, painfully to her feet. Dan watched her naked body swaying a moment in the dim light as she pushed Cicatriz's body away. Sebriana threw herself against him. Dan's breath caught in his chest. Her arms clasped him tightly. He felt the warm softness of her body. His hand slid naturally to the roundness of her buttock. He hugged her to him. Raw emotions like flayed skin, Dan's true feelings were laid bare. In that moment, he loved completely, more than Romeo loved Juliet.

From the doorway came a voice, "Juan," That must have been Cicatriz's name, "can I see her *chichis*?" The great bulk of Tonto blocked the door and their escape.

Sebriana stepped back away from Dan exposing herself. Naked breasts caught Tonto's attention, distracting him and buying Dan time. Tonto's sluggish thoughts were slowed further still by the sight of Dona Loca's naked body. It took the drunken ox long seconds to notice the body of his friend lying on the floor.

Dan rushed for the ox hoping he could make one, good, quick thrust up under Tonto's ribs before he noticed the presence of the rescuer. Dan's blade had barely cut

Tonto's flesh before the big man batted the rescuer aside with the back of his meaty hand, flinging Dan across the room. As his head struck the wall, Dan dropped his Bowie. The big Mexican snorted and stepped in, grabbing Dan one-handed by the throat, raising him off the floor, and pinning him to the wall, choking.

Doña Loca dropped to hands and knees trying for the knife, but the ox kicked her brutally aside. Dan beat at him with his fists. Tonto didn't seem to notice. Dan kicked as well but couldn't gain enough room to make it hurt. With his left hand, the big man hit Dan hard in the belly. Against the wall, Dan had nowhere to go, and his body took all the force of the blow. Blackness began to creep in around the edges of Dan's fading vision. He used his feet to push off from the wall and almost succeeded in toppling the ox, but Tonto didn't loosen the grip on Dan's throat and big man slammed Dan back against the unyielding adobe.

The point of an arrow sprouted bloody from Tonto's throat. The bumbling giant began to topple backward, never loosening his grip on Dan. As they went down together, Dan saw the white glint of Rojo's teeth in his dark face where the Apache stood in the doorway grinning. Rojo didn't hesitate to think who he might have killed if he'd missed. That was his way. Dan untangled himself from the corpse as Rojo stepped back into the darkness to watch for Cabrón, the remaining guard.

Dan stripped the clothing off Cicatriz's cooling body and threw it to Sebriana. She wanted no part of it.

"It's filthy," she whispered, "full of lice, fleas, and worse." She shook her head standing naked and proud.

"You must," Dan hissed. "You'll draw too much attention like that."

She smiled and threw herself at him again. Dan

separated from her reluctantly and grabbing Cicatriz's pantaloons. Kneeling, he helped her step into them her arms and legs stiff with bruised muscles. As Dan raised them to her hips, his hand brushed soft curly hair. The frontiersman went rigid waiting for his heart to restart. She bent and kissed him on the head and, as he stood, on the lips. She snuggled bare breasts against his chest.

"No time for that," hissed Rojo from the door.

Dan finished dressing her, pulling Cicatriz's shirt together over her firm, full breasts. Vest and *zerapé* followed. Sebriana bent painfully trying to fasten rawhide *botas*, leggings, below her knees. Dan helped her. She tied Cicatriz's moccasins tightly to her tiny feet.

Rojo entered suddenly and stepped to one side of the door. He silenced Dan with a gesture and pointed toward the *zaguan*. The third guard, Cabrón, was coming to watch the fun.

He stuck his ugly, grinning, brown-toothed visage with its goat-like beard through the door. His face lit with delight seeing scar-faced Juan, Cicatriz, hovering over the naked body of the woman adjusting his clothes. Then Cicatriz looked up at Cabrón and Cabrón saw a woman's pretty, bruised face where Juan's ugly scar-face should have been. Confusion filled Cabrón's drunken mind.

Neither Rojo nor Dan had time to react before Cicatriz's spear protruded from both sides of Cabrón's torso, dripping blood as the Cabrón coughed up his life. Sebriana spat on him and then hobbled from the room.

Rojo stood amazed. "She drove it all the way through him!" the Jicarilla hissed. "I don't ever want that woman annoyed with me."

Outside, they were about to learn the meaning of annoyed. Doña Loca had gone to the *sala* beside the *zaguan*. There she rummaged for the things she wanted.

Indicating two small casks of black powder, she told her rescuers, "Take those to the doorways of the family quarters."

Returning, Dan and Rojo found her making torches from cooking oil and muslin. She pointed to a few things that would burn and told them to place them with the powder and wet them down with the rest of the oil. She ducked into her room and lit the torches from the candle. The rescuers were in haste to depart, but before Sebriana would leave, she tossed the torches into the pool of oil.

Going over the rooftop, in the flickering glow of burning oil, Dan saw him, the priest, Antonio Jose Martinez. He emerged from a room across the courtyard from the three. Dan knew him, even in the dim light, knew at once that pale face with its deep set eyes, that oval visage framed in black. Dan saw him, and the padre saw the frontiersman.

Outside they found Pedro and Roque waiting for them. Mounting, they rode hard away. Flames crackled in the night behind them and were soon accompanied by two explosions that brought down much of the hacienda.

"She defends her honor like *Española*, a Spanish girl," said Pedro in awe of Sebriana. "That is no woman to trifle with."

"Si!" repeated Roque, "like a Spanish maiden of old, a woman worthy of a conquistador."

"You don't know the half," said Rojo.

Behind them, the *hacienda* was now burning nicely, the fire spreading through the *vigas* and *latillas*.

Pedro spread the story of the brave girl who defended her honor like a Spanish girl. The community west of Santa Cruz along the Rio Grande where the *hacienda* had been was afterwards known as *Española*, the Spanish Girl.

"I think," said Roque, "the *Rio Arriba* may be too hot for Sebriana for a while."

"We should be somewhere else," added Rojo.

"I don't think I was seen," said Pedro Martinez. "I will return to Chimayo."

They bid him farewell near Nambé Pueblo.

"Treat her right, Danito," Pedro called as he waved goodbye. "You don't dare do otherwise." Sebriana grinned sweetly.

"Where shall we go?" asked Roque.

Dan thought a minute. "To the *Abajo*, to *Los Lunas*. Professor Pendarvis entrusted me with a quest. It will be dangerous, but perhaps not as dangerous as it will be where we are known. There are evil forces at work."

"We know," said Roque. "Topper told Rojo and me before he told you."

The two of them grinned at Dan.

"I'm up for anything," said Sebriana, "as long as I can have clean clothes and a bath first."

When they had a moment alone, Dan spoke to Roque. "That priest was there. Padre Antonio Martinez was at the *hacienda.* I saw him, and I think he saw me as we went over the rooftop."

"That place burned," said Roque. "The *Terciarios de Penitencia,* the Penitentes, the Third Order, they may have to find a new leader."

Naming the padre as the leader of the Penitentes set off alarms in Dan's mind. Try as he would, he could get no more from Roque. He would not explain further, and there was no point asking. The priest must be dead. What did it matter?

Two days later, as Dan walked across the Plaza in Santa Fe, he saw Padre Antonio Jose Martinez enter the Palace of the Governors.

Chapter 4

Desperados on the Run

Daniel, Roque, Rojo, and Sebriana had ridden back to Santa Fe to the two-room house Roque and Dan had rented on Water Street and where they had left Topper in care of Father Nighthawk. They found the professor chatting amiably with the Jicarilla medicine man. A blood trail led out the door. Dan looked at it questioningly.

Father Nighthawk said simply, "*Nakaiyeh* come."

"*Nakaiyeh?*" asked Dan puzzled.

"A Mexican," said Topper, but neither of the two old men would say more.

Dan and Roque, with Rojo's frequent assistance, made their living on commissions from merchants for recovering livestock and stolen property. The money was good when they had work, and the work left them their independence. Ranching wasn't profitable. There were too many cows and too few markets. The cities of the States were too far away, and locally, the Indians tended to make off with the profits. Indian trade and trapping were in decline. Only the trade with Mexico was profitable. The three friends fit in best protecting caravans and taking special commissions from Santa Fe traders for special work.

It seemed they had gone unseen or unrecognized at

Santa Cruz, though Dan was certain the padre had recognized him. Dan wondered why Padre Martinez would withhold this information from Don Carlos' family. Sebriana was well known in Santa Fe and word would get around fast once she was seen. The friends kept her hidden, but Doña Loca had other ideas. She wanted her bath, and she wanted to visit a seamstress or maybe two or three. Her bath proved the biggest difficulty. Roque or Dan could go to a barber who kept a tub in the back without arousing suspicion. That would not work for Sebriana. There weren't many *Gavacho*, Anglo, ladies in Santa Fe; Dan could count them on the fingers of one hand. Such ladies as there were, together with Mexican *ricos,* kept their own private tubs at home. Mexican women of a lower status bathed in open air in the river.

"There's no way," pronounced Dan with finality. "Doña Loca cannot go down to the river to bathe. She'd be spotted in an instant!"

While Rojo and Roque rounded up livestock and supplies for their journey, Dan was left the chore of guarding Sebriana and of finding her a tub. A large washtub was finally located, a rarity in Santa Fe where laundry is also done in the river. Water was soon heated, and Doña Loca sat quietly to soak and splash while Dan worked over Topper's notes together with the old man in the next room. Dan had hoped for quiet but Sebriana had her own ideas. She sang and splashed happily and entreated Dan to come and wash her back.

Much to the aged man's delight, she was within Topper's field of view.

"You'll kill him, you know," Dan implored. "He's old and in a weakened condition."

Topper grinned. "I'll be fine. She's lifting my spirits . . . with her singing."

Dan tried to ignore her. He buried himself in the work. Topper had copied codices, scrolls, and inscriptions with precision. Concerning his conclusions and insights, the notes were cryptic, often in code. His journal, on the other hand, was detailed covering his travels and when and where he'd made discoveries. It was hard work, but slowly Dan was recovering Topper's deductions. He was glad he could consult the professor now and then.

Thus occupied, Dan was deep in thought when two wet hands suddenly covered his eyes.

"*Quién es*? Guess who?" a female voice said.

Dan rose and turned. Sebriana snuggled.

"I couldn't find the towel," Sebriana said twisting around in his arms, "but I'm dry now." She pranced away across the room to dress in her new clothes.

Dan and Roque had found both men and women's clothes for her. She'd travel with them dressed as a man.

Roque smiled. "When she dresses as a man, we shall call her Juan."

Reports came daily from Pedro in Chimayo. He didn't risk coming himself but sent sealed notes with friends. At first it was thought Sebriana had died with the others in her room. But as they straightened out the mess she left behind, it became clear the guards had not died from fire or explosion. The marks of a knife, arrow, and spear were identified. Until then, it was thought she'd been blown apart. A *tia*, aunt, and a *primo*, cousin, of Carlos were killed by Sebriana's handiwork. The family was looking for the murderers even as they rebuilt the hacienda. At last, they began to suspect she'd had outside help and started the hunt for the conspirators.

Dan went to Topper. "Is Padre Martinez your friend, so much so that he would protect us?"

Topper wheezed. "Not a friend, no. An adversary and

a very cunning one. He desires the same treasure you do. If he is protecting you, it is with some ulterior motive in mind."

At last, the day came that Dan dreaded in the form of a note from Pedro.

"They have found our tracks against the wall where you climbed over," read the note. "Someone remembered the horse traders at the cantina. They are looking for those traders now. The description is very good: a big, *guero*, a blondie, and a very big Mexicano in very nice clothes, together with one who is so dark he looks like an *Indio*, even an Apache. *Todo es muy feo*, they are all very ugly. Some say there was also a handsome *Mexicano* with a big mustache. Men of this description were seen heading toward Santa Fe."

Dan suspected the last part of the description had been added by Pedro. Nonetheless, it was time for them to move. There was Topper's safety to consider.

Kit Carson assured Dan and Roque that the brothers in the Lodge would be on the watch for pursuit while Father Nighthawk looked after the professor. Rojo hinted there were Apaches watching as well.

"Topper," Dan said, "you have been a good teacher. We will go and look."

Topper smiled weakly. "You are a good lad. Find that which was lost for me. Promise me."

Dan promised.

Topper continued. "I fear for you. There are powerful forces arrayed against you, and I fear I will not see you again on this side. I go to that undiscovered country soon."

"Of course, you'll be here when we get back. We'll only be a few days. A week or two at most." Dan left Topper's side, burdened by the weight of the quest and by fear of losing his friend.

"Sebriana," Dan told her, "Carlos' family is coming to Santa Fe looking for you."

"It's all right," Doña Loca smiled. "I know you will protect me."

"I have to do something for Topper. It will be very dangerous, almost as dangerous as waiting here. I'll take you with us if you want."

She cuddled. "I'll go with you. You will keep me safe."

Dan was terrified. He didn't want to be responsible for her safety. He wasn't sure he wanted to keep her safe in the way she implied. Dan pulled away from her and said, "I've got to talk to Topper."

That night the four rode out of Santa Fe mounted on mules. That is, all of them rode mules except Roque.

"Roque," called Dan, "I see you've found yourself another grulla, a fine dun."

"It is no grulla, gringo," replied the proud Mexican. "It is a *grullo*, a stallion."

Dan grinned. "Mule'd be hardier and Indians less likely to sneak into camp and steal your mount."

"My fine *grullo* stallion stands fifteen hands high and runs like the wind. Besides, the ladies find me *muy bonito*, more handsome, on a stallion."

Sebriana giggled. "He would not want a swift grulla. Such an animal would outrun the stallions and never have any colts.

"Me," continued Sebriana, "I am happy with my pinto jenny. I think I will name my mule Deborah."

"Why?" asked Roque frowning.

"Deborah was a strong judge of Israel who led men into battle."

Rojo cocked his head. "So it is with my people, too.

Sometimes there is a woman warrior." He moved, uncomfortable in the saddle. "I do not like this mule."

Sebriana smiled. "But it is *muy linda*, so pretty, a brindle jack of light and dark buckskin coloring. He looks like a zebra."

"I only ride this creature," muttered the Apache, "because you tell me I must try to look like a Mexican. My mount should have Indian coloring like Dan's Appaloosa. It should not look like a legendary unicorn."

"Zebra," Sebriana corrected him. "And they're not legendary, I think."

"Have you ever seen one?"

Behind them, they led a string of pack-mules and remounts. Oats and corn were included in their supplies to keep their mounts strong when they hadn't time to let them graze and recruit properly.

"I don't know why you bring remounts," said Rojo. "We could just ride these to death and eat them. Then I'll steal some more for you."

"We might need to do that in the weeks ahead," Dan replied, "but, for now I'd like to be able to ride into towns without someone recognizing his brand on the beast I'm riding."

Dan looked long at Sebriana. "She makes a handsome man, young and beardless, a teen."

Roque grinned. "She'll have to watch out for pretty girls and pederasts on the make."

The four made camp away from the road just as the sun was rising.

"Danito," said Roque, "do you still carry that huge axe you claim is only a knife?"

Dan drew his blade. "The smith who made it said it was a Bowie knife, just like Jim Bowie carried at the Alamo." He raised it high so the others could admire it in the rising sun. It was fourteen inches long and four across at its widest with a closed knuckle guard.

Roque laughed. "It is far too heavy, amigo." Roque pulled his long, thin dagger with broad guards.

Dan nodded. "The first time I fought with this knife, I hit a man in the knuckles with the flat of the blade. He dropped his knife and ran, his entire arm numb from the blow. It is a lucky knife." Smiling, he returned it to its sheath. "Besides, you carry a second blade."

Grinning, Roque drew a large blade something like a machete or small sword.

"What you need is this," said Rojo drawing his Green River knife, a kind of butcher's blade. "With this I can do anything. Skin a buffalo, make my dinner, and kill an enemy. Kit Carson says, 'Give it to them up to the Green River.'" He showed them where the eight inch blade was engraved Green River near the handle.

Sebriana pulled forth a dirk and a long thin stiletto, surprising the men who did not know where she kept it concealed any more than they could tell where Roque kept his weapons. Barely half an inch wide at the hilt, the stiletto had three sharp sides.

"I've never seen anything like that before," said Dan.

"It is my *misericorde*," Doña Loca said as if that explained everything. "It has been passed down to me from my grandfather's grandfather who was a conquistador. This knife was called a mercy-giver. When a man in armor was wounded and dying slowly this thin blade could be pushed through the gaps in his armor to give him peace." She smiled. "I would have used it on Don Carlos, but his knife was conveniently located in his belt, and mine was not at hand. Besides he didn't deserve mercy."

Each of the men, Rojo, Roque and Dan, carried two

revolvers, one in a belt holster and the other in a holster on the saddle. They were cap and ball weapons. To load them, they brought the hammer to half-cock and rotated the muzzle skyward. Black powder was poured from a flask in measured quantities into each of the cylinders. One at a time, the cylinders received a .44 caliber ball which was pressed home with a lever under the barrel. A percussion cap containing fulminate of mercury was pushed onto a nipple at the back of each cylinder. Reloading would take a minute or more, and under fire the tiny caps were often dropped.

Nonetheless, two revolvers offered twelve shots before reloading, thirty-six shots among the three of them. The pistols, accurate to about twenty-five yards, lacked the range of Indian arrows, about fifty yards. By firing their bows at a high angle, the Indians intercepted targets sheltering behind cover.

Rojo drew the pistol from his saddle. "It is good that the professor could provide us with arms of the same caliber."

Sebriana had two small, single shot pistols and a pepperbox in .36 caliber.

"It is convenient," she told them, "when all your guns are of the same caliber, *que no?*"

Roque laughed. "You were very insistent with Professor Topper when you demanded that he get you a rifle, in .36 caliber to go with your pistols."

Dan spoke. "I think that weapon won't knock her over when she fires it."

"Yes," said Roque, "and it will be good for hunting. Perhaps it will knock a rabbit over, but I don't think it do very well against a man."

Dan drew his Hawken .50 caliber rifle from its scabbard. "This will knock a man down and give me all the range advantage I need."

Roque smiled. "It was kind of Topper to provide us each with two. That will come as a surprise to someone, I think."

"Yes," said Rojo. "You will be able to say hello at two hundred yards, but these weapons will be slow to reload. I have my bow in my pack."

Roque wouldn't leave his cousin alone. "Maybe if you hit your enemy in an eye," teased Roque, "or an ear or open mouth. That might kill him. But, if you hit him anywhere else, I think all you get is a complaint about *moscos grandes*, big mosquitoes."

"You'd probably hurt him more," added Rojo, "if you waited and threw the little rifle at your enemy."

"I'm more worried about the pepperbox," said Dan. "That thing is scary. You can hit anything with it as long as you're not aiming at it."

The pepperbox had six .36 caliber barrels three inches long. The barrels rotated to come up under the hammer one at a time. The problem was that the barrels tended to ignite each other and all go off at once like the Fourth of July. Even if the weapon functioned properly, it was low powered and not accurate beyond ten feet.

After breakfasting and resting until midday, they followed the Santa Fe Trail east as far as San Miguel on the edge of the *llano*, the prairie. Then they disappeared south into the forest of juniper and piñon, hoping in going this way to throw anyone who might be following off their trail. They stopped here and there to observe their back-trail but saw no one in pursuit. The creak of leather and the jingle of Roque's silver spurs accompanied them, surrounded by the strong smell of mule and the crisp scent of the pine forest.

Rojo led the way. This was country he knew well,

having served his people as their master sheep raider.

"We'll make our way back through Comanche Gap," said Dan, "and then head for Albuquerque and the Rio Grande."

Dusk on the second night overtook them still in the hill country above Galisteo Basin. They camped near a spring where there was good grass. The companions let the mules and Roque's *grullo* stallion drink and roll and then finished drying them with handfuls of last year's grass.

"*Pobrecito*, I shall cook for you," said Sebriana, "and *mi primo* and this Indio shall gather wood and wash the dishes."

"What shall I do?" asked a surprised Dan well aware that she was defensive of her rights and unwilling to be cast as a menial.

"You shall hunt for the table." She grinned.

"Amigo, don't look a gift *caballo* in the mouth," said Roque. "She is a good cook."

Rojo made a small, smokeless fire in a hollow where he hoped its light wouldn't be seen. Doña Loca was good company. Even though they were on the run, dinner was delicious and the company convivial.

"It was a good trade," said Roque patting his belly. "She cooks more better than you two *hombres*."

Around a campfire spreading the warm aroma of piñon talk flowed easily.

Rojo found a rare occasion to ask a question. "What exactly are we looking for? Topper told a lot of stories and hinted at a great treasure, but did not tell me the object of this first quest."

"We're looking," Dan told them, "for a rock with Hebrew letters carved on it in a very ancient script. It might be the Ten Commandments. Topper had heard reports and wanted to go see for himself. He tried at least once, but couldn't find the stone. After that his heart began to bother him. He couldn't make the trip again."

"Are we looking for the original stone," asked Roque crossing himself, "carved by the finger of God?"

Sebriana crossed herself.

Dan looked at the woman. "Brothers, we need to make a decision about Sebriana. She isn't a Mason. We have all sworn not to share Masonic secrets. The professor has shown me secrets deeper than those we swore to protect in Lodge. And he asked us as Masons to keep the secrets of a brother Master Mason."

Roque stood. "Topper has trusted her with secrets and encouraged us to bring her along. He must have known she would need to know everything."

Rojo nodded.

Dan summed up. "Then we've decided she needs to be a full partner except for passwords and signs and the ritual of the Lodge. My brothers, do you agree we must take Sebriana into our confidence?" Roque and Rojo nodded. "Sebriana, will you swear an oath to us like the one we have sworn to each other?"

"Yes," she replied, "but, do you really think you have to make me swear to have my loyalty?" A tear dropped from here eye. Dan feared that if he did not move quickly it would be followed by anger.

"Yes, Sebriana," he said, "but, only because Rojo and Roque and I have sworn together already."

Dan took a Bible from his saddle bag and placed it on the saddle, the best altar he could find at the moment. They knelt around the saddle.

"Sebriana," Dan said, "Place your hands upon the Bible and repeat after me." The three brothers placed their hands on top of hers. "I, Sebriana, known to all as Doña

Loca, promise to keep all the secrets of my sworn brothers even to the point of death knowing that each promise I make to my new brothers they also make in return to me."

She so swore and Dan continued, "I further promise to be loyal to my brothers come what may." She so swore. "I promise not to pry into or to try to learn those secrets of the Masonic Lodge which my brothers are sworn to keep."

"You mean your silly boys club?" asked Sebriana, "Yes, I so swear."

Dan turned to Rojo.

"Sebriana," Rojo said, "do you swear to keep as secret forever the hidden places, trails, and springs, the secrets of the *N'deh*, the Apache people, as your own?"

She had to think a moment about that one. This knowledge would have helped her people fight the hated Apache.

"I so swear," Sebriana sighed and Dan turned to Roque.

"Do you promise," said Roque, "to keep as secret anything you might learn about your brothers that might tend to embarrass them in front of the ladies…"

"Roque," Dan said sternly looking into his eyes.

"I so swear," Sebriana giggled.

"And do you make it your sincerest wish," Dan finished, "that should you reveal any of these secrets or prove unfaithful to your brothers in any way, you might find yourself alone and without hope standing in the trail awaiting the arrival of the family of Don Carlos Baca?"

"I so swear," the bold young woman finished.

"Sebriana," Dan asked, "what do you remember from church about the Ark of the Covenant?"

"The priest said it was very powerful," Doña Loca

replied. "Whenever the Israelites carried it before them into battle, they couldn't lose. The Philistines made a raid a couple of times and captured the Ark and placed it in their temple, but their idols bowed down to the Ark, and it brought them very bad luck."

Roque seemed confused. His recollection of church teaching stood between forgotten and confused. "Why was the Ark so powerful? What did it contain?"

"The tablets," said Sebriana, "carved by the Hand of God in the desert of Sinai. Moses brought down the Law from the mountain and put it in the Ark. The Ark had to be carried on poles because anyone who touched it died. Only the Levites, the priests, were allowed to touch the poles. It was the holiest thing on earth."

"And what became of it?" Roque asked.

"*Primo*, I don't know," Sebriana said. "It disappeared."

"The Bible last mentioned it," said Rojo surprising them with knowledge both deep and broad, "before the Babylonians sacked Jerusalem."

"That's right," Dan said. "That was in 584 B.C. Topper traveled to Jerusalem and to Babylon to find out where it had gone. He found a carved panel in Babylon that showed the Babylonian army carrying off Jews and their temple treasures. The Table of the Presence was there and the Trumpets of Truth and the Menorah, but not the Ark. It was the greatest treasure of the Israelites, and the Babylonians didn't mention capturing it nor did they show it in their art. Seventy years later, when the Babylonian Exile ended, the Israelites were allowed to take back to Jerusalem the Table, the Trumpets, and the Menorah, but not the Ark. What does this suggest?"

Roque understood before the others. "The Babylonians never had it."

"If they didn't capture it," Dan asked, "what happened to it?"

The fire, always small, had guttered down to glowing embers. Faces in the dark were barely visible, faintly glowing orbs.

"They hid it," said Sebriana.

"They did, but where?" Dan asked. "Not in the tunnels under Solomon's Temple. That's where the other treasures were found by the Babylonians.

Dan continued, "I'm still trying to understand it all from Topper's instruction and his notes. He lays out some facts and guesses, but never his conclusions. I will group things together that he learned years apart and in different places around the globe.

"In Egypt," Dan went on, 'Topper found references to long sea voyages and saw the remains of large boats. He saw mummies wrapped in tobacco and coca leaves that can only have come from the Americas.

"On a Greek island, Topper saw a gold ornament with a picture of the Ark of the Covenant on it. It came from a burial circle of a people long forgotten. Homer, according to the professor, referred to a foreign people as Danaoi, from the region known as Mycenae.

"At Roslyn Chapel," Dan went on, "Topper copied part of a document recovered by the Knights Templar from the tunnels beneath the temple. It said, 'Men of Dan traveled with the Egyptians on their voyages even beyond the sunset.' Another fragment said, 'We have taken God's blessing down the great river to a place near its source. We have gone by desert trails to the source of the salt. Follow the Law of the Lord. It shall show you the way.'"

Having given his friends as much as he knew, Dan stopped. "What do you suppose it means?"

"That's easy," said Roque. "They sent the Ark into

hiding 'down' the river, so south along the Nile, and then overland to Ethiopia, the land of the Queen of Sheba, Solomon's girlfriend. I heard a legend that the Ethiopians claim they have the Ark."

"Maybe," said Rojo, whose passion for learning knew no bounds, "but when I was in New Orleans, I was shown some very old maps where north was not up. Some people put west at the top and others east, and I'm told the Chinese put south at the top. So just going down the river might not be meaningful."

His friends were stunned. *Peregrino Rojo*, the Red Pilgrim, was named for his insatiable desire to travel and learn new things. They knew he had gone east with the caravans. He told them he had ridden a riverboat to New Orleans, but none had guessed the full implications.

"If not the Nile," said Roque, "what river then?"

Silence reigned for a time.

Finally the woman spoke. "Why did the professor come to New Mexico?" The men looked at her puzzled. "He thought something important was here. Maybe the river was the Rio Grande."

Dan protested. This point had kept him from accepting Topper's claims as anything more than fantasy. "How could ancient Israelites have gotten to the Rio?"

"I think," continued Doña Loca, "it's there in the notes. The Tribe of Dan traveled with the Egyptians in the time of Moses and before to the New World. They brought back tobacco and coca leaves. Later, as the gold ornament shows, they took the Ark to Greece where they were known as Danaoi and then to the Rio Grande."

"Whether my *prima* is right or wrong," said Roque, "I think this is what Topper believes."

Dan held up the sketch he had made following Topper's journal of what the inscription they sought might look like. "This is what we seek. Topper thinks it was scratched on a rock over two thousand years ago. He has evidence I do not understand that says this rock in near Los Lunas." Dan fell silent.

"On the *llano,* light travels far," said their Jicarilla brother. "I am uneasy. We may have been seen. I do not think it is safe to sleep by the fire."

They found places to sleep separated from each other away from the approaches to their camp. Roque gathered the livestock, which had been hobbled and set to graze, and picketed them some distance from camp near where he would sleep.

"Leave your saddles and packs," said the Apache. "Use them to make it look like you are sleeping near the fire. *Power* tells me they will not attack at night but use the dark to approach. At dawn they will try to kill us."

The others looked at him astonished. This was not the first time Dan had heard this way of expressing a relationship to *Power.* Father Nighthawk also spoke in this manner and sometimes Kit as well. Rojo wasn't saying he had power. *Power* was separate from him. It informed him. *Naawo,* Power, was in life and in the trees and hills and stones. The word was seldom said alone. It was always preceded by a word telling what kind of Power it was, tree power, mountain power, enemy finding power. If Rojo worked with *Power*, was brave, and had integrity in its use, it would aid him; if he went against *Power*, it would depart from him. Enemy Finding Power let Rojo know they would be attacked and when.

"It will only be a small party," Rojo said, "no more than ten men."

Stumbling to his bedroll in near total dark, Dan found he was not alone.

"I don't feel safe unless I'm near you," whispered Sebriana.

Dan concluded that there is no more erotic sound in the world than that a woman's clothing makes as she undresses in total darkness.

In gray, pre-dawn light, Sebriana sprang from their bed. Some sound had awakened her. Still naked, she raised her .36 caliber rifle to her shoulder. Dan, sitting bolt upright, looked where she aimed. A lance wielding Indian was approaching still sleeping Roque. The warrior was naked to the waist, and Dan thought he must be Comanche. Doña Loca fired, and the Comanche collapsed on top of her cousin.

A second Comanche sprang up arm's length from Dan on the other side of the rock Dan had thought concealed the lovers. Sebriana dropped her rifle and flashed out her pepperbox. The pistol chain-fired. All of its cylinders screamed at once, scattering bullets to the four winds. The brave stood there confused. He had been to the heart of the whirlwind where a naked woman had fired a small cannon directly at his head. He'd taken its full blast but felt no pain. He saw the flash, felt the heat that singed his face, and heard whistling missiles pass his ears.

Thinking himself immortal, impervious to bullets, he rose, his hair smoldering, to sing and dance about his new magic.

His confusion gave Dan time to draw his revolver. He pulled the hammer back, but it jammed. A percussion cap had fallen between cylinder and frame and would not let the cylinder advance. Dan reached for his second Colt and his Bowie.

Sebriana meanwhile had located one of her hideout pistols. Firing, she reduced the Comanche to total confusion. She sent a ball up his nose further scrambling his fevered brain. The first two were down, and Doña Loca was responsible for both.

Dan popped the cap loose from where it was lodged with the tip of his Bowie. Taking the knife in his teeth, he replaced the cap with a new one, and then with a pistol in each hand, he advanced on the camp. Sebriana was reloading. Roque was crawling out from under her first kill. A lance passed in front of Dan's nose. He whirled and fired, hitting the lance's owner in the chest. The brave flew backward like a puppet jerked by strings.

In the camp, a Comanche fell spouting blood with an arrow through his neck. Dan looked around for Rojo without seeing the Apache, but it was clear he was nearby. Roque was finally free. Knife and lance in hand, a Comanche leapt through the air toward the recovering Roque. A shot from behind Dan snapped the brave's head to one side. The Comanche knocked Roque to the ground although the brave was dead on arrival.

A noise alerted Dan, and he spun to face another Comanche whose mouth was open in a war cry. Dan saw feathers where the brave's tongue should have been. As he fell forward, Dan saw the point of an arrow protruding from the back of his neck. There was a brief exchange of fire. Dan cracked his pistols at retreating Indians, but the fight was over.

Dan called to his friends. "I count seven riders departing followed by five riderless ponies."

Roque and Rojo joined Dan in the camp.

"Do you always dress like this for battle?" asked Rojo.

"It is a custom of my people. If there is time," Dan replied with dignity, "we paint ourselves blue first. Sometimes we wear a little plaid dress. It frightens the enemy."

Rojo made sure of his kills while Dan went in search of the brave he'd slain. There was a blood trail, but no body. He followed it around the big rock to find a naked Sebriana held with a knife at her throat by the Comanche. He had no target.

Before Dan could think of a plan, Sebriana called out. "I feel faint."

She promptly dropped to her knees exposing the Comanche to Dan's fire. Without conscious thought or aim, Dan's pistol cracked and a round hole opened between the Indian's eyes.

Naked and covered in gore, Sebriana ran to Dan and threw her arms around his neck. He kissed her hard and long, and then as he began shaking uncontrollably, he pushed her away.

"I almost lost you."

Sebriana smiled. "I wasn't scared. I knew you would save me."

Dan turned from her and began dressing, still shaking, his mind and heart in turmoil. He thought, "I cannot risk her life like this. I love her, but I can't let her get any closer. It isn't fair. I'm using her since I can't marry her. She's not an American. She's beneath me. It isn't right, it isn't fair, and I love her so."

Sebriana ran to Dan and grabbed his arm. "*Pobrecito*, you are bleeding."

There was a long gash in his side from an enemy lance. "When did that happen?"

"Let me dress your wound," she said.

Then she dressed Dan who told her, "That's the most fun I've ever had putting clothes on."

His thoughts went black. "I almost lost her."

Still only partially clothed but unable to stay near the woman, he turned from the Sebriana again and stumbled back toward his friends, Roque and Rojo.

Moments later, Sebriana appeared neatly dressed and approached a very bloody Roque. "Is any of that yours?"

"Maybe a little." He grinned.

"Look, *primo*," said Sebriana innocently. "I did as you bade me. Since my gun is so small, only fit for women and children, I had to shoot one through the eye and one through the ear."

The men saw that it was so.

"That girl," said Rojo shaking his head, "is a deadly shot."

"Riders coming," called Rojo.

They hurried to their former places of concealment and checked their weapons.

Dan called to the others. "We need to be away from here before the Comanche return with friends and relatives."

Five riders halted two hundred yards away.

Roque jeered. "They deliberately stay out of range of our weapons."

"Hello the camp!" called the largest one. "We heard shots. Can we help?"

"Hello," Dan called back, "fight's over. We were just leaving. Thanks."

"Can we come in?" the big man called.

"Come," Dan replied unable to think of another excuse to keep him away.

They rode in. The big man looked all around seeing only Dan. "You do all this?" He pointed to the bodies.

"Some," Dan said. "My friends helped."

"Where are your friends now?" he asked. Roque and Juan, the name they'd agreed on for Sebriana, rose from cover. Rojo did not.

"I'm John Rheingold," the big man said. It was clear

he was the leader. Dan guessed he was about six foot four. Long, curly brown hair stuck out from under his sombrero. He dressed in fringed buckskin and tooled boots. He and his men were as heavily armed as Dan and his friends.

Three of John's four men dressed like their leader. One was short, wiry and fidgety. He had dark, shifty eyes and scowled at the world as he played with a pistol. The other two were plain men, plainly dressed. They did not make an impression.

The fourth man had long blond hair under a black, broad-brimmed felt hat. He had cold blue eyes that took in everything as they darted about the camp. What caught Dan's eye was the golden square and compasses that hung on a chain about his neck. He wore corduroy pants and a cotton shirt and black, embroidered vest. He was the dandy of the bunch.

"Where you headed?" blondie asked. He seemed to be second in command and smart.

"Tiler, don't be impolite," said John. "This here is my associate, Tiler Caine. Guess if you're okay, we'll be going."

Dan smiled. "I'm Dan Trelawney, and they are Roque and Juan. Thanks for stopping."

"That Juan's pretty cute for a boy," Tiler sneered.

"Yeah, I've noticed that myself," Dan replied cheerfully. "But it's better not to think about it. The boy fights like a demon and would cut your throat in a second if you tried anything."

A strong gust of wind blew up the blanket Dan had thrown over his saddle at the approach of riders. Beneath it lay Professor Pendarvis's folio. Dan had been about to secure it in his saddlebag.

Tiler's eyes darted to the folio. Dan shuddered, certain

Tiler had seen journal before. The same gust blew back his vest and Dan caught a glimpse of a hammered, Mexican silver-dollar cut out to form a star.

They were Texas Rangers. Dan knew they occasionally entered New Mexico acting as if it were their jurisdiction. Dan prayed that they hadn't noticed his reaction.

The friends gathered as the rangers rode off.

"Texas Rangers?" said Roque. "What are those *pendejos* doing in New Mexico?"

"Maybe he's a former Ranger," Dan mused.

"No. They act too much like soldiers," Roque said and spat.

"I think I've seen them before," Dan offered, "in Santa Fe following Topper."

"You have," said Rojo in confirmation. "Let's get out of here. We should split up, like quail. Go singly and meet tonight."

Dan thought about this. "We don't know the country well enough for that."

Roque suggested they ride up a canyon and set an ambush for those who pursued them.

"There might be more Comanche," said Dan, "than we could handle. We don't have a reason to kill the Texas Rangers, only suspicions."

"We might ride through streams," suggested Sebriana, "double back, change direction whenever we were sure we weren't seen."

The last word came from Rojo. "We might do all those things and we might convince those following that we knew we were followed. It will be obvious to pursuers that we are headed south away from the Santa Fe Trail. The obvious place for us to go is west through Comanche Gap to Albuquerque. They will be waiting."

The others agreed.

Rojo said, "Then we shall be innocents and head directly for Albuquerque. There, among people, we might slip away unnoticed. Many roads lead from the town, and there are many travelers."

Hours later on the trail, Dan spoke of something that had been tormenting him. "Did any of you notice that Tiler Caine was a Mason?"

Rojo turned his head. "They all were, Danito, they all were."

Chapter 5

Decalogue Stone

The four friends made their way through Comanche Gap into the Galisteo Basin. The crumbling ruins of pueblos dotted the countryside. They seemed to Dan to be much like Indian towns of Taos, Santa Clara, or San Ildefanso.

"The stories of my people," said Rojo, "name them and say they were once great towns and great traders."

They turned south to the Estancia Valley where salt could be found and had been, according to Rojo, by Jicarilla in ancient times. To their west were the Manzano and Sandia Mountains, a gentle slope rising high from the east into ponderosa pine country. The Sandia Peak showed *picacho grande*, tall cliffs, on its western side facing the tiny pueblo of Albuquerque. They made their way through the *cañon* that separated the two ranges arriving on the Rio Grande *llano,* the plain, near the pueblo, village that was the Duke City.

The *llano* by the river provided rich farmland. Everything grew there. The climate in the *Abajo,* the south, was warmer than in the *Rio Arriba* north of Santa Fe. There were grape vineyards and apple orchards, fields of squash and pumpkin, tomato and chili. Within two miles of the river, the grasslands, dotted with herds of sheep and cattle, were so green it hurt the eyes of those accustomed to the browns, reds and tans of western lands. The river bottom was crowded with great stands of *alamos*, sycamore and cottonwood. Here and there across the *llano,* like medieval kingdoms protected by self-contained castles, were the *haciendas* of the *ricos*.

In *Rio Arriba*, most men were free. They were poor, but they worked for themselves with few exceptions. In the *Abajo*, most men labored for the *ricos*. In many cases, they were indentured. Many were *Indios* captured as children and given to great families to work in slavery while learning the true and most Catholic religion. Slavery had been prohibited since Spanish times in the mid-eighteenth century, so those who were kidnapped, bought, sold and traded traveled under titles other than slave. They were servants who could be beaten, weren't paid, and could not quit. Little differentiated servant-slaves from *vaqueros* who watched herds and tillers who slaved in fields. *Vaqueros* and tillers received some small pay.

Albuquerque consisted of a large plaza and scattered dwellings and *haciendas*. Behind *salas,* public rooms, and facing the plaza, the homes of the merchants stretched deep and away from the center. These dwellings often contained small, private, enclosed plazas. The friends found *La Posada*, the inn, hired a room for two nights, and then set out to find a meal they hadn't cooked for themselves.

Dan explained his thoughts to the others. "Sebriana is a great cook. It's just that she ain't got the time or the equipment to work with on the trail."

They found a restaurant that actually had tables though the friends found themselves sitting on the *banco,* an adobe bench that ran along the wall. Light came from a decorative chandelier made of cut, hammered, shaped, and soldered tin cans. Cans came over the Santa Fe Trail packed with meat, fruit, and vegetables to metal-poor New Mexico where new use was found for them.

"And plates!" exclaimed Dan. "The times they are a changin.' It used to be a tortilla was plate and spoon."

The restaurant had tin plates on which to serve the food. The mistress of the house brought them rice, beans and *refritos*, grilled chicken and beef, *rellenos*, that is, chilis stuffed with cheese, battered and fried, and *chili con carne*, chili with meat. Of course, there were plenty of newly made, warm *tortillas*. They ate and drank the *vecino* wine and ate some more.

Blessedly sated, the friends stepped out into the night.

Like rats scurrying from a dark room when the door is opened, figures dashed around corners.

"I think I saw that Texian they call Li'l Jim," said Roque.

"I saw two," Dan responded, "that I've seen before in Santa Fe. They wore dark, city clothes and had great bushy beards. That's the way they went," he indicated pointing with his chin.

"Yes," said Rojo, "the two who dress like preachers went that way." He pointed with his lower lip.

It's an easy gesture to miss until you get used to it, Dan thought. Apache consider it impolite to point with a finger. If you point, they're apt to take it that you're a *brujo*, a witch, casting a spell.

"None of you saw the one," said Sebriana, "who watched us from the rooftop. He watched for a long time and only disappeared when I looked at him too long. He was Mexicano, I think."

Dan looked to his friends. "Departing from town unnoticed is going to be difficult. The livery stable won't want to open up in the middle of the night."

"If we prepared our stock early," said Roque, "the fact would be noticed."

"Maybe not," said Dan, who had made arrangements to move the stock to a large fenced paddock outside town to graze. Their packs and tack went along to the small, nearby hay barn.

The next evening they enjoyed another good meal of fresh *tortillas* and green-chili stew made with pork. Sebriana declined the green chili pork stew and *posole,* but ate her fill of fajita, flank steak, and steamed chicken.

Posole, hominy with pork and hot chili, was a dish loved by almost everyone who tried it, tought Dan, noticing that Sebriana took none. "No *posole, amada*?"

She scoffed. "Against my religion."

He looked at her skeptically.

She spoke cryptically. "I was taught to light the candles on Friday night but not let the sacred light get in my eyes." They could get no more from her than they could from the Sphinx.

They bedded down early and arose just after midnight. In turn each of them headed for the privy. On exiting, they continued on in the deepest shadows toward their paddock. Long before sunup, the four friends were already far south on El Camino Real, the Royal Road from Santa Fe to Chihuahua City.

Just after sunup, Rojo gave a sign, and they descended to the river bottoms and rode back upstream in the water for over a mile.

Finding a clearing in the dense growth of *alamos*, Dan called a halt. Rojo moved off among the trees to where he could observe the road and not be observed. Making camp, they waited through the day.

In late morning, Rojo woke Dan. "The five Texians

head south."

Roque replaced him on watch. Within the hour a party of fifteen riders in dark city-style coats and bushy beards passed by going south.

"The circuit preachers" Sebriana called them.

They waited through the afternoon and night. Over the campfire the friends argued about what to do next.

"If we go south, we might ride right into them," Dan said.

Roque shook his handsome head. "I think they will continue south, not come back north."

Dan looked puzzled. "Won't they wonder why no one has seen us?"

Roque replied. "They will think we have by-passed the villages. They know we carried food for many days. They have seen our packs."

"I think," said his Jicarilla friend, Rojo, "We should turn north and ride back to Albuquerque. As we go, we will tell everyone we meet coming south of a big gunfight near Mesilla. Persons unknown attacked four riders. One of those attacked was a very small and very pretty young man, another was a big *guero*, blonde, who dressed like a mountain man, there was also a tall, well-dressed Mexicano and an *Indio* who resembled Adonis."

"We will shift our clothes," suggested Roque, "so that we appear to be a servant and escort for a Spanish lady, Sebriana, who is traveling north to Albuquerque. The four riders, we will say, were driven west toward the Santa Rita Copper Mines by their enemies. We watched from a distance but do not know the outcome. We do not want it to appear strange no one in Mesilla has heard of the fight."

"Oh, good," said Sebriana, "I get to pretend I am a lady."

"I have the hardest part," said the Rojo. They all looked at him. "I must bow my head, walk stooped over, and pretend to be your humble servant."

Humility might prove hard for the proud Apache. Dan dreaded what might happen if some passerby tried to take liberties with him.

Maybe this ruse will buy us a little time, Dan thought. It seemed a better chance than other plans they'd considered. All day long, they passed the story of the fight near Mesilla to everyone they met headed south. By dusk, they were near Albuquerque, Dan could smell the good food they had enjoyed the day before. Another such meal was cooking not far away. But, they didn't dare go into town. In the morning, they turned south again for Los Lunas.

"With luck," said Dan, "we've bought ourselves a few days. We'll need them."

The four approached the tiny plaza of Los Lunas. It was a confused huddle of poor adobes set just far enough back from the river so as not to be swept away in the annual floods. The plain near the river was veined with *acequias*, irrigation ditches, and planted with neat fields.

"How will we find this stone of yours?" Roque asked Dan. "Topper had difficulty."

"I've been thinking about that," the tall Anglo replied. "I think we will tell the villagers that I am one of the brothers Grimm, those collectors of fairytales. Sebriana will be a *rico* from Santa Fe who has invited me here on an expedition to collect the *vecino* stories. You and Rojo will be our guides. We will throw a fandango and invite them here to drink our wine and eat our food and tell us stories."

With the plan agreed upon, they set up outside a cantina on the little plaza. So many people came in response to their offers to pay a few pennies for tales and legends that there was soon a *fandango* going. *Vecino* musicians came and played. The four tipped them for their services. Couples danced the *cuna*, the cradle. The partners grasped each other tight at the waist, shoulders back, and arms extended to form the cradle. They whirled about the plaza. During the next two days, Dan and his friends collected many wonderful fairytales and numerous stories of lost mines and treasures, but nothing about a rock with writing on it quite different from the pictures left by *Indios*. The *Indios'* symbols were not organized like writing. They seemed usually to stand alone or at most to be grouped with a few others linking a few ideas. There was nothing like a text. They learned of many rocks with such *Indio* writing. Nothing sounded promising.

Juan-Sebriana and Dan sat at a table where the people of Los Lunas came one by one to tell them their stories. Children gathered at their feet to listen. Dan copied down what they told him, writing as fast as he could. Anything might prove useful. He'd heard many of the stories before from Roque and from others. Dan and Sebriana thanked everyone for their efforts. None of them went away unhappy, but none of them spoke of the rock the travelers sought.

"I think we are talking to the wrong people," said Sebriana at last.

Dan looked puzzled. "Who should we be talking to?"

"These people," said Doña Loca, "would not recognize Hebrew writing if they saw it. They could walk past our stone and see nothing. We need to talk to the other people; those who might see it for what it is, and I think we will have to go to them."

Dan rubbed his chin. "Who are these people?"

"The *Marranos*," she said.

"What does it mean? It sounds like a word for pig."

Roque growled. "It is. They are pigs, swine, something filthy and dirty that exist only in stories. *Marranos*, there are no *Marranos* here, only *conversos,* converts.

"What are you two talking about?" Dan pleaded.

"*Marranos* are Jews," said Sebriana. "Some tried to come here to practice their faith when they could no longer do so in Spain."

"But," insisted Roque, "they were forced to convert!"

Undaunted Sebriana continued, "Many came here to avoid the Inquisition. When the authorities became suspicious and began their own Inquisition in Mexico City, the *Sephardi* went into hiding or pretended to convert but still kept their religion. In each family, it was different. Many of them came to the places farthest from the capitol."

"This is impossible!" Roque cried.

"You are sworn to keep my secrets," responded Doña Loca, "so I can tell you what I was sworn to keep as secret when I was young. My family lights two candles every Friday. We do not eat pork and avoid meat that has not had the blood drained from it."

"This is impossible," roared Roque. "You are my cousin."

"We only share one great-grandparent out of eight," Sebriana responded. "I think at least six of mine were *Sephardi*. And I think you, too, are *Sephardi*, Roque."

"I do not understand," said Rojo. "Isn't your Jesus Jewish? Isn't yours a Jewish religion?"

"We think so," Dan said quietly. "We believe Jesus was the promised fulfillment of the Jewish faith, the messiah, religious leader, they were waiting for."

"So what's the problem?" said Rojo.

"The Jews," Dan told him, "were looking for a political and military leader, and they thought Jesus' claim to being God a bit extreme. Of course, believing Jesus was God was extreme unless you believed him and believed the proof he gave in rising from the dead. It was Jews who first followed him, and Jews who spread the faith."

"That is *Power*," marveled Rojo.

"The Jews," Dan went on, "have laws that keep them ritually pure and acceptable to God. Like your understandings with *Power*, Ritual purity is how they remain on the proper footing with God. It is very difficult for them to eat with us because they might accidentally break some of the rules, so they separate themselves and get noticed. Remaining separate keeps them distinct and identifiable and opens them to persecution."

Roque fumed and denied the possibility that he was a Jew.

"I think I can find some of these hidden Jews," smiled Sebriana. "I'll need your help. Find a house where the women have cut off the heads of chickens and have hung the bodies upside down to drain the blood."

It took less time than Dan thought possible to find such a house. Juan-Sebriana talked to the women there. It seemed to Dan that she had to convince them she was one of them. He heard her last question. "Where is your rabbi?"

They were directed to a small casa, the home of a butcher, as it turned out. Sanchez, a perceptive and intelligent man guided by much more learning than was expected in the butcher of a tiny village, was short even by Kit Carson standards. His dark eyes were impenetrable taking in everything.

Juan-Sebriana went about convincing him that she

was of the faith. Soon she was calling him rabbi, teacher. She was recognizing him as a religious leader.

"You," said Rabbi Sanchez to Juan, "are a woman, but I believe you are Jewish even though you break our law by dressing as a man. The rest of you are up to something. Explain to me what it is or I will not help you."

"I am Sebriana," said Juan. "You have found me out. We are looking for a stone with Hebrew writing on it."

"Why?" asked the rabbi.

"The writing might be the Ten Commandments," Dan responded.

"Why is this important to you?" asked Sanchez.

"It might indicate," Dan said, "that the Children of Israel had been here a long time ago."

"And so?" Rabbi Sanchez pushed.

"They might have had something," Dan paused looking for a word, "very valuable, very sacred with them."

"The Ark of the Covenant was lost a long time ago," said the rabbi. "I don't see how it could be here, but go and look. I know the rock you seek. It is on Hidden Mountain called hidden for the hidden Jews. I will take you there."

"Are you comfortable having a non-Jew look for the Ark?" Dan asked.

"Will you turn it over to its proper owners the Nation of Israel, if you find it?" he responded.

"I don't see a Nation of Israel to give it to," Dan said.

"Exactly," said the rabbi. "God has let us wander a long time. My family has practiced both religions since we came to New Mexico. God talks to me through both."

They set out the next morning. The ride was about fifteen miles. Hidden Mountain was above the Rio Puerco. The Spanish named every fifth or sixth river *puerco*, filthy. But, *puerco* could also mean a pig, a *marrano*, a Jew.

"It has been six days," said Roque riding his *grullo* close to Dan's Appaloosa mule and signaling Rojo to join them, "since we have seen our friends from the *El Camino Real.*"

Sebriana, dressed as Juan, chatted happily with her rabbi. Noticing Dan looking at the pair, Roque shrugged. His earlier anger had faded.

"We rode south from Albuquerque for one day and waited a day for others to pass," said the Apache. "Then we rode south two days to Los Lunas and this is the third day since we arrived. It is six days since we saw them."

"The Texians and the others would have come to Socorro and the *Jornada Del Muerte* on the second day," Dan said. "Having seen or heard nothing of us, I think, they would have turned around to check more thoroughly."

"And then, they would have met travelers with word of the big fight near Mesilla," said Rojo. "If they believed it, they would have turned again south and crossed the *Jornada*. Not finding anything at Mesilla, they would have headed for the Copper Mines at Santa Rita del Cobre. This would take three or four more days at least. And when they thought to come north again, their horses would be too worn out. They would need to get new stock in Mesilla or rest their animals in good grazing a few days."

"So we have a few days," Dan concluded. "Roque, have you forgiven Sebriana for being a *marrana*?"

"She is *mi prima*. If she is *marrana*, I am *marrano*. What can I do?"

Hidden Mountain rose about 400 feet off the plain ending in a broad, flat summit less than half a mile across.

Rabbi Sanchez led them to the north face and showed them the stone hidden in a fold of the mountain up an *arroyo*, behind a hill.

"The mountain is hidden," said the rabbi, "because it rises little higher than the mesas along the Rio Puerco. You cannot see it until you are very close and then it seems very big."

"And this valley," said Roque in awe, "is hidden by the mountain, folded in its arms like a mother cradling a baby."

Dan stared at the characters incised in stone. He had been taught Greek, Latin and Hebrew but these seemed different. They were not Greek or Roman. Dan almost rejected Hebrew and looked again and spoke. "Characters in stone are different from those drawn with a brush. Rabbi, I honor your scholarship. They are Hebrew, but not the Hebrew I was taught. Can you read them?"

"Yes, because I was taught an older Hebrew. These are the letters of the Babylonian Captivity."

Dan was stunned. "Are you saying this is the Hebrew of the 6th century before Christ?"

Rabbi Sanchez nodded. "We've had centuries to work it out and help from strange quarters. These were first seen by Jacinto Sanchez, my ancestor. Piro Indians showed them to him before 1620 and helped us with the script."

"Piro Indians?" Dan asked.

"They were Pueblo people," said Sanchez, "who lived here and in the Estancia Valley east of the Manzano Mountains before the Pueblo Revolt. They sided with the Spanish in the rebellion against the other *Indios*. When the Spanish withdrew the Piro went with them to *El Paso Del Norte*. Very few ever returned and those that did think of themselves as Spanish. They were expecting us and we were expecting to meet them. It was written but the meaning was not clear until we met."

Dan's mind didn't register that which seemed impossible. The Sephardi had been expecting to meet the Piro.

Almost in answer to Dan's thoughts, the rabbi spoke, "We were told that in ancient times Children of Israel of the tribe of Dan had gone west across the seas. The Piro were told that someone would come who could read these symbols."

"I almost think I can," said Dan. "The symbols look like Hebrew to me."

"Let me help you." Rabbi Sanchez showed Dan the slight changes in shape that came with time to the language and those caused by the crude tools used to carve them on stone. Within the hour, Dan was able to read the inscription. Sebriana hovered near to the huddled scholars while Roque and Rojo explored and watched for danger. This was a country the Navajo liked to raid.

The rabbi rose. "I know my ancestor thought them holy and related to the destiny of our people but he never told me why they were put here .And now I must be going if I am to arrive in Los Lunas before dark."

They thanked him as he blessed them, "may God make his face to shine upon you and grant you peace," and rode off.

"What does the stone say?" asked Roque.

The black veneer of the stone showed light gray when incised.

"First, I will compare the characters," Dan said, "to those that Topper said were ancient Hebrew and Phoenician." He hadn't brought out Topper's book while with the rabbi. He located one character after another until all had been matched or nearly so to what the professor had given him. The result was the same as the rabbi's interpretation.

"It may take me some time to work out what this says," Dan pleaded and spent the rest of the day and the next morning translating.

"See this line?" he asked Sebriana. "It is written smaller than the rest. It threw me for a while. I think it was inserted later and fits into the middle of the second line. Let's get the others."

Rojo and Roque were off tending to the stock and camp. When they arrived, Dan read them the following:

"I, Jehovah, your God have taken you out of Egypt, the house of slaves. There are no other gods before my face. Do not make idols. You will not take the name of Jehovah in vain. Remember the Sabbath day and keep it holy. Honor your father and your mother so that your days may be long in the land that Jehovah your God has given to you. Do not murder. You must not do adultery. You must not steal. You must not give a false witness against your neighbor. You must not desire your neighbor's wife nor anything that is his."

"Sounds like the Ten Commandments," said Roque.

Dan grinned wryly. "That thought had crossed my mind."

"So what does it mean?" asked Rojo.

"What do we know?" Dan asked rhetorically and then ticked off what he thought they had learned on his fingers. "One, it is the Ten Commandments. Two, it is written in a very old script, the one Topper told me to expect with very few differences. He said no one else knew this script except a few who might have seen it at Roslyn, but the rabbi and the Piro seemed to know as well. Three, it seems likely to have been here before the Spanish arrived. The Piro, the Indians who lived hereabouts until 1680, thought it very old and sacred.

"It seems," Dan continued, "to confirm the story on a parchment Topper found at Roslyn. I'll tell you about it tonight by the fire. Until then, find any mark on any rock here, note its location and draw a sketch of it." Dan gave them paper to work with.

Dan turned to Sebriana. She looked beautiful in the late afternoon sun, her hair glistening and black hanging far down her back, her skin clear, smooth and tan. "Topper once told me that a secret shared by two is soon known by many."

"Do we have a secret, *Pobrecito*?"

Dan blushed and turned away. She was Mexican and a crypto-Jew, no fit mate for a New England man.

Hours passed as they searched. Rojo called Dan to him pointing at an inscription on the rock, "This does not look like the work of *Indios* to me."

"Indeed it's not," Dan replied. "It's called a Tetragrammaton, the name of God. I think you've found an altar." The New England man smiled broadly.

Sebriana waved to them. "Come and look here." When they approached she pointed to a figure carved on stone. "See? It is a face with a crown." The crown showed a jagged edge like Hebrew and European crowns.

Rojo scowled. "I have never seen an Indian wear a headdress like that."

"The symbol on the lower left," Dan said, "the x in a circle, looks like a Teth, a Hebrew T."

Roque grinned evilly. "Do you think it's a portrait of Princess Tea Tephi?" He had trouble believing Hebrews might have been here before his heroes, the conquistadors.

Nonetheless Dan thought about what the Mexican said. "Roque, I don't know what it means. It could be, I guess, or some other whose name began with T."

The smell of sagebrush, their firewood, pervaded the camp along with that of roasting meat as Sebriana treated them to a fine meal of beef and chicken, tortillas, and beans. The fire warmed them as the sun turned the sky to blazing crimson shreds. They had time, water and fuel and made the most of it.

After dinner they tried to interpret what they'd found. Dan looked thoughtful. "You've all see the glyphs hammered into the rock here." His friends nodded. "There is no doubt they look like accepted Hebrew writing, different, but of a similar character." Again they agreed.

"Now look at these," he continued turning to a page in Professor Pendarvis's journal.

Perceptive Sebriana was the first to respond. "There is no relationship that I can see."

Dan nodded. "None that I can see either. Topper says these were recorded from the Golden Plates of Joseph Smith and they are supposed to be in some derivative of Hebrew or Reformed Egyptian."

Roque frowned. "So the Golden Bible is a fraud."

Dan cocked his head. "It would appear so, but there is no question that Joseph Smith had knowledge of that which we are seeking. Brigham Young pursues it today. He tells his followers they are the descendants of the Children of Israel and they have come west to seek Zion. That can only mean the place where the Ark of the Covenant is kept. Smith was a Freemason and seems to have gained knowledge from the brotherhood."

"And so they pursue us," said Rojo.

Dan nodded. "It would seem so. Among Topper's papers was a copy of a document he had found at Roslyn. The document was recorded as having been discovered by the Templar Knights when they explored the catacombs under the Temple of Solomon. When the Babylonians threatened Jerusalem," he continued, "it was decided to evacuate the Ark out of their reach. It looked like the Babylonians, unchecked, would take over the world. Even mighty Egypt trembled. The High Priest of the Jews had heard legends of a land far to the west where Egyptians and Danites had sailed in ancient times. The elders of the Tribe of Dan were called to appear before the High Priest. One of them, a very old man, claimed to have made the voyage as a youth to the distant land of tobacco and coca. A company of Levites was assembled including men to fill each of the positions recorded in the Law regarding the Ark and the Tabernacle. Joining them was a crew of the very best sailors of the Tribe of Dan. Their instructions were to ascend a great river to near its source and hide the Ark in some natural temple. They were to send back word when the Ark was safe."

"And then?" asked Roque eyes aglow in the dark excited by the tale. Dan could see he had the attention of the others as well.

"That's where the document ends," Dan concluded. "The Ark was sent to be hidden in the distant west."

"This isn't very helpful," said Rojo.

"It isn't right to end a story like this," chimed Sebriana.

"That is how the story ended," Dan said. "For many years, Topper journeyed the world, going to Jerusalem, Egypt, Istanbul, and Rome. He found nothing until his return to Roslyn where he discovered a badly damaged document, almost impossible to read. Weather and insects had done a great deal of damage. It was found in a jar, in an out-of-the-way side passage under Solomon's Temple, not in the Temple Archives where the other had been found.

"Topper's notes are cryptic," Dan continued. "He translated individual words underlining blanks between them where words and phrases were missing or unreadable in the original. Because the grammar is different from English, words occur in a different order making translation even more difficult. Here's what it said:

Men of Dan, crossing the vast chasm to the setting sun, sailing the eternal deep.

Men of Dan in their boats, the Lord's blessing on the Children of Israel.

They made landfall by the great river whose mouth is guarded by sandbar.

Dan journeyed toward the brilliant East following the great river.

It made a bend toward the gloom, hidden unknown.

The craggy depths forced the men of Dan away from the river through the Negev.

Coming forth from Negev Dan found a muddy river flowing toward brilliant East.

Men of Dan followed the river and journeyed through mountain and waste.

Temple carved by the Hand of the Lord in the cavernous, craggy deep.

Great pillars Jachin and Boaz guard the Holy of Holies

Atop the Well of Souls.

Across vast seas Dan sailed.

Three years the men of Dan journeyed up the river leaving signs for those who follow.

Where the river flows from the impassable deep,

Where the traveler must journey through the desolation,

Where the great river is found again to succor men's hearts, there

The river that flows with mud from the brilliance shall be a sign.

The hidden mountain shall be a sign.

The men of Dan followed the trail of salt to the great chasm…"

Dan paused. "It's pretty broken up after this. Single words, whole lines missing." He continued.

"carved…Lord's Commandments where we left the river…

follow the Salt Road…signs clear to you

Dan's altars mark the road,

Dan's altars where the men of Dan prayed…

mercy on the people of Israel shall be as a sign to you…

Dan returned down the river…

returning to the land of Israel.

We found all in desolation, all destroyed, all of the people gone,

…the Lord's Temple, the pride of Israel laid waste

…Great were our lamentations.

Babylon the Great has taken away the Lord's people."

Dan Trelawney paused.

"What did Topper think it meant?" asked Sebriana.

"Topper," he said, "was a careful man, good at keeping secrets. He thought he had the greatest secret in the world discovered in this document: the location of the lost Ark. He wrote down nothing of his conclusions and speculations. He placed this document with the other document and gave us a translation of the words he could make out. That's all."

"I think," said Sebriana, "this message tells us that it took years to reach the land in the west, but they did reach it, and they sent back word."

"And," Dan said, "when they returned they found the Temple in ruins and everyone gone, the land devastated. The Jews were in the Babylonian Exile. So they hid a message in the ruins of the Temple. They didn't dare be too specific."

Rojo sighed deeply. Unlike him, Dan thought. "So the Master's Word is Lost."

"It seems so," Dan said. "We know they came this far. We know they tried to leave a hidden trail. I wish we had Kit with us. He's good at picking up a cold trail."

"Yes," said Roque, "this one is only..." He started counting on his fingers. "Only..."

"Two thousand, four hundred years old," Sebriana finished for him. "More or less."

Roque's massive shoulders slumped. "Does anything work in our favor?"

"Well," Dan started and then paused thinking deeply, "if a number of Danites and Levites came with the Ark, they might have had descendants; they might have left traces and legends. The professor's sketches of homes in the Middle East look like Pueblo homes. Maybe they have descendants among these people. They seem to say they left a trail of signs. Maybe we can figure out what they were. There might even be a trail of altars. We've found one. There could be others."

Rojo's eyes squinted, and his forehead wrinkled. "Why would they need more than one altar?"

"Sebriana, do you want to explain?" Dan asked.

"I don't think I know," she said. "We kept a few customs, but we couldn't be too obvious. The priests might find out."

Dan nodded. "Then I'll have to do my best to explain. It's at the heart of the difference between our religions, even though we all come from Judaism and two of us are Christians. God created two sets of laws. One governs the physical universe, the other our spiritual life. We all have to be ritually pure in order to be acceptable to God and have any hope of an afterlife.

"Jews," he continued, "are a little vague on the afterlife, but big on purity in this life. They have a long list of rules about what to eat, how to eat it, and what not to eat. They use the term 'abomination,' meaning disgusting for everything from eating clams to having sexual relations with an animal. It's what they have to do to come back into purity that is interesting and shows the seriousness of the crime. For touching something unclean, you separate yourself from the people for the day and take a bath at sundown. Anyone caught being disgusting with an animal should be put to death along with the animal.

"There are many sins," Dan went on, "that require sacrifice to put things right with God. Sacrifice is not the destruction of flesh as you might think. It is ritual killing of things that will be eaten later.

"You can look at this requirement," he continued, "a couple of ways. It may be that death and the spilling of blood are necessary to restore and save the life of the sinner. Or it may be that the killing is symbolic, but the symbolism has to be powerful enough to do the job, so ritual sacrifice and the spilling of blood are required. It is at this point the Jews, Catholics, and Protestants divide."

"Catholics believe," said Roque, "that Jesus who was God was the perfect sacrifice, one time for all. So we don't sacrifice anymore, and we don't have to keep the purity laws, just the Commandments."

"Right," Dan said. "The Catholic confesses his sins and then in the Mass gets a piece of the body of Christ from that sacrifice to stay with him until he sins again. When he does that, he expels or ruins the sacrifice and has to go through the process of confession and Mass again.

"The Protestant," Dan went on, "believes he can pray for forgiveness one on one with God, accepting Christ's sacrifice as saving him. He tries not to sin, and God helps him in that, but if he does, the Protestant asks forgiveness again."

"That's all very well," said Sebriana, "but Jews don't sacrifice. Rabbi Sanchez told me so."

"Here is an altar," said Rojo, "made by Jews we think."

"Maybe it's not," said the woman with finality.

"The Jews," Dan said, "used to sacrifice in the Temple. In the year of our Lord 70, they lost the Temple and were thrown out of Israel. Some think that stopped the sacrifices. Did you notice that Rabbi Sanchez was a butcher?"

"Yes," said Sebriana. "What of it?"

"Why do Jews have a rabbi sacrifice their dinner?" Dan asked. "Is the rabbi still performing the sacrifice albeit in a little different way?"

"This is very interesting," said Rojo, a Jicarilla Apache. "I don't understand the split between Protestant and Catholic. Apaches are more like Jews. If we insult *Power*, we have to purify ourselves. What is the difference between Christians?"

"Taxes," Dan said.

"Taxes?" blurted Roque.

Dan looked at him and said calmly, "The early Protestants realized that salvation was granted by the mercy of God and not by anything man could do. Men put a tax on salvation, and Protestants protested."

"What tax?" asked Roque, his veins bulging in his neck.

"Charges," Dan said, "for marriages, funerals, and baptisms. Priests grow rich on the price of salvation."

"The priests aren't rich," objected Roque, "the church is. Are you saying the Church is bad?" He growled.

"No, Roque," Dan replied, "but men make mistakes, even Protestants. We are not nearly as in awe of God as we should be and we don't build Him very nice houses."

Roque was mollified somewhat. It had been a tough couple of days for him finding out that he might be a Jew, a people he called *Marrano*, pigs. With other men, such revelations might have caused trouble, but Roque thought for himself. He lashed out, defending his love for God, not the priests. He shared some of Dan's doubts about priests.

They sat there smoking their pipes over a low fire and thinking for a very long time. They looked away from the coals so their eyes would not be blind to the night. The land around them was *Dinetah*, as the Navajo called it, their country. The four needed to be on the lookout. *Cimarrones*, wild Indians, did not live this close to the river, but Navajo often raided the *Abajo* for sheep.

"What next?" asked Rojo.

"The parchment the professor found mentioned 'a trail of salt' several times," Sebriana suggested. "Where does salt come from?"

"The Estancia Valley," said the Jicarilla, "where the other Piro villages used to be."

"The brilliance in the Danites' letter might mean east, the brilliant rising sun," Dan said and then thought for a minute. "The river turning toward the 'gloom and unknown,' that could mean north! The river turns north at El Paso."

"The place where they had to leave the river," said Roque, "because of chasms and then crossed desolate land, that sounds like the *Jornada del Muerte*, the land south and west of Rio Grande below Socorro, the journey of death."

"We are north of the *Jornada*," added Sebriana thoughtfully. "And this could be the muddy river and the hidden mountain. But why would they leave their sign in the west if they went east?"

"Secrecy!" exclaimed Roque with finality.

The next day, they rode back to the east, unwilling to be seen and passing far south of town. Across the Rio Grande, they picked up what Rojo said was an Indian trail across the Manzano Mountains to the *llano*. There, near the mountains, stood Abó, the smallest of the ancient villages they sought.

They saw it from a distance, a tower and castle wall of stone surrounded by a crumbling adobe village. As they approached, they could see that the tower was over forty feet high with battlements and a fighting platform at the top. The wall of the rest of the castle enclosed in a large area but was barely over eight feet tall in many places. They rode around the building, amazed at its size and the fine craftsmanship of the stone work.

Roque sat tall and proud in his saddle as he addressed his friends. "These villages were here when the conquistadors arrived, and the people were their friends.

During the Pueblo Revolt of 1680, the people left with the Spaniards and never returned."

His friends looked at him astonished. Roque's knowledge of the past was usually limited to family stories. He blushed. "Topper told me."

The friends prowled the village as well. The masonry was Indian work, and here and there the round depression of an *estufa* showed in the ground.

"The Hopi call those *kivas*," Rojo said. "They are underground chambers where the men stay and do work, like weaving. They also make magic and religion and perform secret ceremonies no one else is allowed to see. Each *kiva* has its own society with its own ceremonials."

"Do the Rio Grande Pueblos have *kivas*?" Dan asked.

"Yes, but they are hidden, very secret," Rojo replied. "The entry is often under their houses, or the *kiva* is out in the mountains. They didn't want the Spanish priests to see and accuse them of being *brujos*, witches. Now they are not so sure of the Yankees, so they still keep them hidden."

The adobes were crumbling as all adobes do when untended. The roofs collapsed and the walls slowly melted and became shorter with each passing year. In time, all that was left was a low hill and a patch of ground a little more barren than the surrounding land. The most obvious sign that people have been there was the litter of broken pottery, flint, and bones.

It was different with stone buildings. In time, the roof leaked, and the *vigas* that supported it rotted and fell. Moisture from rain and snow getting between the stone blocks expanded when it froze, cracking them and forcing them apart. Such weathering was a slow process. Most abandoned buildings were destroyed much more quickly. People came and took the *vigas,* the doors, and the stone blocks reusing them to build their own houses. The walls came down rapidly, melting more swiftly than adobe. At Abó, the stone buildings had been left intact. No one lived near enough to bother taking stones or *vigas*.

"Come quick," called Sebriana. "I have found something."

She showed her friends a paper with her notes. "I paced off the length of walls and drew them here," she said. "See? It forms a cross! We are in a church!"

"How is it that the first to recognize a Christian church is a woman who calls herself *Marrano*?" asked Roque. He looked smug as if this proved she wasn't Jewish; therefore, he wasn't either.

"I had to worship in a Christian church," said Sebriana firmly. "My family practiced Jewish ways in secret. And by the way, please do not call me *Marrano* again, or you might wake some morning to find yourself circumcised."

She showed them the outline of the church.

"Now that you show me," said Dan, "it seems obvious."

Bultos, *santos,* and *retablos*, carved saints and stories painted on wooden boards, were gone, but their *nichos*, alcoves, remained. Baptistery, sacristy, and pulpit soon became clear. The adjoining "castle" was the *convento*, the priest's quarters, which contained space for servants, stored supplies, and trade goods as well as rooms for orphans who would be trained for the priesthood. The *convento* was as big as any casa in Santa Fe. One hundred and eighty years had passed, and still *convento* and *iglesia*, church, were in fine, even beautiful, condition.

"*Un iglesia grande!*" said Roque in awe. "This is the grandest church in all of New Mexico."

"Roque," Dan said quietly, "this is one thing that tells me the love of God is still with the Catholics. They build

Him such fine houses.

"Check the altar," Dan continued. "That is the most likely place. This church was built before 1680. That's two thousand years after the Ark passed this way. If we are correct in thinking it came this way, there should be an altar with a Tetragrammaton carved on it. It might be incorporated in the new altar or a foundation stone. Look for inscriptions."

Both Rojo and Sebriana turned out to have an eye for such details. They found inscriptions and marks Roque and Dan would never have seen. Inscriptions from words to Christian symbols appeared in the most amazing places down near the ground, under lintels, and in places that had become inaccessible with the passage of time.

After a day of searching, Sebriana summed up for them. "No Jewish symbols or letters. There is nothing Jewish here except me."

Dan indicated his agreement. "We could spend a lifetime digging and searching this one ruin. If there had been anything here, I think the Spanish priests would have found it."

"Only if they'd been looking," said Rojo.

Much later, Dan would wish that Rojo's statement had registered with him then. It might have saved them grief later, he thought. At the least, it would have saved them a few days searching.

"Are there more like this?" Dan asked Rojo.

"Two more," the Apache pointed with his lip. "There," indicating northeast, "and there," indicating southeast.

"Let's try that one." Dan pointed northeast extending his lower lip in that direction. Rojo nodded. To the Apache, pointing with a finger is rude.

Hours of riding brought them to the place. Roque was

awed. "This *iglesia* at Quarai is more beautiful than the one at Abó. Look at the setting. Magnifico!" Mountains behind and the *llano* sloped down in front toward dried salt lakes.

"Do you think," Dan asked, "the people and priests grew rich on the salt trade to have built such churches?"

"They must have," Roque said as Rojo nodded.

"If," said Sebriana, "there was so much wealth in salt, wouldn't they have returned after the *Reconquista*? Why abandon three rich cities?"

Later Dan reflected. "I should have listened. We found no altar at Quarai, no sign that Jews had ever been there."

The companions continued south to Gran Quivira. The village was much larger than the other two, and two churches were located there.

"This church," said Roque, "has been torn down and the stone reused on the second one."

So it was. The second church was not as graceful or as tall as those they'd seen at Quarai and Abó, but it was more massive and so was the *convento*. The walls everywhere were very thick. The windows might have been gun embrasures. Windows were a rarity in New Mexico. There was no glass to cover them, but at Gran Quivira they saw at least two large enough to mount cannon.

Still they found neither Jewish altar nor Hebrew inscription!

That night they camped and stabled their stock in what had been the great *convento*. The walls hid their fire and their stock. They were on the *llano* in what had become Comanche country. Comanche were the reason a fine country, the Estancia Valley, remained unsettled by *gavacho* and *Hispano* alike.

Roque looked wistful. "Once the *Faraones* roamed this land."

Dan looked puzzled. "Pharaohs? I thought they were in Egypt."

Roque nodded. "Topper told me."

Rojo spoke. "They were Apaches attacked by the Comanche. Some joined the Jicarilla, some the Mescalero."

Dan thought about the melding of tribes. The Apache had no more than temporary political formation. They spoke the same language even though the names of tribes were different from place to place. Sometimes the remnant of a name was left on a stream or mountain. Rio Puerco where the Jews once were might be a remnant of forgotten knowledge. It was an ironic twist to call a Jew a pig. Hidden Mountain. What was it hiding?

Sebriana made them a fine dinner of turkey they had shot and the last of their *refritos*. They would need to stock up on supplies when next they passed a town. They sat around their fire, warm in its low glow, smoking and thinking.

"Sebriana," Dan commented. "You eat *refritos*."

"Of course. All *paisanos* do."

"But *refritos* are made with lard, pork fat."

She looked puzzled. "I never thought of it that way." She thought for a long time. "Everything is made with lard. How could I avoid it?"

The men settled to smoking their clay pipes and thinking while Sebriana rolled a cigarito. She asked, "Could the priests have found the Ark and taken it away? Or were they even looking for the Ark?"

"I've been thinking about that," Dan said. "The Conquistador Coronado called Marcos de Niza 'that lying priest.' The priest went ahead to scout for the expedition.

Marcos de Niza encouraged the conquistador with stories of golden cities he must have known were untrue. Why?"

"The Knights Templar," Sebriana asked, "were monks who reported directly to the Pope, right? If the Knights found records in the Temple, perhaps they gave copies to the Vatican. When new discoveries made these lands accessible, the Pope would have wanted this great treasure." She faltered.

Dan picked up her thread, "Cabeza de Baca came up the Rio Grande from the Gulf of Mexico on the same path the Danites, the tribe of Dan, must have used. Coronado knew he was entering lands Cabeza de Baca had been through. The Pope wouldn't have wanted the true nature of the expedition known. It was 1540. The Reformation was underway. The Knights Templar were gone, but the Pope might well have had records that showed where they had gone. Papal hostility to the Freemasons is very old. If the Templars became the Freemasons, this might be the reason. Having attacked the Templars, the Papacy could expect their enmity. The Pope would also believe that they too knew about the treasure. Someone might grab the prize ahead of him. The true mission would have to be secret, known only to trusted priests." Dan stopped to muse over his comments.

Roque picked up the train of Dan's thought, "Coronado didn't stay, but the Conquistadors didn't give up! Oñate came in 1598 to settle the land. By then, I think they knew there were no golden cities here, no second Mexico, no riches of any kind. The Spanish Fathers followed the trail here and built these beautiful churches. The Pueblo Revolt drove them out in 1680. The Reconquista took almost twenty years. The land was settled again, but not these wonderful churches. They were abandoned."

"They knew!" breathed Sebriana. "The Pope knew the Ark wasn't here. His people had spent eighty years looking. They knew something was wrong. The Ark was in Nuevo Mexico, but not here."

"What now?" asked Roque.

"We think a little," Dan said. "Rojo, what trails lead from Hidden Mountain? Is there another source of salt?"

Rojo thought for a while.

"The Rio Puerco leads to Acoma, the Sky City," said the Jicarilla. "There are old stories about Acoma having salt to trade, but the salt did not come from Acoma. They got it from Zuni. The road from Acoma to Zuni is called the Salt Trail."

"The *Malpais*, lava flows, cut off Acoma from Zuni," insisted Roque. "*Malpais* are Diablo's own lands. The rocks are razor sharp and destroy boots, moccasins, and horses' hooves. They hide crevasses so deep horse and rider are never seen again. Land that appears solid is only paper thin over deep caves. There is no water, and the heat is oppressive. It is certain death to enter the *Malpais*."

"There is a good trail," said Rojo quietly, "from Acoma to Zuni across the *malpais*."

"Does the salt come from Zuni?" asked Sebriana.

"I think, from a source far beyond Zuni," Rojo said slowly.

"That's the trail we need to follow," Dan said. "I've been thinking about the translation. The Hebrew word for brilliant can mean east or west, the sunrise or the sunset. The gloomy unknown is a poetical way of saying north. I didn't understand Negev in the letter. It's a place in the Middle East, but the word can also be used to mean south because Negev is south of Palestine or it can mean a desert. The altar and the Ten Commandments are west of the Rio Grande. I think those following the Danites were supposed to go west along the Salt Trail."

Avoiding towns and crossing the Rio and the *El Camino Real* only when no one was in sight, the companions made their way back to Hidden Mountain. Roque rode into Los Lunas to the home of Rabbi Sanchez, knowing him to be discreet.

Rabbi Sanchez told him, "Yes, yes. You have been sought. There were men in bushy beards wearing black coats. They were Mormons, I think. What strange beliefs they have. They say they will be God someday. Terrible!

"And the men from *Tejas* were here. They are bad men and look down on Mexicans. They beat three of the *paisonos* very badly. No one would help them willingly, but the people fear them very much. From Socorro to Belen, no one will help them.

"I have heard rumors," said Rabbi Sanchez, "rumors only, from Rio Arriba, the north. The Baca family seeks a murderess that killed six men and an old woman. She drove a knife through the skull of Don Carlos, the heir of the *haciendado*. This Doña Loca, as they call her, is very dangerous, crazy, and vicious. They look for her in Chimayo, Truchas, Taos, and Quemado where she has friends and family."

Sanchez winked and smiled at Roque. "Heed my warning, young man: never cross a Jewish girl."

Roque joined the party at Hidden Mountain after dark and Sebriana found him some dinner.

Dan talked of their plans. "We're going to reconsider the meaning of the stones in the morning."

They were in Navajo lands so they picketed their stock and found places to sleep away from the blankets they'd left by the fire.

In the crisp morning after breakfast, the four friends

began a new search for signs. Pondering, Rojo sat on a stone above the small canyon where the commandants were carved in stone. At midday, he called Dan to him.

"There is something very strange about this place," Rojo said. "It reminds me of another place. The rocks have been rearranged. See they do not match the hillsides above and below us. The bands of rock are out of sequence. It was done a long time ago, so there are few signs of the change now, but the colors are in the same order as in the *Piedre Lumbre* and…"

"And in the big canyon to the west," Dan finished for him. In 1853, Roque, Rojo, and Dan had been to the big canyon of the Colorado River. It was an empty spot in men's knowledge, deep and inaccessible. "Look, there by your hand." Dan pointed.

Rojo hadn't noticed the Hebrew letters carved in the rock. They were faint, exposed to the elements, and could be taken for cracks and irregularities.

Rojo read them to Dan, "It looks like, 7 1 g y, sort of."

"No, they're Hebrew," Dan replied. "It says *tsaphon,* which means hidden, dark, gloomy, unknown, or north."

Rojo frowned, a rare expression of consternation. "Surely, this is the east side of the canyon."

"Let's tell the others and look around some more," Dan replied.

Knowing where and what to look for helped though the signs were faint.

Roque called out. "This looks like 7 I n s."

Dan looked. "*Achor.* It means west." The two friends were near the bottom of the canyon in the north.

"I've found something," called Sebriana. "It looks like a fire followed by sticks stacked for a fire and another fire."

"*Shamesh!*" Dan cried. "Brilliant! You are too, dear. It

means the sunrise or sunset. From its location to north, it must be the sunrise or east even though it's way up canyon here in the south."

They all searched for the final sign and soon found it. Roque thought it looked like an S. Dan saw a river followed by I 7 and a triangle. "It is *mabo,* and it means the entrance or sunset, west."

"Over here," called Rojo.

Dan went to his friend and saw words carved in the rock. *Achor, mezareh* — another word for north — *shamesh* and *darom* — a word for south — were arranged in the proper relationship to the cardinal directions. To the northwest appeared "7 lightning bolt 7"

"That is *halak* to journey," Dan said reading the glyph. "And there beyond it, that series that looks like 7s, chairs and lightning, and ys is two words — *chavran bithron*, the cavernous craggy place. It's followed by *mahamorah*, the abyss."

"I think this whole place is a map," guessed Roque.

"Look there," pointed Sebriana. "We hadn't noticed them before but two pillars were set up near the altar."

"Jachin and Boaz," said Rojo. "The pillars at the entrance to the Holy of Holies. This is a map and directions to our destination."

From up above on the lip of the ravine, the nature of the marks taken together seemed clear. The ravine was a map of the canyon Dan, Rojo, and Roque had seen years before. The "legend" for the map was very faint, up top on rocks that faced skyward. In a few more years, the marks might disappear altogether. As it was, they saw but little. Maybe some inscriptions had already disappeared. Nonetheless, they had a direction and a goal.

"Then," said Sebriana, "we have a *halak* to make, but in the morning as it grows late. A *halak.*" She tasted the

Hebrew word and liked it. It belonged to her, part of her heritage of which she knew so little.

They gathered wood and fed and watered the stock while Sebriana made dinner. In the morning, the companions would begin their *halak*, journey to the west, to *achor shamesh,* and the *tsaphon* in the *mahmorah*, to the brilliant sunset and the mystery in the abyss.

In the cold morning at first light, Dan rolled away from Sebriana awakened by the sound of approaching hooves muffled in the eerie morn. The day had dawned in deep mist bringing the smell of ice. Rocks and hills were shrouded in deathly white. The pounding came from everywhere accentuated by the fog. Vague forms swirled about wreathed in gossamer wisps. Dan peered through the murk as death trundled by in her tiny *carreta,* a female armed with bow and arrow her grinning skull turned in Dan's direction.

As he beheld this nightmare spectacle, four knights in armor mounted on fine chargers emerged from the swirling mists and lowering their lances attacked. They pierced the decoy bedding by the now cold fire. Realizing their mistake, they cast about for new targets to destroy. Ducking back into hiding, Dan thought to wake Sebriana, but he was too late. She was alert and dressed. He dressed hurriedly. The knights vanished back into fog.

Dan made his way to Sebriana's side. "Did you see that?"

Her face ghastly white in the mist, her voice quavered. "Did you see Doña Sebastiana with her bow riding in her little cart?"

Dan was taken aback. It was the first time he had seen his woman terrified since he'd known her. The skeleton, Doña Sebastiana, Lady Death, was the patron of the *Santa Hermandad*, the Holy Brotherhood of Penitentes.

"She looked right at me."

"I saw her, too," Dan replied as calmly as he could.

"In the Bible," she whispered, quivering , "there are four riders. One rides a pale horse. I have seen him."

With the rising sun, the mist began to burn away. The day would be overcast and dark. The clouds low and roiling, but beneath the air was clearing. Dan counted twenty mounted knights and one small cart bearing Doña Sebastiana, the patron saint of the Penitentes, a strange medieval secret society much given to self-flagellation and other bloody acts of faith. The *hermandad* crucified one of their own each Easter. Dan and Roque had seen these ceremonies. Their windowless meetings halls, *moradas*, were a common sight in small pueblos, especially in the mountains of Rio Arriba. They had been in New Mexico since the time of Conquistador Juan de Oñate who settled the territory for Spain in the seventeenth century.

The armor they wore was rusty and antique. They must have kept it hidden in their *moradas,* waiting to be used since the time of the Conquistadors.

Now, one knight rode forward on his high prancing steed and stopped, confronting the hillside. He hadn't spotted the four companions yet. "You have trodden on ground made sacred by the Law of God," he thundered. "Now you must die."

If his display was a ploy to get the four friends to break cover, it didn't work. None of them moved.

Dan considered options. Why threaten them with death? Why not just kill them? He wants information. That's why they've brought Doña Sebastiana and the fancy armor. They want to frighten us into telling what we know.

"Why," Dan whispered, "didn't they attack us the first

time we were here?"

"Maybe," Sebriana said, "they took time coming from the north. Is it *El Puerco Grande's familia* come to fetch me?" By "big pig," she undoubtedly meant her former husband, Carlos, the recently deceased. "That is why Death travels with them looking for me!"

"Don't think so," Dan reassured her. "I think they have been watching this place for a long time. We talked about how the Pope showed undo interest in the conquest and the *Reconquista* of New Mexico. Maybe these are his guards. They weren't very concerned with us after a single visit, nor were they concerned when we departed in what they knew to be the wrong direction. But now we're back showing too much interest.

Dan continued, "I'll bet they want to know what we know. Maybe I can deceive them."

"Don't do it!" she pleaded as Dan rose. "Death is out there."

"*Hola. Como esta?*" he called trying to sound innocent as he stepped from behind the rock that had been their cover.

The leader made a chopping gesture with his hand and pointed at Dan.

Too late, Dan thought. Perhaps they didn't want information, or maybe they just wanted to be sure of total cooperation.

A horseman broke ranks leaping his horse toward Dan, who spun about and ran, making a sliding dive over the rock he'd shared with Sebriana. The long lance caught Dan through the side piercing him from back to front, the tip protruding from Dan's belly.

The lance had hurt going in. The knight laughed at his victim. It hurt far worse when the knight yanked it back out. He laughed again, a cruel almost inhuman cackle.

Thus unencumbered, Dan completed his roll across the rock landing on his back. The knight trotted his horse around, lining up for the *coups de gras*. Dan saw Death coming for him, but was in too much pain to act even in the face of the laughing warrior

Sebriana threw herself across Dan's body. The lance took her through the thigh. The mounted *pendejo* yanked out his lance and aimed to strike her again at center mass, laughing loudly as he lined up his thrust. This was too much for even Dan's pain shrouded mind. Feebly, he drew his pistol and blasted the mounted warrior through the armor plate that covered his chest. As his horse reared, the knight flipped backward over the high cantle of his saddle. He fell to the ground and the horse ran. Rust lay spattered across his ancient armor as more oozed from the hole Dan had made.

A shot came from Roque's hiding place. A miss, perhaps. A knight behind the leader slid sideways from his horse. Roque, Dan thought, would have been aiming at the leader.

The knights mounted a charge, but the rock strewn ground, more than the banging of the friends' rifles, defeated their approach. This ground was not good for lancers. Each of the companions, Dan, Roque, Rojo, and Sebriana, brought down a charging lancer. Six were out of the fight; whether wounded or dead the friends couldn't tell. Three more were wounded but still on horseback. That was almost half their number. They broke off and retreated out of range and formed a semicircle that hemmed the four friends in.

The cliff of Hidden Mountain was behind the four, broken ground and then the Rio Puerco before them. Our mules cannot outrun the enemy's horses, Dan thought.

Roque called out. "Can you ride?"

Dan's reply was weak. "Maybe not. Sebriana is hurt, too."

Rojo called back. "If we break out into their midst, we will be ridden down and lanced. Our pistols will help, but it is difficult to hit anything while riding a running animal."

He's right, Dan thought. Mounted shots need to be placed at almost point blank range. If they bunched up and we charged into them, we might do them some serious harm. If they spread out and then pursue us, we will not likely survive.

Sebriana and Dan patched each other's wounds as the sun rose and burned into the fog. Both wounds were serious enough, being through and through. Fortunately, no arteries were cut.

Dan called to his friends. "We've patched up and stopped the bleeding for now. We might survive and shouldn't bleed to death for a while."

Nearby, the knight Dan had shot began to groan.

"Let me have your *misericorde,*" Dan said to Sebriana.

He took the long thin blade and crawled to the wounded knight. He held the blade before his eyes and watched them grow large behind his visor.

"Promise not to laugh," Dan whispered plunging the iron sliver through the narrow grating into his eye. He drove the blade home until it encountered the back of the man's helmet. He didn't suffer long or needlessly. "Pass the word to your friends," Dan whispered to the corpse. "Leave my girl alone."

The late fall day grew hot with the sun standing directly overhead and nowhere to hide from its unmerciful rays. The stock bawled for water without relief.

Roque called out. "It's a standoff, I think."

Her leg throbbing, Sebriana moaned softly. Dan's side also throbbed, his vision blurred, and his tongue swelled. He prayed the fever was only the heat of the sun.

Rojo appeared suddenly from nowhere it seemed to Dan. He sniffed Dan's side.

"What I smell," Rojo said, "is not good. Like a bad fart. I think the lance cut your intestine a little. You will have an infection, but I will find you some herbs that will help.

"Roque and I have talked," the Apache continued. "At dark, we will light a fire. I will remain here feeding it and walking around it with some of the stock so they will think we are still here. I have showed Roque a path over the mountain behind us. He will lead you away, and I will join you later.

"The Penitentes do not seem to be in any hurry, thinking us penned in. I think they are waiting for reinforcements from other *moradas*."

Having said all he needed, he turned and was gone.

Dan was in the saddle the first night and the next day. Much later he remembered Rojo rejoining the little band and changing his dressing and Sebriana's. After that, Dan was confined to a *travois*, a bed dragged behind a horse made of poles crossed over its back. The trip back to Santa Fe was lost to him.

Chapter 6

Malpais

Dan returned to consciousness warm in his own bed in Santa Fe to the smell of a piñon fire burning in the horno. Dreams of homicidal knights began to fade. A twinge from his side gave him pause to reflect on his condition. He was uncertain how he'd got here. His last recollections were of finding the Hebrew map, and even that was dreamlike. Perhaps all was well, and Topper still alive. Then something warm and soft wriggled against his back under the covers. New smells, strange and bitter, intruded. Although his vision was blurred he realized that there was something moving in the center of the room as well.

Dan blinked several times to clear his eyes. Even the dim room seemed too bright, and his eyes adjusted slowly. Finally, he was confronted with an ageless gnome bedecked in hideous, motley animal and bird skins competing for attention. All about her hung beaded pouches, garlands of talismans that glinted with mirrors and crystals, together with a variety rattles and small drums. The ancient creature was barely five feet tall, unbent by infirmity with wrinkled, sun-darkened skin. She skipped and hopped about merrily, drawing herbs and things less savory or identifiable from the pouches with which she was festooned, grinding some to powder and setting others in pots already boiling on the fire.

"Doña Luna," Dan cried, "you haven't changed a bit." And it seemed to Dan that she hadn't changed at all in the ten years he had known her. Tïéná'áí Izdzáníí, Moon Woman, was a Jicarilla shaman and herbalist reputed to have enormous Power. It was dangerous for her here in Santa Fe. Priests would burn her at the stake for making herbal remedies alone; they would call her a bruja, witch.

"Ah, Breaker of Noses," Doña Luna said cheerfully, "you are awake. Now I can purge you properly!"

Dan would have paid to know where she'd heard that name for him or if it was now general among the Jicarilla. One dark night at Abiquiu, he'd busted an enemy's nose instead of his head. Kit Carson had suggested the name. She'd been threatening to purge him since they'd met. Dan noted the look in her eye. She might be thinking her chance had finally come, or perhaps she knew something of Anglo medicine at that time grounded in bleeding, blistering, and purging.

Dan almost laughed, but the stab in his side returned. Purging might reopen his wound, he thought.

Behind him the soft warmth stirred from sleep.

"Pobrecito," the warmth in his bed chattered, "you are alive. You gave us quite a scare. It has been seven days. See? Doña Luna has come and saved you! She fixed me, too. Roque and Rojo thought sure I would lose my leg. See?" she said again throwing back the covers showing Dan the healing scar high on her inner thigh and revealing much more. "There will be hardly any scar."

As delightful as the sight was, it caused immediate pain in Dan's side and he groaned aloud.

"Oh," said Sebriana lifting the covers, "that looks like it might need attention."

Uncertain what she was looking at, Dan feared her

cure.

"No Sebriana," Dan cried, "you might kill me!"

For the next few weeks, Doña Luna would be his doctor, and she was mindful of the prerogatives this gave her. Sebriana was Dan's nurse with a different set of privileges including bathing the patient. Fortunately, the tub Dan and Roque had acquired for her bath was large enough for two.

Roque and Rojo soon returned with news of the world beyond their walls.

Dan spoke first. "Where is Topper? Is he well?

Roque shook his head. "We buried him yesterday while you yet slept."

Dan was overcome with grief, and their other news had to wait until the next day.

At sight of them, Dan called out. "What ho, travelers.. Tell me of the world. Do they still search for Sebriana? Is she safe here?"

Roque replied, "As long as she doesn't venture outside our walls, she is safe."

Rojo agreed. "No one seems to have recognized us from the cantina in Santa Cruz. Pedro has decided to trade Rio Grande blankets from Chimayo at Bent's Fort on the Arkansas. He is gone and out of reach where the Bacas cannot find him."

"The better part of valor," Dan mumbled glad that Pedro was safe. "The last thing I remember was seeing knights in armor. I must have been delirious. What really happened?"

"You saw knights in armor," said Rojo, the pokerfaced Apache.

"How is that possible?" Dan asked skeptically.

"They were of the Holy Brotherhood, the Penitentes," said Roque. "At one time, I was to be admitted to their order, but my uncle, Sebriana's father, held me back telling me mysteriously there were things I should know first. He died without relating them.

"During the time I was drawing close to the Penitentes, I was shown some of their most precious relics, Doña Sebastiana, Lady Death, with her bow in the little cart and the stored armor of the conquistadors, our ancestors.

"They're not bad men really," added Roque. "In many villages, they provide the only religious services, priests being rare and their prices high. The Penitentes are sincere, flagellating themselves in imitation of the wounds of Christ and crucifying a man to earn the Lord's forgiveness. Their leader is a great priest of the Holy Mother Church, even though this new foreign bishop, Lamy, has outlawed them."

"You told me," said Sebriana, "as you lay there wounded that you thought the Pope had sent them as conquistadors to find the Ark, and they were still protecting its secrets."

Roque looked grim. "It makes sense. They read the map wrong and went east instead of west and built churches. Coronado went east, too, across the Llano Estacado." Roque lapsed into silence.

Dan thought a while. "If the Penitentes are descendants of the Conquistadors and chosen warriors of the Pope, it might explain why they preserve medieval forms of worship. I need to consider Topper's notes and what we've learned so far."

Groaning slightly, Dan turned in his bed to face Sebriana. When he spoke, he addressed all of his friends. "I can't ask you to continue with me on this quest. I promised Topper, so I must continue. You need not. As you've seen, it's dangerous. There are at least three groups pursuing us, not counting the Bacas."

Roque's brows wrinkled into thunderheads. "We are friends. You cannot deny me." He looked threatening behind his drooping mustache.

Sebriana smiled joyfully. "I can't stay here!"

Rojo's face wrinkled into a tiny smile. "The mystery holds my interest. Besides, I promised Topper, too."

Moon Woman spoke eerily and without explanation. "I will be waiting when you near the end of your trail."

As she turned and left the room, Dan asked, "What did that mean?"

Even Rojo shook his head in puzzlement.

Confined to bed often with his "nurse" distracting him, Dan went over Topper's translation of the document found in the Temple again and again, filling in different possibilities for missing words, considering other possible translations for words he did know.

"I may be missing something," he told Sebriana. "I've concluded that this document probably indicates that they followed the Rio Puerco to the west, to some "salt trail," perhaps the one Rojo said started at Acoma."

"Yes, probably." Sebriana swarmed over him, making further study impossible for a time.

Weeks passed as Dan healed. Fall blew away to winter. Reports came from the States that Lincoln had won the election, and states had begun to leave the Union. The fire was cheerful and soothing, and Sebriana kept his bed warm. He felt occasional twinges of guilt. He loved her, but they could never marry.

To Sebriana's annoyance, Dan raised dust leafing through Topper's extensive notes. Old, dry pages crinkled and tore with handling and the dry high altitude winter. Ancient scraps fell to the floor. Dan compared his own notes, twisted pages around, and compared again. Where he could, he retranslated and substituted guessed at words. He searched through their sketches of the artwork from Hidden Mountain. Dan thought it clear that once the Hebrew writing was taken away, there were additional symbols leftover. These resembled glyphs Dan had seen before. Plenty of rocks around New Mexico bore Indian art. Some themes were common, others less so. With the ancient rock art, sometimes it was clear that all the symbols should be understood together as a single picture or theme. In other cases, the glyphs seemed purely random. The glyphs from Hidden Mountain were different. They were not simple pictures. They seemed to convey a common theme though the glyphs were as different as Latin, Greek, Hebrew, and Cyrillic. Or so it seemed to Dan.

On the rocks of a cliff above one of the great houses of Chaco Canyon, Dan had seen a man who either held a shield or had a spiral of Power emerging from his hand. He was surrounded by game animals and birds. The spiral might have been magic calling the animals. It was clear that the pictures should be understood together, animal and man. In many cases though, each symbol seemed to stand alone. Some drawings were more symbol than pictures, concentric circles, spirals, concentric squares, stars, and crosses. There were so many unique symbols Dan couldn't keep track of them all. He tried to discern the single theme.

Rojo and Roque arrived with news.

Proud of his knowledge, Roque spoke first. "Abraham Lincoln has been elected. They say some of the southern states will leave the Union."

Dan could add nothing to this speculation. He was more concerned with the quest and his friends' places in it. He was putting them, especially Sebriana, in danger.

He would continue on his own once he healed and was able. That would be best. But he did need their advice.

"I'm frustrated with Topper's notes and the glyphs we saw on the rock. I can't get them to agree. I can't make sense of what they are trying to tell us."

It seemed madness when Roque said, "Maybe you shouldn't look at what is there. Look for what shouldn't be."

Dan started to object and then paused. "That might be a good idea."

"Look," said Sebriana, "there are different styles." She was right. "Group them by style."

"These were made by Apache," said Rojo, "and these, I think, by Navajo. These were drawn by Pueblo."

When they had grouped them all, Dan smiled. They were left with a handful of symbols, similar in style, that didn't fit into any other category. There was nothing obviously Hebrew, such as a Star of David or tablets. Some resembled Hebrew letters sharing a similar grace but lacking the proper specific form of the letters Dan was familiar with.

It was Roque who noticed something. "Those two vertical parallel lines with globes above might represent the pillars at the entrance to Solomon's Temple."

Rojo nodded. "Jachin and Boaz as we were taught."

A flat horizontal line with a Y-shape rising from it and rays above did not look like it could be grouped with any other set of pictures.

At last Sebriana spoke. "I remember seeing something like that as a child. It might be a symbol of God in the burning bush."

Looking at the floor, Dan shook his hanging head. "There must be a few million rocks out there with symbols on them. How can we find a trail amongst them all? We're looking for a few needles in thousands of haystacks."

Rojo scowled. "We go from water to water. A trail must go where there is water."

Dan picked up on the idea. "If we do not find the special symbols we seek, we'll backtrack and seek water in a new direction."

Roque understood. "We look only a jornada, a day's journey, for next water. The number of points becomes limited."

Dan remained an invalid and unable to leave his bed as a month passed. Rojo and Roque returned one night from Lodge.

"Hola," Dan called on hearing them enter. "Was Kit there?"

"He was," responded Roque, "and he sends his best. He'll be by to see you before he leaves town."

Rarely allowing emotion to show, Rojo was excited about his announcement. "A visiting brother came to Lodge from New Orleans; I have seen him in the city often. He is an important man, a lawyer and a scholar."

Roque interjected. "He is big and tall, a head taller than I, and powerful. He is powerful, too, when he speaks with eyes that glare and hold your attention. His clothes are very fine, too, though in a gavacho style I personally do not prefer. You will want to meet him. His scholarly interests are much like yours."

Dan seemed alarmed. "You didn't tell him about our adventures, did you?"

"No," Rojo reassured him, "he spoke in lodge of our long history, of the Knights Templar, and of the secrets of Roslyn Chapel. He was from New Orleans, and his eyes were like those of a great chief or shaman."

Returning to his studies, Dan heard Rojo discussing

New Orleans with Roque. For one, it was a place of great wonder that he had visited and would never forget; for the other it was a place of mystery and legends.

The next day when the door opened to admit the winter blast, Dan heard the sounds of his friends approaching with a stranger. A fire burned in the horno, warming the room and filling it with the aroma of piñon. Dan hastened to close up the professor's portfolio and conceal it under his thin mattress. Sensing his distress, Sebriana seated herself atop the book, concealing it further.

They entered laughing and joking with a tall man, thickset, fleshy, but powerful, with long, dark hair and beard. His eyes were dark, brooding, and deep-set. His nose was prominent and his forehead high. For all his rude construction, he was affable, even charming when he desired.

"Danito," said Rojo, "meet Brother Albert Pike."

Dan looked up at the tall man. "We've been introduced. Good to see you again

"I understand we have some similar interests," Pike said, extending his hand with a smile.

Roque helped Dan into the next room and seated him at the table where everyone found a place to sit. Sebriana brought them hot chocolate made in the Mexican style. She retired to the bedroom room where Dan suspected she was listening in. "Smart girl," he thought. "She knows Pike will be more relaxed this way."

"Does your girl speak English?" Pike inquired.

"No," Dan said. Rojo and Roque did not react to Dan's lie. Dan imagined Doña Loca was seething in the next room having been referred to as "my girl." Mi esposa she might have liked, but not my girl. She would hate Pike, and for some reason, Dan felt cautious around his

Masonic brother although his friends seemed comfortable in his presence.

"I came here in '31," Pike said without preamble, "searching for a special stone engraved with ancient letters."

Roque's eyes grew large with surprise. Dan wished he had a better poker face, but now supposed he knew why the one lady Roque didn't tamper with was Lady Luck at the card table.

"I searched to the north near Taos and up the Rio Grande close to its source," Pike continued, "but I had no luck. The stone I sought remained hidden from me. There are rumors for those who listen for them. At first, there were only rumors of a stone carved with the Ten Commandments in an ancient form of Hebrew. More recently it is said the stone may lie near Los Lunas.

"I understand you have traveled recently," Pike finished. "Where did you go?"

"To Los Lunas," Dan replied. "We found the stone you describe." Some things, Dan reasoned, were too widely known to try to hide. Visiting these special, mysterious places would raise suspicion. He looked at his two friends.

Pike was charming, even flattering. He was an important man from a big city, New Orleans, as big as they come, treating three country boys as equals.

Pike handed Dan a gold pendant. "Take a look at this."

Dan studied the pendant and passed it to his friends. It showed a large box supported by long poles run through rings on either side surmounted by two angels with their backs to each other wingtips nearly touching. It could have been drawn from the description of the Ark given in the Bible.

Roque, with an air of I've-seen-the-like-before, said, "It's the Ark."

"Aye, it is," said Albert Pike. "You might expect I found it in the Holy Land." His audience nodded politely. "But that's not the case. I found it in a grave on the Greek island Mycenae. Homer refers to those graves and says they belonged to the Danaoi, the sea going tribe of Dan. I think this pendant shows the Ark in the possession of the tribe of Dan on Mycenae."

Some alarm began sounding in Dan's mind. He'd heard this story somewhere before.

Pike continued, "I was able to trace the Danites further. From Mycenae, they continued west and colonized Ireland. Princess Tea Tephi of the royal house of David went with them and stayed there with her people. That is why the Irish harp and the harp of David look the same and why that harp is the symbol of Ireland. That colony was already thriving when the Ark passed through on its westward journey."

Dan relaxed a little. This was new information for him. Pike was sharing information, not prying into what Dan knew. Or was he feeding a little information in hopes of beginning an exchange? Dan hoped his friends would allow him to take the lead in revealing what they knew.

Roque broke the brief silence. "There is something Topper told us I do not understand. We were told that the keys to the trail were hidden in the ritual. I haven't seen anything to indicate this is so."

Roque trusted Pike; otherwise, he would never have asked such a question. Nonetheless, he had changed the subject from the Ark to Masonic Ritual. "Good for him," Dan thought. "I wonder if it was intentional."

Pike sat up gathering his thoughts. "That came later with other seekers and other treasure." Pike turned to

Dan. "Have your friends been told of the other treasures that have joined the Ark in hiding?"

Dan shook his head. "No, I barely understand them myself."

Pike smiled. "Let me tell you of one of the later treasures. Have you heard of the Table of the Presence, the Trumpets of Truth, and the Menorah?"

"Sure," said Rojo. "Those were treasures taken from the Temple of Solomon by the Babylonians."

Roque smiled, glad to demonstrate his superior knowledge. "That's right, but they were returned."

"Correct," said Pike nodding. "But they were taken again, by the Romans in the year of Our Lord 70 when they destroyed Jerusalem and the Temple. The Arch of Titus in Rome clearly shows the Roman army carrying away the Menorah, a table, and trumpets. They were carried to a temple and remained on display until Anno Domini 455 when the Vandals sacked Rome and carried the spoils away to Carthage. Spoils from the Hebrew Temple have always brought bad luck to the possessor. Rome was sacked. In 533, Byzantine Roman Emperor Justinian the First sent General Belisarius to conquer the Vandals. He carried the Hebrew Temple furnishings back to Byzantium. There are representations of these spoils on the arch the emperor erected to celebrate this victory. By 550, the emperor was convinced these trophies brought ill-fortune and should be returned to Jerusalem.

Pike paused before continuing his story. "They couldn't go to the Temple. It was destroyed in A.D. 70 and the site desecrated with a pagan temple to a Roman god. So he had a monastery built in honor of St. John the Divine and stored the Temple treasure there a few leagues from the city of Jerusalem. He didn't want the story of the treasure to get about so he called in a few trusted master masons. The grand master of masons did not want the secret lost, and as he was invited to select the site of the new monastery, he went about it in an odd way which he recorded in verse. Translated from the Greek, the language of the Eastern or Byzantine Roman Empire, that verse runs thus:

> I stand above the ruin of Hiram's pride
> Seeking the lodges of the Holy Saints John.
> I stand upon the first step of a mason
> Measuring a league for each Apostle

Pausing again to gather breath, Pike scanned his enraptured audience and then continued. "Being a grand master mason, he knew how to keep a secret and how to pass along clues. Have you heard anything like this before?"

Rojo was the first to speak. "In the first degree ceremony, there is something similar."

"What is the first step of a mason?" Pike asked.

"A square," Dan replied. "His first tool and the most important angle."

"I submit to you," Pike said, "that if you were to stand in the ruins of the second Temple above the Well of Souls facing east, your left foot would point to the lodge or, to put it another way, monastery of Saint John the Divine at a distance of twelve leagues and your right one to the ruined settlement of the Essenes where the Jordan River reaches the Dead Sea, the lodge of Saint John the Baptist. Each once held a treasure or the keys a wise man might use to find one."

Enthralled, Rojo asked, "So were the treasures found?"

"The lodge of John the Baptist," Pike responded, "was supposed to contain a vast library and in it a treasure map on a copper scroll. The lodge is in ruins on a cliff overlooking the Dead Sea. The library was never found. The treasure from the Monastery of Saint John the Divine was found. As long as the Templars held the Temple treasures in the Holy Land, they were invincible in battle. As the odds rose against them and as the crusader kings squabbled, the Templars began to worry lest the treasure might be lost. The Spear of Longianus was lost. The True Cross was found, cut into pieces, and lost. Finally the treasure was taken to Roslyn in Scotland where it stayed for one hundred years until 1307."

Dan knew that year. It was the year the Pope turned on the Knights Templar. "Friday the 13th. What happened to the treasure then?"

Albert Pike paused until all looked at him. "It was lost."

"That can't be all!" Roque blurted.

Pike smiled. "No, not all, but almost so. The Knights Templar who conveyed the treasure to Roslyn believed they had recovered good evidence of the location of the Ark. During the time the Crusader Kingdoms held Jerusalem, the Templars occupied the site of the Temple. They searched, and they dug into the rock beneath them. Eventually they recovered the archives of the second Temple and took them to Roslyn …"

Roque shook his head like a man bothered by a fly. "Second Temple? You've said that once before. What is a second Temple?"

Pike had the answer. "The first temple was built by King Solomon with the help of Hiram, King of Tyre, and Hiram Abif, the widow's son of the tribe of Napthali, a grand master mason. It was destroyed by the Babylonians. Seventy years later under Governor Zerubbabel, the Israelites rebuilt their temple. Hundreds of years later, Herod the Great renovated this temple, the Second

Temple, the Temple Jesus knew."

Gold gleamed in Roque's eyes. "But what happened to the treasure?"

Pike scowled. "It was sent down the path they believed the Ark had followed and was never heard of again."

The group was quiet for a long while.

Dan thought of all he'd learned and now revealed information that he came to regret later. "Topper spoke of Irish, Scots, and Portuguese fisherman who sailed annually far to the west to rich fishing banks. There were hints and stories but these were not literate men, and their means of navigation were crude.

Dan gathered his thoughts for a moment and continued. "The Templars were on good terms with Robert the Bruce, and they were safe in Scotland."

Pike nodded. "Aye, they were the Bruce's allies and fought alongside him at Bannockburn."

Excitement grew in Dan. "The Templars had a great fleet they used to ferry pilgrims to the Holy Land. There is no record of it after Friday the 13th 1307. . ."

Pike interrupted. "In Masonic Ritual, there is a mystery word that should not be uttered outside of the lodge. Mahabon. Do you remember it?

"Of course," said Roque. "It means . . ."

Pike hastened to cut him off. "Do not say it's meaning to a Mason outside a properly tiled Lodge. I will tell you now its hidden origin. It means Mahdia Bon, in French, Mahdia the Good. Mahdia was a pirate port on the North African coast. They happily received the Templar fleet. In the ritual, you were told you would be brother to pirates and corsairs."

Rojo perked up. "Do you mean Masons are Knights Templar?"

"Isn't it obvious?" asked Pike rhetorically. "Who stands at the door of the Lodge? The Tiler with a sword. Tiler does not mean tile setter in English, and why would the tile setter carry a sword? Tiler is old French for 'the cutter.' You are a Free Mason. In French, a *Frére Maçon*, a brother mason, a monkish title."

Dan now began to muse. "If a missing Templar fleet," he guessed, relying on the knowledge he'd gained from sailors in Greenport, "had sailed south to the Cape Verde Islands, the trade winds and currents would have taken them west to the Caribbean and then north into the Gulf of Mexico. From there they might have sailed up the coast of North America to Cape Fear where the westerlies would have blown them back to Scotland. There are many rivers on those thousands of miles of coastline. The great peninsulas Yucatan and Florida might have served as guides, but that still leaves a lot of space in between and a lot of great rivers. How would they have known which river to pick?"

"The Bible," answered Pike, "in the book of Isaiah and again in II Kings, the writers mention the Sundial of Ahaz.

'Isaiah 38:

[7] "The LORD will do what he says. This is the sign from the LORD to show you:

[8] The sun has made a shadow go down the stairway of Ahaz, but I will make it go back ten steps. So the shadow made by the sun went back up the ten steps it had gone down.'

"To work a sundial you have to know that the sun is a different height from the horizon at noon each day of the year. If you measure the angle of the sun above the horizon at noon and adjust for the day of the year, you know your distance north or south. Measuring an angle would be no great trick for a master mason."

Dan was stunned. "Are you saying Hiram Abif invented latitude?"

"He, or another like him," Pike replied. "It might have been an Egyptian mason a millennium before. The Egyptians and the tribe of Dan were sailing the Atlantic before the Israelites fled Egypt. They had some means of navigation."

There was silence for a long time.

Rojo recovered first. "What became of Princess Tea Tephi and her people?"

"They followed the Scotti to Scotland and occupied a lowland valley," Pike answered, "which they called Rawz Shawlam, meaning something like Hidden Perfection in Hebrew. Barbarous tongues corrupted this to something that lay comfortably on Scotti tongues, Roslyn."

"Wait," said Roque, "you didn't answer Danito's original question. How would Templars or later Danites have known which river to pick?"

Pike smiled. "They had the latitude of its mouth."

"What latitude was that?" asked Roque.

"I don't know," said Pike. "It's lost. It was hard to decipher to begin with. The Israelites used a different system of measurement than we do. The Templars deciphered it. They made many trips, but fewer ships returned each time. Those navigators who knew the latitude were lost."

Dan was puzzled. "Roslyn? The home of the St. Claires, the Sinclair. They were Freemasons." He held back what he'd learned of depictions of maize, a new world crop, among the artwork in the chapel at Roslyn and of the knights in Roslyn and Newport.

"Aye, and Templar Knights before that. Brothers," said Pike, "I think that's enough for now. You've things to consider." With this conclusion, he headed back to his lodgings, the home of a prominent Mason.

As soon as he was gone, Sebriana rushed into the room asking, "What do we do now?"

It was clear to Dan she had been listening, as he was sure she would. Women, like cats, are creatures of curiosity, especially where forbidden fruit is concerned. Roque and Rojo turned to look at Dan, their eyes asking what he wanted to do next.

"As soon as I can ride," he said, "we travel to Acoma and try to pick up the ancient trail."

"What of this Templar trail?" asked Rojo.

Taken aback, Dan had to think for a moment. Everything he'd looked at in Topper's notes so far was related to the ancient Israelites. There were other packets he had yet to open.

Sebriana cut the Gordian knot. "We watch for signs of their passage, too."

"We know too much," said Roque, "and not enough. It is too much to contain. We need to leave town immediately before others suspect."

Rojo looked each of his companions in the eye. "We need to leave before the searchers of the Penitentes, black coats, or Texians can find us."

"Don't forget the Don Carlos' family," said Sebriana.

Quickly was not usually quietly, and they had a need to remain unnoticed. Two determined men, Roque and Rojo, amazed Dan by having them ready for the trail by that evening and doing so without attracting notice.

It may seem strange that Roque and Rojo were able to outfit themselves and their friends for the journey and to acquire the stock and weapons they thought best without thought of money. Dan and Roque were, by Santa Fe standards, comfortable. In 1853, they went with Kit

Carson and took sheep to California to a population that had grown faster than the agriculture supporting it. Sheep cost two dollars a head in New Mexico, and Rojo got them for Dan and Roque for less than that. The less said of his means the better, but many *haciendados ricos* bewailed the loss of their flocks to "Navajos" that year. The sheep sold for six dollars a head in Sacramento. Dan and Roque did well and returning to Santa Fe invested in various projects at the advice of influential friends.

Doña Luna waited as they made ready to depart at midnight. "Take this, young man, and drink it." She handed Dan a cup, and he drank the thick, lumpy, bitter liquid it contained. "Here is more." She handed him a deer's stomach canteen. "It will help the pain." She turned to Rojo. "See that he takes it each evening. I will wait for you at the sweet spring the *Nakaiyeh* call *Dulce* near the river they name Navajo."

Enigmatic, that's what the old woman was, enigmatic, Dan thought. Why would she be waiting for us in a place so far to the west and north at the very edge of Jicarilla territory? The Mexicans, *Nakaiyeh,* as she called them, named the river Navajo for a reason.

"I'll see you then, young man," she said with a crooked smile, her lips not moving. That is the last thing Dan recalled until the four arrived at Acoma. The ride consumed two hard days, forty miles each day. Dan remembered none of it. He should have been in screaming pain from his side. If he was, he did not recall. He simply awoke one morning in their camp at the base of the mesa uncertain of how he had arrived there. His wound, although it gave occasional twinges of pain in the coming months, was completely healed. The smell of coffee and bacon frying wakened him, and he sat up.

Roque looked down at Dan sitting on his bedroll.

"Danito, are you back with us?"

"Yes, I think so," Dan replied. "Where are we?" Upon being told they had arrived at Acoma the evening before, Dan started to consider their position. "There's a church up there, isn't there?"

"The church of San Esteban Rey is up on top of the mesa," said Rojo. "Its graveyard was built by the hands of enslaved *Indios*. Forced by the priests, they built a retaining wall thirty feet high and then were forced to carry soil up there to make it level with the mesa top. The *vigas* of the church were carried by men on foot from Turquoise Mountain thirty miles to the north. Yes, there is a big church, a graveyard, and a *convento*, a palace of two stories for the priest, bigger than the church. These buildings together occupy a third of the mesa top."

"I think we should stay out of sight of priests," Dan said. "Let's pay someone to mind our stock and gear and ascend on foot."

Their presence would be noted and word would get to the priest of the arrival of strangers, but they might delay it a bit and conceal their purpose by going on foot. Dan hated to leave their fine rifles behind, but they didn't want to appear as an invading army. Their pistols, he thought, would be less obvious and as effective in tight quarters.

Acoma, the Sky City, stands on a vertical, white mesa 360 feet high, with a flat summit ten acres in extent. A single, narrow trail leads to the top. It is easily defended. The conquistador Oñate lost a nephew trying to take Acoma and punished the people cruelly for their resistance. Eight hundred Pueblos were killed outright, and the remaining five hundred enslaved. All of the men over twenty-five years of age had their left foot amputated.

Dan reflected on the cruelty of the conquistadors. He

turned to Rojo. "If the Penitentes were descendants, spiritual and otherwise, of the conquistadors, the connection is something to consider."

The Apache nodded. "Indeed, I would expect them to be quite savage."

Dan stopped in his tracks and looked into his friend's face for sign of jest. Finding none, he shook cobwebs from his brain. Beside him, the Jicarilla smiled.

The path led by a large, rock-enclosed natural cistern that held the pueblo's water supply. As the four friends passed by, women came and went with *ollas*, water jars, balanced on their heads. The narrow trail led up steps carved in the rock. On top, an adobe town with broad streets rose to a height of four stories. The houses lacked doors and windows; access was gained by a ladder placed in the rooftop smokehole. The mesa commanded the local countryside with a view all the way to the Rio Puerco.

Pointing to the distant river and what he was sure was Hidden Mountain, Dan spoke to his friends. "The name Rio Puerco, filthy river, can also mean the river of the pig and, by cruel extension, the river of the Jews. Is this a clue? Did conquistadors with special knowledge from the Vatican name the beginning of the trail we seek?"

The city bustled with activity. A crowd of men soon gathered to stare at outlanders. The men wore breechclothes of dark, twilled wool over leather leggings with knee high moccasins below and white cotton shirts cut square above. The hair of men and women was worn long, clubbed in a figure eight behind the head and cut in bangs across the forehead.

Roque approached one of the men and said in Spanish. "*Señor, como esta?* Can you guide me to your wise man?"

Turning to his friends, Roque said in English, "I dare

not say shaman. They will think I'm hunting heretics." He turned back to the man who shrugged, shook his head, and walked away.

Roque tried another who stared at him in apparent incomprehension. No one seemed to be able to speak Spanish.

Rojo had been listening to the speech of the people around him. "I would try speaking the language of the Tiwa, but their talk is like nothing I have ever heard before. It baffles the ear."

Always quick, Sebriana cocked her head birdlike. "I think I hear some Hebrew words." Fascinated, she drew closer to the women and away from her friends. "Their dress is so interesting," she called back. "I wonder if this is how the ancient Hebrews dressed."

She followed a party of young ladies back to the cistern. Their dress was fascinating, consisting of a dark wool manta, a simple dress with tassels along the bottom coming to the knee, worn over a white cotton shirt with sleeves tied under the arms rather than sewn. They wore necklaces of corn kernels in various colors along with strands of turquoise, shell, and silver beads.

That evening Sebriana said to Dan, "What first attracted my attention was their footwear, simple moccasins with thick leggings of clay-whitened leather wrapped around the leg from ankle to knee until the toe can barely be seen."

While Sebriana was away at the cistern, Rojo walked up to one of the men and addressed him in a low tone. The Acoma hurried away. "Father Nighthawk has a friend here, a shaman like himself. They share secrets sometimes. Perhaps the friend, Aa'ku, will help us."

Roque and Dan were puzzled. Rojo had just told them he couldn't understand the local language. Their friend said, "I tried Tiwa even though it is not the language they were speaking."

After Rojo's attempt to speak to them in Tiwa, the crowd lost some of its hostility and began to disperse. The three friends were left standing in an intersection. Rojo was the first to notice. "There is the church." He pointed with his lip down a side street. "Let us move to where we cannot be seen from the *convento*. The priest might be watching."

The man Rojo had spoken to returned and escorted them up ladders and across rooftops to a fourth story roof where an old man sat on a blanket casting a collection of bones and crystals before him.

Aa'ku the Shaman, thin but straight, had skin like smooth red clay. Long white hair bordered a face with deep-set pale eyes that looked fixedly at anything that snagged their attention and sparkled with amusement on occasion, the only sign their owner was pleased. His necklaces carried beads of turquoise, malachite, azurite, copper, silver, coral, and shell as well as a wealth of crystals, bones, and feathers. Leather pouches surrounded him filled with herbs and powders. Dan recognized corn and bulrush pollen caught at the mouths of two bags. A small bundle of sage burned in a bowl nearby. The old man cast his bones one more time and, assessing their configuration, looked up at the three without pleasure. A wave of his arm gestured for Rojo, Roque, and Dan to sit.

Another wave brought an acolyte, a boy of no more than twelve summers, to translate. Aa'ku lit and passed a pipe made of stone carved in the shape of a horned serpent. They each offered smoke to the four directions before discussion could begin. The conversation was difficult with many misunderstandings as the boy spoke Mexican poorly, and there were ideas that did not seem to translate from one language to the other.

"Ancient One," began Rojo, "I am grand-nephew to the mighty Father Nighthawk. I bring his greetings and respect. He told me that if I was ever at Acoma, I must pay my respects to you."

The boy translated, and the Aa'ku directed him to ask a question. After several false starts, the boy asked, "Did Father Nighthawk send you on this errand?"

"No, I come on my own business," Rojo replied. "We seek an object used in worship by the Old Ones long ago."

The conversation was brutal taking a toll on patience and spirit. There were so many problems in translation and so many seemingly trivial questions that Dan began to wonder if the old man was being deliberately difficult.

Aa'ku gestured to his bones and crystals. He spoke to the boy who said, "The Spirits tell me that I should assist three wise men today. You do not seem wise to me."

"*Pobrecito*," called Sebriana from below. Seeing her friends she bounded up ladders and across rooftops annoying the women who worked there until she reached the seated men. "You must see what I've found."

"What?"

Snatching a bag of corn pollen from the old man, she carefully poured some out forming the three symbols they'd concluded might mark the trail they sought.

Aa'ku, leaning forward till his nose almost touched the roof, blew away the pollen. "Where have you seen this?" he asked, speaking in fine cultured Mexican and looking directly into Sebriana's eyes.

She replied without hesitation. "At the cistern and at Hidden Mountain."

Aa'ku looked closely at Sebriana. "What have we got here? A young man who isn't a man? How strange."

Sebriana was dressed as Juan. "You took a risk following the young women to the cistern. Our young men might have mistaken your intentions. Come, show me what you found."

They adjourned to the cistern, a deep pond of trapped rainwater surrounded by high rock walls. Sebriana pointed to the faint symbols high above reach on the far side.

"Where they stopped for water, of course," Dan whispered. Roque raised an eyebrow. "The desert and mountains are large, but trails lead from waterhole to waterhole."

Aa'ku gestured to his acolyte. "Run, go and ask Chongo to meet us at my rooftop." Turning to the four friends, he said, "Let us return to the rooftop. The Spirits mentioned a princess I was to help, and she is wise if you are not."

Chongo, a small man, thin and wiry and shorter than Sebriana, arrived, wearing one constant expression, a relaxed scowl that would have made him tough to beat at poker. His cheek bones were high but not prominent and set in a face of smooth reddish clay framed by long black hair.

Aa'ku said something to him in their native language. Chongo responded at length, bringing forth a speech from Aa'ku. Chongo still resisted, but finally nodded his assent.

Aa'ku turned to his guests. "We are a secretive people. We hide our religion from the priests who would burn us alive as witches. The many clans each hold part of our faith, its details kept from women, children, and other clans. We have ceremonial rooms within this large house." His gesture swept all of Acoma. "They are never shown to strangers, but you will see one today. You must swear to keep our secrets."

Having said where they were going, he gripped Dan's hand in the manner of the Second Degree. Dan returned Aa'ku's grip in kind and felt the shaman's astonishment.

Recovering, Aa'ku turned to Sebriana. "Señorita, you will please sit with me and tell me of your adventures while Chongo takes your friends where women cannot go."

Dan, Roque, and Rojo followed Chongo down a ladder from the topmost level to a smoky room where blankets were rolled along the walls and personal effects hung from the *vigas*. The air was heavy with cedar and the scent of hides. They proceeded through an opening to an adjoining room where the only light came from a tiny fire suspended in large clay dish that smelled of deer fat and then down again to a room filled with storage pots. Chongo moved several pots to reveal a hidden passage, which they crawled through into total darkness. From there, they descended again and then went across and up until Dan was lost in this Theban maze. Still, they continued their dark journey through smoke and the thick smells of people, wool, animal hides, and cooking with strange herbs. They moved a carpet to reveal a trap door, a plug in the floor. *Metates*, heavy grinding stones, set against a wall concealed another crawlway. Finally, Chongo and the three following his lead descended a ladder into a circular room. Light came from a tiny fire suspended in a pottery dish.

His eyes now adjusted to the dark, Dan could see *bancos* around three walls. He perceived objects of wood, bone, feather, shell, and bead hanging from the coffered ceiling above. A faint aroma indicated the ceiling was cedar. An altar stood in front of a stone that served as a deflector shield for a small fireplace set into the wall. The walls were painted in abstract figures of red, brown, green, orange, white, and black, unlike anything Dan had seen before. Highly complex and intricate, the patterns were not the black and white mountain and cloud steps of the pottery found in the dwellings of the ancients. Things that might have been feathers blended with other things that might have been flowers, birds, vines, and antelope, at least in the shape of its antlers. Dan noticed Roque staring fixedly, and then he too saw the angels. They appeared in profile part human, part bird, transcending both. The stylistic elements were missing in these creatures. There were no halos, flowing robes, or flaming sword, such as Christian artwork depicts. These were their own entities, neither animals with human body nor humans with wings.

Chongo called their attention to the altar. Etched faintly and into its surface was the Tetragrammalon, the Hebrew name of God.

Obviously agitated that outlanders were being allowed to view the sacred objects concealed in the *kiva*, Chongo hastily ushered them back up the ladder. He led them by what must have been a different route from that which they had followed going in. They emerged into sunlight on a third floor rooftop at the distant end of the building block far from the fourth floor rooftop where Aa'ku and Sebriana awaited their return.

Rojo looked confused. "I think each family must have several rooms and all of the rooms of a clan must be joined inside. There must be many ways to get to each *kiva,* and all are very confusing."

Roque slowly shook his great head. "I'm amazed that they have kept knowledge of the *kivas* from the priests. They keep secrets as well as the Freemasons."

Aa'ku invited them to sit around him. "Sebriana is

very wise." She beamed at this complement. "She has been telling me of your adventures. You have traveled from west to east and east to west again."

That phrase, the path of a traveling man, got the attention of the three Masonic brothers, for it sounded like a line from the Masonic tradition. The enigmatic old man sat there with a faint smile. He let the moment stretch and then said, "You are not the first travelers to come this way."

Rojo had questions. "Ancient One, Father Nighthawk told me the Acoma were very clever and built square *kivas* to keep them hidden from the priests."

"We can hide round *kivas* as easily as square ones, but Acoma have always built square *kivas*. A man cannot visit the *kivas* of other clans, and women are not allowed at all. The *kiva* is for the men of one association only, either Squash or Turquoise; each has secrets they do not tell. The *kiva* you have seen is neither Turquoise nor Squash; it is something different and very few know of its existence."

Rojo thought about this for a moment. "Ancient One, Acoma designs are admired by all people. We see them on your pottery. Where many others make simple geometric designs of straight lines, Acoma makes designs of curves that show flowers, animals, and birds. What we just saw seemed neither Acoma nor like other Pueblos."

The shaman thought for a moment. "You might have seen the Holy People and pictures of animals, birds, and dancers in other *kivas*. You might have seen such figures as appear on our pottery. I cannot say. I am not a member of all *kivas* and cannot tell their secrets. I am not even at liberty to tell you the secrets of the Turquoise *kiva*. But you have demonstrated that you have earned the right to the secrets of the kiva you were shown."

After a moment's pause he began a story:

"Long ago in the time when the Holy People still walked the earth, bearded men dressed in robes of cloth came to the land of the Acoma. We did not yet live atop the White Rock nor did we yet have houses or farm the land. We dressed in buckskin like the *Indios cimarrones* and wandered here and there gathering plant food and hunting.

"The bearded strangers carried a large parfleche that shone like gold. Four men bore it on their shoulders with long poles afraid ever to touch it. It was a Holy thing come from the God who created the Holy People and First Man and Woman. It had mighty *Power*. Two of the Holy People, like First Eagle, had landed on top of the parfleche where they froze and became shining gold, facing to the front and rear watchful that the Holy Parfleche might never be approached by strangers, their wingtips touching behind them.

"They stayed through a summer on top of the White Rock while they raised crops and hunted, preparing for their next move. Some of our men became their friends and traded with them. They taught us to farm, make, and build houses of adobe and stone.

"They taught my clan about the One God, and we protect His altar. We showed them the path through the *malpais*. After harvest, they departed to the west. We never saw them again, but stories say they went into the Great Chasm that leads to the middle of the earth."

Sebriana couldn't contain herself. "Their God forbad making pictures of Him. I'll bet that's why there were no pictures of animals or people in the *kiva* you saw. The people Aa'ku tells you about didn't eat javelina, which cleave the hoof but do not chew the cud, like pigs, and they made round places of worship. Danito, they were Jews! I'm sure!"

Rojo looked troubled. "Ancient One, don't the stories say corn, beans, and squash were brought by Blue Corn Maiden who taught you to farm? Didn't the Hero Twins teach you to make the bow, and didn't First Woman teach you to build houses?"

"All of this is true," Aa'ku responded. "What these travelers taught us, they taught as secrets. We used the bow, but did not show others. We learned to grow many local plants. Only later did Blue Corn Maiden teach us to grow corn and beans.

"There is more," Aa'ku continued.

"Much later other men came in a time when we had already been living atop the White Rock for many generations. They were bearded, carrying weapons of steel, wearing armor. They offered friendship and had things to trade, so we let them come up to the Sky City. At the cistern, they recognized the signs scratched in the rock, as you did.

"Those of us who knew the secrets of the people of the Holy Parfleche soon realized that these bearded ones knew them, too. We began to exchange secrets. They were shown the altar and admitted they had come in search of those who protected the Holy Parfleche. We helped them all we could, and in turn, they taught us ways to recognize members of their order. They warned us that others might come with evil intentions and that is why we knew we should oppose conquistador Oñate. That is why no Penitente has ever been allowed on the White Rock and why we keep secrets from the priests."

Roque regained his senses first. "They must have been the Knights Templar!"

Dan thought a bit longer. "And this relationship, the continuity of the search, confirms that the Templars became Freemasons and that they, too, passed this way. Pike's theories were correct. The Ark and the Temple furnishings are here in New Mexico."

Rojo, Sebriana, and Roque agreed, and Aa'ku nodded. The exchange of information continued far into the night. Much of what they talked about was secret and could not be revealed. They also talked about the One God and Holy Parfleche. Aa'ku knew more about being Jewish than crypto-Jew, Sebriana.

"You should rest now," Aa'ku said. "In the morning, you will see that you have men pursuing you. You must leave early. Chongo will show you the way on our Salt Road through the *malpais*."

In the morning, Rojo saw the dust from horses ridden hard far to the north near the Rio Puerco and told the others. They didn't wait to find out who it was.

In parting, Aa'ku gave them blessing and advice. "These strangers who ride in so much hurry will catch glimpses of you in the Sky City during the next several days. I will make them think you are here until you are very far away. A *brujo* can do no less for you." His eyes twinkled.

The *malpais* was a land of sharp, jagged black rock as keen as glass. Nothing grew on the black rock, but wind-drifted soil had gathered in low places and a few tough bushes and grasses grew in low spots, salt brush, sage, and *chamisa*, plants as tough as the land.

Rojo looked about in awe. "*Dineh*, the Navajo, tell of

warrior twins, Monster Slayer and Born of Water, who slew the great monsters to make the land safe for the people. They killed an enormous, hideous ogre at Turquoise Mountain, and its black blood flowed down to the valleys and low places. We stand on the monster's dried blood. I had heard of this place, but did not believe existed until now."

Chongo had them tie rawhide boots over their mules' hooves and up their shins and ankles.

Soon Dan understood why. "The sharp rock would have shredded flesh and hoof off our animals even though we've kept to a trail that is often paved in windblown sand and dust."

Chongo would not let them ride. Many sharp rocks overhung the path where the slightest misstep might damage the ankle of a burdened animal. Where they climbed atop the jagged black rocks, the extra weight of a rider might have caused injury to hooves. Some lands were not meant for riding.

Rojo watched Roque struggling. "Your *grullo* can't see the ground in front of his hooves, so he struggles unsure of his footing. The mules can see and walk easier."

Roque growled. "This is part of Hell. I am certain. God did not make this land."

Chongo surprised them by speaking in Mexican. "Do not stray from the path."

Until now, he had been mute to any language except Acoma. He refused to say more when they questioned him.

Roque crossed himself. "This is the land of *Diablo* and his *brujos*. This is a very bad place."

To calm him, Dan said, "The professor thought this black rock came from a lava flow like a volcano a long time ago." The professor's speculations when recalled didn't calm Dan. He recollected that Topper had said there were tubes in the rock below and places where the rocky top was paper thin and would break under a man's weight. Dan thought he had seen some.

Even normally cheerful Sebriana was nervous. "Look at this place, Danito. Even the animals, mice and squirrels, and the insects and rattlesnakes in this *malpais priete*, this *infierno perdido*, are black.'

Chongo led them through cracks in the rock where the black stone towered overhead. The path twisted and writhed like an animal in pain. The way ahead obscure in coiled sunless passage suddenly emerged into a fine small valley of grass and tall pines surrounded by ebony crags only to descend again into a narrow channel. They climbed to the top of the sinister desolation, guided on narrow ways between crusted hummocks only to descend again into a round tube, a tunnel through the earth.

The way was hot, for the black rock absorbed heat from the sun, and there was no shade. After many hours, they came to a small pond, a low spot that trapped rain water and held it. They drank, and the mules and Roque's *grullo* stallion drank.

Sebriana started out across the rock away from the group and the trail.

"Stop!" commanded Chongo.

Sebriana snorted. "Sometimes a lady needs her privacy."

Chongo said nothing. He picked up a melon sized rock and tossed it ten feet from Sebriana in the direction she had been headed. The rock rang like a huge bell as the stone struck. Then it tinkled like broken glass, and a hole opened all the way to her feet. She turned ashen as she looked into its depths and backed away.

"Do not stray from the path!"

Sebriana hurried back to her friends. "Stop grinning and turn around, *pendejos*!"

Dan was astounded. "Topper said the lava forms caves, long tunnels through the rock that might stretch for miles and bubbles. He said the bubbles would be dangerous having thin tops that would splinter like glass. I had no idea why he was telling me this. I thought at the time it must have been some reminiscence from his travels, something he had seen. Do you know what this land matching Topper's lessons means?"

Rojo and Roque shook their heads.

"Topper knew we'd be coming this way. We're on the right trail."

Thus buoyed, they continued their journey, spending only one night in the *malpais*.

At campfire, Dan spoke to his friends. "I cannot accuse those who dwell on *brujos* of being the only ones disturbed by this dark land."

"We all are," said Sebriana, shivering as she leaned close to Dan.

Even pokerfaced Chongo seemed ill at ease. Coyotes howled, and red eyes glowed at the edges of the firelight. There were sounds, groanings, creakings, rustlings, and scuttlings in the gloom.

They were relieved to depart the Devil's Dark Land as Roque named it.

Beyond the land rose into rolling hills thick with pine and lush green meadows. They turned their stock loose early to graze and fatten after hard riding to Acoma and lean times in the *malpais*. The friends took the trail slowly enjoying the ride, certain they were not followed, forgetting that only death is certain.

The fourth day from the *malpais* they came to El Morro, a great white mesa jutting up one hundred feet from the surrounding countryside. It was a landmark known to all and contained a large well inviting to travelers in this land of few springs and fewer streams. For millennia, travelers had scratched their names and messages into the rock.

They searched the rock face for the symbols they had seen before.

"Amigos, come quick!" called Roque. "See what I've found." It was an inscription in Spanish. "Oñate passed this way."

So too had many other travelers. There were many Indian inscriptions, and even one from a Missouri lieutenant who had come out with Doniphan in '46 to subdue the Navajo. Eventually, Sebriana's sharp eyes spotted the inscription they sought, high up out of human reach in a concealing fold in the rock directly above the well. It helped that having decided on a bath, she swam to the far side of the well and was now looking from an angle not available to the rest of her party. She stood up to her thighs in the well, proud and pointing at a symbol not to be seen from the other side.

Dan speculated to his friends. "There's probably another altar near here."

Their search consumed half a day. Rojo discerned a trail up the rock face, and soon they were all one hundred feet above the well gazing on the ruins of an Indian city as large as Acoma. The tops of walls showed here and there. Rectangular depressions revealed where rooms had been, and one stood out amongst walls with sharp angles, a round depression.

Rojo pointed. "I think the altar is there, Danito."

"I agree, but let's leave it undisturbed. We know they were here."

The next three days were spent crossing the Zuñi

Mountains, home to many Navajo.

Rojo talked about the Navajo. "They are not gathered for raid or war and are not likely to molest us. These are their homes. They have women and children with them."

They passed in peace and emerged through a descending cañon to a city standing below tall cliffs at the edge of a vast *llano*.

Ahead of them, the adobe city Hawikuh, known as Zuñi, stood five stories high around a central plaza gained only by narrow passages and dominated by the houses above. Ladders, some mere poles with notches, stuck up through doors in the roofs of this adobe fortress. Oddly shaped pots served as chimneys. Short ladders connected each rooftop to its neighbor, which stood a little higher or lower. Strewn with pots, baskets, *metates* for grinding grain and corn, the roofs served as a workspace. Here and there, they could see a comfortable *ramada*, an open sided shelter providing shade, within the human anthill standing beside the Zuñi River.

Roque swelled with excitement at his first sight of Zuñi. "Seven Cities of *Cíbola y Quivira* were sought by the conquistador Coronado. When the Moors invaded *España,* seven Christian bishops fled west to protect the sacred relics in their trust. They grew wealthy from mines and jewels in the place where they settled and built *ciudad del oro,* cities of gold.

"The priest Marcos de Niza came first and said he'd seen the cities, so Coronado came. He found no gold, only adobe and a hostile people he fought to subdue. The priest had lied."

Dan spoke pedantically. "Marcos de Niza, that means Mark of Nice. He was French, not Spanish."

Rojo raised an eyebrow. "Are you saying he deliberately misled Coronado?"

Sebriana caught on quickly. "An agent of the Pope?"

"The priest," Roque replied, "encouraged Coronado to send men west to the Hopi and the Colorado River. Pedro de Tovar took Hopi guides but could find no way down into the cañon. No one has ever found a way to cross it. Why did the priest want the trail we follow explored?"

Rojo smiled thinly. "The Hopi deceived Tovar who had treated them cruelly. They know a way down into the depths of the cañon. They go there to collect salt. Their ancestors farmed and hunted there."

Considering Roque's question, Dan said, "I think the Pope must have had some idea where the Ark had been taken. We have encountered his Penitente agents. It is likely Marcos de Niza was his agent, too."

Rojo spoke up. "Of the Seven Cities of Gold sought by Coronado in 1540, only one remains."

Roque said proudly, "The Spanish decreed that there should be only one village, the easier to watch and control."

Rojo shook his head. "The Zuñi were distant from Spanish power on the Rio Grande, and it is unlikely they would have complied if it had not suited them. One village is easier to defend from Navajos and Spaniards. This was the farthest outpost of New Mexico and of the Franciscan friars who had overseen the construction of a Christian house of worship."

Sebriana frowned. "The friars who came here sought martyrdom and often found it."

As they approached the town, Roque went up to one of the natives and asked, "Where might we find food and lodging?"

The Zuñi man turned and walked away.

Rojo stepped forward. "I'll show you how it's done." He addressed himself to another of the natives. As before, the man turned and walked away.

"Chilly, isn't it?" said Dan. "Let's camp outside town."

Without a word, Chongo headed into the town and was soon lost from sight.

Roque frowned. "Will that be the last we see of him?"

As dusk was settling and the campfire lit, Chongo returned with a native shaman who walked up to Dan and silently greeted him with an extended hand. Dan trembled when he felt the touch of the Fellowcraft grip. The man then squatted and drew the four Hebrew letters of the Tetragrammalon in the dust, erasing it as soon as the four friends had seen it.

Dan spoke, his face grim. "We have to trust him. He has shown himself a brother."

During dinner, their trust increased as the man showed the same signs and told the same stories as Aa'ku. The shaman said in Mexican, "I will guide as far as the Hopi Mesas." Late in the night, he departed promising to return at dawn.

Dan turned to his friends. "It's strange. We don't know his name, but we trust him."

The next morning, having done what Aa'ku asked of him, Chongo departed for home.

Dan watched his retreating figure. "I'm sad to see him go. If he was not a friend, he was at least a companion who could be trusted."

As they rode out of camp away from Zuñi, Roque brought his horse up beside Dan's mule. "If there is an altar here or carvings on a rock face, I did not see them."

"Nor I," replied Dan who pondered the absence of these signs when others signs were present. "The valley of the Zuñi River is rich and offers many places for travelers to stop and spend a season. No one point stands out from another. We might search for years for such signs as you seek without finding them. The symbols might be up on Corn Mountain where the Zuñi took refuge from the Spanish during the Reconquista.

"Before the conquistadors came, there were seven scattered villages. What we seek might have been near any village or not near any."

Rojo, speaking from behind them where he had been listening, said, "If there is an altar here, like those at Hidden Mountain, Acoma, and El Morro, it will be near water. The Zuñi know."

Roque continued the complaint. "The Pueblos of the Rio Grande are secretive and sullen, rarely opening themselves to outsiders. These people seem even worse."

"Perhaps they have reason," said Dan. "They've blessed more than one priest with the martyrdom he sought."

Sebriana spoke. "I think their secretiveness comes, in part, from their religion. Each *kiva* has its own *kachina* ceremonies and holds them secret from all non-members."

The *kachina*s were gods, talking animal progenitor forms and ancestors. They were represented by dolls and by hooded men in costume. They represented all that was sacred. Each *kiva* had its own *kachinas*. Huddled together in great tenements, they preserve a shred of privacy by being closed and secretive. The need for secrecy also came from long association with the black robes to whom anything but Catholicism was witchcraft.

"These Zuñi are *cimarron,* living on the edge of Mexican civilization," said Roque. "And the Hopi will be wilder still."

Rojo nodded. "They murdered an entire village, one of their own, for becoming Catholic."

Chapter 7

Abyss

West of Zuñi, the San Francisco Peaks became visible distant blue islands in a vast sea of amber grass. Spring, a dry time there on the high mesas, had not yet greened this countryside of high plateaus and deep cañons. Ethereal mountains floating among clouds appeared at the horizons, Turquoise Mountain, Dawn Mountain, Abalone Shell Mountain, Big Mountain Sheep, defining Dinetah, the homeland of the Navajo. Landscape and vista changed so often and so suddenly, it was easy to believe in brujos, magic, and Power. Stories came from this land of petrified forests, about deserts painted in rainbow colors and people who lived in houses high up in cliff walls; such people must have known how to fly. Thirst and hunger lurked though there was plenty for man and mule. It lay hidden, cached in a vast, dry land.

Their nameless Zuñi guide indicated that they must extinguish their smokeless cooking fires at dusk.

"This darkness is eerie," complained Roque as they sat talking in hushed tones about spirits, death, and legend. "Things stir in the night; I can smell them."

Beside Dan, Sebriana shivered and edged closer. Dan thought about their situation. In the land of Navajo enemies where springs were scarce, each waterhole was danger to approach. The friendly campfire was a beacon drawing death from its dwelling in the night as surely as moths fly to flame.

Rojo spoke. "Here we are, deep in Navajo country. They are plentiful, and they hate the Zuñi. We must take more care than before. No fire."

Staying apart from them, their Zuñi guide remained a stranger.

Roque shivered. "It is told that giants visit the Zuñi and are fed by them."

"Shalako," said Rojo. "In the winter, nine-foot tall kachinas, the Zuñi ancestor-gods, with great clacking beaks dance in their plaza. I have seen it. The Zuñi say Shalako bring the rain."

"Were you frightened?" asked Sebriana.

"I watched from a nearby hill. If the Zuñi had known I attended their sacred ceremony, they would have killed me. I think the Shalako were costumes with men inside."

The Zuñi guide made no response to Rojo's statements regarding his gods. He never spoke, and they never learned his name. He must have been an initiate of the secrets the four sought, or the shaman would not have sent him with them. Since he knew their secrets and what they sought it was safe to talk around him.

But Dan thought there might be another reason for their guide's extreme taciturnity. Dan did not think he spoke Mexican or English.

"I've heard stories," Dan said, "even stranger about the country we are going to. Kit told me he and other mountain men had seen little Welshmen less than five feet tall. They live in caves and are very shy, running and hiding at the sight of strangers and pulling in rocks to seal the hole so you can't tell where they are."

Sebriana looked perplexed. "How did Kit know they

were Welsh?"

"Some of the mountain men have heard them speak from afar," Dan replied. "Many of the trappers are Scots and Scots-Irish. They thought they could understand some of the words and concluded the little men must be speaking Welsh."

Roque looked skeptical. "You believe in little Welshmen who live in caves? You must be loco, Danito." He laughed.

"It's true," said Rojo. "The Hopi know them. And the Utahs venerate them thinking them holy. They are prophets for the Utah."

Shaken, Roque changed the subject. "Danito, you have said we seek three treasures, but I only remember you talking of two. What is the third?"

"You know we follow the Ark of the Covenant brought this way by the people of Princess Tea Tephi."

"Wait!" Sebriana was restive. "There is some connection here. Tea Tephi's people lived in Ireland and migrated to Scotland to Roslyn, didn't they? What language did they speak?"

"Hebrew," Dan replied instantly. There was a hush, and then Dan said, "Or maybe Celtic. Why?"

Sebriana shook her head in frustration. "I'm not sure."

"The Ark passed this way," Dan continued. "The Templars followed more than a thousand years later, evacuating the Temple furnishings before the advance of Islam…"

"Wait!" demanded Sebriana. "How did they come by these treasures, Pobrecito?"

"Having descendants of Tea Tephi among them as well as brother Masons among the builders of great cathedrals and monuments, they knew where to look for the lodges of the Holy Saints John and knew what was concealed in each. With Islam all around them, they knew they needed to take possession of the treasures or see it lost to the enemy of Christendom."

Sebriana tilted her head. "You've said that before but I wasn't sure I heard right. Saints John. What does that mean?

Dan nodded. "There were two of them: Saint John the Baptist and Saint John the Beloved. In the Holy Land there are two monastaries near Jerusalem, one dedicated to each. In the First Degree, an initiate points a toe toward each of them forming a square."

Rojo pondered. "That explains the second treasure, but not yet the third."

"The third," Dan replied, "was concealed in Egypt before the Hebrews departed for their forty years wandering in the desert. Do you recall what the Bible says? After the Passover, the Plague that killed the first born sons, the Egyptians hastened to give their golden wealth to the Children of Israel. They couldn't carry it with them, so they hid it in the land of Goshen. The hiding places were recorded on four copper scrolls that went with the People of Israel to the Promised Land. One of them was concealed in the Temple. Of the others, the professor believed that one was at the lodge of Saint John the Baptist, a second went with Tea Tephi, and a third to Israel, as opposed to Judah, and was lost when the kingdom ceased to be.

Dan paused for breath and looked at the dim faces of his friends shrouded in darkness. He had their full attention. "In the Fifth Crusade, the Templar Knights proposed an attack on Egypt to secure the southern flank of the Holy Land. During that attack, they penetrated as far as Amarna, the seat of the Pharaoh Akhenaten and his Empress Nefertiti. The treasure was there and in Goshen, and they recovered most of it.

"The treasure made them fabulously wealthy," he continued. "Perhaps they should have turned it over to the Pope, but they had concerns in Palestine, a frontier to defend. Failing to present the treasure to the Pontiff may have been the beginning of their rift with the Pope. However, Topper thought the Pope didn't know the source of Templar wealth, but that he must have suspected its origin. Nonetheless, in the end the Templar Fleet took it across the sea to be hidden with the rest."

Dan's friends were awestruck. Roque spoke first. "This treasure will make us fabulously wealthy!"

"It's represents more than that, Roque," Dan said. "It's power, more power than any one man or small group was ever meant to have. It was power that God gave to Israel as long as the nation remained true to Him. It's been unlucky for those who haven't kept faith."

Sebriana spoke up. "We haven't got it yet, and there are powerful forces working against us."

"And we haven't seen any Hebrews or Knights Templar," Rojo added. "I think if they were around, the N'deh, the people, would have noticed."

Dan thought for a moment. "Things change over time. Who would have thought the Penitentes were tools of the Pope left in place for hundreds of years? Who would believe that the whole reason for the conquest and reconquest of New Mexico might be this treasure?"

Sebriana seemed troubled. "What other forces might be arrayed against us?"

Roque spat in the dust. "Texain Rangers."

"Who are they working for?" Rojo asked.

Dan considered this question through a silence that would have made most Anglos nervous. He knew of the storm brewing in distant cities. "Maybe they represent the southern states that are talking about breaking away from the Union."

Not satisfied by this answer, Sebriana shook her head. "What about the Knights Templar? Do they still have a stake in this?"

Dan was taken aback. "I think we might be them or at least their successors. Some scholars think that when the Knights disbanded, they sought refuge in the lodges of masons."

"Jews?" suggested Roque. "Don't they seek their ancient treasure?" He snorted. "Who has a stronger claim?"

"I'm here," said Sebriana pointedly, "and so are you. Perhaps this is the reason our ancestors, the crypto-Jews, came to New Mexico."

Rojo looked thoughtful. "We haven't accounted for the bearded ones in the black coats that look like preachers."

Dan shut one eye and frowned. "Something powerful and evil, I think. They killed Topper."

Soon afterwards, they rode through a forest of fallen trees lying shattered like glass on the ground.

Puzzled, Rojo dismounted, and his friends followed his example. He touched the trees and examined them closely. "There is no mistake. These are trees, and they are stone. I can see the growth rings. Our elders tell stories of the time when monsters walked the earth, and one of them turned trees to stone."

The next day they gazed down on a brightly colored desolation. The desert was beautiful in bands of red, yellow, black, white, and orange. Green was missing. Little, perhaps nothing, grew there. The land looked as if it had been poisoned. Their Zuñi guide shook his head and pointed them away.

Sebriana rode close and whispered into Dan's ear. "Is this some effect of the Ark passing by? Perhaps they dropped it, and left this blasted waste and trees turned to stone." Her breath was coming in gasps, and she grew excited. "Maybe someone tried to take it from them and the Ark blasted the attackers! It is very powerful."

Dan shook his head. "I don't know. Perhaps."

"Maybe that is why no one has found it."

Their guide took them by a sure trail, and they camped near water every night in that parched land. His trail went from hidden tank to concealed spring. They drank, filled their canteens, watered their horses, and moved on a mile or two out of sight of water. In the desert, all must come to water, so wells, springs, and tanks are places of ambush. Where rock was exposed near water, they found the signs of the passage of men, and there among the rock pictures, they often found the signs they thought the ancient Hebrews had left.

The Hopi mesas were like a wedding cake that has been dropped. The cake shatters but retains its layers. Decoration and cake from the higher levels breaks loose and tumbles down. Fissures appear everywhere. The homes of the Hopi built of stacked rock the same color as the mesas remained hidden until one was less than a quarter mile away. Only a trickle of smoke from cooking fires gave them away. They had the same shattered and stepped appearance as their surroundings.

Three mesas were occupied by Hopi in 1860, some by more than one village. A fourth, Antelope Mesa, had been home to a village that had converted to Christianity. In a violent rejection of Spanish culture, Awatovi was attacked in the night by the other Hopi, the men killed, and their women and children distributed among the victors. People from the Rio Grande lived at Hano and Payupki, having run from Spanish domination in the Reconquista, the reconquest of New Mexico. They were welcomed and given land so placed that they served as guardians from attackers. The stories of the Hopi say their clans gathered from all over the high desert, from the Cañon of the Colorado and Cañon de Chelly and from south of the Mogollon Rim. They had wandered and returned to the villages of Oraibi, Shongopavi, Mishongnovi, and Walpi.

Below their villages, the Hopi cultivated gardens by capturing the infrequent runoff from Black Mesa. Beans and squash were planted together with the corn which served as trellis for the bean which nourished the roots of the corn. The mounds in which the plants grew were well separated so that roots would spread and capture all possible moisture.

The four friends and their guide followed a procession of stately Kachinas past the melting remains of what had once been a Christian church into the tiny plaza of Oraibi. Centuries' accumulation of refuse, bones, and broken pottery crunched underfoot. Homes rose to three and four stories around them, but the first level came barely to Dan's shoulder, the roadway having gained height through the years. People stood and sat on rooftops. The men were dressed in cotton pants that came to the knee with a breechclout, black with blue border. Many wore belts of huge conchos, hammered silver discs. Smaller conchos appeared along leg seams. A simple tunic belted with a red sash and a band of red holding back long black hair completed the attire. The women wore mantas, a blanket of dark wool fastened along the right side and over the right shoulder, cinched at the waist with a fringed sash in red. The hair of unmarried women was fantastic in concept. Great wheels of hair were coiled over the ears giving the impression of a large butterfly.

The town smelled of smoke and ash, of too many people living too close together for too many centuries mixed with the sweet smell of corn, the musty scent of beans and the clean smell of summer squash and onion. The aroma of sage and piñon forest wafted through it, all heavily mixed with dust. The town was complex, old, and paradoxical. Adobes seemed to have been built with less care than at Acoma or Zuñi but were more at one with the setting flowing down lines of the mesa following its contours, melting into the terrain.

A villager said to them, "Niman Kachina."

And Rojo told them, "I think it is the farewell to the Kachinas who will return to their home in the San Francisco Peaks until next winter." Deference, awe, and wonder were written on his face.

Dan was surprised. Peregrino Rojo, the Red Pilgrim, had seen many parts and blended in with them all. Rojo acted as if the Kachinas were real and not men in masks.

They danced raising their knees high each making the hollow hoot or click of its kind. The Kachina masks, decorated with fur and feather that told its name and nature, covered the entire head of the dancer. The dancing gods carried whips of yucca and wands of juniper. They were followed by bands of clowns painted in stripes of black and white who behaved in outlandish and obscene ways suggesting gluttony, foolishness, and mistreatment of relatives. One clown ascended and descended a ladder upside-down, his head toward the ground the entire time.

The travelers camped on the mesa beyond the town hobbling their stock so that they would not wander into gardens. When the ceremony was ended, the Zuñi guide took them to the home of a shaman, a holy man. They climbed ladders from one rooftop to a higher rooftop in the red glow of the setting sun and finally stood beside a smoke hole as their guide called down the ladder. A voice within invited them down.

In the dim light of a tiny fire suspended in a pot near the vigas, they saw a viejo, an ancient, with long white hair that reached the ground all around him as he sat cross-legged on the floor. He was clad in fine white elk hide adorned with fringe, bells, mirrors, and tinklers made of the lids of tin cans twisted into bell shapes. His eyes were of the uniform gray rainbow luster of pearls, his cheeks shrunken, his lips receding over gums, more skeleton than man.

He greeted them in Spanish. "I am called He Who Wanders. Sit. Aa'ku's message that you would be coming arrived many days ago."

Dan was surprised, and glancing at his friends, thought they were, too. Doubly so, he thought, that word could have gotten here from Acoma ahead of them and that the ancient one spoke Spanish. Few of the Hopi did. They were cimarron, wild, from beyond the edges of civilization even if they did dwell in villages. They lived in the old way and practiced a religion that had existed before Christianity came. Any who spoke Spanish here had probably been slaves in Mexican households.

Rojo was the first to speak. "Father, how came you to speak Spanish?"

"I was born soon after Governor Oñate came from the south with his turtle backed men to conquer the people of the Rio Grande. I remember when Hano was being built. When I was young I went to see the Pueblos on the big river and learned the language of the foreigners."

Dan began calculating years as the old man continued. "When I was older, I traveled with Padre Garces and Juan Bautista de Anza to visit the Great Salt Sea in the west."

Roque spoke up. "Is that how you came to be called

He Who Wanders?"

"No," said the ancient one. "In my old age, I learned new ways to see and to travel. I soar above the earth and visit friends like Aa'ku and Tïéná'áí Izdzáníí."

Rojo turned to Dan. "He knows our Doña Luna."

He Who Travels nodded. "Yes, I know her."

Roque was counting on his fingers. Dan thought he might pull off his moccasins and start on toes. "He must be 150 years old. I don't believe it."

He Who Wanders began speaking in a surprisingly clear voice for one so old. "The truth does not require your belief, young man. Listen for time grows short, and I have much to tell you." He rose from sitting on the floor in one fluid motion, raising hands overhead making a gesture Dan had only seen once before on the night he was raised in Lodge. Even Rojo looked surprised. He Who Wanders continued his narrative.

"I do not use this sign lightly, knowing well its meaning. Dark forces are gathering about you. I think you are the ones we have been expecting, and I hope to live to see the completion of your quest. It is you who are in great danger and distress, and I will do all in my power to help you.

"My *kiva* possesses knowledge no other *kiva* remembers. We know of the One God and His Ten Laws. When most Hopi were still wandering, our *kiva* was already settled at Oraibi. Among the people was a very old couple who remained childless long past the age when the old woman could bear children. The old man prayed for a child. He prayed to Storm, Wind, Thunder, and Lightening with no effect. He prayed to lakes and mountains and to the earth itself, but no one answered.

"Finally, he prayed to the Unseen God who created the earth, and soon his wife began to swell with child. When the child was born, the old man felt he should make an offering to the Unseen God. He took the child with him to a place far from the village but could think of nothing good enough to sacrifice for such a great blessing. It came to him that he must sacrifice the child. The old man explained this to the boy who said he understood and lay peacefully on the ground while his father raised the knife to stab him.

"Only then did they notice a mountain sheep that had caught its leg in a cleft in the rock. They freed it and killed it burning the best parts on the fire as an offering.

"As the child grew he became a mighty hunter. Out hunting alone, he had time to think, and it came to him that he wanted to be a shaman. He told his parents of his desire. Soon afterward, he was out hunting and killed a deer. As he approached it to butcher it, an idea came to him. He broke the deer's leg and then tried to use his powers and knowledge and singing to heal the leg.

"While he was thus engaged, a man dressed in strange clothing approached and asked what he was doing. The boy explained that he wanted to be a shaman. The man said that if this is what he truly wanted he should meet the man in this same place the next day and come prepared for a very long hunt. The boy took the deer home and explained to his parents that he would be gone for a long time on a special hunt.

"The boy met the man, and they walked to the west until dusk and came upon a bear which they mounted and rode at high speed all through the night until they came to the deep cañon. They dismounted and climbed down until they came to a *kiva*.

"They called out and were invited to enter. There were kachinas inside waiting for them, preparing a ceremony. They had yucca whips and told the boy they must whip him to pieces and then resurrect him if he wished to be a shaman. He said that would be fine, and they told him to strip. Once he was naked they whipped him until he bled in many places. Then one of them approached with a sharp flint knife and cut off a piece of skin from the end of the boy's penis.

"'This will be enough,' the kachina said. 'It is a symbol of your bond to the Unseen God and of how He has saved you as His own.'

"They then taught the boy many things about what he could and could not eat and about the Ten Laws. The boy returned home and was a powerful shaman and healer among us all of his days. He was the first of my *kiva*."

The four companions sat in rapt attention through these stories. Sebriana's eyes especially grew large and round.

"You must go to the great cañon," He Who Wanders said. "One of my kiva will guide you along the Salt Road. You will find part of what you seek there. Leave your stock here. We will care for it. Where you go, you must go on foot.

"When you return, I will have more to tell you. Save your questions until then. Now sleep, for you must depart early in the morning."

Thus invited, beds, skins thick with fur, and blankets,

were brought, and the friends slept there in the ancient one's room. Arising in the morning before daylight, they joined the old man on the roof to sprinkle pollen and greet the sun. They breakfasted on cornmeal mush, *piki* bread, and venison before they hastened to the west on foot.

Dan hated to leave Topper's parfleche, his valise, behind, but consoled himself by entrusting it to He Who Wanders. For the rest, each took one rifle each and two pistols with a bit of powder and shot. They brought canteens and Roque insisted they take a length of lariat. "You never know when rope will come in handy," said Roque earnestly. Somehow Dan got stuck with carrying it.

They made up packs with their bedrolls, filling them with dried vegetables, cornmeal, beans, pemmican, and jerky.

He Who Wanders assigned two young Hopi men to guide them. Dan never learned their names, for they spoke but little Spanish, and none of the four friends spoke Hopi. Rojo communicated with them by signs and in Navajo, though neither he nor they spoke it well. Roque referred to them, and they responded good-naturedly, as Nando and Nacho. They led the group at a fast pace. Dan thought they would have run had he and his friends been up to it. Four days of haste and worn moccasins brought them to the edge of the abyss. They had traveled west from Oraibi, crossing the Little Colorado and then following it northwest in the lee of a great mesa that rose high above them on the west.

Roque, Rojo, and Dan had seen the mesa before from farther west where, if anything, the canyon was deeper for their having been atop the mesa that now loomed. For Sebriana, it was a first, and she stood in awe as the sun set, turning the red, orange, and yellow of the rocks to even brighter and more vibrant hues. The cañon defies description. It was like being in the clouds and looking down on a mountain range of vibrant color.

The night was dark and moonless lit by a million stars. As the fire died away, the sense of void so near brought a hush over them. The warm smell of cedar engulfed them in the early spring chill.

They backtracked a few miles to a tiny cañon whose floor fell steeply and twisted into the earth. The sky was not visible above from within. The cañon lit with light contorted and reflected down routes as tortured as the one they trod. In places, Dan could reach out and touch both walls, whose stone glowed crimson, ochre, topaz, white, and apricot in the strange light. For miles, the course was almost level, the bottom sandy. Then it would descend again so that they had to scramble, using hands as much as feet. When they finally emerged, they were far down in the big canyon, but not yet near its bottom. Before them the cliff fell away sharply for hundreds of feet.

Roque whistled in awe. "When it rains, this will be a waterfall. Very high. Very impressive."

They turned toward the cliff face following their guides along a narrow ledge. Hours later, between exhaustion and terror of the heights, Dan could scarcely guess the time as they came to a plain that sloped downward from the cliff toward the river far below. It would end in cliffs long before it arrived at the final chasm.

"Look at this," said Rojo. He directed their attention to the ground nearby where stones had once been laid in piles forming straight lines and right angles. Rojo reached down, picked something from the ground, and handed it to Dan.

Dan examined the object. "Pottery. It's painted with designs in black and white." He handed it to Sebriana and

Roque.

Rojo nodded. "These are walls. This place was once farmed."

They would see these signs again and again as they traveled along the side of the cañon. They learned from their guides that the small hollows in the rock that meandered up many slopes were hand and footholds, stony stairways.

Roque snarled in disbelief. "Why would anyone farm here?"

They climbed and scrambled through the coming days. Trails led away from the one they followed, going up and descending. Theirs was evidently a main connecting trail.

Dan quipped. "I believe we're following the Grand Trunk Road."

Camping near water was not a problem, for streams and springs were numerous. They worked their way along narrow ledges that fell off to terrifying depths and across surprisingly broad meadows.

Sebriana commented on the people who had lived here. "They must have been birds or angels with wings"

The first days were constant terror. Roque balked at the first bridge, an ancient log and stone affair set across a deep side-cañon. "We can't cross that. The logs are old. It's too narrow anyway."

The Hopi had already crossed ahead of them. Rojo stepped forward. "I'll go," and he did, shaming Roque into following.

Sebriana was fearless, or so Dan thought. She seemed to sweat a bit more than the weather could account for. In the evening, she cuddled, and Dan felt her shivering from the day's trials and exertions, but she never said a word of complaint.

At the end of their first day, Dan told his friends, "These paths were made by human mountain goats or monkeys." No one contradicted him. As days went by, they learned new skills and became almost used to their environment. Balance improved, and they became more sure-footed. "The people who made them were born to this life. I'm surprised they didn't all fall to their deaths as toddlers."

Roque nodded. "Perhaps their mothers carried them in cradleboards until they were teenagers."

On the fourth day while climbing ancient stairs, mere shallow depressions in the rock, Roque became entangled with himself. The next hold was on the wrong side, and he tried to cross a leg under the one whose toe gripped rock knocking his foot free. High on rock that slopped toward cliff, he held on momentarily with only his fingers and began to slide, slowly at first and then faster. Below him, Dan balled his fist in a handhold and braced for the shock. Roque struck, and for an instant they both were in danger of going down, but he caught with toes and fingers. Newfound confidence was shattered.

"Gracias, amigo," he breathed and resumed his climb.

Dan found that perception in the cañon was distorted. It was often difficult to discern whether objects were on one side of the river or the other because the river twisted and wound unseen below.

One morning, their guides led them up to a small tower like a pulpit with a top a beam's length on a side. As they stood there, the rising sun cast a brilliant shaft of light through a window, a cave, in the rock between two massive pillars.

"*Ventana*," said Roque, "a window in the rock."

"Behold, Jachin and Boaz!" Dan joked referring to the two pillars that stood at the entrance to Solomon's

Temple. As it turned out, the pillars were across the river, but the cave was on the same side as the travelers. They arrived at the *ventana*, window, within a few hours.

They approached along a wide, well-watered bench high above the river. As they got close, they saw signs of ruined houses and long ago human occupation. A narrow path cut into the cliff face led upward.

Roque breathed a sigh of relief. "Stairs! Real stairs. The kind I grew up with." He started upward on them.

At the top of the stairs, they found a flat forecourt. Inspection showed it had been created by human hands and built up with loads of stone and earth and a rock retaining wall. Cathedral-like, the cave had a high ceiling and flat floor.

Rojo gestured toward the back. "There is a second chamber."

Entering they saw that light was admitted from a window above. Falling on the sandy floor the light illuminated the center of the room.

"Stop," Dan cried. "Look at the floor!"

"It looks like a box once sat there," said Roque.

With arm and hand and pace Dan began to measure the unmarked space.

Roque watched his friend's strange behavior. "What are you doing?"

"Measuring. A cubit is the length of a man's forearm and so forth. Biblical measurements were made with the body not rulers."

After a few minutes, Dan stood. "Yes, it's smooth and the right dimensions for the Ark. Look closely. There are the marks of passage all around. These are the marks of sandals. There are none there in the middle. No foot has trodden there."

Behind them in the outer room Sebriana called.

"Come look. See these paintings."

Tall men with broad shoulders and triangular bodies clad in long robes looked down on them. Colorfully painted priests wore imaginative crowns and oblong pendants. The comrades stared in amazement.

Awed, Dan said, "These could have been twelve Levites from the Bible led in procession by their high priest. Look, there on his breast, Aaron's ephod and golden breastplate. And those must be the Urim and Thummim, the prophesying stones."

"Jews wouldn't paint pictures of men on the walls of their temple," said Sebriana confidently.

Roque seemed puzzled. "Have we come to the wrong place?"

"I think the place is right," Dan replied. "Sebriana is right as well. I think the Hopi, their ancestors or someone like them, must have painted these pictures. They painted the men they saw. It was here, but the Ark is gone. We've come a long way to find such disappointment."

Rojo spoke philosophically. "I do not regret the trip."

They inspected the site for signs of where the Danites and their priests might have gone.

Roque growled. "Even Kit Carson can't read a millennia old trail."

"We don't know that," Dan responded. "They might have left last century or last week."

Sebriana looked at her lover. "I think the condition of their houses suggests they've been gone a very long time, but the painting in the cave could have been made yesterday."

"Caves do that," Dan said. "They preserve things."

Their explorations were interrupted by Nacho and Nando, the Hopi guides. They made signs that the travelers should turn back.

"We would never have found this on our own," said Rojo. "I think we should continue to follow them."

"Before we go," said Sebriana, "shouldn't we check this village for signs of Hebrew occupation?" She referred to the ruined village below what they'd come to think of as The Temple. "Shouldn't there be metal or other things here that would prove who lived here?"

Dan thought about her question. "Topper wrote about this problem. He thought that in time metal would corrode and disappear unless something was done to preserve it. Tools wear out and get thrown away. The people who came here might have been farmers, soldiers, and sailors who didn't know how to work metal. They would have known bronze and copper, but they'd have needed a fresh source of ore.

"I'm sure they brought Old World crops with them, but in all this time, the crops might have become so widespread that we think of them as New World species. They may have farmed new crops in the same fields as the old. It has been a very long time. We could look and dig and sift through the soil. In time, we might find something. And we might miss it, too. This place is isolated. The cañon protects it."

He stopped to think and recall. "The pictures on the wall of The Temple indicate someone held the ones who lived here in awe. In time, without outside trade, isolated, they may have come to look a lot like their neighbors and ended up using the same technologies. It might be hard to tell them from the Indians."

Roque smiled. "Maybe they are still here. I thought I saw some little Welshmen ducking into caves as we made our way here."

Rojo scowled. "I saw ringtail cats and raccoons."

Roque wasn't easily put off. "These were bigger than

that, much bigger, the size of a mountain lion maybe. Small for a man but large for an animal, although usually all I saw was a head disappearing into a hole."

"So," said Rojo, "something hairy and the size of a ringtail."

Sebriana's eyes flashed with insight. "They carried the Ark away. Think of the work and skill that took. They could not touch it. It was too holy and a touch would kill, so the carry poles were as close as they could get. Think what that journey would have been like. They left here because they wanted to leave. They didn't become shy little men who hide in caves."

"If there is anyone here," Dan added, "they must be watchmen replaced at frequent intervals."

"I suppose," responded Rojo, "that a group that looked like Indians might live here and hunt and gather unnoticed if they were careful. They might pass through the desert like ghosts in small parties at times when they knew the Hopi and Navajo were busy with ceremonials. But I think if they were here I'd have seen them, not Roque."

Roque scowled.

Sebriana smiled. "Perhaps they have studied to fool your trained eyes, but they cannot deceive the eyes of the foolish."

Roque's scowl deepened as he tried to puzzle out his *prima's* meaning. He sought to recover his dignity by asking something wise. "Why haven't we seen signs of the Knights Templar if they came this way?"

Dan shook his head. "I don't know."

Journeying back to Oraibi, Dan saw the trail with new eyes, saw how it was chosen to make it possible for four men to pass carrying the Ark between them and where the way the path led down a pitch might have made it easier for men to lower an object carried on poles by rope. Dan watched for Welshmen, but didn't see any, though he did have the feeling they were watched.

Rojo had the same feeling. "I don't want to alarm the others, but we are being watched from the other side of the river."

Sunlight glinted then as it does from the lens of a telescope. Dan and Rojo both saw it. Rojo shook his head. "Make no sign. Don't let them, whoever they are, know we are aware of them. They are too far away to hurt us now, but they travel in the same direction we do."

They came to the place where they had entered the cañon. At this point, the river made a great bend from flowing east to west to flowing from the north. Dan almost missed the small flash of light from a mirror pointed north, but he did catch the unmistakable answer from far north on the near side. The light flashed so many times that Dan began to perceive pattern, a mix of long and short flashes.

"What is that?" asked Sebriana.

"We seem to have company," Dan replied.

"They won't be able to reach us," said Rojo, "before the crossing of the Little Colorado, even if they have horses. As we move directly through the cañons on foot, going where their horses can't, they will remain days behind us."

He referred to a place almost forty miles from the big cañon where the river started its descent into the abyss. At the crossing, the cañon was only one hundred feet deep while further west, it was over one thousand feet deep with sheer walls.

For once, Sebriana seemed concerned. "Who are they?"

Rojo thought for a moment as he considered the

possibilities. "People who use telescopes and mirrors. Paiutes live on that side of the river. I doubt it's them."

Dan added his thoughts. "Probably not the Texians. Our pursuers are on both sides of the river and must be numerous."

"I doubt," said Rojo, "the Penitentes could have come this far without a fight with the Navajo."

Sebriana persisted. "Who then?"

Dan answered, "The ones in black. They seemed numerous."

"But who are they?" Something in the dark, unknown menace troubled Sebriana, and she shivered.

Dan sought to comfort her by making the unknown known. "Topper said Joe Smith was privy to Lodge secrets. So Brigham Young must know them, too. Perhaps the treasure is why he brought his people west."

"We must move quickly," said Roque, "and keep careful watch."

They made their way back up through the labyrinth of the narrow cañon that led to the desert far above. Color, light, and texture were in contradiction. The stone was polished with lines as sharp as glass but soft in color and sandy of texture glowing in filtered light, although the companions felt completely enclosed in the earth.

Dan wondered why the ancient Hebrews had come so far. What more secure cathedral could they have found? He thought about what the country might have been like more than two thousand years before: did the Indians build stone and adobe houses as they did now in 1860? Did they farm or were they nomads? They certainly left ruins enough.

In camp that night, Dan had a story to tell. "Before we left, Kit had me read a letter to him from his friend Major Carleton. Two years ago, Carleton was assigned to look into the disappearance of a wagon train not too far from here at a place called Mountain Meadows."

"I heard about that," said Roque. "The Fancher Party had about one hundred and twenty people and they disappeared completely. It was very mysterious. There were all kinds of strange rumors. The Mormons put about that it was Paiutes that killed them. That would have taken three hundred Paiutes. Who ever heard of that many together in one place? Those Digger Indians scrounge a few things to eat from the desert. They live all spread out. And how could the Fanchers just disappear?"

"They didn't disappear," Dan went on. "Carleton found them. Their bones were all spread out and scattered around Mountain Meadows. He said every skull had a neat hole in it like they'd been shot from close range.

"There were things the major couldn't put in his official report, rumors and whispers and things told in confidence. People up there are scared. Half of them are murderers and the other half live in fear of them. According to Carleton, a group of Mormon militia called Danites ambushed the wagon train using a few Paiutes to make it look like an Indian attack to the Fanchers. The Mormons offered to mediate, telling the Fanchers the Paiutes would let them go only if they were disarmed and escorted by Mormons. The Fanchers agreed and were led out each man with a Mormon beside him. At a prearranged signal, each Mormon killed the man next to him. Then they killed the women. They left little children alive thinking them too young to remember."

"¡*Cabrónes!*" yelled Roque.

Sebriana wept. "That's the ugliest thing I've ever heard. What possible reason could they have had to do such a terrible thing?"

"Carleton concluded it was robbery. The Fancher

party was carrying a lot of money, and their wagons held tools and supplies the Mormons needed. Brigham Young had ordered the Mormons not to trade with them although they were in need of food and had money to pay. Carleton was certain Brigham Young had ordered the attack. He didn't think the Danites would move without orders, especially not to do something this terrible. The major went through the remains and it was clear to him that everything of value had been taken."

"Danites, that's a strange name," said Rojo. "We've heard it before. Wasn't that the name of the Hebrew tribe that was sent out with the Ark?"

"Yes," Dan replied. "It seems strange that the Mormon militia would carry such a name. The Israelite tribe of Dan was made up of sailors and warriors who protected Israel. I remember stories about the Mormons using that name for their militia in Missouri."

Roque squinted one eye trying to remember things he'd heard. "Danites are enforcers for Young. I've heard they enforce religious discipline and protect the community from outsiders. They are said to be some bad hombres. But I never heard why they were called Danites."

Roque thought deep and long and then exhaled. "Topper told me that Joseph Smith, the Mormon founder, was a Freemason."

"He was," Dan replied. "The Grand Master of Masons in Illinois, who was also the governor, raised Smith himself. Smith started having ceremonies to make all of his people Masons. The Grand Lodge told him to stop because he wasn't bothering to make them do the proficiencies; they didn't have to learn all the things which Masons must demonstrate they understand. Smith just pronounced them Masons and gave them the passwords and signs. They started using Masonic symbols in all sorts of strange ways, like putting them on their small clothes for protection from evil.

"Sebriana, we are talking about symbols that are used to remind us of lessons and great truths. They used them as if they were magic. So, the Grand Lodge expelled Smith."

Sebriana pondered the man being expelled from the lodge. "Why did they come west?"

Dan replied, "There was unpleasantness in Illinois and Missouri. Everywhere they went, they raised militias and harassed their neighbors. Smith was arrested. As he waited for the Mormon Militia to come and rescue him, a mob attacked the jail. Smith had a pistol and used it to defend himself. He was shot."

Roque cocked his head strangely. "How could he have a pistol in jail?"

"That, amigo," Dan replied, "is only one of the strange things in the whole affair. Afterward, Brigham Young took over leadership. When the United States went to war with Mexico and was distracted with the fighting, Young moved his people in without firing a shot to take over much of the land the Union had just acquired."

Sebriana looked thoughtful. "But, *Pobrecito*, why call the militia Danites?"

"Not just militia, *mija*, a special force that enforces religious order. If you decide you want to leave their church, they cut your throat. If you speak out against some doctrine, they do the same. It is a good question, though, and there are hints in Topper's notes. He learned much of what he knew from Masonic libraries. He shared his knowledge with other Masons. There was a letter from the Grand Master of Illinois giving warning about Joseph Smith."

Her jaw dropped. "Are you suggesting that the real

purpose of the Danites is to find the Ark brought here by Hebrew Danites? That the name is some sort of cruel joke?"

"I think it could be so," Dan concluded. "If we ever find out who killed Topper or who pursues us from north of the Rio Colorado, we may have an answer."

Roque had a gift for understatement. "I think we are in a whole lot of trouble."

Arriving at the place where they intended to cross the Little Colorado, Rojo saw dust to the north. The friends and their guides went to ground and sought cover. It is easier for men afoot to hide than it is for riders and easier to hide than outrun men on horseback. Light flashed from a telescope. Before long they could make out thirty riders dressed in black and leading remounts and a pack train.

Dan thought, "If they are pursuing us, they are taking the job seriously."

The black coated men left a small party to guard the crossing and made their way down to the river bottom where they spread out and followed the river southeast looking for signs of a party crossing.

There are many places where the Little Colorado can be crossed by men afoot.

Dan calculated their chances of going unseen and found this a point in his party's favor. On horseback, the strangers had fewer choices. The Little Colorado, which they were now following, was not deep or wide. In a dry season, winter and spring, there were times when there was no water. Dan could tell a great deal from the debris piled alongside the riverbed. When the rains were heavy, it was a rushing torrent, tossing uprooted plants and trees many feet up the cañon-side. Most of the time, it was a slow, muddy trickle barely knee deep.

The Hopi guides were sure to know places to cross.

Dan suspected that they knew many that no one else knew, and that was another point in his party's favor.

Then Dan realized that the pursuers, for such he was sure they were, had an advantage. Anyone traveling this way, especially on foot, was likely to head to the Hopi mesas, for they were the nearest villages, there not being a Spanish town until they neared the Rio Grande. Travelers moved from water to water choosing the shortest distance possible between; in this way the trail system grew. Some waterholes disappeared in dry weather, so primary trails develop branches that run to more permanent water. Dan's party had options for travel, but they were limited.

The sandy bottom of the Little Colorado posed a problem. Dan's group would leave tracks. They might follow in one another's footsteps disguising their number, but there would be at least one set of tracks. Brushing them out with a wand of desert broom would only make sign more visible. Wind and water make their own tracks, and they could not to be duplicated. Rock and rocky places were an option, but on the rocky ground, Dan thought, the river offered long, straight vistas that would make the group easy to spot in daylight.

Rojo and their Hopi guides realized how vulnerable the river bottom would make them and kept the small party hidden until nightfall. The moon was almost full, lighting their way as they traveled southeast, their guides leading them to what Dan hoped would be an unguarded ford.

Chapter 8

Oraibi

Still on the south or opposite side of the Little Colorado from Hopi, they slept the next day in an ancient ruined village. Dan was glad they had no livestock.

Rojo pointed. "The Hopi wish us to hide in here." He indicated the ruin. "I do not like houses of the dead, but I think we have little choice."

It would have been difficult to shield the mules and Roque's grullo stallion from observation. The ruin was made of stone blocks. Roque commented, "If we have to fight, this stone heap will be a fine fortress. We can move through doorways from level to level and side to side without being seen while firing from windows. We'll be in the shadows where our enemies can't see us."

Dan thought Roque might prefer fighting to running even at these bad odds.

"Let's go," Rojo said. "Our guides are ready."

The sun was down and the moon had not yet risen, When it did, it would be nearly full. They walked in darkness back toward the river.

"Shh!" whispered Sebriana. "Horses."

Then Nando heard them and stopped as they all did. He indicated that the friends should follow him quickly.

Dan could see his companions only as dark shadows

against a dark background. Their guides, Nacho and Nando, moved forward again, and they followed over the brink and down into the broad river. Moccasined feet make little noise. In the dark, uncertain footing is difficult to detect and missteps send rocks clattering into the deep.

Dan knocked loose a stone as big as a watermelon. It tumbled into space just missing Roque's head as it fell to strike with a ringing clank and starting a small landslide below. Noise echoed down the valley.

From both sides, they heard voices calling and horse hooves beating down the riverbed coming their way. A rifle fired into the air; Dan saw its flame. Another answered and another.

"They gather toward us," said Rojo in hushed tones. "It will take time, perhaps even a day for all of them to arrive, but five or six will be here in minutes and many more will arrive within the hour."

Dan nodded a gesture that was lost on the others in the dark. "Retreat is our only choice."

Roque seemed to want a fight. "We don't want to be caught in the flat open of the river bottom."

Rojo agreed. "We must move back to the llano from which we came."

"It seems our only hope," said Dan. "Move quickly. Riders are bearing down on us from either side."

Waving his arms, Nando signaled to them, and they followed into a cleft in the rock. On the river side, the opening was barely large enough for a man's body to pass through, but it opened a little inside, and soon they could stand and walk upright. Above them, Dan could see the cleft narrowed to mere inches in breadth where a few stars shone in the sky.

A slot cañon, Dan thought, but a small one like the ones they'd used to descend to Rio Colorado.

The ring of hooves transmitted through the rock alerted them before the riders arrived. Above Dan, a large body blocked the stars. The rider's horse staled, and Dan dared not move to avoid a drenching.

"They're here somewhere. I'm sure," said a voice somewhere above.

"You're sure this is where the noise came from?" asked a second voice.

"I'm sure," the first voice answered.

There were sounds of a horse approaching and then a third voice. "I heard it, too, and thought it near this spot. Didn't sound like an animal. They make small noises or none at all. This was big, and I thought I heard a yelp."

"Spread out then. We'll wait for the others," said the second voice. "We'll stake out this place." The riders moved away from the cleft.

"This is the second night I'll spend in the saddle," said the first voice. "Wish I were back in my own bed."

"That's no attitude for a Danite, Micajah," said the second voice. "We have our duty, and our reward will be great. Think what the prize is and how pleased the Prophet will be when we bring it to him."

"I know, I know," said the voice they now knew as Micajah. "We're the Children of Israel, gathered back from all nations, and now we seek our Ark lest it fall into the hands of Gentiles."

"Hush and do as you're told."

Dan's party continued on, away from the river, back the way they'd come or so Dan thought. It was hard to tell. The going was slow as the slot cañon was narrow and in places they had to crawl. In other spots, it opened up, and they could see the arc of the sky. Moonrise found them in such a place and slowed them further still. They could still hear the riders. More had arrived, and they were searching for the travelers. In the open places, Dan and his companions had to proceed slowly and quietly hoping not to attract attention lest they be seen.

False dawn found them in the arroyo miles from the river and out of the covered way. Only the banks of the slot cañon now kept them hidden. Anyone passing within a few hundred yards above or below them was sure to see them. Now and then, Dan could see the tops of hills.

"Anyone on those heights might see us," Dan warned.

Roque spoke up. "We're in the drainage we followed to the river back near the ruins."

Rojo signaled them to move faster.

As the sun rose, Dan in the lead with the two Hopi called back to the others. "I can see the ruin where we stayed yesterday."

A few more minutes undetected, he thought, would bring them to welcome concealment.

"We've covered miles since we left the river," said Rojo. "Those pursuing us will have a very great area to search."

Roque chuckled. "Maybe we have slipped through their net, and they are now far behind us."

It was a possibility, Dan thought.

Rojo pointed. The rising sun flashed and reflected off of something on a hilltop miles to their west and was followed by the report of a rifle and puff of smoke.

Sebriana was concerned. "That mirror flickering long and short flashes may be sending a message in code."

Half a mile behind them a rifle answered.

Rojo shouted. "They've spotted us! Run!"

Dan had heard that a man can outrun a horse on broken ground over short distances, but eventually the horse will wear him down. Dan ran for the safety of the ruin dodging between boulders knowing that above the slot cañon's banks the land was flat and a horse could hit its stride. It wasn't far.

Even as Sebriana ducked through a doorway, Dan heard hooves behind him and saw Roque drop to one knee as he turned to fire on their pursuer. Dan heard the shot and heard the body fall. Then he was in the ruin and already organizing their defense.

Surveying their fortress, Dan realized that on three sides they were safe. The ruin stood on a stone outcrop that rose twenty feet above the banks of the cañon and could only be accessed with great difficulty from those sides. On the east, it faced the banks and was connected to them by a narrow strip of stone like a drawbridge. Nacho and Nando served as lookouts watching the back trail and the distance. The small party had four rifles and eight pistols to face the onslaught. Somewhere below Dan, Roque was reloading his rifle.

"Good shot, Roque," Dan called, his chest heaving with exertion. There was no answer. "Roque?" Dan stuck his head up to look down their back trail. A bullet clanged on stone spraying his face with biting chips. A shot answered from one of Dan's companions, and he heard a cry of pain.

"Cabrón!" A female voice cursed the man she'd shot. Although he could not see her, Dan knew Sebriana must be busy reloading.

Dan contented himself with watching from well within windows and doors where he would be in shadow. They had access to six rooms on two floors and a parapetted roof that was their tower. Dan thought he could move unseen between the rooms.

"Roque, are you okay?" No answer. Dan pondered that Roque might be up to something and not wish to be disturbed or to give away his location.

Before them at one hundred yards, Dan could see four Danites and their horses. Dan whispered to his companions, hoping they would hear. "They must think themselves beyond our range. We'll soon surprise them."

How should they use that surprise to best advantage, Dan wondered. If they could take the black coats, who he was now sure were Mormons, and seize their horses, they might escape before the rest arrived. Peeking over the rock he used for cover, Dan saw that a fifth enemy lay writhing on the ground. That would be the one Sebriana had wounded. One Danite went to his wounded friend while the others wrestled with something else on the ground.

"Anyone got any ideas?" Dan called. "They can't get to us. We have the perfect fortress, but we'll run out of water soon if they lay siege. I don't see a way to disappear and get away. I suppose we could light fires and slip out in the dark tonight, hoping that they're fooled while we leave. Kit showed me a way to stack the wood so that it burns very slowly and keeps feeding into the fire. There's wood enough in the latillas and vigas..."

From somewhere above, Dan heard Rojo's voice. "Nacho says we left one of the enemy dead behind us..."

"That'll be the one I saw Roque turn to shoot."

"Nando says a Danite rider came in behind Roque and knocked him on the head," Rojo finished.

A sixth Danite rode to join the others as one of them called to him pointing to the bundle at his feet. "Brother Pratt, what do you want us to do with him?"

"That's Sergeant Pratt, Private Micajah, or Bishop Pratt. Keep the gentile under guard. I'm sure Captain Brannan will want to question him when he arrives."

"Yes, sir, Marsah Pratt, sir!" Dan detected a hint of sarcasm in Micajah's voice. Brother Pratt was not well liked.

"My name is Amasa Pratt. Sergeant Pratt to you, private."

Pratt had a telescope on a strap around his neck.

Sebriana called over to Dan, "That must be the telescope that you saw reflecting the rising sun, the one that shone up on that hilltop where someone was directing the others."

Dan considered his adversary. "Seems likely."

The man he watched was below medium height, dark, and stocky. Dan called to his mija. "He sure has got the small man's need to push others around." A white shirt showed under the dark woolens that covered him while a broad-brimmed hat with a rounded crown rested on his head. The belt strapped on over his long jacket supported two single-shot horse pistols and a large knife.

Rojo commented. "Revolvers must still be rare in Utah."

Dan laughed as Pratt dismounted awkwardly. "He's not much of a horseman." Dark hair and bushy beard concealed most of his face showing only two glinting, beady, dark eyes.

The dark woolen suit and white shirt were more suited to city streets than to the lonesome high desert, but now well coated in dust and grime, appeared to be the uniform of this militia. Unwittingly, Amasa Pratt had revealed to Dan that Roque was still alive. If Roque needed guarding he must be in good shape, too.

Rojo spoke just loud enough for Dan to hear. "I think it strange that Pratt is content to wait on his leader doing nothing through the day."

Dan agreed. "He must have fear of his captain's wrath, or I'm sure he would try interrogating Roque or negotiating with us."

Dan's Jicarilla friend affirmed his suspicions. "These

are good things to know, Pratt is indecisive, a bully and disliked by his men."

Dan chuckled. "If the bishop is only a sergeant, Brigham Young must be handing out religious titles like there was no tomorrow."

Pratt had his men carry the dead Danite to a spot under a tree away from their camp. They gathered stones and stacked them over him.

Dan had heard about their captain, Porter Brannan. He was a tough guy, an enforcer for the Prophet, and many said a completely unscrupulous, cold-blooded murderer. The nicest things Dan had ever heard said about him were that he was tenacious and deadly with a pistol.

Bishop Sergeant Pratt sent riders to the river and to the hilltop. Dan saw the flash of their signaling. More riders came in hourly. Dan was glad Pratt had made no more preparation than he did.

Dan and his friends improved their position as much as they could.

Dan moved over near Rojo. "Marsah Pratt seems to assume that our three blind sides are of no use to us or him. He's posted no guards there, concentrating on our front."

Nando showed Dan and Rojo what looked like a small door now bricked up on the side away from the Danites.

Rojo smiled. "Hopi are like prairie dogs. They always have a hidden backdoor. It must have been their clan that lived here. They knew where to look." As he spoke, the two Hopi loosened the stones, removed them, and then put them back in place loosely. "When darkness comes, we can slip out this way. We'll need a rope."

Dan protested. "I'm not leaving Roque."

"Even to save Sebriana?" Rojo countered. Dan looked into his dark eyes. He posed a good question, well put. It would be a hard decision.

Sebriana butted the Jicarilla back to the wall. Looking up, her nose almost touching his chin, she glared at Rojo. "I'm not leaving him either," she snarled.

Rojo smiled. "Then we must work on a plan."

Toward dusk, Captain Brannan arrived with ten more riders. Looking out at him still mounted on his horse, Dan saw a man with long blond hair and guessed he was of medium height. He wore a broad-brimmed, black hat with a round crown and a silver-concho hat band. An Arkansas toothpick and an ivory handled revolver hung from his belt while a cased telescope hung over his shoulder. A rifle rested across the pommel of his saddle. Unlike his men, he wore fringed buckskin.

Pratt ran to make his report even before Brannan dismounted. The captain barely acknowledged him but listened as he looked over how things lay.

"Have you tried rushing the gentiles, brother?" Dan heard the captain ask.

Bishop Sergeant Pratt replied, "Captain, I've got one dead and one likely to die as it is."

Brannan turned his horse and started off at a slow walk circling all the way around the fortress.

Dan was surprised that neither he, Rojo, nor Sebriana tried to shoot the captain as he rode so close to the ruin well within range.

Dan shook his head. "I could shoot him easily."

Rojo scowled. "Perhaps Brannon thinks himself beyond our range."

"He's well within it," Sebriana observed.

"Perhaps this one may just be over bold," said Rojo.

Dan had second thoughts about firing. If he killed Brannon, what would his men do to Roque?

Finishing his circuit, Brannan rode right up to the

front of the fortress and dismounted. "Mind if I come in. I'd like to talk to you."

"I do mind actually," Dan replied. "You can talk from where you are." Dan didn't want the Danite to get a clear idea of his defenses or numbers though he suspected Brannon could see both from where he was. Letting him stand was an act of defiance.

Up close, Dan could see that his face lacked the hardness that comes from making difficult decisions. He lacked the hunch shouldered shiftiness of those who knew they'd done wrong and might have to answer for it, and he did not show the haughty arrogance of those who laugh at God and dare Him to do His worst. He showed the world the bland features of an angel or an idiot. Dan guessed his blank expression came of surrendering his conscience to the Prophet so that he no longer worried about morals or ethics, right or wrong.

"Very well, gentile. You have information that the Prophet wants. Where is the Ark?"

Dan hoped he could bluff. "I don't know what you are talking about."

"Nonsense. We've been following Professor Pendarvis for years. We know what he was looking for."

There it was as good as a confession, Dan thought, and his heat rose. He'd killed Topper. Dan raised his rifle, but wrestled himself back under control. Under his breath, Dan vowed that the day would come when he would kill Brannan. "Topper was too good a man to be squandered by a fanatic," he said aloud. Louder, so that Brannon could hear him, Dan said. "All fairytales and legends. What makes you think I'd waste time chasing a chimera?"

Brannon responded, "The Prophet Joseph Smith translated the Golden Plates from Reformed Egyptian. Therein we learned that Lehi, the Israelite of old, and his family escaped the ancient holocaust that was the Babylonian destruction of Jerusalem and the Temple. They had two crystals with spindles inside that guided their way. Not all are given the Strong Meat. The knowledge that the Ark also escaped and was taken east by the children of Dan to this land, this Deseret, the new Zion of the Latter Day Saints, is not given to all. Lehi's people found the land occupied by evil Jaredites who had fled the Tower of Babel, their way guided by sixteen glowing stones. Some of the Nephites fell into evil ways and became known as Lamanites. The fought their brother Nephites for a thousand years and built up huge mounds of bodies."

Dan thought the fanatic was in love with his fairytales.

The captain continued. "But I suspect you already know much of this. Beware. There are others seeking the Ark as well, Secessionists and Papists. It would be a terrible thing if either got to it first. Your party is not strong enough to resist them. They'll kill you. You don't need to die. The Ark is ours by right and God's will. You travel with Jaredites, those who slew God's chosen. Their crime was no less because they acted as God's instrument."

"That's funny," said Dan. "I mistook my companions for Lamanites and thus Children of Israel. Isn't that the story you tell the Indians? And the Ark and ourselves would be better off in your hands? But I won't have to decide. I don't have the information you want."

"That's a shame. It will go badly for your friend if he doesn't have the information you are concealing." He mounted and rode back to where his men held Roque.

"Bind the gentile's arms to his sides, Pratt, then hoist him by his feet up into that juniper."

Soon Roque was suspended upside down his head

about three feet from the ground. They built a tiny fire on the ground below him between the roots of the tree. The Chiricahua Apaches had perfected this technique which slowly boiled a man's brains. They could keep a man alive in agony for three or even four days at a time while his head slowly cooked. Brannon seemed to have learned the finer points of the method.

Dan could hear Roque taunting them. "Pinche cabrón, you make the fire too small, and you don't let me have a blanket. I am growing cold. Build up the fire."

"Bravo! Mucho Hombre!" called Sebriana.

Roque's bravado was exceptional, Dan thought, but it wasn't long before they heard Roque groan a little in the dark.

Dan sniffed the air. There was piñon smoke, but no touch of burning human flesh as yet. Maybe Roque would be all right.

Rojo suggested a plan. "Shoot and kill the sentries. Then follow Nando, Natcho, and me out through the hole in the wall. I have set a rope you can use to drop down. Go south and around the camp. Rescue Roque, if you can. We will ride through camp driving their horses, trying to sound like a war party."

Dan could think of nothing better. Sebriana agreed. Roque's rope, after all the miles Dan had carried it, would finally be useful.

"It will be time," said Rojo, "to make your move when the Great Scorpion stands just there." He pointed to a spot above a hill on the southwest horizon referring to the constellation Scorpio which, Dan thought, looks as much like a scorpion to his people as it does to ours.

They let hours pass watching the Danites, little more than one hundred yards away, build a fire and cook their dinner. They sat around laughing and joking, looking into the fire, all except one. Brannan kept his back to the fire and watched the night. He posted two sentinels, one to feed Roque's fire, the other to watch the picketed horses. One by one, the others found their bedrolls. The three companions and their Hopi guides continued to wait. The sentinels finished their watch and were replaced by others. The new guards nearing the end of their watch dozed. Scorpio paraded silently across the southern horizon until he stood centered where Rojo had chosen above a distinctive hill. The moon was just rising.

Sebriana and Dan carefully sighted their rifles on targets near the limits of their range with only moonlight and firelight to guide their aim. It was unlikely we'll hit anything, Dan thought, but we'll certainly stir them up.

Sebriana must have been thinking the same thing. "Pobrecito, you think you cannot hit this target, but I have seen you. In a fight calm comes over you. You shoot swiftly and accurately."

As Kit had taught, the rifle became another limb. In a fight, Dan reflected, I have no conscious memory of aiming or squeezing the trigger. It's all one thing. It's as if I 'thought' the bullet to the target.

"Sebriana, corazon, you are always deadly."

She clicked her tongue three times in signal, and they fired as one. Both sentinels crumpled to the ground. Dan wasn't sure either of them had struck their mark. The sentries might have been seeking cover.

"Quick now!" Dan hissed, but she was already out the backdoor. Sliding to the ground, they made their way south along the arroyo away from the Little Colorado, circling wide around the Danite camp.

As they ran, Dan caught glimpses of the turmoil in the camp. Danites were awake tangled in blankets, half-dressed and stumbling over each other, firing at the empty fortress. Indian war cries shattered the night as Rojo, Nacho and Nando drove the horse herd through the camp. There had not been such a night since Gideon attacked the Midianites with trumpets and torches. The Danites whirled about shooting wildly at fleeing Indians, at the fortress, at each other. Two attacked each other with knives and fell headlong into the fire. Because they didn't rise again, Dan assumed both were successful in slaying their opponent. There were cries of "Indians," "Navajos," and even "Apaches!"

As the Indios cimarrones tore through the camp driving the Danites' stock, a horse reared, a rider on its back. Dan was certain the rider must have been thrown. Another horse went down to gunfire.

In the midst of it all stood Brannan trying to restore order, knocking men about, pushing them into line firing outward. Rojo deliberately let a few of the horses run loose two hundred yards from camp. It was a ruse. The Danites desperately needed horses. If they recaptured a few they might be able to pursue the Indios and recapture the herd.

Brannan saw the stock. "You two guard this one and keep the others from coming out of the ruin. The rest of you, go after the horses!" Brannan disappeared into the dark.

They ran, and the stock ran from them. Even some of the wounded tried to help. It was as Rojo had hoped. Deafened by their own firing, they did not hear Dan and Sebriana approach. Distracted by the rodeo, they did not see the pair coming. Sebriana and Dan fell upon those left by the fire with tomahawk and rifle butt.

Dan hit his man with the flat side of his 'hawk so hard he lost his grip, but the blow only annoyed the big Mormon. Dan pulled his Bowie as the Mormon drew his own knife. They danced silently in the night. Neither Sebriana nor Dan wished to alert the others by firing a pistol, for the Mormons were now running northeast a quarter mile away from the camp chasing their stock. Dan's attention was on his opponent, but he could see that Sebriana had no more initial success than he. Needing to finish fast, so that he could help her, Dan closed in on the Mormon, accepting a bad gash in his arm in exchange for tactical advantage. The big man clasped Dan in a bear hug and pinned Dan's arms at his sides. He sought to crush Dan. Dan couldn't move his blade, nor could he breathe. His vision closed down to a tunnel surrounded in darkness. With final forlorn hope, Dan smashed the Mormon's nose with his forehead, and as the Mormon's grip loosened, Dan slid his knife upward from the groin to the Mormon's breastbone and gutted the big man.

As the big man fell away, grasping at his innards, Dan turned to see Sebriana prone under her man. Clenching a knife, the Danite raised his arm and prepared to thrust it into her neck. Too far away to reach with hand or knife, Dan dropped his Bowie and grabbed for a pistol, knowing he'd be too late. Doña Loca arched up and kissed the Danite on the lips. Startled, he backed off her and paused, giving her time to insert her misericorde, her mercy-giving dagger, into his ear. He fell forward, covering her completely.

Dan glanced around. Two men lay dead in the fire. It hadn't been Dan's imagination. Roused from sleep by gunfire and Indian war cries, the Danites found their mind seized by confusion. They defended themselves from the first enemy that came to hand, often another Danite. The guard lay dead near the tree where Roque hung suspended. A bullet-pierced hand over his mouth testified that Dan had caught him yawning. Sebriana and Dan had only fired two shots; however, three men they hadn't fired on and hadn't fought lay injured though still moving. Gideon would have been proud of how successfully his plan had worked. The Mormons had acted just like the Midianites and started killing each other. None seemed to pose a threat. Nevertheless, Dan paused to kick weapons out of reach of two of them.

Gathering his weapons, Dan ran to Roque and kicked aside the tiny fire at the base of the tree. Dan cut Roque's feet free and lowered him to the ground then cut his bindings. Roque didn't move. Dan shook him.

"Leave me alone," growled Roque. "It's the middle of the night. I was sleeping."

"Roque, are you all right? Do you know where you are?"

"Oh," he responded, "they didn't singe my hair did they? Does it look okay?" He got unsteadily to his feet and stumbled around camp, amazingly locating his pack and weapons. "Okay, I'm ready."

"Hhumph. Cabrón! Get me out of here!" Unable to roll the dead man off, Sebriana was still trapped under him. Dan kicked him aside, and she rose, her face a mask of blood.

"Are you all right?" Dan gasped.

"Of course. This is all his," she replied.

They took off in a run back down the arroyo to the north, heading toward the Little Colorado and their rendezvous with Rojo and the horses.

Something nagged at the back of Dan's mind. Where was Brannon? Had he gone off chasing horses?

Dan looked at Roque who was limping painfully. "Roque, I'll carry you if you like. Your feet must hurt badly."

Roque grunted and kept running. The pain must have

been excruciating. He'd been bound for hours and the blood flow restricted.

They'd covered no more than a mile when Rojo met them. Mounted now they galloped through the night across the river and on toward Hopi and the dawn. At daybreak, they paused for breakfast, searching Danite packs and their own pockets for things to eat. Dan looked about and saw that his friends and allies were all there. Suddenly, he felt faint.

Sebriana seized his arm and began binding it. "You've lost a lot of blood."

Dan turned to look into her pretty face and was stupefied by a grisly horror mask, her face caked in dried blood "Don't worry," she said. "It isn't mine."

Nando and Nacho were happy. They were returning home with a fine small herd of horses and a war story for their friends. Roque sat rubbing his feet but grinning. Rojo was happiest of all.

Dan grinned at his friend. "That was quite a plan you came up with. Impossible odds, no chance of success, certain death for all, but it worked."

Rojo grinned, a terrifying sight on an Apache face. "My people have a saying about that. If it's stupid but it works, it isn't stupid. When their supply train comes up, the Danites will have horses again."

The Hopi conferred with Rojo at length. "They say they have never seen such excellent shooting. Both Big Shoulders and Hunter Woman killed their targets."

Nando stepped up to Dan, smiled, and said in halting English, "Thank you for inviting us to your party."

Rojo turned his head away to conceal a grin. "You know, Indians are just taciturn."

The ride to Oraibi was uneventful.

He Who Wanders stood atop a roof at the edge of the

village, facing southwest as if expecting the travelers. From a distance, Dan was sure he saw a second figure beside him.

The old man gestured to the four companions to let Nando and Nacho attend to the horse herd. "You must hurry as you are pursued by an enemy greater and more dangerous than you suspect. Climb up and join me in my dwelling. Time is short, and I have much to tell you."

Once they were seated and food placed before them, He Who Wanders began to speak. "This is my friend, Hosteen Béézh, a hataahli of the Navajo, a singer of powerful songs and a man of knowledge who cures the unwell."

Hosteen Béézh's long hair showed a mix of gray and black and was clasped in a pony-tail behind bound by a scarlet headband above an unwrinkled visage. He wore moccasins that came to his knees adorned with conchos under loose-legged cloth trousers supported by a belt of huge silver conchos from which hung a cloth breechclout broad as an apron. His shoulders were covered by a poncho of cloth in a flowered pattern and a folded blanket in broad stripes of white and gray that hung to his shins and closed in the front like a coat.

"What have you learned on your travels, my friends?" He Who Wanders asked.

Looking around and getting the nod from his friends, Dan responded for the group. "We found what we think must have been their temple, but it was empty and clear sign that they left carrying their possessions. We did not see any indication of where they might have gone."

"The years grew long for them," said the ancient shaman. "No one came for them. The world above their new home changed. Blue Corn Maiden came teaching the People to grow corn, beans, and squash and to keep turkeys. The people in the cañon intermarried with their neighbors. One day, they decided to follow the trail back the way they had come, but the time had been long and they had forgotten much."

Dan thought about how this special people had become something else and forgotten their way back to the Promised Land. Their weapons of bronze corroded away to nothing over the centuries. How would they replace them? Many tasks require specialists, but for specialists to have a place a society must be large enough to support them. They would have grown the old crops until the new ones came and then abandoned them for ones more suited to the environment. Buckskin would have replaced cloth. Not having a place in the new world, many customs would have fallen away. They might have lost most of their language through intermarriage. They might have been so rigid in their rules that they could not replace the Books of the Law when the old ones grew worn. With a change in language and no paper, they might have lost writing. After 2,000 years of change, how would Dan or anyone recognize the villages of these long forgotten Children of Israel?

Dan suppressed a laugh, and Sebriana looked at him. He shrugged. Would they find circumcised skeletons? Perhaps not. Would they have rebelled in anger at having been abandoned for so long and melded into the local population? Dan's head whirled with possibilities and ached at the thought that what emerged from the abyss might have become unrecognizable. Was there a tribe of circumcised Indians? Perhaps the rite was kept in some kiva. It's not like Dan could ask someone to show him.

His head swimming, Dan became aware that He Who Wanders was still speaking. "We were here and knew them. Our Eagle, Sparrow Hawk, Tobacco, Cottontail,

Rabbit Brush, and Bamboo clans intermarried with the Danae whose clans were Katsina, who were Masaw's servants, and Parrot. Masaw, the God of Heaven, told them where to plant their footsteps. They journeyed east through our lands, east of the Chuska Mountains to Yupkoyvi where Dineh, the Navajo, dwelt on the distant mountainsides. There was usually peace between the two peoples. Yupkoyvi was a gathering place for the Katsina and Parrot clans who spoke a language different from our own. The Danae made large villages where the streams emerge from the mountains, and there they farmed. They had special wisdom from Masaw. Their Katsina priests knew when drought would come to the land. They gathered in food stuffs in good years to eat in the drought years and stored it in their great houses. The greatest of these were at Yupkoyvi where they built a great round temple for their ceremonies. Hosteen Béézh will tell you about them."

The Hosteen, an honored elder, began his tale, speaking in Spanish and Navajo.

"Some call him the Gambler, but that is not correct. He was *Haahwihlbeehi*, the Winner of People. He came from the far west, from the depths of the Great Chasm. Pueblo Bonito was already a great center of trade when the he came there where all peoples bartered for decorated pottery, the blue stone called turquoise, food, clothing, herbs, parrots, and ceremonial items. It was also a place of vice or prostitution, incest, gambling, and sexual deviancy. The Gambler was of a clan that had stayed behind in the west.

"The Gambler played his games with the people, and he always won. First, he would win their turquoise and fine clothing and anything they had of value. Then, he would gamble for their food, and he always won. He would gamble for their labor and force the people to build many great houses where he stored the food he had won. Finally, he gambled for the people themselves, and he won them all.

"He forced them to work harder and harder. He was unmerciful. His houses grew great and full of food, and even though he owned all the people and made them work hard, vice continued among them as before.

"A great drought fell on the land, and the Gambler fed the people with the food he had won from them. And vice continued. Food stores diminished and the people began to worry.

"A young man arrived from the south with a band of followers. He saw what the Gambler had done and challenged him to games of skill and chance. Young Warrior won everything back, what little was left, and then he won the Gambler. With his warriors, the young one cast out the Gambler, sending him back to the Great Chasm from which he had emerged. The newcomers, warriors from the east with powerful weapons, then settled down in the houses of the Gambler and built new ones as well. For a time, they flourished and had great wealth, but they continued in wickedness, learning vice from the people of *Yupkoyvi*. The people of *Yupkoyvi* were greatly weakened by famine and drought, but they continued their wickedness. Starvation drove the clans to scatter until the people of *Yupkoyvi* were no more."

Dan and his companions all sat open mouthed for a

while. There was something familiar in this story. Joseph had done something like this for Pharaoh. Was Gambler an echo of Joseph or was he simply a man who remembered Joseph's story and knew how to prepare for drought? The Ark and the Children of Israel might await them at *Yupkoyvi*.

Sebriana spoke softly. "There is a story like this in the Bible. When Joseph was in Egypt, he was asked to interpret the Pharaoh's dream of seven fat cows consumed by seven skinny cows. Joseph told him there would be seven years of plenty followed by seven years of famine, but Egypt could be saved if they stored food from the years of plenty and ate it in the lean years. Joseph was put in charge of collection and storage.

"It happened as Joseph foretold, but he didn't give the grain away. He sold it to the people. At the end of the first year, Pharaoh, through Joseph, gathered all the money in the land. The next year, people sold him their livestock, and the year after their land. The year after that they sold their children to Joseph, and in the end they sold themselves and all of the Egyptians became slaves of Pharaoh.

"It sounds like *Yupkoyvi* had a system of food collection and storage for drought years. It makes sense. Rain is uncertain here."

"Child," He Who Wanders responded, "the stories of our people say it is so. The people of *Yupkoyvi* understood the cycles of drought and plenty. They stored food for drought years and had many great houses across the land, but *Yupkoyvi* was the center. That is where the greatest cache was and where they went for their most important ceremonies."

"Grandfather," she replied, "our story also says that in time the Egyptians became angry and turned on Joseph and his family who held the best farmland in Egypt and made them slaves."

"You have learned all I have to give," said He Who Wanders. "Now you must make haste to be on your journey again."

"Those who follow you," said *Hosteen Béézh*, "do not know what happened after the people emerged from the Great Chasm and lived at *Yupkoyvi*. If they do not see you go or find your trail, it will be long before they find you again. You must hurry. Leave tomorrow night. I will go with you and show you the way."

"Where is *Yupkoyvi*?" Roque asked. "It sounds mythical."

Rojo responded. "Chaco."

Chapter 9

The Gambler's House

The four companions made their arrangements quietly. Setting out one at a time the next day, they made their way along Oraibi Wash gathering at a spot two miles north of the pueblo. Nando and Nacho brought their stock along with supplies they would need and their stored possessions. They packed and made ready for a departure after nightfall. The moon, now past full, rose late in the night. Its light was welcome once they were away from the village.

Nacho and Nando accompanied them for many miles, driving their entire herd of stolen horses. Nando told Rojo not to worry about them. When the Danites showed up, it was certain in all minds that they, the people of Oraibi, would tell them that the horses had been purchased from passing Navajo. Meanwhile, the two Hopi young men would drive the horses down all of the trails covering any tracks. During the night they made a wide circle to the east, south, west and then back to Oraibi.

As they rode through the night, Sebriana urged Deborah, her mule, up beside Dan's Appaloosa. "Have you been there? Tell me about Chaco."

"Chaco," Dan replied, "is Chaco Canyon. Rojo, Roque, and I were there six years ago. It is an amazing place. There are great houses five stories high built of stone beautifully laid. They may have been taller once. We estimated that some of them had more than six hundred houses within them plus many underground *kivas* and even some *kivas* surrounded by houses, which were towers many stories high. As far as the eye can see, there are more of these huge buildings with no more than a half mile between them."

Hosteen Béézh turned in his saddle. "There is more you have yet to learn. There are more great houses, many more. They are spread from the San Juan River in the north to the Zuñi Mountains in the south, from the Chuska Mountains in the west to the Turquoise Mountain in the east."

Dan was puzzled and asked Hosteen Béézh, "How can you be sure these are all the same people?"

Hosteen Béézh cocked his head thinking for a moment. "From the shape of the houses and the shapes of and designs on their pottery you can still tell today. But I know because my people have been here, and the story has been passed from generation to generation."

Dan was struck by the first part of his response. He had a moment of epiphany, a revelation. These shamans who had helped them so much were scholars in their own right. They were a lot like Topper. He would have liked them and learned from them, and they would have liked him. They studied nature, questioned the why of things, and even recorded the histories of their people in the songs and stories they memorized. The superstitious dancing shaman shaking rattles while he sings to chase away evil spirits was an incomplete picture. Singing was done to reassure patients and provide a physical presence to cures whose most powerful elements were not always obvious to patients and their families.

Hosteen Béézh, explained it to Dan one evening. "Just knowing family and friends have gathered to help them and care for them puts sick people's minds at ease. The songs soothe and comfort them so the herbs can do their work."

Coming back to the present, Dan took up his narrative, continuing to tell Sebriana about the wonders of Chaco. "The walls are fitted together in perfection with stones of the same size and shape. The builders included decorative bands of stone in smaller sizes and different hues. The structures are beautiful and harmonize with the surrounding terrain."

Hosteen Béézh overheard Dan's narrative and added. "When they were new the walls were covered with adobe fine and smooth."

Sebriana was puzzled. "Why would they hide the beauty?"

"To keep out the drafts," the shaman smiled.

Proud and stubborn Sebriana persisted. "Then why take the time to decorate if you're just going to hide it?"

"They knew it was there, and that satisfied them." Hosteen Béézh cocked his head quizzically, wondering if Dan understood.

Back in Greenport, Long Island, Dan's long ago home, a sailor once showed him two Japanese flutes. They looked much the same, brilliantly finished in black lacquer with a finish so clear it was like looking into a deep, reflective pool of water.

"Very different prices I paid for these." The sailor blew a few notes on each which sounded much the same to Dan. "This one has four or five coats of polished lacquer, gets shinier with each one applied, but this one has forty coats. What's more, the tenth coat is gold leaf. Furthermore, the bamboo was boiled in water until it was soft then turned inside out. Only one in ten doesn't crack or rip in the process. This is best quality."

Being young, Dan asked, "But why turn it inside out if it doesn't improve the tone? And why have a layer of gold thirty layers down where you can't see it?"

The sailor winked. "The man who made it and the man who bought it know the gold is there. It is enough."

This was a strange lesson. Anything well done should have beauty and perfection all the way through. Dan recalled what a rabbi once told him of the techniques used in the production of the woven blue cord that hung from his shawl. To him how things were achieved was as important as the final product.

Looking at Sebriana's quizzical expression, Dan awoke from his reverie and realized he had not finished his tale. "Chaco is a place of mystery. Many houses packed together crowd a stream that is a mere trickle. It could not produce enough water for them all. Far from the mountains, it is unlikely the cañon had ever been home to much game or with so little water ever to have grown many crops. Firewood is scarce. Logs for *vigas* and *latillas* must have been brought from Turquoise Mountain forty miles away."

Rojo spoke up. "Of all the rooms we looked into, only a few showed signs of ever having had cook-fires within them."

Ever practical Sebriana said, "They might have cooked outdoors."

Rojo added, "Nor was there sign of heating fires. The *vigas* and *latillas* are still in place but are not blackened or greasy. They look clean as in a house that has just been built."

Days passed as they rode east through Navajo country. They encountered Navajo often but never had trouble. Their guide was a respected and well-known elder. Herds of sheep, goats, and cows tended by young boys and dogs were no surprise. They knew that Navajo stole sheep in tens of thousands.

Anywhere there was moisture, there were farms of young wheat, corn, pumpkins, squash, and beans, though this early in the season only sprouts showed. In water rich cañons there were orchards of peach trees. The wealth of this people surprised Dan. Selecting sites of great natural beauty could not have been an accident. There they built six-sided homes of log or stone topped by an earthen roof with doors facing east in clusters of three and four.

"The first *hogan* belongs to an elder woman," *Hosteen Béézh* told Dan. "Her married daughters bring their husbands to live near her, but they are never supposed to look at her or see her. That is our custom."

Around the homes stood neat corrals for horses and sheep, and fine *ramadas,* brush-covered sunshades, where they saw people working in the shadow as they passed, and looms strung from juniper trees so that a woman might work at her weaving in shaded comfort.

Roque was impressed. "These places are as good as any of ours. I thought they were simple nomads. Living so well, why must they raid us for sheep?"

Hosteen Béézh looked sadly at Roque. "The young men must bring many sheep and horses to get a good wife, to show they can support her and make her rich. They will not steal from their cousins, so they must go to the Mexicans to get sheep. Besides, the Mexicans raid us and steal our young for slaves. This warfare and raiding is not one-sided."

"That's not true!" Roque exploded. "Slavery was outlawed among my people long ago."

"That's true," the shaman responded. "You outlawed

it, and now you call it something else, but Navajo children are still taken against their will to be servants in your homes without pay."

"They are compensated," Roque insisted. "They get to learn our language and the ways of civilization. Most important they get to learn about the *santa fe*, the Holy Catholic Faith."

"Ah yes," said *Hosteen Béézh*, "I know a little of Mexican customs and religion. Jesus made you a free gift of his sacrifice, and you pass it along at such a low price, only ten or twenty years of service are required."

Roque spurred and turned his horse, riding back a little ways.

So he does not have to be near the shaman, Dan thought. Roque, he was sure, had his doubts about the black robes who sold sacraments at prices most could not afford, but he was proud of his heritage. He was a man, and a man should be proud of himself and his people. With wisdom, one could see the faults as well without losing heart, hope, or one's faith.

They rode across the wooded upland of Black Mesa studded with juniper and piñon, dodging in and out of canyons too numerous to name and descending into a broad valley bordered on the far side by the Chuska Range. Navajo farms dotted the water courses they passed. Crossing the valley, they entered a narrow cañon. At the entrance, the walls could not have been over twenty feet high, but as they advanced, the mesa rose above them until the cañon was hundreds of feet deep.

Roque urged his horse close to Dan's. "Danito, come away a little bit. I have something to say to you that I don't want *mi prima* to overhear."

They moved away from the others. "This must be Cañon de Chelly, the Navajo stronghold. See the fortifications they have made in the cliffs."

Dan had noticed them. Pueblos sheltered in the cliffs, some of them hundreds of feet above the cañon floor.

Roque continued. "The old man must be leading us into a trap. They would never let us see this and live. They can fall on us from behind, in front, and from high above. We would stand no chance."

"There is no trap," said *Hosteen Béézh*.

Roque griped. "The ancient one has ears like a bat!"

They passed farms, *hogans*, flocks, and peach orchards. Many people came out to look them over and on seeing the shaman had called greeting and gone about their business unconcerned.

The shaman pointed to the dwellings in the high cliffs. "Hopi clans once dwelt there. They can still tell you who lived in each house."

They followed the right hand branch of the cañon. It was a Navajo paradise. A stream flowed along the bottoms providing water for man, animal, and crops. The grass was good. Cliffs, smooth, unbroken, and streaked in russet, brown, yellow, tan, and rust rose a thousand feet around them.

The canyon walls had been chipped and rubbed into pictures. Rojo pointed all around. "They know a hundred easy trails to the top of the cliffs. For them, the mesa top is easily reached. Look at the pictures left by the ancient Hopi clans. They show mountain sheep and deer."

They went deeper and passed a tall spire as high as the cañon rim. It seemed no bigger around than a house, but it rose and rose, vertical and never getting smaller. It was an impossible monument.

Awed, Rojo whispered, "Spider Rock. Many stories include references to it."

Hosteen Béézh nodded. "It is the home of Spider

Women who taught our Navajo women to weave so well."

They passed to the left of the tower and continued up the cañon with the ground now slowing rising beneath them. On the second day, they emerged onto the mesa at the foot of the Chuskas and climbed into tall pine country which they traversed through a succession of valleys only slightly wider than the canyons behind them. They were able to take game from time to time though it was not plentiful. Turkey and deer were welcome additions to their diet.

Late one afternoon after they had begun the descent of the east side of the Chuska Mountains, *Hosteen Béézh* called a halt. "We will rest here for several days and let the mules and horses feed on the good grass and drink their fill of fine mountain water. They must grow fat for the journey ahead. We have a hard land to cross and must reach the springs on the far side in one day."

Speed and endurance in riding stock depends on the animals' condition. Stock must be exercised, fed, and rested. To give them rest, the four friends tried to ride theirs every other day leading a *remuda* of spare mounts. Stock being ridden can't feed until evening. Even the remounts could only graze a little in the day when they were on the trail. They'd feed at night on grass, but grass wasn't very nourishing unless it was in seed. When they could, they fed the stock grain, corn, and even beans, though the last have unfortunate side effects. Grain and corn kept the stock strong. Grazing at night on grass didn't, but it did keep them alive.

The halt gave Dan time to study over Topper's notes. *Hosteen Béézh*, Roque, and Rojo went hunting. Sebriana stayed to assist Dan in his scholarly pursuits, but first she insisted they search for plants to savor their food. She and

Dan picked and set sage to dry and then searched along the stream for wild onions and garlic, cattail roots, and watercress. They found all of it in good quantity.

Coming to a deep pool where water flowed in from a hot spring, Sebriana began disrobing. "It is the birthright of woman that she is allowed to bathe whenever occasion permits."

"Go right ahead," Dan said watching her clothes fall away. The early spring day was unseasonably warm. "I'll take these vegetables back to camp and get started on my studies."

"You have begun to stink. If you were any kind of gentleman, you would wash yourself. What's more, you'd help a lady wash her back."

There was no use arguing with Sebriana. Scholarship would have to wait. Dan crumbled. "One can sympathize with medieval monks who wanted peace to study and wouldn't take women into their monasteries."

After two days of more or less uninterrupted study, Dan tossed the leg bone of the turkey they'd just eaten for dinner over his shoulder and looked across the fire at his friends. "I've reviewed my Hebrew letters and the few words I know. We've seen no engraved messages coming this way from the cañon."

Roque looked thoughtful. "They may have lost language, or they may have come a different way."

"True," Dan replied. "What really puzzles me is that we have seen no sign of the Knights Templar. Topper's notes indicate they made more than one trip. They came this way much more recently."

Rojo cocked his head in thought. "Maybe we have heard stories about them. The warrior who challenged the Gambler isn't given a name. He is very mysterious. If he freed the people, why was Chaco abandoned?"

Hosteen Béézh said, "I will show you the place they say was the Gambler's house and that of the warrior who challenged him."

Sebriana spoke next. "The Templars thought they were being pursued, and they were secretive anyway. Think of what they've passed on to you Freemasons. They didn't leave marks for others to follow, and they may have gone out of their way not to be seen, not to make contact with anyone.

"They were carrying a fortune and a treasure to be hidden with the greatest treasure of all. The most powerful force in the world of their day sought them. They didn't carve anything on the rock. They were the finest military force in their world. They sent scouts ahead and followed the trail to the cañon. When they realized the chasm had been abandoned, they followed the trail to the Hebrews' new home, obliterating all signs as they went. Having found the Hebrews, they returned for the other knights of their order and led them to the Ark."

She sat back looking very pleased with herself. Her friends were stunned but could not fault her reasoning.

As they rode down from the Chuska Mountains the next day following a creek that disappeared in the dry plain ahead, *Hosteen Béézh* called a halt and then led them up a low ridge to the north. He waved his arm above the plain below. Nestled into the side of the mountain, a large pueblo lay in ruins and blanketed in windblown dust. Three stories high along its curving back wall, low along its straight front, the pueblo looked like a large letter D.

The old man looked at Dan. "This was the edge of their world. There are many like this near the Chuskas, south almost to the Zuñi Mountains and north to the San Juan River, all like this, uninhabited."

They resumed their ride, leaving behind the cool, pine-scented mountains and descending to the hot alkali plain thick with fine white dust and scarce of vegetation. Dust devils spun about the plain stinging them with hard-blown sand that blinded eyes and pricked noses.

The old shaman grimaced. "The Hard Flint Boys are at play." He pointed to the north with his lip. "The Navajo call it *Tsé Bit'a'i*, Rock with Wings."

Far to their north, they saw a black pinnacle against the sky. They tied kerchiefs over their faces. They helped but little. The dust stung their eyes and nostrils and clogged their throats. The mules complained becoming noisy, lethargic, and difficult to handle. Dan and his companions pushed them hard to make better speed and stopped occasionally to give them water from canteens, which the stock lapped from Sebriana's cooking pot. They rode on into the dusk and twilight and then into the full dark of a moonless night.

When the shaman finally called a halt, Dan sensed there were trees around them again, juniper and piñon, and heard the gurgle of a cañon spring. They cared for their stock first before eating or resting. The mules and Roque's *grullo* stallion needed to be unpacked and unsaddled, rubbed down with dry grass, watered, and hobbled. Only then did the companions make a fire and eat.

They rose late and rode east through a maze of cañons.

Roque looked nervously around. "We are forced to ride the bottom of the cañon. This would be a good place for an ambush and a bad place to be ambushed. I am lost as well. I do not know where we are or what direction we are going."

"I know, Roque," Dan replied. "I'm waiting to be

confronted by the Minotaur."

Roque raised an eyebrow and looked at Dan strangely.

Days later, they emerged into what seemed an endless flat plain. The sun beat down on them. These low lands were the hottest place Dan had been since coming to New Mexico. His friends commented on it as well. Only Sebriana seemed not to mind the heat. The party followed a water course first east, then south and north, and finally east again until they entered a cañon where cliffs one hundred feet high rose on either side of them. A trickle of water ran in a deeply cut arroyo.

Roque rode to Sebriana's side. "When we get there, *prima*, you will see that Chaco is very much like this place, tall cliffs and a tiny stream. But Chaco is crowded with many great houses. You will see. Do you see the layering in the stone of that rock wall? The stone of the great houses is laid just that carefully."

As they passed Roque's wall, Sebriana looked into its interior rooms. "Do Chaco's great houses look like this, too?" She smiled sweetly while Roque blushed. They had arrived.

They rode on to the fourth great house, by Dan's count, but he admitted he may have missed some. It was a five story colossus in the external shape of a letter D with its curved back almost against the cliff. A rock like a huge chimney one hundred feet high hung above part of the city, threatening to obliterate the building below. It had separated from the cliff and leaned out from it.

Looking up, Dan said, "I don't see anything that keeps that rock from falling."

"I will call this Pueblo Bonito, the handsome village," pronounced Roque. "Sebriana may name the rest."

"I think we should camp here," Dan said. "This seems to be the biggest pueblo and the center of things."

The Navajo shaman nodded his assent. "Tomorrow I will introduce you to the Navajo families that live here and I will show you the Gambler's house."

"What do we do now?" asked Rojo.

"We explore," Dan replied. "I think I should sketch all of the pueblos here and draw a map of their relationship to one another. We should look for trails and study the picture writing on the rocks. We should look from the cañon rim as well as from down here."

"Remember the pottery," said Sebriana. "Gather a pot and some broken pieces from each house and remember where you got them."

Roque scratched his head. "As I recall, there were lots of complete pots here. Why gather broken pieces?"

"Because you can carry more," she said. "We can compare the designs like hosteen told us."

Roque mocked her. "And what will we learn, *prima*?"

Dan interceded. "We don't know, Roque. We need to look at everything and find a pattern, even a pattern in what is not there."

The next day they rode around the canyon, noting buildings, rock art, odd depressions, and stairs in the cliffs. They met the Navajos who lived in and farmed the cañon and hired two boys to tend their stock. Navajos proved useful with information as the weeks went by. They were good observers and were aware of things it would have taken the companions years to discover.

"Now I will show you the House of the Gambler as I promised," Hosteen Béézh said.

They rode back past their campsite and past a pueblo that was being undermined by Chaco Wash to a building of right angles with sides four stories high that stood very close to the cliffs.

Sebriana looked it up and down. "Looks like a castle."

"Ha," responded Roque. "What about the one by the *arroyo*? That has many levels like the towers of a castle."

Sebriana snickered. "The one by the *arroyo* looks like it was built by two different men who argued about what they wanted."

She was right, Dan realized. Part of the structure was in the D-shape. The rest was square like the one near the cliffs. There was also a round structure of concentric rings attached to one side.

"Sebriana," Dan said, "you've hit on something. There are two very different kinds of building here, the D-shaped and the square, well rectangular, but square comes close enough. They have obvious right angles where the D-shaped buildings look more organic, like they'd grown from the land."

Sebriana stuck her nose up proudly. "I will name this square building The Castle."

They left their mounts with the Navajo boys and climbed to the top of the cliff by way of a slot in the rock hidden behind The Castle.

Dan called attention to their path. "Human hands have worked on this slot at times leveling the grade until it is both a stairway and ramp."

They emerged on the cliff far above the cañon floor where they were able to observe many of the pueblos.

Dan pointed. "There don't seem to be many buildings on the far side of the arroyo. But look there at that huge round depression."

"It's strange," muttered Roque. "They face south from the north wall of the cañon. They have entrances east, west, and south, but the north wall, the high one, facing the cliff, is featureless with no entrance. If they built it for defense, it should be the reverse. The cliff side is protected and low walls and entrances there could easily be controlled."

Rojo noticed something. "The pueblos grew higher toward the back, the cliff side. The side away from the cliff is only one, or rarely two, stories high."

Clever Sebriana noticed something else. "The late afternoon sun casts long shadows throwing into relief structures that are not visible at other times of the day."

They realized that what she observed was so.

"Now I'm sure," said Sebriana as they climbed up a stone shelf. "We are following a road. See? There are steps beneath us. Look ahead and behind. See? The path has been cleared of stone which now serves as a curb. The road is very straight."

Hosteen Béézh spoke. "I have always thought so. It leads to Gambler's House. There it is." He pointed to a low, damaged pueblo to their right on the east.

"What about that?" Dan asked, indicating a tall, square structure that stood to their left and no more than one hundred yards from Gambler's House.

"That was the home of the young warrior who beat the Gambler. Look about you," Hosteen Béézh commanded. "See the mountains around us on the horizon. This was the limit of their world. The Gambler's houses can be found this far and no farther. He owned everything as far as you can see, everything except the Navajo."

The day was growing short as Sebriana gathered bits of broken pottery while Rojo walked about muttering. Roque and Dan poked about, hoping something would jump out at them. The western sky blazed in crimson glory when they descended canyon walls.

In camp that night after dinner, Sebriana spread out her pottery. "Look. This comes from the Gambler's house and this from the other. The designs are different, and one is more skillfully done than the other." She was right.

Dan expressed a thought. "The more skillful ones with the more complex design might come from a later period."

"So I have thought," said Hosteen Béézh.

"I noticed something today," said Rojo. "At Gambler's House and at Young Warrior's House there was a difference. There seemed to be enough stone lying about to repair the Young Warrior's House completely. This was not the case at Gambler's House where some of the walls looked like they were pushed down and the stone carried away. Some of the *vigas* were missing, too. There should have been some trace of them, but it looked like they had been removed."

Hosteen Béézh nodded. "At Hopi they often pull down an old house and reuse the stone and *vigas*. Why not? The stone must be found or shaped to fit into houses and new *vigas* must be carried from far away. The stone from an old house is already the right size and shape."

Rojo was excited. "So if a pueblo is missing stone and vigas, it must be older than one that is not. I will check this tomorrow. It seems to me that the square fortresses could have been repaired with the stone and vigas lying about, and the D-shaped pueblos were missing too much."

Roque was fascinated by roads and stairs. Sebriana wanted to visit all of the pueblos, poke about in them, and sketch them. Hosteen Béézh promised to find them both Navajo guides to assist. Dan would climb to the top of the south mesa and draw a map.

The day dawned hot with a sky blue from horizon to horizon and it grew hotter. Dan hiked across the valley and waded the shallow stream scarcely getting his feet wet, intending to search the south mesa for some trail or crevice that would take him to the top. Near the base of the cliffs, Dan stumbled into the great round depression they had seen the day before. It had an angular structure at the north end, like a rectangle but narrowing at the end closest to the circle, a giant keyhole. Later Dan located another squarish structure on the south end.

The roof had collapsed inward, but there were gaps reaching all the way to the floor twenty feet below. In the structure on the north, Dan found a broad stairway leading south into the subterranean room and a hidden passageway covered by a flagstone. Too much of the subterranean building had collapsed by the stairs for Dan to gain easy access that way, but the hidden passage allowed him to squirm almost to the center, emerging vertically through the floor. Dust stood thick everywhere except in the recess at the end furthest from where Dan had entered. An alcove extended beyond the circular room, and in it stood a raised dais large enough to support the Ark they sought while leaving room on the sides for men to approach and lift the thing by its handles. It might be coincidence, but this area was exquisitely plastered and painted with geometric signs in turquoise and blue and the whole was intact and free of dust, pristine, as if preserved by some higher power.

Clearance from the sagging roof never exceeded four feet and was usually much less. Light filtered in from gaps and by its dim glow Dan made out three evenly-spaced, low circular structures and the spot where a fourth might have been but was now concealed by debris. Chunks of rotted log stood almost upright in two of them. Columns to support the roof, Dan thought.

The function of a rectangular stone box standing twenty inches high between the columns eluded him. Wooden boards gray with age covered the top. Dan struck out with his Bowie at a scorpion rapidly advancing toward him, severing it. His effort was rewarded with a kettle drum boom that in the enclosed space nearly deafened him as it raised gritty dust to his nose and eyes. He struck the foot drum, for that was how he thought of it, again and again amazed at the clear, musical quality of the note before the first board, aged and brittle, shattered and fell.

Then the ceiling began to settle. His heart pounding, Dan scurried down his hole, hoping that down was not the wrong way out. Ancient *vigas* cracked and dropped in bursts of choking dust. The once coffered ceiling came apart log by log. Down under the stone floor, Dan squirmed as the walls of his sarcophagus shook.

He crawled as fast as he could, but the settling was pushing the sub floor walls of his secret passage out of alignment.

The crawlway grew tighter as he moved ahead. Soon between dust and constricting walls, he couldn't breathe. He felt the stone squeezing him to death, getting tighter. His heart pounded.

Odd thoughts arrive as death approaches. "What will my friends think has become of me? Will they guess? Have Sebriana's sharp ears heard my booming drum?"

His vision became a white tunnel edged with advancing black. Convinced his situation was hopeless, Dan calmed himself. His lungs stopped heaving, and his chest and arm muscles relaxed. He could move again. And breathe if he took shallow breaths and exhaled before trying to move. As soon as he pulled with his arms, muscles expanded again, and he was stuck. He tried pushing with his toes. He slid a little along the floor! Pushing, guiding with arms straight ahead and squirming, he made his way slowly back out to daylight.

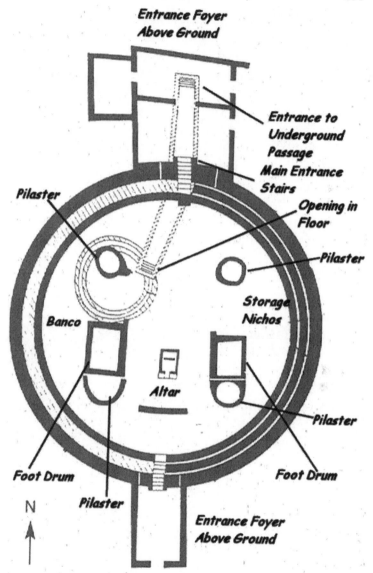

Entrance Foyer
Above Ground

Entrance to
Underground
Passage

Main Entrance
Stairs

Opening in
Floor

Pilaster

Pilaster

Storage
Nichos

Banco

Altar

Pilaster

Foot Drum

Foot Drum

N

Pilaster

Entrance Foyer
Above Ground

Great Underground Temple

The settling ceased as he climbed into the light; he quickly said a prayer of thanks. Dust stood thick over the depression that had nearly been Dan's grave. He coughed mud and snorted black snot while his eyes oozed slime. He collapsed onto the flagstone cover. Behind him in the subterranean passage, Dan thought he could hear his heart racing to catch up. When it finally arrived, he was sufficiently recovered to begin the process of recording his find in Topper's journal. He paced off the structure's circumference at three hundred and fifty feet. It was not yet noon.

He continued with his original investigation, locating first a convenient talus slope and then a cleft in the face of the cliff. Above, he found carved steps such as he and his friends had used in the great cañon of the Colorado River of the west. He crawled up them, clinging to the rock with fingertips and toes.

Dan spoke aloud to the steps trying to stem his terror. "I don't know if age has worn you steps shallow or if your makers simply thought the depth sufficient. The latter I suspect since you are shallow even where overhangs and caves protect you from the weather."

Emerging onto the mesa top, Dan saw before him half a mile distant the silhouette of a pueblo. Turning, he looked at the cañon and noticed that the Gambler's House atop the north mesa was in line with the pueblo behind him and the circular structure he'd just explored.

Dan spoke aloud to his muses. "That underground building I explored must have been some kind of Temple and these other pueblos are in line with it."

He thought about his conclusion. The interior had once been open with a *banco*, a seat, along the wall as far as he could see. It seemed an appropriate place for large meetings. The *kivas* of the Hopi and other Pueblos were meeting places for secret societies and religious groups. He had never seen any this large, but he had heard that there were such hidden in places where they could not be observed by black robed priests. Dan looked at his sketch and realized that by connecting the more distant entrance north or south to the furthest pillars a Star of David was formed.

Again he spoke aloud into the mesa winds. "It must be coincidence."

He sat and drew a sketch of the cañon, marking the spots where he knew there were pueblos. The map he had drawn confused him. "I'll have to get Sebriana to name the pueblos for me."

On his map, he assigned the D-shaped pueblos numbers and the square ones letters and placed David's Star over the Temple.

An hour before sunset, Rojo rode up and found Dan taking measurements. With the Jicarilla rode one of the cañon Navajo they had met. "What are you doing, some strange white man's rain dance?" He smiled.

Dan smiled, too. "I'm measuring angles with my compass and using a bit of geometry to calculate distance. I take a reading, turn a 90° angle, walk one hundred paces, turn, and take a reading on the original target. You know geometry, don't you?"

Dan thought that it might seem a strange thing to ask a *cimarron* Jicarilla Apache raised in a tepee, but Rojo had acquired education in many strange places. He was insatiable in his quest for knowledge.

Rojo dismounted to look at Dan's map. "When I traveled with Captain Aubrey to Missouri, he taught me reading, writing, mathematics, and geometry. I thought about all I had learned the night before during the day's march. I even did math problems in my head. Toward the end of our journey, the merchants in the caravan found it amusing to teach me double-entry bookkeeping.

Rojo stood. "The day grows short. Mount up behind me, and I will take you back to camp."

Dan considered the distances involved and the offer of a ride. Rojo had come up from the south side of mesa and had a ride of several miles ahead of him. He shook his head no. "Too hard on the mule. I'll race you though."

Dan gathered his things and took off at a run north to the staircase he had ascended while Rojo galloped south. Sliding down the stairs, Dan risked breaking a limb, but he landed safe if hard in the rock crevice, skipping through it to the talus slope. He worked his way down and sprinted across the cañon floor, leaping the tiny stream and scrambling up the banks of the *arroyo*. Still a quarter mile from their camp, he glanced behind to see Rojo and the Navajo approaching the *arroyo* further west. Dan put on a final burst of speed. They entered camp almost together.

Breathless Dan looked up at Rojo and mouthed the words: "I won."

Rojo smiled down at him. "Well done, *Mangani.* You almost beat us."

The sun set in another blaze of glory. The towering clouds on the western horizon spoke of powerful thunderstorms soon to come.

Caught out in the dark, Rojo's Navajo companion stayed with them for dinner and through the night. After eating, they went over what they had learned. Dan told them about the Temple and about the alignment of the two pueblos with the Temple, and then he showed them his map.

Rojo looked at it. "There is another D-shaped pueblo above the cliff near the mouth of the cañon and the one south of you on the mesa was also D-shaped."

Dan placed them on the map where he had already entered the pueblo near where they camped and its close neighbor to the east as well as the Gambler's House. From the mesa, he had seen two more to the east, but the distance was too great for him to determine shape. Sebriana produced her notes and sketches. Both were D-shaped.

Looking up Dan told them. "That makes seven."

Conversation ceased for a long moment as the number hung there, bringing some recollection to each of them. There was something important about that number.

Dan couldn't let it go. Seven cities, why should there be seven cities? What did that have to do with the evacuation of ancient Jerusalem? Nothing came to mind.

This evening was the first of many spent comparing what they had learned. The spring of 1860 was passing, and they lingered in Chaco Canyon learning more each day. The Navajo helped with information and by showing them glyphs and houses that might otherwise have gone unnoticed. They helped as well by selling the friends supplies so that their time in the canyon extended through the spring. Evening was consultation time.

One evening, Rojo spoke after the long silence. "Today I looked into many pueblos. The square ones don't show evidence of stones and *vigas* being carried away. The D-shaped pueblos often show such signs. In places I can see where walls were deliberately pushed down. But not all of them are like this, only the ones near square pueblos."

Sebriana summed up their findings. "So, the square pueblos were built later. Look at my pottery. I've laid the pieces out in groups based on where they came from. I tried to pick up only the most common kinds of pottery at each site. They must have traded with each other. So I guessed the most common types were made in the pueblo where I found them. Do any of these belong together?"

Roque was the first to see something. "Those mugs are different from these. There are two different shapes, I'm sure."

"The designs are all black on white," Dan said. "I guess that means the same clay was used. Now that I think about it, we've seen different colors and qualities of pottery along the Rio Grande. The clay looks the same, but the paint is different."

Rojo joined in. "That's right. Where the black covers most of the pot, the black is almost brown. On the others, it is very black and almost shines."

Very pleased, Hosteen Béézh nodded. "The woman has shown you. The black comes from the D-shaped pueblos and the brown from the square."

Sebriana beamed pleased with the praise. "And I didn't find any of the brown and white in the D-shaped pueblos. The designs show differences, too, but they are more subtle and harder to describe. If you look, you will see it."

Dan turned to Roque who often seemed left out conducting a long search that took him great distances but didn't seem to yield immediate results. "Roque, what did you find?"

"Roads, Danito, many roads. And they run straight. They never turn. If they come to a cliff, there are stairs even when it would have been easy to go around. They run from pueblo to pueblo and point to places far away. The biggest of all runs south from the *fajada picacho*, the mesa that looks like it is wearing a belt."

And so their evenings progressed even as week succeeded week. Rojo decided to look at the inscriptions on cañon walls. He didn't want to enter any rooms. Dan spent further days sketching and mapping and then joined Sebriana in poking into the pueblos. Roque was still fascinated with staircases and roads. He followed them as far as he could. They hired a Navajo woman to cook for them and bought sheep from the Navajos for food. Fortunately, the Navajo liked receiving silver pesos in payment.

Hosteen Béézh explained, "They use them to make jewelry."

It was a country idyll for the friends after so much fighting, running, and climbing. They stopped worrying about the outside world. Although the spring advancing toward summer, it was hotter than any Dan had known in New Mexico. They made the most of it. Sebriana found a deep pool in Chaco Creek where they could bathe the dust and salt from their hair and bodies.

Each night they reviewed what they had learned that day sharing with each other facts and theorizing about them. They kept a small fire as even in summer the desert evenings were cool, and it provided light for their discussions. Many weeks passed untroubled.

Something gnawed at Dan's mind as they talked around the fire. "Rojo, I thought your people did not like to be near the spirits of the dead. Yours and the Navajo as well, yet the Navajo live here among these houses even using their stones to build their *hogans*."

"It is true," he replied. "The Pueblos bury their dead in old store rooms and under the floors of their houses. I can sense them there, and I am uncomfortable enclosed in Pueblo houses. There are many spirits trapped there. The same was done here in the square castles, and I do not wish to enter those houses because they are houses of the dead. The spirits here are very old. I feel very few of them around me. There should be more. I do not think many people lived here. More lived in the square castles than the D-shaped buildings if the number of spirits means anything."

"Strange," Dan said. "The D-shaped pueblos seem to have been occupied much longer, yet they show the least signs of occupation. There are few signs of cook fires and you say few spirits."

Sebriana cut in. "Maybe it's not so strange. Jewish people do not bury their dead nearby. They take them at least a half a mile away. Maybe the lack of burials is a sign that the ones who lived here are the Danites we seek."

Roque was troubled. "But where are they?"

"Gone," said Rojo. Roque frowned at him though the answer was not a jest.

Dan spoke to quell rising anger and frustration. "Why? Why are they gone?"

Sebriana looked thoughtful. "Drought maybe or maybe war."

"Drought brings famine, and famine brings war," said Rojo.

Dan thought about famine and war. "I don't think we are seeing any signs of war. If it was war, we might have seen unburied skeletons with arrowheads stuck in bones. Stones would have been blackened where pueblos had been burned down, *vigas* charred instead of reused."

Rojo added information. "If the fire were hot, the stones might be red, but I have only seen these red stones in the kivas of the house by the *arroyo*."

Dan wrinkled his forehead in thought. "Maybe there is a deeper question. Why did they ever come here? There isn't much land for crops, no game, no wood for construction, no firewood, little water. It's hot and dry and one of the most undesirable places around. It's indefensible because enemies can roll boulders off the cliffs onto the pueblos which are built right up to them."

"It is true," said Sebriana. "And there are signs that very few people ever lived here."

"Then why build such big houses?" demanded Roque. He was never comfortable with bafflement or an unsolved puzzle. He liked his world comfortable and concrete without mystery.

"If they were the Danites we seek," she responded, "they might have remembered the story of Joseph and stored corn and beans against drought. Each clan would have had storage rooms and places to stay when they came here. Great ceremonies would have reinforced the need to make the sacrifice of storing for the future. Roads directed them here. A few lived here year round to protect their stores. Because they were Jews, their few burials were at a distance from their homes."

Roque was still not satisfied. "Why here?"

The light of epiphany came on in Rojo's eyes. "Because it is the central place! Their civilization made its homes at the foot of the mountains at the edge of the basin where there is game, water, and wood."

"It is called the Central Place," said Hosteen Béézh nodding.

Sebriana came to her feet in excitement. "The story . . . the Gambler. Maybe the Navajo didn't understand the system of storage and exchange. They were outsiders to it. Or maybe at the very end, when supplies were low, those who lived here charged for what was not theirs just as Joseph did, thereby enslaving the people of Egypt.

"Think of it. There are always local droughts. All clans and pueblos would have brought their surplus here. Those in need would have received it with proper ceremony. It would have worked until there was a long and deep drought affecting all. Then they would have had to leave."

"What would the departure have looked like?" Dan asked.

Rojo responded. "I have seen this and heard about it from the Pueblos. Families would have left and gone to stay with their clans in other locations. If things were bad enough, whole clans might have left. It would always have been just a few people, never the whole group. The whole group might go in times of great surplus, but in bad times, the land will not support a large migration. It might have taken years for a pueblo to empty. A few always stay behind.

He paused for breath. "My grandfather told about the time when the Pecos pueblo became empty. There were too many greedy people who wanted their land and too many Comanches making war. Some went to live with relatives at Jemez. Some are still there living near Pecos as Mexicans among the people with whom they have long intermarried."

"What would they have done with the Ark?" Dan asked.

Sebriana frowned. "They would have taken it to some safe place. If the society was breaking up, that would have been some place hidden. I think they'd have left a message hoping someday people from the Holy Land would follow them."

Dan nodded. "What evidence do we have that they were our Danites?"

Rojo smiled. "The stories of the Hopi and Navajo and Acoma say they came here. There are no stories to our knowledge telling what happened when this society fell apart. The end must have come slowly."

Sebriana looked thoughtful. "The lack of burials inside the pueblos shows they might be Jewish. Some of what we think are kivas might be ritual baths filled by capturing rainwater. The circular grand kiva, the Temple, seems Jewish. Animal and human motifs are lacking in their pottery art and from the woven items, baskets and cloth, which we have found. All the designs are geometric, and that carries over to all of the Pueblos. Maybe they learned pottery making from the Danites."

Dan agreed. "We have found some other things, though I don't know what they mean. The front of this big D-shaped pueblo is colonnaded as if there had been shops at one time. We have found parrot feathers, copper bells, turquoise necklaces, and sandals of woven yucca, cloth with geometric patterns and doorways shaped like a T. These appear in both types of pueblo. The doors are wide as a man's hips from the waist-level down and a hand-breadth wider on each side from there up, wide as a man's shoulders.

He thought a moment and then addressed the others. "What of the square pueblos? How are they different."

Roque grew excited. "They look like castles to me, much more defensible than the others, more compact with less outer wall to defend."

Sebriana interrupted. "Have you found any metal tools there? I haven't. The castles were inhabited by people different from, but related to, the Danites."

Dan reflected awhile. "Tell them how we know this."

Sebriana thought for a moment. "Both contain the same kind of cloth, feathers, and sandals. The pottery is similar though the designs are different. *Indios* lived in those houses. I am certain of it."

No one disputed her. Rojo spoke next. "Today on a cañon wall I found a picture of a procession. Three men rode horses. All carried spears and swords. The most striking thing was their mantles, white with a large, dark cross."

"A red cross?" Dan guessed. "All of the legs the same length but broader toward the outer end?

Roque shook his head. "Franciscan priests accompanied some expeditions against the Navajo."

Sebriana challenged him. "Then the mantles would have been black with a white cross."

They realized that the difference in dress between Franciscan and Templar was properly depicted on the cañon wall. None of the Spanish or Mexicans wore a light mantle with a dark cross. Their crosses were always white.

Dan was astonished. "Could it be the Knights Templar? Could they have occupied the castle pueblos? Is that why they look like castles?"

Sebriana was practical. "What does the picture tell us? That they were few in number and had only a few horses. Could they have faced some great disaster and lost most of their horses, men, and metal? Is that why we find so few signs? I think that they prized metal and did not let it go easily."

Roque looked puzzled. "Then why are there so many castles?"

Dan turned to look at him. "There are only three or four, all small, all near D-shaped pueblos where they quarried, eh borrowed, stone and *vigas*. These castles were also occupied by an *Indio* people, shared, maybe by allies. Did they still have the two treasures they had brought? What did they do with them?"

There was no answer for a long time. Finally, Rojo spoke. "The Navajo story only mentions one warrior. This might have been a party of scouts."

"I do not think so," said Sebriana. "They stayed long enough to build castles. There would have been a few Danites left. At least, that's what the Navajo story indicates. I think that both sides, weakened by strife, united to survive, and then joined the treasures together and hid them."

"But where?" asked Roque.

This question brought on another long period of quiet thought. Dan broke the silence. "Have we seen any writing, a message perhaps?"

Troubled, Roque shook his head and wrinkled his forehead as he thought and tried to remember the remarkable tales he had been told as a child and loved so much. "The Knights Templar may not have been literate. I have heard that knights despised book learning in favor of manly skills. The few literate priests among them may have died."

Rojo nodded slowly. "I have seen no writing on the cañon walls. Not for certain. There are a few marks that might have been Hebrew letters, but they also resembled figures seen in all rock pictures."

Dan reprised their conjectures. "I have noticed something strange in the construction of the great D-shaped pueblos. In my sketchbook, the walls I've drawn and the kivas have begun to look like Hebrew letters. There aren't enough of them in any one pueblo to spell out a word. Collapsed and missing walls make it hard to tell, but they seem to be the initials of well-known blessings. This can only be seen from above on the mesas, as if they wanted God to see it."

There was silence. Suddenly Rojo sprang to his feet. He turned slowly in a circle his arms extended, his hands upright from the wrist, the palms facing out. He stopped while facing west-south-west for a long moment and then continued, halting again in the east.

Dan saw Rojo's palms and was shocked. Despite his amazement, most of his mental energy still gnawed on a problem. They were so red they almost seemed to glow. One moment they were pale and then as Rojo turned to the west-south-west they blushed red.

Rojo stopped. "Enemies approach!"

Chapter 10

On the Chaco Meridian

Rojo stood there a moment before he spoke again. "*Power* informs me, many enemies approach from the west, perhaps as many as thirty, even forty. They are mounted but still a few days away, uncertain where we are.

"A small band of men, perhaps four or five, approaches from the east, only one or two days away. *Power* is uncertain about them. They may be enemies or allies."

Dan barely heard him. The slow cogs of his brain had finally meshed around to a conclusion. He sprang to his feet. "That's it!"

Rojo scowled. "You seem pleased that enemies are coming. Perhaps you doubt me."

"No, no, Rojo," Dan replied. "We need to deal with the enemies. I believe you. It is important, but I just had a revelation, an epiphany. There are seven D-shaped pueblos here. These are the Seven Cities of Gold! Coronado was hunting too far south. He had trouble with Zuñi, Hopi, and Acoma. They never told him the ruins of Chaco Canyon were here! These Seven Cities of Chaco are what the Pope sent Marcos de Niza to find! The Pope knew the Templars and the Danites had come this way. The Pope sent the priest, Marcos, after the three treasures. The priest was given a cover story to fool Coronado. The Pope didn't want Coronado and his conquistadors to know how truly valuable the treasure was. This is Cibola! Coronado would have gotten some of the Templar gold, but the Pope would have had the real treasures."

Roque looked slightly puzzeled. "Danito, explain to me again about the three treasures."

Dan smiled. "The first is the Ark of the Covenant which disappeared during the Babylonian captivity. The second is the furniture of Solomon's Temple: the Menorah, the Table of the Show Bread or Presence and the Trumpets of Truth. These were taken by the Romans in A.D. 70. The third is the gold and silver the Eyptians forced upon the Children of Isreal as they departed after the Ten Plagues. Most of this was buried in the land of Goshen and its hiding places recorded on copper scrolls. It was recovered by the Templars during the last crusade when Richard the Lionheart led the Templars into Eygpt to Goshen. It was hidden on the Temple Mount for a time."

There was still a piece missing. Dan knew it but couldn't recall what it was. Something about seven bishops fleeing Moors.

Rojo looked at Dan and asked. "About our enemies, what should we do?"

Roque stood folding his arms across his chest. "Mountains full of Utahs lie to our north and more mountains full of Gila Apaches to our south. East and west are blocked by enemies. Let's stay and fight. We could prepare a defense from one of the castles."

He wants to be a knight, Dan thought as he heard Sebriana suppressing a laugh, but he considered this option. "When an assault on a castle will be too costly, and you have time on your side, you lay siege. Which of the castles has a well? How long will our water last?"

Rojo replied, "The answer is obvious. There is no well. We can't store water for more than a few days.

Dan agreed. "If we run, we should go east. It is clear the Danites and the Templars are no longer here. Which way did they go? That should guide us."

The direction in which the ancients had departed was not at all clear to any of them.

"Rojo," said Dan, "you say we still have days before our enemies arrive. We must sleep on this question and tomorrow we will look in our own ways for an answer."

In the morning, Dan consulted Hosteen Béézh.

"You must find your own answer. The old stories don't provide a clear answer," Hosteen Béézh told Dan.

They worked on their projects through the day and met after supper at the campfire. Dan, Rojo, and Sebriana thought themselves stumped. They discussed the issue well into the night.

Sebriana held herself and shook as if she were cold. "I think they went north. Hosteen Béézh says there are great houses there on the San Juan River."

"That is Utah country," said Roque.

"They are allies of the Jicarilla," said Rojo.

Roque insisted that they were *muy cimarron* and not safe to be around.

Rojo snorted at Roque's assessment of these mountain Indians. "My grandmother was a Utah."

Roque wasn't in favor of going east or west toward enemies. He was leading up to something. He might not be able to express his logic, but he had an opinion, thought Dan. He wants us to suggest it.

A glance at the stars told Dan this night's discussion

had gone too long. It was after midnight. No one seemed to have any clear idea of how to proceed.

Finally, Sebriana spoke. "I think the Danites would have left a message if they were able even though they must have thought themselves abandoned. And the Templars would have as well. The Danites may have been discouraged though the appearance of the Templars was sure to have confirmed their most ancient stories of their origin. Yes, they would have left a message."

Roque cried out. "Isn't it obvious? They followed the great south road! The road is the message." Roads had been Roque's special project.

Rojo was not as excited as he dug for something in his possibles bag. "I found this today and meant to show it to you. Before today, we have found copper bells and parrot feathers that came from the south.

Finding the object, he withdrew it from the pouch. "This stone has been lacquered, had part of the lacquer cut away, and had been painted in the slots created." He displayed a colorfully decorated round stone about as big around as a teacup. "I have seen its like before far to the south at Casas Grandes beyond Mesilla."

Dan broke in. "The Temple and the two D-shaped pueblos on the mesa tops form three points of a line that aligns with Roque's great south road. I think we should go south."

Rojo frowned. "It is not wise to journey south through the mountains of the Gila Apaches, especially with a woman."

Roque laughed. "My *prima* will have to become Juan again. I think she likes it."

Dan thought for a moment. "Rojo, can you sketch us a map that would show our position in relation to Casas Grandes?" Roque nodded and taking pen and paper from

Dan drew a map.

Dan looked at the map. "It's due south of here?"

"I think so, yes, exactly south."

Dan nodded. Odd. South was indicated. Everything lined up. How strange, he thought, that Indians could keep a straight line over such a distance using only line of sight from one object or mountain top to another. It was a remarkable feat. "Then, I think we can travel along the Rio Grande through Los Lunas, Socorro, Mesilla, and Janos."

"That would take us first east," said Sebriana. "What about the approaching enemies?"

Dan thought for a moment. "I suppose those in the west are the black coated Danites we encountered before. But who is coming from the east?"

"Possible allies," Rojo reminded them.

Dan shook his head in consternation. "We need to know. With allies and a little preparation, we might discourage the Danites permanently."

Roque looked worried. "Trails and waterholes are limited in number. If we go east, and I think we must, we might run into one set of enemies while avoiding the other and find ourselves in their crossfire."

Sebriana cocked an eyebrow. "Then let's meet those coming from the east and find out who they are."

Rojo considered the countryside. "Let's move into the pueblo by the arroyo and camp there. I think we can defend it. We can invite allies in or insist that it is too crowded, and they must camp outside."

"Sure," Dan said, "and we can dig a few holes and collect a few pots and things telling them we are collecting artifacts to send to an archaeologist. It gives us further reason to ask them to camp away from our diggings and provides a rationale for our being here."

Roque and Sebriana both looked at Dan quizzically. Finally, Sebriana couldn't contain her curiosity any longer. "What is an archeologist?"

"A kind of historian who digs up antiquities and old pots," Dan informed her. "They dig in old ruins to study the past and to find treasures."

Roque thought a minute. "That's awfully close to what we are doing."

Dan smiled. "All the better as there will be some truth in our claims to make them seem real. And we have concluded the treasure is not here since both Templars and the Hebrew Danites have departed."

Rojo indicated he would talk with their Navajo friends. "They will watch for the approach of the black-coated ones. Should we find both parties dangerous to us, they can assist us in departing undetected."

The next evening Juan-Sebriana and Dan sat in the golden glow of the dying sun to the smell of lamb roasting on *appolas*, sticks sharpened at both ends, stuck in the ground around the cedar fire. They sprinkled the roasts with sage gathered in the desert.

"Hello, the camp!" Five riders approached on well-made horses. "May we come in."

"Come in and sit," Dan replied, recognizing two of them immediately despite the growing dark. "Never turned a man away at dinnertime yet. Get yourself some coffee and some lamb and beans."

"Lamb?" asked John Rheingold. "I didn't expect lamb out here. Venison maybe, or mountain sheep."

Dan replied. "Navajos have got plenty. We buy from them."

As his men tended to their horses, tall, broad-shouldered Rheingold, dressed in backcountry buckskin and wearing tooled boots covering feet and legs to the knee, strolled in. "I think we've met. Dan Trelawney, isn't it, and the handsome Juan?"

Sebriana smiled happy to be called handsome.

"That's correct, Mr. Rheingold," Dan replied. "I assume you're not going much further tonight, and I'd appreciate it if you'd camp away from us. We've been digging pots and such for a museum back east and wouldn't want you or your stock to step in a hole or to trip over anything valuable."

Rheingold gave the necessary instructions and his party moved further back from the ruin. His men gathered into camp as the Navajo cook poured coffee and set more items on the fire.

Rheingold glanced about. "You had two other friends as I recall."

Dan eyed Rheingold's companions. They were armed, of course, for this was Navajo country, but the tie-down loops were over pistol hammers and rifles weren't cocked. They weren't looking for immediate trouble, Dan thought.

"They're about," Dan replied, "tending to one thing and another."

Hearing Dan mention them, Roque and Rojo eased down their hammers and walked casually into camp from their places of concealment.

As the meal progressed, a bottle went round and round the fire from hand to hand as they packed and smoked their clay pipes and talked. The Texans did not seem to hold back on drink though the four friends were sparing as they sipped. Blond, city-dressed, Tiler Caine worked his way around to be near Juan.

Dan heard him mumble to sour-faced Pennington, "That's the prettiest man I've ever seen."

Dan noticed Juan's *misericorde*, Sebriana's thin

dagger of mercy, was missing from its case undoubtedly concealed in her sleeve ready for action if gunman Caine got fresh.

"Caine," Dan said recalling the Square and Compass pendant that hung about Tiler's neck, "have you ever traveled?"

"From west to east and east to west again," he said giving the Masonic response.

Dan rose, extending his hand, and Caine did likewise, gripping Dan's the way he'd done before in the Lodge. Dan returned the grip. From this start, it soon emerged that all of the Texans were Freemasons.

Dan told the visitors that he and his friends, Roque and Rojo, were as well.

Thinking himself mocked, Pennington was enraged. "What? An Injun and a Roman Catholic?"

Dan looked directly at him. "They believe in God, so why not? Perhaps next year, we'll get to raise Juan. He's still too young.

"If you don't mind me asking, what are you Texians doing out here in Navajo country, Brother Rheingold?"

"Prospecting," the Texan said.

Dan thought the notion of Texans prospecting without the proper tools was an obvious lie. This country showed no mineral promise, they didn't appear to have the gear for prospecting and, of course, Dan knew them to be Texas Rangers though he doubted they were aware that he knew.

Rheingold tried to reinforce his lie. "You know there's a war coming, Dan. Folks will have to choose sides, especially out here. We're from Texas, and Texas will need mineral wealth to support and defend the Lone Star Republic against invaders.

"The natural place for us to get it is here in New

Mexico and on west in California. When we took our independence from Mexico, Santa Anna gave us the land all the way to the Rio Grande. Santa Fe is in Texas. When we joined the Union, the Yankees cheated us out of what was ours by drawing the line between the two much further east. The Yankees knew Sonora and Chihuahua were in rebellion against Mexico City and would have fallen in with us giving the southern states access to the Pacific Ocean. They put a buffer between us. The Rio Arriba rebelled just after Texas did."

Roque growled deep in his throat. "I know. I was there. Mexico City made laws that robbed us of our living, taxed us on money we did not have, and sent governors who were not elected. We wanted redress, not independence. That does not mean we wanted to quit Mexico or join Texas."

In the years between Texas independence in 1836 and her joining the Union ten years later, a horrible war was fought in the Nueces Strip, a one hundred mile-wide territory north of the Rio Grande, which both sides claimed and tried to control by massacre and atrocity. The word came to New Mexico, and her people learned to hate and fear Texans.

"That's exactly my point," interjected Rheingold. "This Abraham Lincoln that the Northerners like and the Yankees, in general, want to do to us what Mexico City did to you. The Republicans want to raise high tariffs on imported goods, forcing us to buy from the North at ruinous prices and forcing us to sell our cotton to them and not to Europe where we can get more for it. They have more population, newcomers from Ireland and Europe, and they use that to overpower us in the House of Representatives. It was not supposed to be like this. The Constitution was not intended to create a Yankee dictatorship. The States have rights reserved to them never delegated to the Congress."

Dan realized that states had already left the Union during the past winter. No word had come about Texas, but he was sure it would secede. Perhaps it already had. Dan and his friends had been away from civilization and news for many months. Did these Texans know? Probably. They were coming from the direction of the Rio Grande.

"You hold slaves," accused Roque, proud that his people had outlawed slavery almost a century before, outlawed it, but didn't stop practicing it where Indians were concerned.

Rheingold looked Roque in the eye. "Slavery will go away soon of its own accord. Machinery is reducing the need for manpower. People have their wealth tied up in slaves but as the need decreases, the value of the slave decreases. Soon they won't be worth their keep."

"Perhaps the Federal government could buy them and free them," Dan suggested.

Sebriana looked at him oddly. "*Pobrecito*, you usually know these things. That would ensure a market and keep the price up."

"And it would just be wrong," said Roque with moral certainty. On most points his morals were somewhat slippery. For all that, Dan thought, he's still a good man and my friend.

"Buying slaves says the government approves," Roque finished.

"Slave and free," continued Rheingold, "it sets us apart as two different economies. States come into the Union as one free and one slave. It maintains the balance in the Senate so the Yankee population doesn't overwhelm Southern tradition. The Founding Fathers intended a balance of power."

At this point, volatile Tiler Caine jumped in with both feet. "Why slavery is right there in the Constitution. All the states held slaves back then. The Yankees didn't need slaves no more, so now they're getting all self-righteous on the South, them that made their wealth carrying slaves from Africa."

Tiler lifted his chin. "Well, you can bet the Knights of the Golden Circle will stand up for Southern rights. We'll extend slavery into Chihuahua and Sonora. That degenerate culture that proceeds from Mexico City can't hold onto their border provinces. Their government don't run there now. We'll take 'em same as we did New Mexico and California in the War and for the same reasons, except this time, it will be Southern manhood making a way to the Pacific."

Dan was shocked to hear the Knights of the Golden Circle mentioned so casually along with the implication that these men were Knights as well as Masons. Perhaps that explained some things. The KGC and others like them had mounted filibusters into Mexico before this. Whether Mexican culture was degenerate or not, Dan kept a careful eye on Roque for fear his anger would rise, Mexico City abused the outer provinces economically and as a result could not control them. Armed filibusters had been launched but so far had met with bloody disasters, surrender ending in execution.

He mused. It was understandable that the South did not want to end up an impoverished colony of the Yankees, another Ireland, Sonora, or Chihuahua with policies dictated by a distant government in which there was no equal say.

Morose Jim Pennington spoke up. "We'll see to Arizona as well."

"Arizona?" Dan asked.

"You might think of it as the Gadsden Purchase," Pennington replied. "It's more than that. It's the passes for railroad and wagon that stretch from Texas to the Colorado, the road to San Diego. The Yankees won't do anything with it. There's no law. The nearest judge is in Santa Fe. He comes twice a year to Mesilla. That's three hundred miles from Tubac and Tucson. Thieves and murderers run wild there. We arrest them, but there is no way to try them, so they go free."

We? thought Dan. Was he from the Gadsden Purchase lands? The Oregon and California Trails used South Pass way up north in the land of the Sioux. Kit Carson and Fremont on behalf of Fremont's father-in-law, Senator Benton of Missouri, had tried four times without success to find a middle route. Such passes would preserve the economic strength of Missouri as gateway to Santa Fe and the West. South Pass was a gateway for the Yankee states. Passes and a railroad linked to San Antonio would help the South.

Pennington continued. "Apaches and Mexicans make lives hell in Arizona. The latter come across the border and commit murder with axe and bludgeon and disappear into Mexico where the authorities are of no help. The Indians steal from miners, ranchers, and farmers alike. No one is safe. There is not enough Army to keep the savages under control. It's a miracle the Butterfield Road stays open."

Then the Butterfield Overland Mail is still running. That's good, thought Dan, who realized that he needed to step in before Pennington and Tiler Caine offended Roque, Sebriana, and Rojo beyond endurance. The two men might hold their temper, but Juan was apt to skewer someone's brain with that steel toothpick of hers.

Dan spoke up. "What I heard from big, one-eyed Mose Carson last time he came through was that the Butterfield Road stays open because the Chiricahua and Gila Apaches are at peace with the United States, though the Gilas don't much care for the miners tearing up the earth at Pinos Altos."

The Texans, Dan thought, had strong Constitutional arguments in their favor, and he supposed they felt cheated out of eastern New Mexico. It was clear they also had imperial plans for a takeover of Mexico and possibly of California and the western territories. The states had rights and had delegated a short list of very specific powers to the Congress withholding all the powers not specifically delegated to themselves and the people. States had to ratify changes to the Constitution before they became law. It was clear that states, not the Federal government, were intended to be the supreme power since superior delegates to inferior, not the reverse. If the Federal government exceeded or abused its power, the only way the states could retain their rights was to withdraw, to secede from the Union.

Dan's head buzzed with the tangled arguments. The problem was that slavery, even if the Constitution passively accepted it, was evil, and it bred evil. It bred men who thought they were better than other men. Congressman Philemon Herbert, an Alabaman representing California, had shot and killed an Irish headwaiter for refusing to serve him breakfast after the stated hour. The congressman was acquitted by a southern court. Dan had heard he was living down near Tucson with a lot of other killers and scoundrels.

An imperial South would be dangerous to United States interests. Texas would go after the part of New Mexico that these men called "Arizona." And it sounded like they wanted Sonora, Chihuahua, and California as well. Whatever they might say about their rights, they didn't seem to have much respect for those of others, Dan concluded.

Rheingold looked at him. "You seem troubled by slavery. It's not as bad as the abolitionists try to make out. Most slaves are well treated, even loved. They're a bit like family. They're also a substantial investment, like a good horse. People take good care of expensive property. They nurture and care for it. It's very rare for a man to abuse valuable property."

Roque growled again. "You just compared a man to an animal. I know men who beat their horses."

Enraged Tiler Caine sprang to his feet. "Come on then, grease!"

Rheingold looked at Caine his eyes gray steel and ice. "Tiler, sit down. These are our friends and Masonic brothers."

Roque stalked out into the darkness. Dan guessed he wasn't feeling very brotherly just then. Discussion turned to other topics, and the bottle passed from hand to hand. After half an hour Roque returned smiling and nodding to all at the fire. Dan thought he must have gotten over his anger for now.

"It's late," Dan said. "Time we turned in. We've got a very early day planned for tomorrow."

The Texans left the camp moving off to their own one hundred yards away.

Hosteen Béézh came into the circle of firelight from where he'd been listening in the shadows. He was always there to inform their councils. "The Danites are camped beyond the end of the cañon where you can't see the light from their fires. They may suspect your presence, but the local Navajos tell me no scouts have been close enough to see you."

"They'll be here in the morning," said Rojo. "We should depart now. The hosteen and I have talked this over. We will slip away now, one at a time and meet by the Temple. The Navajo will come into camp with their horses replacing us and feeding the fire. They will stay until the Texians can see they are not us. By then, the Danites should be close."

They packed and left, meeting up at the Temple. Dan could see problems with the plan. The Texans would also be in pursuit soon. He and his friends might gain six hours on them if they were lucky.

They hurriedly bid farewell to Hosteen Béézh and their cook; both had been good friends.

Rojo directed them to take his mules. "I've bought a horse from the Navajo. I have some things to discuss with Hosteen Béézh. I will join you soon after daybreak."

They covered many miles in the dark. At daybreak, they chewed a little jerky as they changed their saddles to fresh animals. Sound carries far in desert air. Far behind them they heard a rifle fire. The shot was followed by a barrage that went on for several minutes. Thereafter, they heard occasional firing until finally they were too far away, and the sound was too faint.

Two hours after sunup, Rojo, riding hard on a lathered horse, joined them. They halted while he moved his saddle to a mule.

Rojo grinned. "Danites were almost to our castle, our campsite, when someone fired on them. Danites charged, but the Texians' position was too strong for them. I tried to help out, but the range was too long, and I missed Porter Brannan." He displayed his teeth in an evil Apache grin. "As soon as the Danites broke off the first charge, the Texians tried to get mounted and flee, but they had trouble with their saddles and tack."

Roque looked very pleased with himself. "Guess they'll be stuck there a while making repairs. Texians really ought to learn to take better care of their tack and not let anyone loosen up the seams and cut straps halfway through where it won't be noticed, at least not until they try to mount up. Hope they can learn to get along with the Danites in the meantime. It would be good for them to learn to respect other people, religious dissenters, slaves, Mexicanos, *Indios*." He ticked them off on his fingers.

Dan had qualms. "They're lodge brothers faced with dozens of Danites."

"Tough lodge brothers," said Rojo, "holding a very strong position evens things out. Besides, the Danites think they are lodge brothers, too, since Joe Smith made 'em all Masons. Brotherly love ought to just overwhelm them all any minute now."

Sebriana and Dan were flabbergasted.

They watched their back trail and kept a sentinel at night, but the journey to Santa Fe was uneventful. In Santa Fe, they planned to get money and supplies and time to rest, but returning to the city of the holy faith posed a problem. They had Sebriana's in-laws to consider.

"I could get my cousins and steal all of the Don Esteban Baca's cattle and sheep," suggested Rojo, "My people need the meat. That should intimidate him."

Dan shook his head. "The Army and Kit Carson already pursue Jicarilla for crimes smaller than you propose. Such an adventure would bring too much trouble on them."

Sebriana twisted a wicked smile. "We could ride into their hacienda one night killing all the guards, and I could cut out Don Esteban's heart for ever having bred such a son."

"In which case, you'd be almost certain to hang for murder," Dan said. "A few *vaqueros* killed in fights are accepted by everyone, but a don slain in his bed is another matter. Imagine the spectacle. People would be sure to come from Las Vegas, Taos, and Socorro to witness the hanging of a woman."

They rode down long valleys skirting the Jemez Mountains to the south on their way to the Rio Grande. They rode with the smell of mule and saddle, the creak of leather straps, and clop of hooves through fields of fragrant sage exhausted from months on the trail.

"I am not afraid," Sebriana declared.

"I never thought you were. In jail, they'll give you a sackcloth dress. They probably won't allow you to brush your hair or put on makeup. You'll look terrible, and that's before they snap your neck and the contents of your belly run down around your feet."

She looked less pleased at this prospect. Dying as a proud and dignified lady was one thing, but not being allowed to look your best was another matter. "But you have given me an idea."

As they approached Santa Fe, the smell of chili overwhelmed them. It was mid-summer 1860, and the roasters were everywhere. The outer skin must be burned away to reach the sweet green flesh below. Then the chilis could be stuffed with cheese or ground meat, coated in egg batter, and deep fried to make *rellenos* or cooked in savory stews. The red chili powder and the beautiful *ristras* of dry red pods that hang from *vigas* were present all year long. Only in the mid- summer did the town breathe chili, masking the odor of too many people and animals and too many latrines too close together. On cool mountain evenings spice blends with the scent of burning piñon. No finer incense was known to man.

The four travelers saw to their stock and opened up Dan and Roque's casa, having barely done so when Kit Carson arrived. Down from Taos to see the governor on business relating to the Jicarilla and Utah agencies, Kit dressed in his city best, long-wasted, fringed buckskin jacket beaded at the shoulders, the belt in the middle supporting Bowie knife and Colt's pistol. A fine, beaver felt hat of unblocked, bowl-shaped crown and broad brim made this costume not just his best but his city best. His face was clean shaven, calm, mild, and broad.

"Señor Cristobal," howled Roque in delight, his approaching arms wide like Old Ephraim, the griz, grasping Kit in a hug that lifted the smaller man six inches off the floor. Kit might have been small, but he was broad and powerful through the shoulders. He returned the hug giving better than he got. It was Roque who gasped first and released his hold. "Not bad for a fifty-year-old man," Roque grunted.

Sebriana back to dressing as herself was confined to the casa so none of her enemies would know she was back. She made hot chocolate with ground clove, cinnamon, piñon nuts and *piloncillo*, brown sugar cones and served it to Kit, Roque, Rojo, and Dan. Then she seated herself with the men. They lit their pipes while Sebriana rolled a corn husk *cigarito* for herself. With *aguardiente*, brandy, at hand it was time to relate their adventures and troubles.

After a long while, Kit mused. "I'd heard of those tiny Welshmen living in caves by the big cañon of the Colorado. Can't say I believed it. I've heard stories too about the people of Chaco being kind of special. Think you may have the right of it. You should talk your discoveries and theories over with Brother Albert Pike. He's a very learned man."

Their talk drifted to Sebriana's difficulties. Kit thought for a long time. "You can't kill Don Esteban Baca y Armijo. Folks would notice. You'd hang. You've got to go down and reason with him. Won't do any good; he's too arrogant, and he's lost a son. But you have to give him the chance. It's only right. Sebriana ought to stand trial and be acquitted by reason of self-defense, but Don Esteban has allies, and a fair trial is unlikely."

"The governor could pardon her," Dan suggested.

"The governor don't like you or me, Danny."

Roque swelled with anger. "Baca will hire hunters to kill her so he doesn't get his hands dirty. Is there nothing we can do?"

"Well, I've got an idea. Danny you ever think about making Sebriana an honest woman?" There was more to Kit's plan. The mortality rate among Sebriana's husbands was a stumbling block for Dan. "You got a good woman there. You need to start taking her seriously."

Take her seriously? Dan knew he couldn't. He might feel like he was in love with her, but that wasn't enough. It was easy for Kit. He was from the frontier. Frontiersmen didn't have to worry about social standing and their families' reputations. Did it matter? Would word get back? Was he ever going back Out East?

During the long months of their journeys, he'd put the issue out of mind having other pursuits to keep his mind occupied. He simply enjoyed her company, her wit, her insights, and other benefits. But now he had to consider her problems. She was widowed five times, at least one by her own hand. Dan wasn't sure he wanted to tempt fate. He knew he didn't want to be on the run from the Baca family forever nor did he want Sebriana to suffer being caught by them. The Bacas had returned to their homes for now, but Dan was sure they had men out looking for her. When spotted, she might be slain or dragged to court. Any of the relatives might kill her on sight.

He realized their time together on the trail had changed his feelings for her, them. She was a good friend and companion and kept the bedroll warm. The trail had changed Dan, too. He was no longer content to run. He wanted to turn and fight, to do something positive, to take action.

Kit relayed other news. "Albert Pike is in town, and I hear Texas is talking about annexing New Mexico again."

Roque said, "The *Paisanos* don't like it. They tell stories of Texas terror and what Texians do to Mexicanos."

"There are people," said Kit, "some of the traders, who say we'd be better off under Texas rule than as a territory."

Roque blustered. "No Mexicano feels that way."

Dan tried to calm him. "The matter was settled by Congress. They set the boundary out on the Llano Estacado. Texas has no claim."

Kit spoke softly. "Albert Pike thinks they do. And he thinks war is coming. Texas will secede and lay claim to New Mexico if Abraham Lincoln is elected."

"What will the Mormons do?" asked Dan, thinking back to their recent encounters.

Kit shook his head. "No one seems to know. They've just finished their little war with the United States. They may be hostile. They may close the trails again."

"I heard," said Roque, "they don't like the slavers and had trouble with them before in Missouri."

"Kit," said Dan, "I think they might be up to

something, something that will be very bad for the United States if they pull it off. It'll take time to explain."

"Then it will have to wait," said the mountain man. "I promised Mr. Pike that I'd meet him."

Sebriana spoke up. "What are Texas Rangers doing here?"

"*Cabrones!*" yelled Roque. "Those *putos* are spies!"

Dan wandered the town looking for old friends and checking up on military acquaintances and traders.

"We have to worry," one officer told him, "that one of the Southerners will try to take his whole unit with him or turn over supplies to the South."

"What about invasion from Texas?" Dan asked.

"Not much chance of that," his acquaintance replied. "Too much desert to cross."

Days later the morning dawned warm and muggy, rare for Santa Fe. With piñon fires out for the day, the smell of manure and too many latrines pervaded the city. Dan longed for the chili roasters to start their work. Leaving Rojo to guard Sebriana, Roque and Dan went in search of Albert Pike. They found him breakfasting at La Fonda in company of Rheingold who sprang to his feet and reached for his gun. Roque shifted his Hawkin subtly but meaningfully aligning it with the Ranger's belly.

Rheingold growled deep in his throat. "You abandoned us!"

Dan looked the Ranger in the eye. "Didn't know I was accountable to you for my comings and goings."

"You knew those Mormons was coming," Rheingold accused.

Dan nodded. "I did. Didn't know they had truck with you. Thought they were after us, not you."

The Ranger glared at Dan. "They weren't after us until someone fired a shot at them."

"Must have been the Navajos," Dan said. "They don't like strangers in their valley."

The Ranger had more accusations. "Someone cut up our tack."

Roque spoke up. "Probably the Navajos. The cook, she heard the bad things Caine and Pennington said about *Indios*. Probably made her angry."

"I see you got away all right," Dan said.

"They kept us pinned down for days and then we had to repair our tack," Rheingold responded. "We had to kill several of the Mormons. Made it difficult to make the peace. Pennington and Smith were wounded."

Dan tried to look concerned. "Will they recover?"

"I think so, but Smith will be known as Three-finger Joe-Bob." There wasn't a hint of humor in Rheingold's tone. The loss of a digit was a score to be settled.

Dan glanced at Pike. "I can see you two have lots to discuss. We'll be going."

Pike stood gallantly. "You're on the trail of something very important. There are evil forces at work that will try to thwart you. It would be terrible if what you seek fell into their hands.

"There's a war coming," Pike continued. "This treasure could be very important to the side with right and justice and the Constitution on its side. Those who bring it in will be heralded with laurels and riches, honors and position."

That tore it, Dan thought. He liked a dollar same as the next man, but suggesting that he could be motivated by anything other than conscience in matters of loyalty to his country annoyed him deeply and told him a lot about the man he was dealing with.

"We'll be going now," Dan said as they backed out into the street unwilling to turn their backs on the

Southerners.

In the street, Dan looked earnestly at Roque. "We've got to get going again. I want to leave Sebriana behind and deal with the Bacas first."

"O ho, *mi amigo*." He smiled. "This will not be so easy. This woman, she has her own mind and is very stubborn."

She wouldn't hear of it. She threw a heavy wooden crucifix at Dan.

He ducked. "I want you to be safe in the care of friends."

Roque and Rojo argued she would be unpredictable in this fight, especially this fight.

"She might blow up the *hacienda* like before," said Rojo.

In the end, she had her way, of course. Her insistence on having her own way, thought Dan, was another good reason not to marry her. Who could hope to control such a woman?

They made contact with Pedro Martinez when he came to Santa Fe on a trading expedition with Rio Grande blankets to sell. He curled the ends of his long mustaches as he told them about events in Chimayo. "Doña Loca's casa and fields have been untended since you went away. I guess the don doesn't want to appear too greedy.

"There are strange men around all the time, hunters. They watch her casa. They watch Sebriana's relatives. They look for a sign that she is near.

"I don't think I should ride with you," Pedro went on. "I would be too easily recognized, and it would go hard with my family. I can spy for you."

And he did, providing invaluable information.

They timed their ride to arrive after midnight. Staking

their mules and Roque's *grullo* stallion a half mile from the Baca *hacienda*, they worked their way up to the *zaguan* where two guards were posted. As they'd expected, both were asleep. It was difficult for men to stay alert when nothing happens night after night especially on warm summer nights. In the army, wakefulness was induced by the threat of being shot for sleeping on guard. Among civilians, except in the most exciting times, guards slept.

Rojo and Dan made their ways to the opposite ends of the wall where they could approach the recessed *zaguan*, the gate, in the center unseen by anyone sheltering inside.

The plan was that Roque and Sebriana would raise a diversion if the guards awoke. Silently they moved toward the gate. Arriving together, they awakened the guards by cocking their pistols in their ears. Sebriana and Roque joined them, disarming and gagging the pair. They threw a few turns of rope about their bodies to bind their feet together and their arms at their sides. Then they hoisted them to the *vigas* like fat *ristras* of chili.

Dan and his friends followed Sebriana to the *don's* bed chamber where they found him asleep in his four-poster bed next to a comely lass of perhaps fifteen years. Dan cocked a pistol in the *don's* nose putting his off-hand index finger to his lips. *Don* Esteban Baca understood and remained quiet. Roque gagged the girl and bound her naked to a bedpost. They bound the *don* to another although he was far less lovely to look at.

"*Don* Esteban," Dan began, "Sebriana Ruiz is under our protection."

Esteban snorted. They had entered his bedchamber and proved they could kill him in his sleep, but he knew they dared not, so he was unimpressed. "She is a murderess wanted by the law!"

"Have the charges dropped," Dan suggested. "Return her home and lands and molest her no further. Call off your hunters."

Dan had prepared quit-claim deeds on all of Sebriana's lands, and he presented them for the *don's* signature. He scoffed. Dan pulled his oversized Bowie from its sheath. "I will start by cutting off your toes, one by one. Then I'll move on to your fingers starting with the left hand."

The Don sighed and snickered even as he signed. "This will do you no good." Dan waited for Esteban to remind them that she was subject to arrest, but he did not. "I have hired men to hunt her down and kill her. They will hunt you, too."

"If anything happens to Doña Loca," said Roque, "I will return for you."

"And I will be with him," said Rojo through his twisted Apache grin. "I will cut off your *cajones* and feed them to the girl while you watch." For emphasis he flicked out with his knife and cut the don's *cajones* deeply enough that they bled.

Sebriana, unable to constrain herself further, laughed at the sight of his blood. Turning to the girl, she asked, "Does he pleasure you? Or just selfishly pleasure himself as his son did?" Tied to the bedpost, the girl tried to conceal her mirth.

They gagged Don Esteban and departed. They had accomplished little. Dan realized that some men are just too convinced of their own power, position, and importance to be intimidated by reality.

As they rode, Dan talked about their new problem. "The difficulty with back-shooters is that they shoot you in the back. You don't know who they are or when they are going to attack. How do you defend against them?"

Sebriana took the lead. "You have to draw them out in the open. Set a trap and bait it. I'll be the bait." She smiled.

"Why should they hurry to a trap?" asked Roque.

She nodded. "Because I'm going to use the deeds the don just signed to sell off all of the property. He'll want to stop the sale, and they'll want to hurry to get their pay."

They set her up in her casa in Chimayo where she began selling off her property. Roque and Dan guarded her, and any watcher might have noticed them there during the day. She was safe enough because they were there. Dan never left her alone. Rojo watched secretly from a distance searching for those who sought Sebriana.

A fight with guns was a dangerous thing. No one entered one without thinking he had the upper hand. Unwillingness to enter a fight without a clear edge was the hallmark of hired assassins who fought for money, not honor or country. They wanted to live to collect and enjoy their pay. The sight of Dan and Roque with Sebriana was enough to keep them at bay. They were in Chimayo, and there were people around. They did not want to be seen springing an ambush. They would wait.

Rojo rode up to Sebriana's casa. "Hurry, we must leave."

When they were safely away, Rojo explained the emergency. "The sheriff came from Santa Fe. I think he had a warrant for Sebriana's arrest."

Fortunately, Dan thought, the sheriff can't wait forever in one place to make an arrest, especially when the people are in sympathy with the one sought.

They tried to identify those who watched them. Strangers in the village were easy to detect. Chimayo was on the High Road to Taos from Santa Fe, and travelers did pass through, but those who lurked and stayed soon became obvious. Dan spotted one. He rode a dark horse and wore a black, hooded cape that concealed his features although Dan soon saw that he was dark with a large hooked nose. A golden hoop dangled from his ear and a gold tooth flashed in his mouth. Dan thought this wraith that often shadowed them looked like a gypsy. Dan felt certain he would be a knife man.

Roque spotted two hunters he thought to be half-breeds. Indian women on the fringes of their own tribes and white men, many of them French-Canadian, bred their off-spring to a difficult life outside both cultures accepted by neither. Some became great hunters and explorers among the best of the mountain men. Others were dissolute malcontents and dangerous to all around them. These two assassins wore stained buckskin and long, greasy hair uncombed. Even from a distance, they smelled bad. They had the cruel look of men who kill for pleasure.

Sebriana spotted the dandies, three of them. They dressed in styles rarely seen north of Mexico City. Their clothes and weapons were adorned with silver. They wore tooled boots to the knee, spurs with large, cruel Spanish rowels, embroidered vests and jackets, and huge *sombreros*. Their hats shaded their dark and evil faces.

Rojo spotted the most dangerous man, a *gavacho* hunter. He always stayed far away cradling a well-maintained Hawkin. He wore buckskin clothing, neat and well cut. This was a man of business who knew his trade and went about it methodically.

Dan wrinkled his brow. "That sounds like a man I might have liked under other circumstances."

Roque nodded. "We both might if he weren't a hunter of men."

"Lacks some kind of scruples," Dan agreed.

Only Rojo ever saw him. He was that careful and that elusive.

The specter of the grim reaper followed them. The hooded figure often carrying a lance dogged their paths silhouetting himself occasionally on hilltops. Dan thought the man must have figured he would frighten the companions in some way, deriving some advantage when he finally struck.

The fancy boys jostled them on the road in minor attacks that could have turned murderous in moments. Too obvious, they didn't want to be seen as assassins. They would wait their time.

In times past, when Roque and Dan hunted buffalo with him on the *llano*, Chief Chacón of the Jicarilla demonstrated the way to fight a superior foe. The Comanche menaced his people so he made it appear that the Jicarilla were weak and fleeing from them. He lured them in until he had them surrounded on all sides and then struck hard and fast. Very few Comanche escaped his net. Dan and Rojo agreed that they would have to do the same.

One day Rojo told them, "I need to return to my people for a while." He rode off in daylight when all could see him go. Roque and Dan would be enough guard, but standing guard was boring work, and Roque craved excitement.

That same evening a *fandango* was held, and Roque elected to go. "It has been a long time. She is safe enough with you." He and Dan argued loudly.

"She's your *prima*, dammit!" Dan insisted.

"She's your lover. You care for her." Roque stalked

off angrily and headed for the *baile*. He was as angry as Dan had ever seen him, and he didn't care who knew it.

"I want to go, too," pouted Sebriana stamping her foot.

"It's too dangerous," Dan pronounced thrusting out his chin.

"I wasn't meant to live like a monk," she countered. "I want to get out and have fun."

"I'm the only one left to guard you. It's too dangerous."

"Get out of my casa, Daniel. Be gone. I will take care of myself." She pushed him out the door into the deepening twilight.

Drifting across the Santa Cruz River, Dan could hear the sounds of the *baile*. *Farolitos* lighted the way inviting everyone to the party. There would be food and dancing. Behind him through her open door Dan could see Doña Loca secreting weapons about her person. She'd be safe enough he thought angrily and stalked off toward the dance. Sebriana blew out the light and stepped out into the evening. The hunters wouldn't try to kill her in front of witnesses, but there was risk on the way there and back.

In the gathering twilight, Dan returned to her and took her hand. She squeezed his. He was sure the hunters watched them and knew she had a reduced guard. They'd be safe enough at the *fandango* within the circle of firelight with people around. Away from it with eyes night-blind, danger lurked.

Pumpkins decorated the pathways. *Ristras* hung from *vigas*. The harvest had been good. They ate beef and lamb cooked with savory spices and wrapped in tortillas. Sebriana avoided the pork. Rolled tortillas were their spoons lifting spicy stews to their hungry mouths. They danced the *cuna*, hips together, shoulders back, arms extended rocking the baby in the cradle. Across the *plaza,* avoiding contact with the lovers, Roque had gathered a covey of female admirers. Dan and Sebriana made a show of drinking the strong *aguardiente*. Exhausted, Sebriana and Dan retreated to a corner to eat a little more their backs to the firelight.

Staggering, she gave sign that she had lady-business to attend to in the dark. Dan objected. She pushed him away drunkenly and strode into the night. No sooner had she squatted down than a hooded figure hovered above her, and Dan saw the flash of a knife.

It was a close run thing. Dan had not been drinking only giving the appearance. His night vision was restored from having his back to the fire and though he appeared to be staggering out to take a leak, he was following Sebriana closely.

A quick rush brought his knee to the assailant's back. Dan's left hand under the cloaked figure's chin pulled his head back exposing his neck. Dan's blade across his neck ended his life. Bowie finished the job of separating head with its dark hair and gold earring from shoulders. Dan lowered him to the ground, propping him against a wall as if napping. Then he stuck a pumpkin under his hood in place of his head. Dan doubted there were many in Chimayo familiar with events in the tiny New York hamlet, Sleepy Hollow. The pumpkin shouldn't incite much panic.

"You've soaked my clothes in his blood," Sebriana complained. She still held her *misericorde* at the ready just in case Dan didn't appear in time.

"Couldn't be helped. Time to leave the party anyway," he replied.

They started back with Dan carrying the head in his left hand. His right was free to grasp his pistol. This was a dangerous time. Ambush could be expected. They circled far around following different paths than they had come by.

Ahead, a light appeared from her casa as the door was opened to reveal two men crossing the threshold. A shotgun blast from within propelled them back the way they had come. A third charged the door. The steady, rhythmic firing of a pistol followed. Roque had left the *baile* before Dan and Sebriana and had concealed himself in the casa with a directional light aimed at the door. All three knew the chance was good that the assassins would seek to conceal themselves there awaiting Sebriana's return, but Roque had beat them to it. Crouched in shadow with the light blinding anyone who entered, Roque gave himself additional advantage.

Somewhere in the gloom, an Indian flitted from shadow to deeper shadow. Rojo, who hadn't returned to his people, guarded their flank. Ahead of them a dark figure broke cover and raised a rifle to his shoulder, aiming at Roque in the lighted doorway. Dan drew his pistol and fired at the center of the silhouette, taking the man down with the first shot. Dan continued firing until six cylinders were empty and then drew his second weapon and waited. Dan's hearing and sight were impaired from the flash and thunder of his revolver. At his side, Sebriana stood ready with her pepperbox. Off to their right, a death scream rent the night, and Dan knew Rojo had his man. The *gavacho* hunter was dead.

A fleeing figure almost knocked Dan over. Doña Loca's little pistol cracked once, and then it exploded in flame. Their assailant was dead before Dan took his head and that of the man he had killed. The two half-breeds were accounted for.

Dan looked up at Sebriana. "Effective but you have to teach that pepperbox not to fire all its barrels at once."

As they approached her casa, Dan and Sebriana met an excited Roque. "I got two of them as they entered the door. The flash of the shotgun blinded me for a moment as the third man entered. I was sure I was *muerte*, so I fired and fired. When I could see again, the third *hombre* lay dead at my feet with the handle of Pedro's knife on one side of his neck and the tip sticking out on the other. Pedro has already gone. He did not want to be seen."

They visited *Don* Esteban late that same night entering as they had before and tying the *don* to his bedpost again. Dan set out seven heads at his feet to stare at him in accusation.

"I will get more hunters!" Esteban protested. "You are dead, all of you. I will never stop."

They had impugned his courage and his honor, not that he had either. Dan supposed he'd continue the hunt, for Doña Loca had killed Carlos, his son.

Both Roque and Rojo stole a kiss from the pretty, naked lass tied to the other bedpost. She returned their affections with warmth. Grateful, Dan supposed, at not having to eat the don's *cajones*.

As they rode away Roque turned in the saddle to face Dan. "He may think himself secure enough to continue the hunt, but after this night, he will have difficulty finding assassins."

"It's time to continue our quest," said Dan. Before they could leave Santa Fe, word came that Kit had been injured in a fall. His horse rolled down a mountainside with him aboard. He was never quite the same after that. Dan and his friends rode to Taos to be at his side and to assist his wife, Josefa. They were delayed many months as Kit slowly healed. During this time, word came that Lincoln had been elected, and New Mexico began a slow slide into chaos.

Chapter 11

Into the Southland

In time, Sebriana liquidated her assets reinvesting in commercial ventures with the Santa Fe merchants Roque and Dan knew well. Investments might soon become risky, for thunderclouds were gathering on the horizon. Risk meant high profit for those bold enough to pursue it. South Carolina seceded from the Union; others followed. Winter dragged on toward spring. Kit began to heal but only slowly, and it appeared he would carry internal wounds for a long time to come.

Lieutenant Dubois in from Fort Union told Dan he was only sure of the loyalty of three officers, one of them the surgeon. Disloyalty among Army officers was bad news indeed. Fort Union, the largest base and supply depot in the territory out beyond Las Vegas on the *llano* stood astride the junction of the Mountain Branch and Cimarron Cut-off of the Santa Fe Trail, protecting New Mexico Territory's supply-line to the States. Without it, New Mexicans would become Confederates whether they liked it or not. Most Mexicanos didn't like it but many Anglos did.

In late February, Rojo went back with his people for a while. Returning to Santa Fe, Roque and Dan sat in the *sala* at *La Fonda* wrapped in a thick mist of fragrant piñon smoke. Drinks in hand, they watched a covey of officers as they played cards at the next table. Far along in their cups, they spoke loudly enough for all to overhear.

"We should resign our commissions now," insisted a lanky lieutenant.

A bald captain nodded. "Aye, those who get there first will reap the greatest rewards and positions. A Confederate government has been formed at Montgomery, Alabama, with Jeff Davis as President. We could be generals or territorial governors." Rumors emanating from the South suggested he was correct. Office seekers of all kinds were flocking to Southern state capitals.

And not just to the South. Many officers loyal to the Union but tired of long years in the West with little hope of promotion, sought high rank in the volunteer units the Northern states were forming. Men tended to identify with their home states more strongly than they did with the Union as the Founding Fathers had intended. Dan sympathized with men who felt their homes were threatened. However, it seemed for every man who wanted to defend his home, there were five who sought advancement.

"Have you heard the news from Texas?" asked a thick set major. The others shook their heads. "General Davey Twiggs has surrendered all the Federal property there to the state government."

News was slow in coming, taking weeks to arrive from the States. This word must have come by military express.

Dan turned to Roque and spoke in a low voice. "This is bad news. Texas now has military arms of uniform caliber, cannon, powder, and shells. They'll soon form an army."

The thick set major went on. "We have to be careful. Some officers may think they can take their whole unit with them or take supplies the way Twiggs has done. They may wait until the last moment when Texas is invading."

Roque spoke low in his throat. "I thought officers placed honor above everything else."

Dan replied. "Most do. Most have honorably resigned their commissions before leaving. Davey Twiggs, hero of the Mexican War, may have had southern sympathies as eastern papers claim, but he also had little choice in surrendering the Federal property in Texas. His men were scattered, many of them on the march, when he was confronted and surrounded."

Spring arrived with more bad news and more resignations. The military had difficulty functioning, and Apache and Navajo raided at will. Only the Jicarilla were quiet.

In May of 1861, Colonel William Loring, Military Commander for New Mexico Territory, turned his command over to Lieutenant Colonel Edward Canby and went south after telling his officers, "The South is my home, and I am going to throw up my commission and shall join the Southern Army, and each of you can do as you think best."

Sebriana came to Dan the next day. "*Pobrecito*, it is time you continued the search. Mesilla and Tucson, I am told, have held conventions declaring their region to be Arizona and part of the Confederacy." They hadn't as yet declared, but they were making noises in that direction. "It would be very bad if the Texians found the treasure."

"I haven't seen Albert Pike," Dan argued, "or the Texas Knights of the Golden Circle in months. Perhaps they've given up. Besides, I can't leave you here alone."

She smiled. "I'm glad that's settled so easily. Juan will have to go with you."

Dan made his way to the Plaza and spoke to *Guust Cha'du*, a Jicarilla woman who sat before the Palace of the Governors with baskets to sell. He told her that he needed to speak with Rojo. Two days later Rojo rode into town.

The four friends made careful preparation then headed out for Casas Grandes in May, 1861. They had heard rumors of immense ruins. After witnessing Chaco Canyon they were sure whatever they sought must be monumental, too. The Great South Road at Chaco pointed directly toward Casas Grandes. Following the South Road through the mountains was not an option to their liking. *Cuchillo Negro* and *Mangas Coloradas,* Black Knife and Red Sleeves, leaders of the Gila Apaches were on the warpath. In the spring of 1860, Americans had discovered gold and silver at Pinos Altos near Santa Rita del Cobre, the copper mines, on the southern edge of the Apaches' range. Drunken miners had tied Mangas Coloradas to a tree and whipped him for sport. The chief, who stood inches over six feet, was not amused. Not long after atrocities began along the southern immigrant road which ran through the chief's territory. For each actual brutality, ten rumors grew.

Rojo rode out of town to the north the day before their departure. He rejoined the party near Santo Domingo on *El Camino Real*, the Royal Road, which led from Santa Fe to Mexico City along the Rio Grande. "You are followed. There were two teams of watchers lurking in Santa Fe. Each sent a rider to report on your progress. Two men so far unaware of each other continue to follow you."

"Who do you think they are?" asked Roque.

"One seemed to be *Nakaiyeh*," Rojo responded, "so I think this must be the Penitentes. The other I don't know. He was *Mangani*, white man. I think he is not from Texas. He rode like a farmer, so maybe he is a Danite of the Mormons." *Nakaiyeh* was an insulting term by which Jicarilla referred to Mexicans.

In the gathering heat and dust of the dry spring, Dan thought for a long time about the nature of their pursuers as they rode south. "Roque, what do you think our pursuers will try next?"

Roque doffed his sombrero and massaged his scalp. "So far the Penitentes have attacked us only when we invaded a site they were guarding. They have an ancient charge to uphold, but it is based on a mistaken idea."

Dan thought about what an ancient charge from the Pope implied. "I agree. If we are correct, de Niza and Coronado mistook Zuñi for Chaco. We visited Zuñi and that probably kept them interested in us."

Sebriana reached the next conclusion. "But if they haven't identified Chaco as the Seven Cities of Gold, our trip south might lessen their interest."

The center of New Mexico west of the Rio Grande was dominated by the Mogollon Rim, which was framed by the mountain ranges of Gila, White, Mogollon, Pinal, Blue, Black and others, providing streams and springs in plenty. In a dry land, the mountains were home to ancient trails by which forgotten people traded goods over vast distances. On horseback or on foot, a man could travel by many paths though wagons would have difficulty. Apache lived in the mountains, and all others entered at their peril.

East of the Rio Grande were mountains and then the *Llano Estacado*, the country of the Comanche and Mescalero Apache where there were no towns in 1861. The Pecos River flowed south to join the Rio Grande in

Texas.

Trails in dry country led from water to water by the shortest route, thereby limiting the ways a path could run. Going south from Santa Fe, the friends followed the Rio Grande along the *Camino Real.* The Penitentes would see them. When they came back north, they would ride again along the *Camino Real,* and the descendants of the conquistadors would pick up their trail again.

Chewing on dust as much as on the problem of pursuit, Dan rode with the smell of mule and leather in his nostrils and a blazing sun on his back. Near the river and the *acequias,* the smell of water and grass dominated, but on the high ground the road they followed, there was only dust, mule, and leather. Dust devils danced in brown pastures, masters of the land until the summer rains banished their power.

Dan pondered and shared his thoughts with his friends. "The Mormon Danites have information from the Freemasons and thus from the Knights Templar in the form of puzzles, hints, clues, mysteries, and enigmas. They know the game, but they haven't solved the riddles. They're counting on us to do that."

"*Si,*" said Roque, "When they attacked us, they demanded information."

Rojo now added his thoughts. "When we stop at Casas Grandes, I think they will attack again if we do not break their pursuit first."

"I agree," said Dan, "but not before they think we have found the treasure."

They passed Socorro, its name meaning succor or salvation. It was the last town before Mesilla and the traditional beginning of the *Jornada del Muerto*, the Journey of the Dead Man. The Rio surrendered its plain to a narrow gorge, and *El Camino Real* followed the high bench away from the river. For a hundred miles there would be no water and little grass. It was rough country haunted by Mescalero and Gila Apaches.

At Socorro, they ate well and restocked their supplies and fed and rested their livestock before taking on the Jornada. Ten miles south of Socorro, they forded the Rio at Valverde near Ft. Craig.

"Roque," said Dan through cracked, parched, white lips, "I'd as soon forget my memories of the Jornada.

Roque tried to speak, cleared his dry throat, and tried again. "What? You don't like distant craggy brown peaks, hard rocky ground, heat and dust, the smell of cold rock, skeletons of man and beast, some decorated with arrows."

Sebriana giggled weakly. "Let us not forget the endless movement one foot ahead of the other walking the stock, falling asleep riding to awaken miles away finding nothing had changed."

They elected to push straight through without camping.

Roque coughed up dust. "Halt awhile and El Diablo catches up with you on the Jornada."

They did not stop at Doña Ana where there was water and grass. Instead, they pushed on to Mesilla.

"The Crosses," whispered Roque as they passed *las cruces*, "belong to travelers who having found good water and grass after the *despoblado*, the desolation that is the Jornada, rested and lowered their guard. Their crosses stand where they will rest until Judgment Day."

Mesilla, county seat of what was coming to be called Arizona, included everything south of Socorro from the Pecos River to Yuma on the Colorado, a distance of well over six hundred miles. It was over three hundred miles to Tucson. In all this vast territory, there were only Butterfield Stations and a few small towns. The only justice was a circuit judge who came down twice per year from Santa Fe. Without effective courts, it was a land of murder and mayhem dominated by Apaches who until recently had been peaceful.

As they rode into town, a bearded Anglo in a wide sombrero eyed them.

Dan turned to Roque. "Texian, or I miss my guess."

Roque nodded. "There are many seditionists in Mesilla. It is close to *Tejas*."

Dan scowled. "We best be careful."

As they dismounted, they were approached by a man in neat city clothes. "Meeting tonight to elect a delegate to Congress. You might want to attend."

"Which Congress?" asked Dan and wished he hadn't.

The well-dressed stranger looked surprised. "Why the one that's going to give us territorial status."

Dan switched gears offering no new information about himself and his friends. "Sure, we might do that." Seemingly content, the stranger departed. "If he can be that confident with strangers, this place must be a hotbed of sedition."

Roque growled. "This is not a good place. Many of the people had lived in Doña Ana since their ancestors were expelled from the Rio Abajo by the Pueblo Revolt. They wished to remain in Mexico, and when Nuevo Mexico passed to the United States, they came south. They didn't come far enough."

"Just because they don't want to be in the United States doesn't mean they want to join the Confederates," said Sebriana.

The newer of two plazas bustling with activity consisted of wood frame houses and buildings in the *gavacho* style where goods were bought and sold at exorbitant prices. At this last outpost of civilization before wilderness, merchants rarely had necessities nor had them in sufficient quantity. The town would profit by war. Southern armies would march through on their way north and west. The Mesilla Valley would be the supply depot for conquest. Armies would arrive bit by bit, a few companies at a time, as they waited for grass to grow, supplies to come forward, and springs and basins to refill.

Sitting against the wall in the older plaza, a man in a green top hat worked silver into jewelry with a set of small portable tools.

"It can't be!" exclaimed Roque. "He cannot be here!"

"But it is," replied Rojo.

"Juan," said Dan, "look over there. It's a wee Leprechaun."

Still clad in her traveling clothes playing the part of Juan, Sebriana frowned. "I've met *Rodado Verde*, the Green Vagabond. He is a silversmith. I have bought from him before, and I like him." She crossed her arms.

Verde doffed his hat. "I hope the day finds you well, but I can see you're in grave trouble as you travel with that baboon, Roque Vigil and his ill-mannered partner, Dan."

She smiled. "He is my *primo*."

"Careful, mija," said Dan. "He's like a snake and strikes for no reason. I've never heard any name but Verde for him, so he must be hiding his true name being on the run from the law somewhere.

Dan turned to his friends, "I think he might be from Ireland and on the run from an English court that has him scheduled to hang for insulting their Queen."

Sebriana laughed. "He's bound to be wanted for something somewhere."

"That one," said Rojo, "he likes to stir up trouble almost as much as he likes to drink."

Verde was short, a few inches over five foot tall, and of an indeterminate age. Dan guessed somewhere between fifty and one hundred and twenty years, though spry for his age.

The Green Vagabond had been dressed like a mountain man on other occasions the friends had seen him, though he always wore the green top hat. Today, however, he wore loose white cotton and a serape. The green hat was out of place.

Roque snarled. "He looks like the *alcalde*, the mayor, of a Mexican pueblo in Ireland."

"You gone blind or somethin' since I last saw you, greaser? Of course, it's me. And you, blanket-ass, you're usually more perceptive than that. Daniel, I see you're still running with a bad crowd, and it looks like you've picked up a fancy-boy. And here I thought you liked girls. Just goes to show, you never can tell."

Dan was only stunned for a moment. There was, after all, affection in the way Verde snarled "greaser" or called Rojo "blanket-ass."

Shaking his head, Roque looked Verde up and down. "Don't I want to kill you for something? I can't remember."

Rojo chided. "He is a warrior deserving of our respect. He has stood beside us in many fights."

"Yes," said Dan, "At least as many as he's gotten us into."

Sebriana smiled. "I think he's cute."

"That's right!" Roque roared, his memory returning. "It was your voice in the Jicarilla camp that started the fight at Cieneguilla. I know it was your voice."

Verde held up his hands. "I was there and for sure, but I'm innocent as a saint. I tried to warn those poor dragoons. 'Be comin' up if 't's a fight you're after,' I cried to let them know there'd be trouble."

Roque challenged the little man. "And then you fought on the Jicarilla side."

"Nay, lad," Verde replied. "I sat out that fight, and a grand one it was to miss. I had too many friends on both sides and couldn't be after shootin' 'em."

"Gentlemen," Dan said pointing to Verde, "you are undoubtedly looking at the cause for Arizona wanting to secede to the Confederacy."

Verde smiled roguishly. "And what brings you to my domain?"

They were taken aback; they had not thought about a cover story.

Roque responded. "I wanted to deliver a letter to the Jackass Mail to send to my *primo* in Los Angeles."

"You're too late, boyo," Verde replied. "The Butterfield ain't runnin' anymore, nor is the San Antonio and San Diego. Mail goes by a northern route now."

Dan tried to look surprised. "You don't say! Without it, Tucson must be completely isolated."

"Yup, it's time to get out of Mesilla. Mind if I ride along with you?"

Evading a straight answer or a lie, Dan said, "You don't know where we're going."

"It's never mattered before." Verde chuckled. "Besides, you get into the best kind of fun." His eyes twinkled like stars disappearing behind storm clouds.

They rode southwest across a sea of brown grass dotted here and there with islands of craggy rock showing dark gray or black on the horizon. Few of these rose far enough to be covered in forest. Once, they met Apaches, men who dressed much like the local Mexicanos in white cotton trousers, colorful shirts, and vests with the difference that they also wore broad cotton breechcloths and knee-high moccasins with a turned up toe in the shape of a prickly pear. Rojo had lived among them and spoke their language, which was close to his own.

Rojo spoke to them and then to his friends. "They are at war with Americanos and Mexicanos whom they intend to drive from the land."

Roque and Dan reached for guns.

Rojo held up his hand. "They are quite willing to accept a private truce with me and my friends."

Along the way, the trail crossed the border into Mexico, and they passed into a mean little town, Janos, whose people seemed to be of mostly Indian blood.

Rojo scowled. "These vermin will trade with the Apache or feed them poisoned whiskey depending on the season."

"Watch who you call vermin, Injun," said Verde. "These folks speak a kind of Apache among themselves and were once your allies."

As they neared the Sierra Madre, they entered a broad river valley. Roque expressed his approval. "Good farmland. It would be easy to irrigate."

"So it would, boyo," said Verde, "especially when you consider that the locals adopted an ancient irrigation system that only needed repair."

Roque growled. "How do you know this thing?"

Verde grinned but said nothing.

They followed the road south to Casas Grandes, a town of some importance with a small military garrison.

Verde spat. "These people are currently at peace with the Apache. The people of this prosperous outpost trade with them for goods and livestock stolen from Mexicanos in Sonora just across the mountains. They pay the Apache tribute for being left in peace. Or poison them if they think they can get away with it."

The town was surrounded by adobe ruins rising as much as three stories, the *casas grandes*, big houses, for which the town was named.

Dan led the others out to one fine section of especially large ruins south of town. "Those large round depressions might have been kivas. Do you realize that we are due south of Chaco Canyon and exactly where the Great South Road points?"

"Of course 'tis, boyo." Verde did his impression of the Sphinx.

They searched acres of ruins separately and in pairs, each turning to those things peculiar to his or her imagination, those that caught their interest or fancy. They found cloisonné stone discs similar to those at Chaco.

Sebriana was the first to notice pottery discontinuity. "This is not Chaco pottery. It is different. There are three and four colors where Chaco was only black or brown and white, and there are pictures of flowers, birds, animals and people where Chaco had only geometric patterns."

The style was distinctive and unmistakable.

"These people were not Hebrews," Sebriana, still dressed as Juan, told Dan. "They would not be making gods of things in nature. The Law forbids it."

Dan nodded. "It is a difference from Chaco, though I think the colors just tell us this pottery comes from a later date than we have seen before."

That night, they held counsel amongst the ruins. Rodado Verde rose first to speak. "I'd be after gettin' a few things off me chest. There's things I notice. Fer instance, Juan avoids talking to me and he's the first lad I ever seen squat to pee. What I'm saying is, Doña Loca, I recognized you way back in Mesilla.

"And something else." He stepped around the fire and extending his hand greeted Rojo, Roque, and Dan with the grip of a Mason. "Can't you open up to a Traveling Man?"

"Where were you raised?" Dan asked. Raising is the final ceremony of initiation for a Freemason.

"In Scotland at Roslyn Chapel."

"Scotland?" blurted Roque. "I thought you were from Ireland."

Verde cocked an eyebrow. "I spent time there, too, but I never said I was born there."

"So where are you from?" demanded Roque.

"Here."

"Here? America?!?"

"Here, Casas Grandes," replied Verde.

"You're not Mexican," insisted Roque.

"No, I'm not."

"You're not old enough to have been born in these ruins," challenged Sebriana.

The Green Vagabond smiled. "No, I'm not. My ancestors lived here long before I was born."

Roque pressed him. "Where were you born?"

"Rancho near the mouth of the Rio Grande," Verde replied.

"A Texian!" blurted Roque. "I knew there was something about him I didn't like." Dan thought that seemed to settle some things . . . for a while, maybe. Still something nagged and seemed unanswered to Dan.

They continued their discussion of what they'd observed that day amongst the ruins.

Rojo had searched for T-shaped doors and found them. "It seems an odd thing. Pueblos don't use them that I know of. Why would the Ancient Ones make their doors so, and if the Pueblos are descended from the people of

Chaco, why would they stop making their doors this way?"

Verde perked up. "It has to do with ventilation and draughts, boyo. These old casas were more comfortable than you might think though it doesn't look it now. They ran streams through them to bring in drinking water and flush away sewage. It looks like all the rooms would be dark, but they left round windows to let in light. The lowest floors were dark, but they were only used for storage and burials. The big houses were sited to catch the sun so that the adobes took in heat in the daytime and warmed the house at night. These people were clever builders.

"The T-doors were a wonder unto themselves," Verde continued. "Man's bigger at the shoulder than the hip. If you want less draught through the opening, you make the bottom smaller. They found that by blocking top and bottom separately, they could bring in cooling draughts or vent away smoke while holding in heat. The people down along the big river had to do things different when the Mexicans came. Priests might accuse them of witchcraft for making a T-door."

Rojo was almost angry. He did not like being lied to. "How can you know this?"

"I told you, me lad. My people lived here," answered Verde.

Rojo snarled. "This place has been abandoned a very long time."

Verde smiled. "Didn't say they lived here recently. Look, you lads haven't been exactly forthcoming with your Masonic brother. You know I'm sworn to keep your secrets. I'm going to open up and tell you mine.

"But first, let me tell you what I know of your secrets. You're searching for the Ark of the Covenant and the treasure of the Templar Knights."

Roque jumped to his feet. "*Brujo*! How can you know this? You've been spying on us!"

Verde's eyes twinkled. "You just confirmed it now, didn't you, boyo?"

Dan shook his head thinking, one day Roque would lose his temper to Verde's undoing.

Dan stood and touched Roque's arm. "I think he'll tell us if we let him. You can kill him later if you really need to." Dan nodded to Verde to continue.

Verde stroked his chin and cocked his head quizzically, perhaps wondering if he'd get out of this alive. "Sit down and rest yourselves. I need to tell you a long story, my story.

"Long ago, the evil pope seeking after the treasure of the Knights Templar sent out a decree that the knights should be arrested and tortured to death. They had grown wealthy. Their crime was the desire to use their wealth to free the Holy Land. Many were able to escape to Scotland where they fought against tyranny alongside Robert the Bruce at Bannockburn. They had brought great treasures back from the Jerusalem, excavations in the Temple of Solomon itself. Treasure also came from Egypt.

"This wealth was stored at Roslyn for a time. Scholars among the knights poured over scrolls brought from the Temple finding reference to the hiding place of the Ark. Learning of the Western Paradise and having a fleet, they decided their own treasures needed to be taken to greater safety. They found the great river, the Rio Grande, and began unloading their ships at its mouth. A storm scattered ships and sank many others. Most of the horses were lost. The treasure though had already been unloaded. They waited through the winter and into the next spring, able to support themselves by hunting and trade and also able to defend themselves. No ship came.

"Leaving signs should any come to follow them, the surviving Knights Templar, about one hundred and fifty in all, started inland in search of the Ark. Eventually they found the Danites at Chaco Cañon. Only a few hundred Hebrew Danites remained by then. Drought and cold had forced many away from the Central Place. Most had gone to the Rio Grande and quickly lost their identity among the peoples there. Two groups retained their identity. One of these went north to a large river, the San Juan, I think, though in those days it must have been running very low as drought had long been on the land. Another group had gone south and prospered, gone south to where we now sit.

"There was mistrust between the Knights and the Danites and dissension among the Knights who built their own castles in opposition to the nearly empty houses of the Hebrew Danites. One group who lived atop the mesa claimed to own everything even the other Danites. Their domination of the others was clear and was a hindrance to negotiations between the Knights and the Danites…"

Rojo had grown excited. "Gambler's House. You're telling the Navajo story of the Gambler."

Verde resumed his narrative. "Gambler, yes, so the *Dineh* call him.

"In time, the Knights intermarried with the women of the Danites. Eventually, they overcame the Gambler or, to be more correct, his descendants, and learned that the Ark had gone north with a group of priests and their followers. Using Chaco as a base, the Knights went north and opened negotiations with the people there. The amount of gold they were carrying was difficult to transport without pack animals. It was decided to combine the treasures and conceal them in a place of safety.

"The land could no longer bear so many people. From Chaco and San Juan, most headed south to what is now Casas Grandes, though we had another name for it, *Pacimé*. A party of one hundred was to conceal the treasure and follow. To my knowledge, this party was never seen again. From Pacimé a party of ten men and their wives was sent to establish a station to watch for ships near the mouth of the Rio Grande. Every five years, a party was sent from the river mouth to report to the leaders at Pacimé. In 1458, all was well at Pacimé. Times were hard for my family. It was fourteen years before they could mount another expedition. In 1472, they found this place deserted. "

Roque was enthralled. "What happened to the people? Where had they gone?"

"I don't know," replied Verde. "There was no sign of them. That is to say of the Knights and the Hebrews. It wasn't long before the younger generations were more Indian than Templar or Danite although warrior societies still used these names. Each generation fewer and fewer maintained the old identity, and then they were gone. They may have left due to drought. They may have moved away for some other reason. They might have died of some epidemic. I think one of the powerful empires in the south, the Aztecs, perhaps, came and carried them away as slaves. There were a few *Indios* left, but they admitted nothing.

"There's not much more to tell," Verde went on. "We continued to live near the mouth of the Rio Grande and to send an expedition to Pacimé each generation in hopes someone would be there to meet us. We saw the emissaries of the Pope and avoided them, hoping someday an expedition of Knights Templar or Hebrews would come and we could share our knowledge with them. And now here you are!"

Dan shook his head. "You left out a few things about yourself."

"So I did, too," Verde replied. "My family, for our small group intermarried as well by taking native wives, never prospered or grew. We lived in frequent warfare with our neighbors. There were one hundred and sixty-seven, four women with child, in the village when I was sent away to school in Ireland and Scotland. I was gone twenty-one years wandering and learning. Then I returned to take my place among the sentinels. In my absence, Texas had become an independent country, and my village had been massacred in the fighting over the Nueces Strip. I am the last sentinel, the last Templar Knight."

"You poor man," said Sebriana. Overwhelmed by the sad story, she rose and went to hug him.

"Be careful," chided Roque. "You'll catch something." Sebriana sniffed at Roque, disgusted with his rude ill-will.

Gazing into the embers of the fire, Dan thought for a while as Sebriana hugged a delighted Verde. Preoccupied, he fixed on a minor distraction, an alien smell. "Why does the fire smell so? Like burnt sugar."

Rojo said, "It is the mesquite, the tree that grows thorns and beans."

Dan's mind continued to gnaw at puzzles. Coals glowed and disappeared. Logs collapsed in bursts of sparks. The fire was dying, but Dan did not move to feed it. The night was still and warm. Coyotes sang their disappointment to the stars. An owl hoo-hooed and flapped its wings, a dark shadow passing across the twinkling void.

Rojo muttered. "Someone will die tonight."

"One of us?" asked Roque.

"I think not," the Jicarilla replied.

"Our dreams then," Sebriana whispered.

Dan was agitated. He had to be sure. Aloud he said, "I can't let the quest die unless I'm sure." Suddenly his mind flooded with new questions. "Verde, did you meet Topper, Professor Pendarvis, at Roslyn?"

"Met him," the Last Templar replied, "liked him, traveled with him. Before you ask, I've known Al Pike, too. Nice enough fellow but I don't trust him. It seems to me, he can rationalize most anything."

"Did you know," Dan asked, "that Topper has preceded us into that Undiscovered Country . . ."

"From whose borne no traveler returns," Verde finished for Dan. "I heard. The world has lost a good man. Was it the work of Mormon Danites?"

"I think so," Dan replied. They lapsed into silence again as they mourned the loss of a brother. After a time Dan spoke. "He sent us, you know."

"I thought as much," Verde replied.

"You've implied the Ark was never here," Dan said, "nor is at Chaco any longer. Where is it?"

"That, Danny me lad, I don't know, and I've spent years looking. My family spent generations on the quest. As soon as the Knights realized the party sent out to hide the treasure was long overdue, they had men out searching. It's well hid wherever it is."

"Is there no hope?" Dan asked.

"Lad," Verde began, "there is always hope. The

Masters' Word is lost only until future generations shall find it anew. From massacres and catastrophes there are always survivors. It's clear from things I saw at Roslyn that some of the Templars made it back to Scotland from the scattering of the fleet and that they returned and made contact with someone who knew of the hiding place. Did Topper tell you of a line from the tower at Newport?" Dan nodded. "Did he tell you it passes north of Taos?"

Dan nodded. They were silent for a moment.

Verde looked at Dan. "What's the last thing Topper told you?"

"Hidden in the ritual," Dan replied. "The secret is hidden in the ritual."

"Did you do that?" Verde asked.

"Do what?" Dan asked.

"Let the ritual guide you," said the Last Knight. "Look, you've already performed a remarkable feat. You've followed a trail already 2,500 years cold all the way to Chaco. So I ask you again, did you let the ritual guide you?"

It was Rojo who answered. "We could have done more. We'd been following other sign up till then."

Verde responded. "Exactly. Up till then you'd been following old sign laid down by Hebrews come fresh from the Holy Land. Their descendants could no longer leave such clear sign. They'd lost most of their identity. The Templars took over laying signs, and they got the word back to Roslyn. Somewhere at the library, there must be a story long hid about the Knight or Knights who made that journey. The Freemasons took over the story, and they hid clues deep in the ritual."

They sat sucking on their pipes, except Sebriana who fashioned a huge cigarito from tobacco and corn husk. They were cheered by what they'd heard and were soon lost in deep reflection. The stars whirled overhead in their long slow dance. Time passed unnoticed. The sweet odor of burning mesquite became pleasant.

Then Verde spoke again. "There was a story told among my people of a man who laid out the plan of the Lodge using Pacimé as the Junior Warden's seat, somewhere far to the east is the Master's seat and far away in the west is the Senior Warden's seat. He drew a map. Afore you ask, no, I've never found it."

Roque scratched his head. "So how do we find it?"

"Ask the *N'deh*," Rojo responded. "If it is in Apache country, they will know."

"They are at war with the United States!" Dan exclaimed.

"Then we must ride boldly into their *rancheria* and ask hospitality," Rojo replied.

Roque spat out his pipe. "We can't take a woman into an Apache camp!"

Sebriana glared at him. "No, you can't, but she can take herself."

"Well, that's settled then," smiled Verde. "We ride with little chance of success into almost certain death. And we're bound to run into a fight with banditos Mexicanos, Apaches, or secesh or maybe all of them. What could be better?"

The next day they rode west into the Sierra Madre where the Apache were hunting *gavachos* and Mexicanos to slay. They sought the Apache and certain death probably by extended torture. As they rode, Dan checked his Hawkin. He thought it might be best to fire it and reload making sure he had fresh powder and a new cap. Then he'd do the same for his pistols. The noon halt was going to be noisy.

Taking in his surroundings, Dan realized that no one

description fit the Sierra Madre. Where he crossed the range, it had no more depth than forty miles, two days travel at most by mule. Uplands were covered in pine forest with piñon, live oak, and juniper below giving way to barren wastes. Dan noted an unfamiliar shrub. Roque called it the *manzanita*, little apple. Its limbs were covered in tiny hard berries this time of year. Dan realized they looked and tasted like tiny apples. Its bark was smooth and red as blood.

Mountains that seemed steep but not craggy came to abrupt cliffs that fell away one thousand feet.

A troop of animals crossed their path, pointed snouts low to the ground, rumps two feet high ending in long tapering tails. They reminded Dan of raccoons. Rojo called them coatimundi. Javelina, the desert pigs, Dan had seen before but never in such numbers. Toward dusk of the first night, a black cat larger than a bobcat leapt from a tree, screamed like a banshee, and vanished into the twilight.

Beyond the Sierra Madre, mountains sprouted like islands in a grassy sea. The land was divided by deep cañons. Working their way north, they crossed a well-watered grassland, green as Ireland, and entered a land of cinders pocked with cones of black rock. Ahead a large mountain loomed.

"*Sierra nevada*," Roque breathed, "snowy mountains, *muy alto*, very high."

Verde snorted. "Mountain men call these the Cherry Cows."

Sebriana smiled sweetly. "Civilized folk call them the Chiricahuas."

They followed a small stream into a cañon of that mountain.

"These are their mountains, I think," said Rojo, "the

Chiricahua. We are watched. Ride boldly, show no fear."

The cañon opened into a bowl ringed with pine, aspen, and oak. Scattered about the grassy meadow on both sides of the clear stream were fifteen dome shaped wikiups. Willow poles set in the ground, bent to shape, and tied with yucca strings formed the frame which was covered with a thatch of bear grass. Boys tended horses and cattle herds while others played at games of skill and daring. They dodged blunted spears and arrows launched by their fellows. The men wore broad breechclouts of white cotton whose sides almost touched on their hips and whose bottoms fell below their knees front and back. They wore loose-fitting shirts of cotton cloth, both white and patterned. Their moccasins were boot-like, rising to the knee with the rawhide sole turned up distinctly in the front to protect the toes. Their hair, bobbed in bangs across the front, reached to shoulder length at side and back and was bound with a red cloth headband. On the whole, they were a well-made people with nut brown skin and high, broad cheekbones. The women dressed in long, loose dresses gathered at the waist, let their hair grow long. The young women wore their hair gathered in the back around a cloth covered device creating a shape like a bone or butterfly.

Rojo hailed the camp and was confronted by a group of men. Their dark, brooding faces seemed threatening. However, the companions were soon invited to dismount and were then offered food.

Accepting a wooden bowl, Dan asked Rojo, "What is this?"

"A soup of roast meat and tule root."

Dan tasted. "It is most remarkably like potato."

Rojo nodded. "There is also acorn mash, young yucca shoots, and a sweet mash of baked mescal heart."

Dan swallowed and said, "We must offer them gifts." He rose and brought from the pack mules a small cask of black powder, plugs of tobacco, and skeins of trade beads.

They soon learned that most of the men spoke Spanish with varying degrees of skill which gave everyone a common language. The Apache passed around a pipe, and Verde passed back a bottle of rye. The Apache relaxed and told deadpan stories that soon had everyone laughing. They capered around, performing feats of skill and comedy making the friends welcome.

Rojo leaned in to Dan. "We need to talk to their shaman." Dan nodded his agreement. Rojo turned to the Apache leaders. "We need to speak to your keeper of wisdom."

"He lives apart from us, higher up the mountain, nearer to the Ghan, the mountain spirits. Tomorrow this young warrior will guide you to him." The leader lapsed into Apache.

Roque drew Dan and Rojo aside while Sebriana prattled with women and children. "Somewhere near at hand, Cochise and Mangas Coloradas are killing every white man they can find. They are close kin to these people. These are Cochise's warriors who have killed for his anger."

Rojo looked from one friend to the other. "They have honor. They have accepted us as guests. They might slay us on another day, but for now we are safe. A young warrior will guide us through their land as far as Ft. Buchanan. He will be our passport through *Apacheria*."

They made their beds near the edge of the Apache camp and arose early in the morning. Their guide led them through a maze of passes and cañons to a place on the east side of the mountains. They crossed a landscape of black, volcanic rock, sharp and hard on the feet of horse and man, coming ever closer to the tall, snow-capped mountains.

"We're walking on cinders," said Dan. "It's like the whole country has been burned up.

A tiny stream flowed out of the canyon they followed whose sides loomed far overhead.

A voice called in Spanish from above them. "I've been waiting for you." An ancient Indian sat upon a flat rock like a high pulpit.

"Never be astonished by the words of a shaman," whispered Roque. "It's all tricks and lies."

"That is often the case, Roque Vigil," boomed the shaman from above. He was at least one hundred meters distant.

Roque was startled. "There is no way he could have heard me." Roque had the sense to say no more.

"Hail to you, Ancient One," said Rojo greeting the shaman for all of them. The shaman dressed as did the other Chiricahua with the addition of numerous pouches, adorned and unadorned, and ornaments of metal, bone, feather, fur, and glass.

"Come up!" bade the shaman. "I have something to show you."

They dismounted, ground-staking their mules and Roque's *grullo* stallion, and began the steep climb. "Come to the top of my seat of *Power*. See here. Look on the sign."

"Saints preserve us," said Verde. "After all these years, here 'tis."

The seat faced east toward the rising sun. To one side, facing up from the rock was a sign. The influence of Pacimé was clear in its form. It might have been an elaborately decorated sword or, though carved in the stone with obvious care, a poorly executed *pajo*, the fancifully arrayed prayer stick made from an agave sword. More clearly it was the emblem on the symbolic pikes carried by the deacons, escorts, and sentinels of the Senior Warden who sits in the west with the deacons to his left and right controlling the doors.

"But how?" Dan murmured overwhelmed by what he saw.

"Follow me," cried the shaman leading them down the hillside to a boulder that towered twenty-five feet above the streambed. It was covered in miraculous signs, in the style of Pacimé and Mimbres, elegantly carved into the rock facing the sky.

Sebriana searched the signs. "This is wonderful! I see mountain sheep, mountains, and a bat. Those wavy lines must be a river, and the curlicues that look like waves must represent rapids."

Rojo addressed himself to the shaman. "Ancient One, Revered Father, what can it mean?"

The shaman smiled. "How would I know? I am but a poor Chiricahua shaman who comes to this place to draw on its *Power*. Can't you feel it throbbing through you? Draw it in. Absorb it. Hold it. You will need it for the future. You have a very difficult path to travel."

Dan nodded. He could feel it. The ground seemed to vibrate as if some great water-wheel were turning a millstone or as if a steam train on the Long Island Rail Road was passing by. "It is a map, but its conventions are unknown to me. Is south at the top as the Chinese draw maps or north as we do?"

"Maybe I can help, Danny-mi-lad," said Verde stepping into the void. "Some things I know that you do not. The bat which we see here between peaceful river and rapids is the name my ancestors gave to the San Juan, River of the Bat. The mountain sheep with the so carefully drawn entrails appearing inside a mountain might indicate the San Juan Mountains from which the river flows up by Wolf Creek Pass. They called those mountains Heart or Spirit of the Mountain Sheep."

"I will copy each sign and the whole map into Topper's book," Dan said. "We have our map, and it takes us back north to Chaco and beyond."

Not all of the symbols made sense to them, making it important to copy exactly and not let interpretation sway them. Sebriana came up with the idea of using a bolt of gingham they'd brought with them as trade-stuff to make a rubbing of the whole. A mix of charcoal bound in lard was the best rub they could come up with. It worked well enough.

One set of symbols consisted of concentric circles, something that might have been two towers and a mountain topped by a mountain sheep. A line touched the side of the concentric circles and passed between the towers touching both before ending at the mountain. Dan couldn't guess its meaning, and even Sebriana and Verde were befuddled.

"Noon approaches," said Dan searching their baggage for his sextant. He took the noon siting and recorded the location in Topper's book.

They camped there that night by the Seat of *Power* talking with and questioning the shaman. He did not give them his name.

Rojo explained to Dan. "The Apache feel telling their name gives others *Power* over them. That's why we use nicknames and why we do not tell even those to strangers. Calling him Ancient One is good enough."

Their Apache guide signaled that they should continue upstream. A hawk cried and circled overhead, staying with them as they made their way. The Chiricahua pointed with his lip up the steeply sloping hillside to where the hawk landed on a boulder. Climbing, they discovered more symbols like they had seen. There were no more animals, only abstract figures similar to those on the flat rock.

Suddenly Dan stopped bemused. "I can read these. The word 'king' is repeated three times."

"I don't see it," said Roque.

"In Greenport, a Chinese sailor taught me a little of his language. The word king is very simple. It is a family name, and here it is, crudely made as if the person was illiterate, knowing only how to write his name. Look for more."

"These symbols have *Power*," said Rojo.

"The Chinese think so." Dan searched the hillside and found more. "This one that looks like legs with something shiny set on top means bright. And this other with a big head and small arms like a baby wrapped in a blanket means child."

"Who could have put them here?" asked Roque.

"Well, there's too many that look like Chinese," said Dan, "for them not to be. They don't look like other rock art we've seen. Chinese sailors had stories about a great sailor who lived a thousand years ago. Cheng Ho, they called him, and said that on his fourth voyage he discovered America. Until now, I didn't believe it."

Verde spoke up. "Bishops and apostles went to the East long ago. My people knew of their going but not what became of them. They sought a home of safety and the protection of the Ark. Perhaps they sailed with Cheng Ho."

Dan thought a while. "In Topper's journal there are vague references to Chinese Christians. The churches in Rome and Constantinople lost track of them when the Western Empire began to crumble. "

"What can the symbols mean?" asked Roque still puzzled.

Sebriana brightened. "Isn't it obvious? Three kings, the triune God. The bright one must be a spirit and the last is a son. Father, Son, and Holy Ghost. There were Chinese Christians here."

Dan pondered what could have brought Chinese Christians across a broad ocean and desert. They'd gone east when Rome was still receiving goods from China across the Silk Road. There had always been rurmors of their existence in Cathay. That much seemed right. But, what brought them over the ocean to these remote and dangerous mountains? Only a prize as great as the Ark of the Covenant would have been sufficient. Something was drawing men from East and West to this place and had been for a long time.

Roque and Verde thought they had come this far seeking the seat of the Senior Warden in the West. And they had found it near the Chinese symbols. The clues all pointed to the Ark being the Altar in the middle of the Lodge. That would have meant the Ark was at Pacqimé, but they did not find it there. And the symbolism was repeated at Chaco where the great *kiva* should have been home to the Ark. Dan thought it almost surely had been at one time. The road that joined Pacqimé to Chaco also went north up a flight of winding stairs. And the symbols near the Senior Warden's seat pointed to a location north of Chaco in the San Juan Mountains.

Dan rode in silence with his thoughts through mountains and dusty plains wondering why the Ancient One had directed them to the west instead of to the north back to Chaco. Near springs in a river that rose in the mountains and disappeared in the plain their guide halted, gestured and spoke.

"What does he say?" asked Dan looking at Rojo.

"He talks of men like turtles mounted on horses, the first horses the People ever saw, passing this way heading north searching for Seven Cities."

Roque swelled with pride. "He must mean Coronado."

"I think so," said Dan. "More people seeking Seven Cities in the north."

"And treasure!" howled Verde. "The Pope would only have sent them after great treasure. We're on the right path, boyos me lads."

Dan thought, then why is the Ancient One pointing us west?

Dan and his companions continued westward with their guide, crossing the mountains and descending into a great valley and following a clear stream that settled into intermittent pools choked with water plants. Their stock was coming from a day of resting on fat grass. The Apache pushed them hard through a low pass between two ranges. Cottonwood and sycamores hid a river that snaked through the valley.

"It is called San Pedro by the Spanish," said Rojo. "They say the conquistador Coronado came this way. The mountain men call it the Beaver River."

The north-flowing river moved slowly through beaver dams many of which were in decay, their beaver trapped in years past. They camped there and had a swim, Sebriana inviting Dan to guard her private pool.

They rode across the valley of the San Pedro joining a stream that flowed from the west. Coming near a small mountain range, they passed an aging adobe fortified rancho long abandoned. Beyond the grass grew thick, and hillsides were abundant with oak, juniper, and manzanita. The stream they followed grew small and wandered away south while they continued west passing a hollow that was the start of a northward flowing stream.

Dan asked Rojo about this, and he conferred with their guide. "Three streams start here, he says. One flows southwest. We'll come to it soon. One north, one east, and on the other side of those southern hills, not far, a fourth goes south."

"Strange," Dan replied. "We are surrounded with mountains."

It was a good land and a fine place to ranch with many necessities close at hand.

Near the headwaters of the stream that flowed to the southwest, called Sonoita Creek, they found Ft. Buchanan. A more miserable place Dan had never seen. Its ill-made adobes were of the type called *jacal*, corner posts stuck in the ground, branches woven between and mud daubed on top. There was no discernible pattern in the layout of the fort. It was as if someone had spilled a greasy stew and let the mess lie. Flies were drawn to the horses of the dragoons. Worst of all, it was the feeding ground of swarms of mosquitoes, so thick they blocked the sun.

Dan looked around for their guide, but he was nowhere to be seen.

Rojo grinned. "Apaches don't believe in long farewells."

South along the creek in the gathering dusk, noise and light beckoned them. Large adobe buildings on either side of the creek exuded music, laughter, and the smell of good cooking. They were drawn to the quieter of the two by the aroma of food. Under a *ramada*, a brush shelter, in the courtyard, tables were set out and thickly occupied by soldiers and civilians alike eating and drinking. At one table, a Mexican girl dealt *monte* and smoked a cigarito, putting Dan in mind of Santa Fe's Doña Tules.

The proprietor, a statuesque woman well over six feet tall with hair as red as the recent sunset, guided them to a table whose only occupant was a young, bearded lieutenant.

"Mind if we join you?" Dan asked.

"Not at all," he replied. "I'd enjoy the company. As commander of Company C, my men and even the civilians hesitate to socialize with me. The only officers here now are myself and Colonel Pitcairn Morrison. My name's George Bascom, Seventh Infantry."

"I'm Dan Trelawney, and this is Roque Vigil, Doña Sebriana Ruiz, Rodado Verde, and Peregrino Rojo."

The lieutenant rose from his chair and bowed toward Sebriana. Shaking Rojo's hand, he stared fixedly at Rojo's face and eyes. "You're dressed like a Mexican don, but you look Apache. Have you come to kill me?"

"I am Jicarilla Apache, but, no, *mangani*, I will let you live…for now."

"It wasn't my idea, you know," Bascom said. "I'll own to havin' done the deed, if reluctantly. Where did you come from?"

"Santa Fe," Dan replied.

"Really? No one has gotten through without an escort in months. Even the mail has stopped," said the lieutenant.

Dan pointed to his friend with his lip. "Rojo is our escort. We've heard about your confrontation with Cochise. I'm sure you're pestered for details, so I won't ask."

"With the soldiers, I am a hero," Bascom said. "Most of the civilians are less enthused because the mail has stopped, and Cochise has become unmanageable. But what can we do? Too few men, too few mules, and the dragoons are too far from the settlements.

He looked up at the tall woman. "Western, fetch these folks some dinner, please."

"Western?" Roque questioned.

Bascom smiled. "That's what they call her. Comes from Great Western, the big ship. She's been with the Army for a long time. A hero of the Mexican War, she manned a cannon at Ft. Brown in Texas. Now she provides everything a soldier needs, laundry and sewing, home cooked food, gambling, liquor, good company. Some of her girls cozy up to the boys, and Western protects them and keeps them safe. She's quite a lady."

Mexican girls bustled about serving food and drinks. Western returned with their dinner of beef stew and bread.

Roque looked up at her. Dan had never seen such admiration in his eyes. And she was returning the look.

"Western," Dan said, "why have you built an enclosed courtyard?"

"Is he kidding?" she asked looking at Bascom. "George, haven't you told him?"

"Told him what, Sarah?" he responded. "That the night watch hides for fear the officers moving between buildings with cocked and ready pistols will shoot them? Or that the Apache are inside Fort Buchanan after dark stealing stock and anything that isn't nailed down? Do you want me to tell them that the Apache go where they like and steal what they wish, and we can't do much about it, or that Baldy Ewell was the only one who ever had any success pursuing them? Should I tell them that everyone between here and Tucson has lost friends and family? That Mowry's mine is under siege? It's all true."

Western grabbed a chair and sat with them as the full dark closed in. Her helpers lighted lanterns around the courtyard. She was with them but intent on Roque.

Roque gazed into her green eyes. "Señora, your eyes

are green emeralds. I have never seen the like."

"Call me Sarah," she replied.

"Your cooking," he continued, "is *muy delicioso* even if it lacks chili." Roque never lapsed into speaking Mexican, nor did he show much of an accent when talking to *gavachos* unless he was angry.

Dan thought his friend's attraction to the redhead might be getting serious, though he didn't think anger was the emotion driving Roque.

They finished dinner. Verde's attention had been attracted by a character with huge mustaches and attired in a broad-brimmed hat and knee high boots. He swaggered, bragged, twirled his pistol, told tall tales, and boasted loudly though with a gentle touch and a good deal of self-deprecating humor. Their green-hatted friend went to drink with the group gathering around the stranger joining in the fun.

"Jack Swilling," said Bascom indicating the stranger. "Apparently, he's really done most of those things he brags about, and he's quite deadly with those pistols."

Dan looked around the table. Roque and Western had disappeared. Sebriana cuddled against him. Rojo sat calmly.

"What brought people here?" Dan asked Bascom.

"The mines," he replied. "Mowry's aren't far away, a few miles down a side cañon. There are more at Cerro Colorado beyond the Santa Cruz River. The miners need protection from the Indians, so Fort Buchanan is here. The soldiers and the miners need to eat, so there are farmers and stockmen all along Sonoita Creek all the way to the Santa Cruz and north up the Santa Cruz to Tucson. These Santa Rita Mountains west of us separate the Sonoita Valley from the Santa Cruz. The climate's better on this side. It's hot as Hell on the other."

A great commotion arose below them along the creek. Cattle bawled, and horses' hooves pounded, speeding up the valley toward Fort Buchanan. Streaks of flame stabbed the night followed by the thunder of pistol shots. The ruckus moved rapidly up valley and through the fort. Sometime later, they heard horses approaching. A large man in a broad straw sombrero dismounted, pouring powder and dropping ball into the cylinders of his pistol even as he approached. Long tangled gray hair and greasy fringed buckskins marked him as a mountain man. Missing fingers and a patch over one eye marked him as one Dan had met before.

He roared to the serving girls and assembly in general. "Whiskey, bring whiskey. None of your mescal now. Whiskey for my riders."

"And beer for his horses," said Rojo under his breath.

"Hey, Ole Mose, you ketch 'em?" hollered Jack Swilling.

Mose bellowed again. "Thievin' devils got clean away. They drove Grundy's stock straight through Ft. Buchanan. We had to stop lest the sentries shoot us. Git bolder every day, they do." He looked around for open tables and chairs.

"Wagh, Trelawney, Danny Trelawney, wal, ah'll be et fer a tater. It's you indeed. Does that mean my brother Kit is here, too?"

"If he were, you'd be paying a debt," Dan said. Moses Carson was Kit's half-brother and older by almost two decades. In Santa Fe, he'd run up debts against Kit's credit and skipped town. Dan didn't think Kit minded as much as he did. There's no accounting for kin-feeling even though they had never known each other well. Mose joined Bascom's table unbidden.

"Pinal Apaches, Lieutenant," Moses continued. A

strange vision passed through Dan's mind, a patch-eyed Moses leading the Children of Israel to the Promised Land from the quarterdeck of a pirate ship. "Not Cherry-cows! Cochise's people don't raid over here. The Pinals would consider it poaching and they don't team up 'cause they don't like each other much, even if they are kin." Mose fixed his one eye on Dan daring him to say anything.

"I understand, Mr. Carson," replied Bascom, "but the scouts followed the trail of the oxen and Felix Ward as far as the Dragoon Mountains, right to Cherry-cow, eh, Chiricahua country."

Ole Mose grunted and belched while Dan held his eye. "I heard this country is full of scoundrels and murderers."

"It is that," said the lieutenant apparently unaware that Dan was needling Mose. "When I first arrived here, Major Ewell was holding a murderer at the fort where he'd kept the assassin fully four months. The closest a judge would come was Mesilla. There was no way to transport the villain and the witnesses there so the major had to let him go. The worst ones stay up by Tucson where they can rob travelers and soldiers and *vaqueros* in town for a good time and don't have to worry as much about Apaches."

"Lookee here, Danny," said Mose, "it takes strong men to build such country, men with tough bark on who know which away the stick floats. These are shinin' times if you're daring enough and strong enough. You gots to be ready to put it to yer enemies right up to the Green River and willing to make your own justice."

Dan thought, that's right the country needs men who would willingly ram home their blade right up to the Green River, the maker's mark stamped on the blade of a knife at the hilt, even into the back of a brother. His nose wrinkled in distaste. Mose was one such. He'd borrowed against his brother's name driving Kit almost to bankruptcy.

Bascom stood tall and straight in his uniform, a fine soldier. "Gentlemen and lady, forgive me. I've finished my dinner and must return to the fort."

"I'll be goin', too," said Mose. "I'm greeze hungry, and I wanna git me some arwerdenty 'n' git *loco* drunk. This ole coon is gonna have him some fun, m'be find him a robe-warmer fer the night." He winked at Sebriana.

Dan loved Kit like a father, but Mose, old enough to be his grandfather, was hard to take, though he was real and had surely done a thing or two in his time. Dan thought Mose could be hard to understand, even for those who've been around mountain men.

Content, Sebriana snuggled against Dan's side. Rojo looked at him. "So, Dan, what are we doing here and how long do we stay?"

"We need what supplies we can gather and to let the stock graze and fatten," Dan replied. "We'll stay a week or so. We've a long trip ahead of us, all the way to Chaco by way of Mesilla."

Dan didn't realize then just how long that trip would be. The last thing he saw before Sebriana and he found their bedroll was a sight more heinous than any Dan had seen before. He prayed never to see it again. A drunken Moses Carson was dancing with an inebriated Rodado Verde.

Dan and Sebriana spent the night on the ground. It was too late to find a room when they turned in. Tomorrow, Dan promised himself, tomorrow we will sleep in a bed.

The early summer morning dawned fresh and clear, the sky blue from horizon to horizon, a shinin' day as Mose might say. Toward noon, clouds blew in from the southwest gathering behind the mountains and then tumbling over into the Sonoita Valley. The day grew blazing hot. The clouds reared up higher and higher, turning from white billows to black, threatening thunderheads. The billows boiled and surged like breakers on a sea of blue.

The storm was late in arriving; so was Roque. Dan didn't expect to see Verde until the sound of cork pulled from a jug woke him. Roque was excited when he entered the room.

"Danito, I am in love. Doña Colorada is everything I have ever wanted in a woman. She is smart and knows how to make money and keep it, too. She is powerful and directs her own business. All people respect her. She has soft skin smooth like cream and smells like flowers in a dream. She makes love with purpose like a man. She really enjoys it. She has my heart. I will never love another. Perhaps I will stay here with her."

Dan was concerned. "Are you sure, Roque? Are you sure that she's the one. You have had many lovers and fine things to say of each and every one of them."

"I loved them all. Each one was special in her way, but there has never been one like this," he replied. "This is one I can respect. I think about her every moment. She is my heart, my life. I cannot live without her."

"There is going to be a storm," Dan told him. "We need to find rooms."

Roque was unconcerned. "The rooms here are already held, but I think Western will let you sleep in her *sala*."

Dan thought some privacy and comfort might be in order. "Let's see if we can find beds. The Boundary Hotel is just across the valley. Let's get the others. See if Western will let us leave our stock in her corral. I don't want to be busy moving them when this storm breaks."

The air was hushed, humid, and expectant as they set out across the valley. Sudden gusts carried cobwebs, dust, and dry grass.

The storm broke behind them as they stepped into the common room of the Boundary. A bolt of lightning flashed, splitting an oak tree a dozen yards behind them followed by a continuous roll of thunder like battery after battery of artillery firing. Wind blew the rain until it didn't fall but flew across the ground in fist-sized packets that pummeled the door. The fury of the storm blew tree limbs before it. Lightning flashed along the underside of the clouds. Their bastion held for the moment though outside the storm flattened the world before it. Water gushed from *canales* and ran down paths cutting ravines where men had walked.

"The first storm of the season is always the worst," said Paddy Graydon from behind his bar. "I'm for having another drink to fortify me ag'inst it. What about you, Sergeant Dunn, and you, Pengelly?"

"Aye, that first bolt of lightning must have killed me," said Verde, "to see the likes of these standing before me. I thought they'd died and gone to Hell. Is this then the canteen at Fiddlers Green?"

"Is the whole Regiment of Dragoons here then?" Dan asked.

"You know it's not, Danny," replied Sergeant Pengelly. "Just Baldly Ewell's old company."

"Is Ewell here?" Dan asked.

"Was here," said Dunn, "and well loved by the people. He was an effective fighter in this desert, but he's gone for months to Fort Bliss on business, and I t'ink from there he may a gone south, don't ye know. The new commander is still learning, and we've have come down from Fort Breckenridge to educate him.""

"How comes Sergeant Graydon to be behind the bar?" asked Roque.

"He's sergeant no more," replied Pengelly. "Took his retirement and built him this fine hotel."

Graydon's face darkened. "Trelawney, you know better than to bring a woman in here." He looked at Sebriana more closely. "Never be minding now, I see it's Doña Loca. Doña, be after making ye'self to home. Ye're welcome here."

"We need rooms, Paddy," Dan said to Graydon.

"And I'd be having them, too."

Dunn caught Roque's eye. "Are y' still larnin' to play the pipes, laddie?"

"I'm getting quite good," replied Roque smiling. "Everyone knows it except Danito who constantly insults the way I play."

Dan gave his friend an evil eye. "I'm the only one that's heard him play that wasn't in a position to run away."

"Have ye got your pipes with you, me lad?" cried Dunn. Roque nodded. "Then ye shall have a wee audience this ev'n. Nothin' like the pipes to hold the monsters of night and storm at bay."

They fell to handshaking, backslapping, and exchanging toasts with old comrades. Graydon, short and thickset with curly black hair, had rooms for them all. Graydon knew Rojo and Sebriana well and so gave no further argument to woman or Indian being in his establishment. Proper women tended to cause problems in establishments where there was drinking, gambling and working women, some of them Indian and prepared to provide close companionship. Outside the storm raged.

The morning air was washed and scrubbed crystal clear. The ground was a tangle of torn tree limbs, uprooted manzanita, and desert broom hiding a maze of new rivulets and clefts.

One of Western's betties, the servant girls who assisted her, told Sebriana about deep pools in the stream that were well screened by trees and brush. A half hour's walk took Dan and Sebriana to the pools, and the day being hot they stripped off and had a swim.

Lying on the bank afterwards enjoying their privacy and the warm sun, Dan and Sebriana were aroused by a crashing and splashing in the brush upstream.

"It must be *el oso*, a grizzly bear," yelped Sebriana reaching for one of her pistols.

Dan jumped up the bank grabbing for his Hawkin and bringing it to full cock at his shoulder in one motion. Brush crowding the stream above their pool wavered and shook with the passage of some huge animal growling hideously, splashing down the creek. Deep in the thicket someone screamed. Dan drew bead where the beast must emerge and waited.

Dan saw dark hair and beady black eyes first and sighted between them, beginning the slow squeeze of the trigger. Only then did he recognize Roque and aim behind him. Roque came bursting from the brush into Dan and Sebriana's pool. His clothing was completely ripped from his body, his mouth gaped in silent scream, his eyes wide in terror as he looked back over his shoulder. Behind him came Sarah, her arms extended toward Roque, red hair streaming, and dressed as her mother first saw her. Their apparent screams resolved into laughter as they sped across the pool oblivious to the presence of observers.

From downstream, they heard Roque's plaintive call.

"Queen of my heart, I love you but sometimes a man must rest!"

Sebriana fell back laughing, a lovely sight, and then jumped to her feet savagery clouding her face. "You didn't look, did you?"

"No, *mija*, I would never look at another woman, only enough to see her hair is red everywhere."

"*Pendejo*," she cried, fell naked on Dan's body, and forced her will upon him.

It was mid-afternoon before they noticed the world again, having slept and bathed and made love and done it all again. Sebriana glanced over northeast. Dan turned and seeing smoke came alert. It came thick and black from the direction of Fort Buchanan. Dan realized that grass burns with a white smoke and brush brown. Pine trees send up black smoke and so do burning houses. There were no pine trees near the fort.

Roque ran back up stream holding his shirt as he fastened his britches. Western was close behind him. They ran for their mules and Roque's *grullo* stallion in Western's corral and saddled them. They were soon joined by Rojo, Verde, and Graydon. Before they arrived at the fort, most of the men who lived along the valley were with them. The fort was burning.

The infantry and dragoons were drawn up in march order. The major in charge was locked in heated debate with Mose Carson.

"That's a load o' buffler wood," Mose yelled. "Ye can't just up an' 'banden usns. Y' know which way the stick floats. There's more injuns than we can handle. What with the Jackass Mail gone, we can't even get a letter t' other settlements 'r Santa Fee. Y' could at least ha' lef' us yer supplies."

"Orders, Mr. Carson," replied the major. "I don't like

'em, but I'm sworn to follow 'em. They arrived by courier last night. I was ordered to march immediately for Fort Craig on the Rio Grande and burn the fort and all supplies behind me so that they don't fall into the hands of the secesh."

Dan realized he meant secessionists. They weren't called Rebs; they were secesh.

Paddy Graydon saw Dan's puzzlement. "Folks in Tucson elected Granville Oury their representative to the secech South. It seems the Army has reason to be concerned."

Dan recognized how hard-to-come-by supplies were in Arizona where everything came from far away and how important they would be to either Army.

Dan looked at Paddy. "He's cuttin' these people's throats."

Like a great grizzly bear, Mose Carson was reared up on his hind legs towering over the major. "There's gonna be a damn site more secesh aroun' here win yer gone. Leave us somethin' to fight with. At least the Texians is offerin' t' defen' us."

The major turned on his heel and stalked back to his column. Mose hurled a road apple after him striking him in the back of the head. Twisting his neck, jutting his chin, and straightening his hat, the major deigned not to notice. Mose picked up another horse apple.

Dan grabbed his arm. "No, Mose, don't. One more, and he'll have to shoot you for sedition. These are perilous times."

The column marched away leaving the Gadsden Purchase, Arizona, west of Mesilla undefended. Dan figured the soldiers would stop on the Rio Grande to defend Santa Fe and Colorado. Like a lot of folks on the frontier, he had some sympathy with the Southern states that were paying high tariffs and getting little in return. Roads, canals, railroads, and harbors were being built in the north. It was one thing for Texas to secede, at the same time it was clear to Dan that Texas intended an empire in the west, and the local residents would be given little say. There were secesh, those who favored secession, in Arizona, and though they were few, they were a very vocal minority.

Hours later, Paddy Graydon galloped after the military, pausing long enough to tell Dan that without the military he had no business. Now in complete possession of Graydon's Boundary Hotel, the friends made themselves at home. Sebriana organized the girls in the kitchen.

That night a rider came in from the south. "Mowry's gold mines have been raided!"

Verde sucked on his pipe, withdrew it, and blew a smoke ring. "Who done it, boyo?"

The rider gathered his wits. "Pinal 'paches most like, I think. Stock was takened, and the workers was hole up fur three days." He stopped to pant. "Mr. Mowry says he's decided that he kin no longer operate without pertection."

Dan learned later that Mowry stayed and continued to operate the mine; however, with the military gone, other mines closed. Soon there was no reason for anyone to remain along Sonoita Creek. A prosperous community packed up and left, heading for Tubac where they intended to weather the war. Dan and his friends followed the wagon train.

They descended from piney lofts, oaken groves, and manzanita glens into chaparral scrubland of craggy rock. Scrub gave way to cactus wasteland. Down its center ran a tiny stream, the Santa Cruz, flowing north to Tucson and the low desert, a narrow band of green in an earthly

Hell. The heat made breathing and talking difficult. Sunbaked Tubac tried feebly to shelter in the shadow below its hill and tiny presidio without much luck. Even the tall cottonwoods along the Santa Cruz River were too far off to be much help. Its lone street ran parallel to the river ending at a building labeled Sonoran Exploration and Mining Company. Church and presidio topped the hill. Dust drifted toward the ground from adobe buildings that seemed to have sprouted from the earth like untidy mushrooms. Juan Largo sat in the shade of a slowly crumbling building and stretched his game leg. The strangers would find him in time.

Sebriana tried to be discrete with her questions. There was no need to tell strangers that they sought an object of *Power* and gold. Verde, Dan, and Roque showed less discretion in asking about old trade routes and other mysteries. Rojo observed and it was he who detected Juan Largo watching the friends.

"That one watches us," said Rojo to Dan pointing with his lip. "He is Apache Manso."

"I don't know that tribe."

"It means 'tame Apache.' His people live near Bac and work as scouts for the Mexicans."

Dan considered this. "Are we in danger? Is he working for one of the groups that follow us?"

Rojo was silent for an uncomfortably long time. Dan almost asked him again when Rojo replied. "I do not think so. He is an old man. He might have much to teach us."

Rojo walked to the old man and spoke in Apache. "Ancient one, can I get you some food and tequila?"

"Your speech is strange. I do not understand some words, but I think you offer me food and wine. Yes, you can give me these things. Where do you come from?"

Juan Largo rose to his full height. He was taller than Rojo dressed in a broad, high-peaked, straw hat and loose-fitting cotton trousers and shirt, frayed at cuff and wrist. A serape covered his shoulders. His thin cheeks spoke of long intervals between meals.

Watching, Dan realized this man had been large and powerful and might still be counted a dangerous man though sitting, his back to an adobe wall, he hid it well.

They turned in at a cantina where Juan Largo ate heartily and edged closer to Sebriana.

She asked, "Juan Largo, how old are you?"

"Many summers. Mature enough to appreciate a woman like you."

She blushed.

"You are not Indio," he said, "or you would not blush so. You would know it is true."

Roque squirmed in his chair. "*Viejo*, do you know the secrets of the old ones?"

Largo ignored him.

Verde jeered. "He don't know nothin'."

"Senior Juan," Dan addressed him, "we seek news of our ancestors who passed this way long ago."

Juan ate hungrily, scooping frijoles and meat into his mouth with a tortilla. When the beans were gone, *posole*, hominy with chili and pork, was put before him and, that too, soon disappeared. "A *pollo* would be nice," said Juan, and it was set before him. Roque and Verde squirmed impatiently. Dan tried not to show what he was feeling. Juan Largo belched quietly as he poured himself a glass of tequila.

It was late afternoon. Except for the friends and Juan Largo, the dark, low ceilinged cantina was deserted.

"Father," said Rojo, "tell me a story of long ago and of the very place where it happened. I want to know of white men who visited long before Padre Kino."

Dan noticed Largo's eyes flash at the mention of the priest. Dan looked closely at Juan Largo who was so very tall. Mexicans would call him *guido*, blonde, though Anglos would call his coloring auburn or brown. His features looked more German than Indian. Dan wouldn't accuse the padre of breaking his oath, but Juan Largo looked like he might descend from the tall, Austrian Jesuit.

The old man became quiet, his whole body silenced as he thought and remembered. "It is a very old tale, seldom told. I heard it from my grandfather when I was very young. Long, long ago it happened at Painted Cave, in that very place. Two men came across the desert from the rising sun. They followed the river you call Babocomari. They had light hair and metal skin and hats. Their skin was burned red by the sun. We had never seen that before. The N'deh, the People, do not burn. They had come far carrying strange weapons. They carried a bow as tall as a man. None of our people could draw the bow. We thought it strange. We watched them from afar as one watches wild game to learn what it will do.

Juan drank a glass of tequila and continued, "One was very weak. His friend helped him, but soon he fell and did not rise. His friend lifted him on his shoulders and carried him. That is when we approached. The man was too tired to resist. We soon showed him that his friend had already started his journey to the next life. By signs, the living man showed us that he wanted to bury his friend in some high place that could be seen from a distance and found again should he return. Or so we thought and took him to Painted Cave.

"The People do not like to touch the dead. The stranger carried his friend by himself. It was very hard, for the way to Painted Cave is steep and difficult. The Painted Cave contains the *Power* symbols of the ancient ones. It is a place of *Power*. We helped the one dig a hole for grave. He spent the night with a small fire chipping the rock making symbols we did not understand. In the morning, he thanked us and began anew his journey heading back the way he had come. It was long ago, my ancestors have said. It is a strange story." Juan went silent.

Roque glared. "*Viejo*, you cannot expect us to believe this story. You made it up."

Rojo looked at Roque reproachfully.

Juan Largo spoke. "My grandfather taught me. He taught me to remember and recite stories exactly as they were told to me. This is what happened long ago at Painted Cave at that very place."

"Father," said Sebriana softly, "will you take us there?"

"If it were not for this Coyote," Juan looked at Roque, "I would gladly. Since he thinks the story is not true, he will have to pay. I need a horse and saddle . . ."

"Done," said Dan.

Juan smiled. "And a rifle and a revolver."

Dan smiled. "That seems fair."

"And a . . ."

"Enough, father, enough. No more."

Juan looked at Dan. "You have some wisdom, young man. I would have gone for just the horse and saddle."

They started out in the morning ascending to jagged mountains from the river in the desert. Slogging through dust that smelled of horse sweat and saddle-leather, they descended into the lush, green valley of Sonoita Creek and ascended passing Fort Buchanan. Mountains rose blue in the distance across a rolling, grassy plain.

"There." Juan pointed with his lip. Ahead a mountain rose like a thumb from the smallest range in view.

He led them into a valley hemmed by mountains to a wash that rose steeply.

"We go on foot."

The climb was brutal, the stones in the trail sharp and loose. Gaining the pass that looked out across a stream, the Babocomari, to a tall range.

"This way," said Juan leading them down a narrow path where the cap-rock rose sheer on their right and the scree slope, decomposed shale slick as grease, fell away steeply to the valley far below. "In here."

It was an aerie, a place a Valkyrie might call home, but one which would terrify mere mortals, Dan thought. A pile of sticks housed eggshell and downy feathers, signs it might have been an eagle's home. The cave was as Juan had said, painted in swirls and concentric circles that seemed to form a night sky constellation. There was no doubt this place held *Power*, *Power* of the Air and of the Mountain's Heart, *Power* of the Eagle and of the Sky.

"I'll take a sighting on the noon sun," said Dan feeling as though he might be desecrating the place.

Rojo stood rooted, his breath coming in gasps. He could feel the *Power*.

"I do not see a grave." Roque chuckled.

Juan pointed with his lip back to the entrance and a flat stone covered deep in dust. Dan knelt beside it and blew into the dust. As it flew away, runes were revealed. Dan swept with his hand and blew again to clear the signs.

Dan looked up. "These weren't made by Indians."

"No," responded Roque. "I think an eagle has scratched the rock with his talons."

Verde spoke. "I've seen such before, in England and

Scotland on the standing stones left by the Saxon invaders. I can read them a little."

"There are notes in Topper's journal." Dan copied the runes afraid to pause here long enough to translate them. He didn't want to get caught here for the night unable to descend the trail in the dark.

An eagle cried and riding a thermal buffeted by the wind held itself steady outside the cave and gazed in. Sebriana turned and stood looking directly into the creature's eyes, enthralled. She stood still until the eagle cried and banked away. And still she stood transfixed.

Dan noticed her odd behavior. "Sebriana, are you all right?"

She said nothing. He stood and looked into her eyes. She was far away, it seemed, for he saw no one looking back.

Fearful, he said, "We must get out of here."

Dan led Sebriana by the hand; she did not resist.

They camped in the valley at the mouth of the wash near a good spring. Dan worried about Sebriana who made the evening meal without speaking. Distracted, Dan worked through Topper's notes with Verde's help.

"She'll be all right, boyo."

Dan nodded without conviction. "Topper recorded the story of a 12th century Englishman who sailed west with friends. There was some suggestion that this was not unusual, that fishermen made this trip frequently. But there was something special about Rough Hurech. He was in search of rumored churches in the west."

In time, with Verde's help and Topper's notes, they worked out a translation of the runes Dan had copied.

> The body lays,
> Rough Hurech here,

He enjoyed life and merriment
The Secret he stole coming hence
Rough Hurech's body, fame and glory
Now lie in dust beyond Eden

"What does it mean?" Roque asked.

"I think," said Dan, "only that we've found Rough Hurech."

"He sought something," Rojo said, "and came this far to find it."

Verde glanced at him. "Aye, laddie, he did. He came a long way, and if he came, others must have come, too. That cross on the stone, it was the Cross of Lorraine, a Templar symbol."

"And Masonic, too," said Dan. "It seems odd that Topper had part of the inscription and its translation in his notes."

Verde cleared his throat. "Part of the story is missing. Rough Hurech's friend, Bold Sutton he was called, returned alone to England. He was a broken man, and worse, no one believed his tales. He died soon after."

Roque scowled. "How could one man make such a journey alone? Where did he get a boat to sail to England?"

Dan looked at his friend. "He carried a good English bow to get his food and frighten foes."

Roque snorted.

Verde responded. "Yet here he lies, and his story is there in Topper's book and in the tales I sought in Scotland."

"The place holds *Power*," said Rojo. "He left here imbued with great *Power*. Men are content to master one kind of *Power*. Sutton mastered four. It was enough to get him home."

Dan spoke slowly gazing into the fire. "Hurech, according to Topper's notes, sought seven Christian churches established by seven bishops who came this way seeking the Ark of the Covenant. Hurech was allied with the Templars who came to Roslin and he sailed on one of their voyages to the west."

Roque turned to Dan. "I have heard something of these bishops. The Conquistadors followed their trail seeking the Seven Cities of Gold. They left Santa Espania, heading to the west across the sea. They sought the Ark of the Covenant to bring home where the Moors were conquering the land and killing the Christians. They were sure the Moors were the Anti-Christ and only the Ark could turn them back."

Juan Largo hugged his lean knees and rocked back and forth humming, a quiet smile illuminating his face. He had found the men his grandfather had told him would come.

Sebriana said nothing, but went absently about her work.

Roque scratched his head. "If they came, others might have come, too."

"It is so," said Juan Largo. "Long ago before these men. I will lead you."

That night, Dan slept with his arms around Sebriana fearful of what had befallen her. He held her close against the evening chill. He dreamed she was an eagle who broke his grasp and flew away to circle far above, far beyond his reach and then far beyond his vision. He shuddered. He had lost her and awoke to find himself still holding her.

"Good morning, *Pobrecito*."

"Sebriana, I worried about you."

She seemed different he thought, more powerful and confident.

Sebriana smiled. "I dreamed of flying."

He shuddered.

"Danito," she whispered, "I love you."

He turned away. He loved her, but he could never marry her. She was Mexican, and he was a New England man of good family. She was Catholic, or perhaps Jewish. He had been raised a Protestant. He couldn't speak of love to her. It would be a promise he couldn't keep.

"Don't worry, *Pobrecito*. I am content to love you."

Juan Largo led them west and north between the tall mountains toward a distant towering range deep into Pinal Apache country, the country of a people not friendly to Anglos, Mexicans, or Apaches Mansos. They followed a wash that became a canyon. They passed a Butterfield Station where two canyons joined, and there was water.

They did not know the country, or they might have recognized Seneca Station and Pantano Wash, which they continued to follow. Low in the wash they caught only glimpses of towering mountains to their right.

Roque squirmed in the saddle. "This country is hotter than the Inferno."

"You'd know, boyo," responded Verde cackling.

Hot as it was, Juan Largo led them to water time and again. He knew the way.

They camped for the night where the stream was wide and the mountains in full view.

Juan pointed with his lip to jagged peaks in the west where dark clouds gathered. "Soon it will rain."

The clouds added humidity to the unbearable heat. Sleep came hard, if at all. Dan wanted to hold Sebriana, but the night was not cool enough. Clothing chaffed. One exposed bare skin at peril.

Verde howled and cursed in a tongue they did not know but which Dan thought might be Gaelic. "Left my rifle in the sun. It's too hot to touch."

Soon they all had burns on hands and arms. Hats were pulled down low to shade faces and necks, and sweat ran freely from under the brims. Their shirts were stained white.

Toward dusk they came to a river that ran with thick warm water. It flowed but little though the water was soothing. Clothing and bodies were rinsed. For a few cool moments Dan and Sebriana were able to touch. Juan Largo chose a camping ground, and they staked their livestock on poor grass.

Sebriana prepared dinner and afterwards they sat unable to sleep.

Juan Largo began a tale. "Long ago there was a church, Santa Catarina, I am told, in this very place. It was founded by Padre Kino himself and was the farthest north of all his missions. He himself chose the spot. He had a map and writings. Some thought he came here because there was a silver mine and a lead mine nearby. But how would the Padre have known this? He was the first priest to come here.

"There are stories on the rocks," the old man continued, "left by the ancients who used up the land and departed. They lived here so long ago that men cannot count the years. Their pictures tell of a strange people, a people who carried spears harder than wood, hard like stone, but not stone. They carried shining knives harder than stone and less brittle. They lived here and made farms, and they used a crossed sign."

Sebriana and Dan stepped away from the others to seek a place to sleep.

"*Pobrecito*," she whispered, "there are spirits here. I see them."

"Fireflies, Sebriana. Don't be alarmed. They're just fireflies."

"No, Danito. I can see their faces and their clothing. I have never seen anything like this before. They have helmets with horsehair plumes and wear leather skirts and carry tall wooden shields."

"I don't understand," Dan said fearing for her.

"Neither do I, but I am not afraid. They carry a cross with two cross bars. You have called it the Cross of Lorraine." She sat, and he joined her.

She shuddered, and he hugged her shoulders. Dan did not remember falling asleep, but when they woke, it was morning.

"Dig here," said Juan Largo without explanation.

The men hesitated.

Sebriana turned to Dan. "I saw something in the night. It is all right. Dig."

Rojo spoke. "There is *Power* here. It calls to me."

They dug in the hard, hot earth, breaking their way with hard tree limbs, knives, and anything sharp they found among their supplies.

"There is something here," said Verde clearing dirt from a hard, flat, smooth metallic surface. He pulled a cross from the ground.

Dan looked it over. "It's made of lead, and it's been in the ground a long time. There's writing on it. The language is Latin. Perhaps there was a church here."

Their excitement grew, and despite the heat, they dug faster. They found swords of lead and an implement that seemed to be for making communion wafers. There were more crosses and fanciful implements that defied explanation.

Dan cleaned a cross with his hand and read the inscription, slowly, haltingly.

"We are carried north over the sea to Calalus an unknown land where
People . . . ruling.
The Toltesus were led over the wooded land.
Theodorus brings up his army to a city, Rhodda, . . . seven hundred taken.
No gold . . . from the city.
Theodorus, man of great courage, rules fourteen years.
Iago rules six years.
With God's help . . . afraid of something
In the name of Israel
Iago . . . the city.
With God's help Iago rules mighty hand . . . of his ancestors
Sing to the Lord
May his fame last forever."

"What does it mean?" asked Roque.

Verde answered when Dan shook his head. "There is a legend of a Roman from Constantinople who went west with his people across the sea. Most thought he was headed for England."

With a sudden intake of breath, Rojo straightened. Dan watched as a scorpion sidled down the cross Rojo was holding and jumped to the ground. As his arm reddened, and a huge lump rose, Rojo dropped the cross. His eyes drawn to it, Dan saw a date. "814 A.D.," he said softly.

Roque caught Rojo as he fell. "What happens now?" the big Mexican asked.

"Perhaps he dies," said Juan Largo.

"Help me," said Roque lifting Rojo.

Dan and Verde joined him, and they carried Rojo to a spot under a mesquite tree where Sebriana spread a blanket. She knelt beside him and cooled his head with water from a canteen and her handkerchief.

Juan Largo showed them how to rig a blanket above him to provide more shade. "Now pour water on it, so that the air around him might be cool."

"Put them back," Rojo mumbled. "*Power* has been disturbed."

Dan started to comply when Verde put his hand on Dan's arm. "First copy them into the book."

Dan copied feverishly while Sebriana tended to the Jicarilla. Roque brought water and all that she asked. Rojo stiffened and lay still ceasing his mumbling. Only faint fog on Sebriana's looking glass showed that he still lived. Juan Largo sat equally still, the sombrero over his eyes in the shade of a boulder.

Verde looked over Dan's shoulder at the work making occasional corrections. "I think the old one prays to his gods."

When the drawings were finished, the artifacts went back in the hole and were covered up. Sebriana continued to nurse Rojo who seemed unchanged. Juan continued whatever he was doing.

Dan wished for Sebriana's wisdom and insight as he sat and thought. "It seems strange. The artifacts were all lead. There was no steel and no porcelain, no glass, only lead."

Verde mulled on this while Roque tended to his cousin and Rojo. "Think, boyo, perhaps they hadn't the means to make steel. They'd need rich iron ore and a man who knew the secret of steel."

"Secret of steel?"

"Sure, laddie, steel doesn't happen by accident. If you don't know the secret, all you get is soft iron."

"The Romans knew," said Dan, "and how to make glass and porcelain, too."

Verde nodded vigorously. "Sure, but the artisans know. Not soldiers, not priests. Maybe their artisans died. Maybe they lacked the right artisans, and maybe they couldn't find the right materials."

Dan frowned. "There's plenty of material around here for glass."

"There still has to be somebody who knows how to work it."

"Still," said Dan, "just lead? It doesn't seem right. The Romans would have carried gladius swords and pilum javelins and scutum shields. We didn't find any of that."

Dan and Verde fell silent for a time.

Finally, Verde spoke. "Boyo, did it seem to you these things were rather well organized? Intentionally buried? Not dropped or thrown away?"

Dan thought about this. "Yes, it did. These seem to be religious artifacts. Perhaps they were given special burial."

Rojo writhed and groaned. "An army is coming," he moaned. Sebriana mopped his brow.

Juan Largo rose and walked to Dan. "This is a place of *Power*. Long, long ago the ancients knew this and painted and adorned the rocks. Much later Padre Kino built a church."

Dan pondered. "When you say long, long ago, do you mean the ones the Papago call 'all used up'?"

"The Hohokam? Long before the Hohokam. The people who buried these things were here when the Hohokam were young." The old man returned to his rock adjusting himself to where the shade now stood.

Rojo sat bolt upright. "An army comes." He pointed with his hand and arm while Sebriana tried without success to lower him back down. "They carry long shields that hide their bodies and carry sharp spears. The people of the land dare not fight them. There is peace." He fell back and was still.

Sebriana cooled his forehead. "He's still hot, burning."

Roque took an interest. "I thought the Roman Empire was something of the distant past, long before the Moors came." He didn't seem to grasp the years but knew the order and relation of events.

Dan replied. "The Western Empire fell until only the Roman Church remained and Charlemagne, who stopped the Moors around 800, declared a Holy Roman Empire. But the Eastern Empire didn't fall until 1453."

Roque paced and thought. "What would have brought them here in 800?"

"Pleas for help from the Seven Bishops of Antilla?" said Dan.

Verde shook his head. "I don't think it was so. There was a rift between Eastern and Western Church. They may have sought the Ark of the Covenant. The Eastern Church drew in artifacts and holy relics from the East. Before Mohammed, they ruled the Holy Land."

"Look here, Verde, on this sword. It's the Cross of Lorraine."

"Boyo, do we know anyone who uses that?"

Dan considered. "The Freemasons and the Knights Templar."

"Laddie, neither of them was around in Anno Domini 800. Who came before?"

Dan inhaled sharply. "The masons at King Solomon's

Temple."

"The same, boyo, the same."

"Then how would Padre Kino have known to come here?"

Verde grinned. "He was a Jesuit from Austria. The Jesuits, they has their secrets and their learnin'."

Dan thought about this. The men who had buried these things used Latin, the Roman language, but anyone in the Roman Catholic Church used Latin and so did most of the countries of the old Roman Empire. It seemed clear to Dan that the people who left these artifacts behind were from the Western Empire, not the Eastern. The people of the Eastern Empire used Greek.

Sebriana spoke to Dan. "The ones who buried these things may have been the bishops of Antilla. They got word back to the Pope that they had reached this place. Kino knew where to look, where to build his church."

Roque looked almost angry. "Are you saying that this is as far as the seven Bishops came?"

Sebriana smiled. "Maybe."

"Who built the seven cities at Chaco?" Roque was sure he had stumped her.

But Sebriana was clever. "Maybe they found the Ark in the Grand Canyon and they are the reason the Hebrew Danites brought the Ark to Chaco. Maybe they worked together."

Verde danced a jig in the dust grinning all the while. "Maybe, boyo, maybe. Maybe not. Maybe these ones got no further than here. Maybe they went on to Chaco."

Dan stood. "The only thing clear to me is that our search takes us back to Chaco. The Ark isn't here, but the signs point north."They fell silent again until late afternoon. Heat made conversation difficult.

Roque watched the skies in the west where clouds

piled high and dark, rank on rank. "Do you see it? Marching armies with spears and tall shields. They're led by priests carrying crosses and swords and the strange devices we have seen. There," he pointed, "do you see it?"

None of the others did.

Rojo sat up again. "They are led by men with crosses." He fell back again, but there was a change: he seemed peaceful, at rest.

Sebriana felt his head. "His fever has broken."

Juan Largo stood. "He will live. *Power* found him worthy."

In the morning, Rojo was up and about, seemingly his old self, but like Sebriana, Dan sensed a new *Power* in him. They headed south passing Tucson, a few streets of crumbling adobes burned by the sun. Toward dusk, the sun reflected off the white bell towers of San Xavier del Bac.

"It is a Franciscan mission to the Wac with whom my people live," said Juan. "But the Franciscans are all gone, sent away by the Mexican government. There are no priests now in this whole country."

"The Wac?" asked Dan.

"A people who speak the language of the Papago."

Close inspection showed the mission crumbling, left without care for too many years. Roque was overwhelmed by the grandeur. None of the churches of New Mexico made of patched adobe could compare. He entered the church under statues of headless saints to be awed by paintings stained by a leaking roof. Seeing his interest, the local Indians came out of hiding and brought forth the church furnishings they had saved and hidden.

"Are you the new priest?" one asked.

Roque shook his head.

The Indians brought food to share with the party led by Juan Largo. After dinner, Dan looked about for his friend. An Indian indicated the church and Dan stepped inside to see Roque on his knees by the altar in prayer. Roque fell forward stretched out in the position of the cross. Dan could hear his murmured prayers and left his friend alone.

In the morning, Roque emerged from the church. To Dan, his step seemed more confident, more powerful. They would sleep in Tubac that night.

Mose Carson met the friends at the edge of town. "Wagh, now this ole coon is glad to see y'. Step down, we've need of yer bullthrowers. Heep a trouble brewin,' 'n' we haven't enough men, not by a long chalk. 'Paches seen about. Over t' the Cerro Colorado diggin's, miners have gone under, falling at the hands of Mexicans armed with axe and hammer. Galena pills gonna fly. Be a fight sure."

Fifty-three people from Sonoita, by Dan's count, had gathered at Tubac, twelve of them women and children. There were another twenty-six folks from Tubac. Though some were tough men, they were not near enough to hold the place effectively. The ends of the streets were barricaded with wagons, barrels, and sacks flour and grain. Anything that came to hand was used. Stock were brought inside and corralled in the *presidio*, the old Spanish fort, along with their feed. Outside, trees, brush, and *arroyos* would offer good cover to an approaching enemy. There was little to be done about it. Tubac would not be easily defended.

That night the defenders built a bonfire and stood around.

"Now what?" asked Dan. Having spent the last ten

years in New Mexico, he was familiar with frontier notions of a town hall meeting.

Verde grinned under his green top hat. "Why now, laddie, they'll fall to speechifying. And won't it be more like an Indian war dance with first one and then another tellin' us his feats in war and how brave he is. Soon the whole place will be on high cockalorum with this one telling how many Indians he kilt all by hisself and his neighbor claiming he could handle an equal number of Mexicans."

Mose Carson stepped up behind him. "Wagh, now this ole coon is sure gonna injoy th' war dance, wagh!"

Soon it became clear to Dan that most of the Sonoita Creek people wanted to pull out for the Rio Grande, as soon as the road was safe, while others, Tubac men among them, wanted to declare for the Confederacy and beg Colonel Baylor to send troops. Apaches had been seen in great numbers at the edge of town. The large band of Apaches was no raiding party. Apache raiders took livestock and supplies. The band was a war party and for Apaches, war meant killing. They had come to take the town. A man called Grundy Ake proposed putting together a wagon train. There was talk of the Arizona Rangers defending the settlements. They'd been formed at Pinos Altos to fight Apaches and were said to be having some success. Men boasted they could handle twenty Apaches all by themselves.

An arrow flew through the night, hitting the boastful speaker in the neck. The party broke up as people scattered to rooftops and barricades. A brave group returned with buckets of water to douse the fire and drench the village in darkness. Dan and his companions stood next to a barricade near the old presidio. More well aimed arrows came. Now and then a scream rang as an arrow found its mark.

Dan turned to Roque. "I haven't even seen movement out there. Do you think it's just one or two?"

Verde responded. "I'd be after informing you it ain't the Apache you see that kills you. It's the one you don't see, which is most of them."

Dan didn't see Rojo anywhere. The thought crossed Dan's mind that his friend might have run and joined his people. He quickly rejected it. But the unseen enemy still troubled him, growing in number and ferocity in his imagination. The stories he'd heard of these southern Apaches modes of torture came back to nettle him. He thought of what they were said to do to women. "Sebriana, I shall save my last shot for you."

"*Cabrón!* Save your last shot for yourself." She growled low in her throat like a wildcat.

Shots sounded from rooftops at irregular intervals as men fired at phantoms in the dark. The flickering light of muzzle flashes illuminated specters moving among the defenders. A spectral warrior loomed yards from Dan, his 'hawk raised to strike. He turned to fight the brave waiting in vain. The flash of a rifle fired across the plaza revealed a group of five Apaches armed with knives, 'hawks, and bow already in among the adobes of the town. Rifles and pistols fired at them, but they disappeared like vapor.

Boom, boom. Down beyond the river, a pistol fired again and again followed by the drumming of hundreds of hooves. The night went quiet. An hour went by, and no more arrows arrived. Lanterns were lit, and men scoured the street searching for warriors within their lines.

Rojo appeared at Dan's side and grinned. "There were more than one hundred ponies guarded by two boys in the meadow across the river." He pointed to the place with his lower lip. "My pistol scared the boys away, and the horses followed them. The Pinal will spend the day trying to catch their stock. We'll have time to prepare a proper welcome for them."

Dan considered this good news. "How will they attack?"

Rojo thought for a minute. "In the daytime, they will try to remain hidden firing at those who move about and at people going outside the plaza. They will not try to rush us. They know our strength and can wait. At night, they will steal and murder anyone they find isolated. In the early morning, they will attack."

Dan looked around to see if all his companions had come through. Roque was nowhere to be seen. Sensing Dan's concern, Sebriana pointed. "*Mi primo* and *Señora* Western went that way."

By the dawn's light, they counted two dead and eight wounded. Most of the wounded could still fight. The defenders dared not move outside the main street and presidio. One man stepped out to retrieve a sack of money he had buried behind the *horno* in his cabin. On his way, he stepped out of sight for a moment and was never seen again. Shortly afterwards, the screams began. They continued through most of the day.

Dusk found shadowy figures among the adobes. A man screamed and was found with his throat cut. Two days had passed and most of the defenders had been without sleep. In the pre-dawn twilight following a quiet night, men began to doze.

There was no chance to fire a volley or two. The Apaches crept close and were among the defenders. Sleeping sentries screamed once and died. A warrior pounced on Dan who threw him to the ground. The two faced off with 'hawk and knife. A long slash went through Dan's shirt, painful but not deep. Dan responded with a kick to the man's belly. Then he drew his pistol and shot him. Dan searched for targets.

As suddenly as the attack began, it was over. There were more men dead and wounded. Most of Dan's party ranked among the wounded but none seriously so. The day dawned clear and mercilessly hot. The sun singed exposed skin. Lips turned black, and tongues expanded until breathing was difficult. The heat singed nostrils. Venturing forth in the open for water was worth a man's life.

A scream came from nearby. Dan turned to see that a man had lifted his rifle touching the barrel. "Don't leave it in the sun. Keep it shaded." The man nursed his blistered palm.

In the shade of an adobe, Dan watched a scorpion marching toward him. A small dust devil, the Hard Flint Boys playing as the Navajo would say, happened by, swallowed the stinging insect, and then twisted off down the street. Flying scorpions, Dan thought, Satan's punishment of the damned. By late morning, all was quiet.

Dan saw Rojo and Old Mose head out into the chaparral.

It wasn't long before Mose Carson returned. "Wagh. I see which ways the stick floats. Time we wuz goin' elsewhere. Hitch wagons and git."

Out of nowhere, Rojo was at Dan's side. "They have gone."

Despite the heat, the wagon train was soon formed though cries and curses rose from men touching iron left a moment in the sun. Every inhabitant of Tubac joined the affair and by noon they were moving north to Tucson and hoped-for safety. Like Lot's wife they turned back to look one last time on their city.

Dan nudged his mule closer to Roque's *grullo*. "We've returned Juan Largo to his home."

Roque turned to to Dan. "And now Juan Largo's home is gone."

Overhearing, Rojo said, "His home is with the Wac and he has been away too long. He stays with us until he reaches them. He needed to return but did not know how. He has made himself right with *Power*."

Dan started to ask his meaning but thought better of it.

In the heat of mid-afternoon, out of the wavering haze and dust in the south, appeared an army of Mexicans. Two hundred riders charged down on the town. Most were armed with lances and machetes. Only a few had guns. Overhead thunderclouds piled high and black, blocking out the sun.

Finding the town empty and devoid of anything of any value, the Mexicans set fire to anything that would burn.

Ten miles out the wagon train stopped briefly on a rise, and the Arizonans watched the thick column of smoke. Tubac was burning. Many of the women and children wept. Home and new beginnings were gone. Tucson was now the only place in the Gadsden Purchase west of Pinos Altos and Mesilla occupied by people from the States.

Dan turned to his friends. "And where do we go from here?"

Roque sat up tall in his saddle. Sensing Roque's mood the *grullo* danced under him. Calming the horse, Roque said, "We follow the trail of the Conquistadors. We go up through the tall mountains to Zuñi and Chaco. Our path is clear."

Dan tilted his head to one side as he answered. "I don't know. With Apaches attacking towns they must be pretty excited. It can't be safe to go through the heart of their country which no white man has trod since Coronado and which we avoided as we came south."

"We have Rojo."

"And we almost lost him," Dan responded. "We almost lost Sebriana, too. I think we may be unworthy. God has closed the road to us."

Roque's brow furrowed deeply as he thought. He cheered thinking of a tall redhead, but said nothing to Dan. His love was with the wagon train and he would be with her a little longer.

The storm broke too late to quench Tubac's fires. It tore at the desert and at the canvas on the wagons. Thunder roared its hostility at the earth and cracked its lightning whips to scourge the ground. Dan set his hat aside and stepped into the face of the gale to howl his fury. Alongside him, Roque, Sebriana, and Rojo roared as well. A figure ducked under a wagon to shelter from the storm. The green vagabond smiled, pleased by their rage. "They'll learn."

In appearance, Tucson was somewhere between children's mud pies and sun baked cow pies. Its mean streets, hot and refuse strewn, twisted haphazardly between crumbling adobes. If Santa Fe was Mud Town, Tucson was mud town in shambles.

Dan thought he might not be giving Tucson a fair shot. He'd heard so much about the town that had been at Mexico's furthest reach. It was also beyond the reach of U.S. law and a haven for men on the run from California committees of vigilance. It was a place for men with no other place to go. Tucson was a town of gamblers, thugs, grifters, wastrels, smugglers, scalp hunters, filibusters, murderers, highwaymen, and harlots. It had once been a Mexican garrison town, a *presidio,* but that was gone, and the town lacked a purpose. Major Steen had moved his dragoons away from Tucson because the town was harder on his men than the desert was.

Dan told Sebriana, "I wish I could see this town in a better light."

Roque overheard. "What light would that be? A dim candle in a saloon?"

"Where can we go?" asked Dan.

"Perhaps we can stay here and wait until the wars pass us by, the Apache and the Texians," responded Roque. "I could be happy here with my Western." He referred to the tall Sarah Bowman his latest true love.

Dan smiled, then scowled. "Mail and newspapers have stopped coming from Mesilla. Perhaps the Texians have invaded as expected."

Grundy Ake soon had his caravan organized for the Rio Grande. Very few chose to stay in Tucson. The companions departed with the caravan hoping to make Mesilla before the Texans' invasion.

Dan rode up beside Sebriana. "It may be slow, but at least there is safety in numbers."

Sebriana shook herself in a way Dan could see meant she was unhappy. She didn't say anything. Like the others, she quietly accepted Dan's leadership, but that didn't mean she always agreed with him. Putting spurs to her horse she left him.

They headed east, dropping down into the Cienaga and passing Butterfield's now vacant Seneca Station. Without incident, they passed San Pedro Station, Dragoon Springs, and Ewell's. The caravan watered in Apache Pass, once Cochise's home, and continued on to San Simon.

Roque looked ahead to the Peloncillo Mountains and frowned. "Doubtful Cañon will be our test. These people say that in March and April Cochise and Mangas Coloradas attacked everything that came this way, killing many and torturing those who survived."

They entered the narrow pass and climbed the steep grade without incident. Their first real trouble came after aptly named Doubtful Canyon when they entered the playas of the Animas Valley. Extensive dry lakebeds full of loose sand, silt, and salt that raised clouds of dust so thick a man couldn't see his hand in front of his face when the wind blew. Usually the summer rains filled the playas with water, fresh sand, and silt, but rains in New Mexico fell locally and were known to soak one valley and leave the next dry. The wind blew hot and dry for the Sonoita Wagon Train.

Grundy signaled the wagons to pull in close facing the stock away from the wind. It was a small train of only ten wagons of various types. If they'd continued, the wagons would have become separated and lost, unable to see the next in line ahead. Besides, they couldn't breathe.

Roque suggested they use some of their precious water to moisten their bandanas.

"Why?" asked Sebriana.

"So you can breathe through them."

The bandanas soon dried but still served as filters for all but the eyes. They tied the kerchiefs over their faces to keep out the grit. Eyes clogged with it until sight was impossible. A featureless gray world howled at them. It closed in and suffocated, a pillow over the face.

Dan choked on the wind. "We need water."

Rojo shook his head. "Wander out there without landmarks, and you'll end up farther from it than we began."

They sat and waited, listening to the shrieking gale and complaining stock, hoping and praying, it would end soon.

Sebriana prayed. "Is God angry with us for leaving Arizona or for being here at all?"

Dan shuddered. He was headed away from Chaco Cañon and the Ark. He had been led to Tubac and signs of Christians seeking the great relic a thousand years ahead of him. Their road had been the ancient Indian trace that Coronado had followed. At Doubtful Cañon he'd turned aside from that path and made his own. It was then the bad luck had struck. Icy fingers tickled Dan's spine.

Grundy rode up near Dan and jokingly said to someone shrouded in the dust, "I think we've got a Jonah among us."

Chapter 12

Road to Val Verde

The mud falling from the sky was a welcome relief after two days of constant wind and dust. The storm broke in thunder, lightning, and falling mud, which gave way to rain. They hitched up and started moving before the rain let up.

Dan told Sebriana, "If we wait, the playa will begin to fill and movement will become difficult."

The stock watered in hollows and washes. At Dan's suggestion, Grundy spread the wagons abreast of each other in broad files, as was done on the Santa Fe Trail for protection. Here they spread out so that they did not churn the muddy earth with their passing as they might if they traveled in a long column. Muddy they might be but cheerful, too, relieved of water worries in dry country. The rain brought up the grass deep, green and lush.

As they passed from playa into hill country, it worried Dan that they again traveled in column with their strength spread out.

Dan went to Ake. "Grundy, an enemy could hit our front, center, or rear and help would be long in coming from the other parts of the caravan. There were enemies out there. Both Cochise and Mangas Coloradas raid in this area, and between them they have over three hundred warriors."

Rojo agreed. "Mr. Ake, both chiefs have been given strong reasons to hate Americans. Now that the government has withdrawn its soldiers, they think they are winning."

Not trusting an Indian, Grundy Ake looked at Rojo suspiciously. Grundy and General Wadsworth were the leaders of the caravan, and to Dan, they didn't seem as concerned as they ought to be.

A military expressman riding hard approached from the east. He pulled up by the lead wagon, Wadsworth's open carriage. Grundy, Dan, Rojo, and others rode in close to listen.

The rider spoke. "Where you folks headed? Don't matter nohow. Head north to Fort Craig on the Rio."

General Wadsworth spoke. "What? Why?

The soldier replied, "Mesilla and Fort Fillmore are in Texan hands. I'm taking word to Fort McLane and Pinos Altos."

Wadsworth, who was supposed to have some military experience, seemed to be calculating odds and strategy. He'd been elected general of an Arizona militia that never formed at Tubac or the Sonoita Valley. Arizona Rangers had formed near Pinos Altos and the Mimbres Valley to protect miners and settlers there, but it was doubtful he had any authority over them or that he claimed such.

Wadsworth finally replied. "Thank you, young man. We'll consider what you've said."

Dan overheard Ake grumbling. "I know we got us a Jonah."

Roque indicated he wanted to speak to Dan privately. Dan thought perhaps he'd seen some sign of Chiricahuas, so they rode a little way from the others, and Roque brought his horse close to Dan's mule. "She left me,

Danito. It breaks my heart. Sarah had a business at Yuma and is returning to it. She said she loved me but treasured her independence. If the Apache attack, I will ride out alone to face them and end my suffering forever."

"There'll be another," Dan said consoling him.

Sometimes kindly intended words only make the matter worse. "There can never be another like the Western. She has torn out my heart. Such love as ours has never been since the days of the ancient heroes. Perhaps a monastery will take me."

Dan tried to picture Roque in a monastery. "Now, let's not go doing anything hasty or drastic. Death is preferable to celibacy."

Roque started weeping. "It is so. I will miss her always. My heart will ache forever. Only death can free me from the pain. What have I done to earn this torture? I will follow the monastic life so I can learn and be forgiven."

Dan wondered why the announcement of Roque's heartbreak had been so long in coming. Sarah Bowman, the Great Western, had stayed behind in Tucson ten days before. He wondered if Roque had been so pained that he couldn't speak until now. Dan didn't dare crack a smile, but he could not envision Roque in monk's robes chanting psalms. Dan had no doubt his friend was deeply and truly in love with the Great Western, and she with him for that matter. She had the better sense, knowing them both too headstrong to make a match and that her independent lifestyle would soon offend his Spanish honor. Casting him adrift was the kindest thing she could do. Roque kicked his grullo gently and put some distance between himself and the caravan.

Dan thought, I'd best remember to call it a grullo today. New Mexicans see the grulla as a mare or gelding, not just a color. Roque was in a bad mood and sensitive about things.

Sebriana guided her pinto mule up alongside Dan's Appaloosa. "He mourns the loss of Western. It could not be. She was not meant to be a meek and obedient wife."

"She's been happily married several times," Dan replied. "How would marriage have been different with Roque?"

"She was an army wife," Sebriana said. "Soldiers have different expectations. They expect their wives to be independent and take care of themselves when the soldier can't be with them. Roque would have wanted to smother Western with protection. He would have expected her to act like a great lady so others could see in her what he sees. She is great and brave and proud but not a lady. Airs and fine clothes are not for her."

Dan grew silent for a moment and thought about women. Every man wants to win a woman he can put up on a pedestal and admire. She should be a woman of refinement and great beauty, and their love should burn with hot passion. A pretty girl comfortable as an old, though favored, shoe comes in a distant second and might leave one wishing he'd waited for a goddess to come along.

"Besides," Dan muttered aloud unthinking, "the risk is too high, too many dead husbands."

Sebriana smacked him open-handed up the back of his head so hard she loosened his teeth.

Dan realized she'd known about the broken heart. He had assumed Roque had just shaken off another romance. "How did you know? He said nothing until today. How long have you known?"

"Since Tucson, of course." Reigning in her mule, she held back until Verde came alongside her, letting Dan know that Verde was more pleasant company than he was.

The days slipped by, dawning clear with blue skies, the afternoon bringing thunderclouds and frequent storms. Dan was glad they weren't trailing the herds of sheep and cattle that followed behind the caravan. They proceeded at the pace of the plodding oxen pulling Grundy's wagons in the lead, constantly on alert for Chiricahuas and Texans. Roque and Dan on one side, Rojo and Verde on the other, they rode a few hundred yards ahead and to the side of the caravan, scouting for lurking marauders.

They returned to the column one afternoon to find Grundy and Mose arguing. Mose was insisting loudly, "Y've gotta bunch 'em up more!"

"We're out of Pinal country," replied Grundy. "The Chiricahuas have been friendly to us."

"Not by a long chalk," said Mose. "Ain't you bin listenin' to the talk outa Pinos Altos?"

They camped near the Santa Rita copper mines not far from Pinos Altos. Captain Mastin and the Arizona Guards came down to greet them. The Guards had been formed mostly from men who farmed and ranched along the Mimbres River. Raids had made economic pursuits impossible, but the mines were thought to be rich and close enough to the Rio and Mesilla to give them hope. They hoped that after a few retaliations, battles as they called them, they'd be able to return home and go unmolested. Dan saw that Jack Swilling had signed on as second in command.

After supper, Mastin addressed the leaders, Grundy and Wadsworth. "Don't go through Cooke's Canyon. They'll be waiting for you."

Grundy argued back. "We've got to. Don't wanna get too close to Mesilla. I understand the Texians have taken over. The Texians need supplies. They could take everything I've got left, including cattle and sheep. I'll give the Chiricahuas a couple of steers and they'll go away happy."

"Grundy," said Swilling, "You don't know what it's been like here. They tried to wipe out Pinos Altos."

Despite the warning the General headed for Cooke's Canyon. It would bring them to the Rio Grande fifty miles above Mesilla and save them a week getting to Fort Craig. The caravan forded the Mimbres River without incident. The next day they approached the cañon.

Grundy sent some of the sheep and their herders on ahead. "It's getting late. Let's camp here."

The next morning, the rest of the herd was sent in, followed by wagons and riders. Rock strewn cañon walls, neither high nor especially steep, made passage difficult for riders and impossible for wagons everywhere except in single file at the bottom.

Grundy called in the scouts. "General Wadsworth, we need them to help keep the wagons moving. Besides, they're sky-lining themselves up on the rim."

Things went well all morning. The entire caravan entered the cañon strung out over two and a half miles. Grundy moved the cattle and sheep, about 500 head, out first. They moved slowly wanting to spread out and graze. The wagons too moved slowly impeded by the rough terrain. The riders in the rear ate dust. Dan thought it the reverse of what was usual. He wondered what Grundy was thinking. Everyone except the drovers had their fill of dust for lunch.

Dan shook his head. "Roque, we riders should be out front. If anything happens, we're best able to maneuver and adapt."

"Sí, amigo, if we are attacked the cattle and sheep will

be scattered all over the place."

"I'm going to talk to Grundy." Dan rode off toward the lead wagon.

Dan saw Tommy Farrell out ahead of the herd wave his arms and point. The distant rider dismounted to look at something on the ground and then called back that he'd found the dead bodies of herdsmen who had gone ahead into Cooke's Cañon the day before.

Three wagons ahead of Dan, John Sinclair suddenly stood up, dropped the reins, and then tumbled over to the ground dead. Only then did Dan hear the shot followed closely by the thunder of dozens of rifles echoing up and down the valley. The Apache seemed to be everywhere. The mules pulling the lead wagon were soon slain by rifle and arrow fire. Apache riders charged out of side cañons and were soon amidst the herds driving them away and overpowering the drovers. Fire directed at the second wagon killed the oxen and the driver.

Dan rode back down the line searching for Sebriana.

As they passed, Roque called to him. "I'm headed for General Wadsworth's carriage. He tries to turn around."

People on the wagons were beginning to return fire. Old Mose was trying to organize them and get women and children to relative safety under the wagons. The foe was elusive, never reappearing to fire from the same spot twice. If fired on, he'd fall as if dead only to scurry away out of sight. The hillsides offered him the perfect cover for this game. As Roque arrived, fire intensified against the third wagon where Mose was organizing the defense.

"Sebriana!" Dan called.

"Pendejos! Cowards!" Sebriana was watching five of the riders galloping away in the direction the wagon train had come.

Dan yelled to the remaining riders. "Come on! We've

got to organize a defense around the lead wagons until we can evacuate the women and children."

To a man the remaining frontiersmen followed Dan.

"I will fight, too!" yelled Sebriana riding at Dan's side.

Dan knew better than to argue. "Protect the women and children. Then get under a wagon."

With drivers dead or wounded in the lead wagons, those behind could not move forward. And like Wadsworth the wagons were finding themselves unable to turn around.

As Dan rode up, Moses Carson called out. "Wagh! See which way the stick floats, pilgrim. Theyuns'll be pickin' us oft by onesies. Teckin' theys time 'bout it, too."

Roque's grullo pranced in a circle as Roque brought the stallion under control facing up the hillside. Tomahawk in one hand, pistol in the other, knife in his teeth, he was a magnificent sight. Dan was startled into inaction.

Rojo fired his rifle and then raised a pistol to give Roque cover.

"Give the man cover, boyo!" howled Verde, firing his own rifle, clearly enjoying the mayhem.

Dan and Sebriana fired at the same time. Roque charged. The Apache scattered before him like Moses parting the Red Sea.

Dan grabbed the driver of the third wagon while Sebriana grabbed the driver's woman. Rojo and Verde continued providing covering fire.

Beside Dan, Sebriana spoke softly, "Don't worry, mijo. Soon, Roque will remember how much he enjoys finding new lovers."

General Wadsworth had abandoned his carriage and

started calling orders. "We've got to try to get everyone back to the rear and form a defense there!"

Mose Carson steadied the line and directed fire calming the men as he went.

Dan turned to look back as they approached the fifth wagon in line and saw Apaches swarm the lead wagons. He called out to Mose, "Let's give them a volley!"

With a touch here and there, arm signals, and his strange speech, Old Mose organized the volley. The Apache busy robbing the wagons were startled. They broke and ran when Roque charged down the hill into their midst.

"Magnifico! Bravo! Olé!" roared Sebriana.

The Chiricahua soon returned to the lead wagons. Ignoring the people huddling a few wagons away, they proceeded to loot them, fighting among themselves over choice items. They opened trunks and looted them, too.

Grundy called out. "Don't no one fire on them, and maybe they'll leave us alone."

From atop his charger, Roque looked down on his friends. "Most of them have gone off chasing the sheep and cattle."

So swift and cunning were the attackers that Dan was uncertain whether they'd killed many of them. There were men who later would brag of having slain five or six by themselves. The Apache 'possum act may have deceived some who honestly believed their count.

Old Mose summed it up. "Wagh! They's critters claims the Patches carry away their dead. Seems right unlikely. The Patches don't keep the dead around longer than it takes to roll them into an arroyo."

"If anyone killed an Apache today," Roque told Dan and Sebriana, "it would have been Mose Carson."

Kit's brother was everywhere, directing fire, pulling

in the wounded, and setting up barricades and defenses. At intervals, he stopped and aimed carefully, heedless of incoming fire. Dan's respect for the old man grew that day.

"No one killed any," said Rojo. "They fought well. The Chiricahua came today to raid, to steal supplies. They did not come to see us all dead, to make war."

Verde spoke quietly to Sebriana. "He's a good'n that boyo, Dan. Coolness comes over him in battle. The nervous energy that makes his shots waiver in competition is gone. He fires without conscious thought. Fears that grip him at other times do not hamper action."

Sebriana agreed. "They say it comes from accepting that one is already dead. Perhaps, but I think it comes from letting the conscious mind go and trained responses take over. Even so, he says he thinks he did not kill anyone today."

Mose had raised a barricade of wagons and was pushing folks inside. At the very end of the line, some men had succeeded in turning a wagon around by brute force. With the wagon hitched up, they loaded the wounded into it and drove hard for Pinos Altos hoping to find Mastin's Arizona Guards still there. General Wadsworth set men to work on turning a second wagon. For a while, it looked to Dan like they might survive.

The Apache soon renewed their attack. Dan watched in horror as Sebriana turned in the saddle and aimed her rifle only to start and fall to the ground. She leapt up drawing her pistol and loosed three shots at an enemy Dan couldn't see before swinging back up into the saddle of her pinto mule. Roque, grim faced, leaving his empty rifles hang from his saddle horn, was firing a pistol in each hand. An arrow hit Verde, and Dan lost sight of him. Rojo was dragging wounded to safety. Dan wondered if he did not wish to fire on Apaches.

Dan turned in the saddle and saw death coming for him on swift wings. A spear rushed toward him. Dan saw the flying missile without ever seeing the one who hurled it though he must have been close. He fended successfully with one arm knocking the instrument of death away.

"To the barricade!" someone yelled and pointed. Few heard him over the noise of battle. Dan rode to Sebriana and pointed. She nodded and headed for Mose. Roque was already on his way, and Verde was lost to sight. Dan headed in.

Miraculously, Dan and his friends still had most of their stock and now led them inside and secured themselves in Mose's barricade. The firing slacked off. They had become a more difficult target for the Apache. Their controlled fire kept the enemy at bay. Four men lay dead. Twice that many had wounds that left them beyond helping with the fight.

As dusk arrived, Dan went to Sebriana's side. "I thought you were dead."

She smiled. "It's only a little furrow in my shoulder. It stung."

"That's but a wee bit o' nothin,' boyo," said Verde. "Lookee here. Arrow went through me side, feathers and all, an' right along its way sweet as you please leaving only a hole."

Roque looked at the little man. "Shame. But I hear the Chiricahua put poison on their arrows."

Roque's saddle bore three arrows sticking up like porcupine quills, none of which had penetrated either Roque or the horse. He'd fought well, Dan thought. He did try to get himself killed. But he seemed to have forgotten about his broken heart.

Dan had a long gouge in his forearm from fending off a thrown spear.

Roque looked at the arrows. "See that one by the saddle horn? One inch closer, and I'd have had no choice but to join a monastery and chant psalms in a girlish voice."

The next morning, having ridden all night, Mastin and the Arizona Guards rode in chasing the last of the Apache from the hillsides above Cooke's Canyon. With them, riding at the rear, were three men Dan recognized as having been with the caravan. Dan wondered if they had they deserted at the first gun shots or ridden to find help at Pinos Altos.

"If you'll ride guard," Grundy told Mastin, "we'll get this train through the cañon yet. But I've lost all my livestock to the raiders."

"The only way to make Apaches stop raiding is to make it too expensive for them," said Mastin.

"This raid has been pure profit," said his lieutenant, Jack Swilling. "Ain't cost them nothing yet. They'll be moving slow on account of the cattle and sheep. We kin ketch 'em if we leave right now."

"Mount up," called Mastin to his men. "We're going after the scoundrels."

"Hang on," Dan said. "We're going with you." Roque and he mounted. Rojo shook his head.

Sebriana was angry with Dan for offering to go. Indicating Verde she said, "I'm staying with this poor wounded man."

She turned around trying a new tack. "Pobrecito, mijo, mi Danito, stay with me. I have such a bad feeling about this. We will never see each other again. Stay with me."

Dan was torn, but he knew his duty. He had to get the stock. The Indians had to be punished. Besides, he was getting too close to this woman. She could never be his wife. It was better to make a break from her now than to assert his independence later.

They rode off south after the Chiricahua raiders.

"Amigo," Roque said to Dan, "you say this is your duty but what about your promise and the quest?"

Dan frowned thinking briefly of Jonah. "It can wait. We need the stock. Then we can head for the Rio Grande and the north. We'll soon be on our way again."

Roque shuddered. "What of mi prima?"

"We'll see her again soon."

They rode all day out of the cañon and into the grassy plain beyond flanked by mountains and cut by deep arroyos. In the red light of the setting sun they stopped for a rest break in a deep arroyo well out of sight.

Roque's head snapped up and swiveled, listening. "I heard hooves. A lot of hooves. A herd is coming this way."

Mastin stood on his saddle and peeked over the edge of the arroyo. He whispered to his men. "Pass the word. We passed them along the way. Now they are coming right to us. Get your weapons ready and wait my signal."

At his signal, the Arizona Guards and the men from the caravan who had joined them charged up out of the arroyo onto the plain. Mastin had picked the perfect moment. Instantly, they were among the Apache and the herd. Dan and Mose had estimated that at least sixty Apache had attacked the day prior. The Apache must have split up because only twenty remained as drovers. Nonetheless, they fought like tigers.

Half of them began stampeding the cattle away from the Arizona Guards while the others fought a rearguard. Two of these went down as Guards raced among them firing at point blank range. Then Mastin took a bullet through the arm and fell from his horse. His men rushed to him when he didn't rise.

"Circle the cattle in," yelled Jack Swilling dismounting beside his leader. They had recaptured about half the herd. The rest were on the run with the Apache. "They'll soon be joined by the others, and they're headed for more cañon country. It's too risky to follow. They know we're here and they'll set an ambush."

No one in the group had any medical training. They'd all seen wounds before, and they all knew that Mastin was in serious trouble. The bone had been shattered by the bullet, and most of the flesh blown away.

Roque spoke up. "The Apache get lead in rods a foot long and big around as your finger. They don't cast bullets. They cut off a piece of lead and chew it into shape. The ball isn't round or even, so it tumbles when it hits anything hard, like bone. It makes a mess like you see."

To Dan, it looked like at least two inches of bone near Mastin's shoulder were completely missing. He was in terrible pain and bleeding profusely. They tried to staunch the bleeding. A poultice of the inner bark of juniper helped slow it, but it didn't halt the flow. There wasn't enough left of the upper arm to fit a tourniquet.

"I'm no doctor," said Swilling, "but I think that arm needs to come off."

"I think we'd kill him," Dan said. "It would be too easy to make a mistake and make it worse."

"Then let's make a travois," said Swilling, "and take him to the doctor in Pinos Altos." Dan noticed Jack drinking from the same brown bottle he'd been feeding to Mastin to ease the pain.

Noticing Dan looking, Swilling met his eye. "Old back injury."

Laudanum thought Dan. Not a good sign. The tincture of opium could rob good men of all judgment. Swilling was a functional hophead. That explained a few things about his reckless nature and tendency to brag.

They dragged Mastin along behind his horse. At every bump he groaned, gasped, or cried out. They went as fast as they dared, but the large bumps started the bleeding again. They'd see the blood trail starting beneath him and stop to tighten his bandages. Toward dusk, he cried out loudly. They camped there and buried him, a good man gone before his time. Swilling did a remarkably fine job saying farewell words to wish him on his way.

Dawn broke gray and overcast, a rarity for that country and time of year. The unit moved slowly, in no hurry to move on from that lonely grave. A rider approached them from the south. As he drew near, Dan saw the man was John Rheingold now wearing the uniform of a captain in the 2nd Regiment of Texas Mounted Rifles.

Captain Rheingold rode up to Lieutenant Jack Swilling. "Would you boys be kind enough to stack your arms? I wouldn't want there should be any misunderstandings between us."

"Excuse me?" said Jack. "I kinda missed the import of yer speech. What'd you want?"

"If you'd be kind enough to assemble over here without your weapons, I'll explain."

"Explain first," said Jack.

"All right." Captain Rheingold raised his arm and sixty men of the 2nd Texas, armed to the teeth, exposed themselves on the hills encircling the Arizona Guards position. Among them, Dan saw Jim Pennington, Three-fingered Joe-Bob, and Tiler Caine. The twenty-five Arizona Guards were outnumbered and outmaneuvered.

"Now if you'll please assemble, I've something to read to you."

They assembled.

"This is a proclamation from Governor Baylor of the Territory of Arizona…"

"Who, say what? The Territory of which?" demanded Jack.

Rheingold continued. "Governor Baylor has come to Arizona from Texas in command of the 2nd Texas with the authority to institute government and raise troops for defense of the Territory of Arizona. Formerly a portion of New Mexico but legally the property of Texas since Santa Anna surrendered it after the Battle of San Jacinto, Texas has now asserted its legal authority."

"It's about time!" and "Hurrah for Arizona!" was heard from a few of the Arizona Guards before Jack Swilling silenced them with a glare.

Rheingold started speaking again. "Pursuant to his orders, the new governor has proclaimed that all residents of Arizona found under arms in organized groups are hereby conscripted into the Army of Arizona."

"Con-whated?" called out one of the Guards.

"Means you're in the Texas Army now," responded Jack. "Listen here, Captain, I don't know about this conscription. A lot of us are Union men."

Rheingold nodded. "You'll mostly be used for home defense and protection against Indians which I understand is what you're already doing. So it shouldn't be too much of a problem for your scruples. Your people need protection. We'll keep you supplied and paid.

The captain continued, "The alternative is that we have to execute you as spies taken under arms. You are rebels and resisters to the law of conscription."

Swilling thought about this. "Well, if we only have to fight Indians."

Rheingold countered. "You'll fight whoever we say or face a firing squad."

"Looks like we don't have much choice, boys," said Jack. "We're secesh now and in their army t' boot. We get to keep our weapons?"

"Wouldn't be much good fightin' Injuns without 'em," replied Rheingold.

Rheingold detached a squad of men to Cooke's Canyon to take the cattle back to Grundy Ake. He led the Arizona Guards south to Mesilla to meet the new Governor, their commander in chief. Along the way, they learned that there were other companies operating against the Apaches. One was led by Captain James Tevis and the other by Roy Bean. Bean's men who had come out of Texas with him were referred to as the Forty Thieves. Dan never heard of any case where they fought Indians, but more than once he heard rumors they'd killed peaceful Mexicans.

Governor John R. Baylor was a southern aristocrat who affected a military uniform. Before he declared himself governor, he'd been colonel of the 2nd Texas. He was tall and lean with a high forehead and black hair and beard. It was his eyes that you noticed first. They were the stern, glaring eyes of a man who knew he was always in the right. He was a man for whom his ends would justify any means he chose. Dan didn't recall much of the speech he made to the Arizona Guards. He was too busy watching those eyes.

During the rest of the summer and fall of 1861, boundaries were uncertain and there were no caravans west or north. Depredations were constant. In the past, they had been erratic and involved stock rustling and the occasional disappearance of a lone traveler. Now they usually resulted in one or two people killed or children and women abducted as well as livestock taken. Small parties of travelers were in grave danger. Usually the Arizona Guards arrived too late to do more than bury the dead and try to recover the stock. Apache camps were far back in the Gila Mountains. The unit didn't dare try to raid that deep with only twenty men. Five had already deserted and more would follow them.

A rider warned them of an attack on a Rio Grande pueblo, Doña Ana. They rode out and found the village smoldering and, a few villagers sitting about looking confused. They ran at the sight of mounted men. Roque spurred his horse and tossed his lariat over one then led him back to Captain Jack Swilling.

"Why do you run?" Jack asked.

"Please don't kill me!" the villager begged.

"We won't," promised Jack. "What's your name?"

"Manuel, Manuel Ortega."

"Well, Señor Ortega, we are here to help you," said Jack. "Why do you run from us?"

"First the Apaches came and killed two people and robbed us a little," said Ortega. "Then men like you came and took everything of any value left, killed everyone who resisted, and burned the town. Don't worry. We promised not to tell the governor in Santa Fe. You are safe. We are your obedient servants."

Jack looked at him. "Did you hear any names?"

Manuel shook his head up and down. "Si, I hear one man called King Frijole. It is a strange name, no?"

Jack looked puzzled, so Dan told him, "That would be Roy Bean, Rey Frijole."

The unit did what they could for the villagers. Dan thought it was no wonder these people, New Mexicans in general, hated and feared Texians. He chuckled to himself about Sibley's notions of raising a rebel army in New Mexico because the Mexicans didn't like Americans. Maybe they didn't, but they'd never join a Texian army. They hated Texians.

In late September, a rider on a lathered horse found them up near Cooke's Spring. Pino Altos was under attack. Hundreds of Apaches were in the town between the houses which were holding out as individual fortresses. Fearing they were already too late, the Arizona Guards pushed their horses and mules to their limit.

The fight had been raging for a day and half when the fifteen men of the Arizona Guards arrived to find the women of the town, stalwart ladies of the evening, entrenched with a small cannon. They had been doing serious murder on the Apaches. It amazed Dan that the Apaches hadn't managed to take the ladies' position. Their effort had saved the town.

Roque smiled at Dan. "They do not like it when anyone interferes with their income. The miners must keep mining, no, to make them rich."

The unit charged into the Apache directly and for a change, taking them by surprise, executed twelve of them, losing two of their own dead and two wounded.

Dan looked around and said to Roque, "Worst fight we've ever been in."

Roque nodded. "Guards are losing too many men to desertion and arrows. Soon it will be us."

The Guards and miners buried the dead, patched the wounded, and tried to repair and improve the town's defenses. Everyone thought the Apache would soon return and finish the job. As large as the Apache force was, the eleven remaining men of the Arizona Guards added little to the defense.

"Sure, we stay another night," said Roque. "The chiquitas are offering a half price special for one night only. That's like two for one almost."

The attack never came.

Swilling explained the situation to Dan. "Apache don't like to mount a siege. Once an attack has failed, they consider it unlucky to try again. It will be a long while before they attack Pinos Altos again."

The Guards were still there a week later when a courier arrived from Mesilla with a new proclamation from the Confederate governor.

Jack Swilling read it to himself and muttered, "I'll be damned if I will."

Then he assembled the Guards and read the proclamation to all of them.

> Use all means to persuade the Apaches or any tribe to come in for the purpose of making peace, and when you get them together kill all the grown Indians and take the children prisoners and sell them to defray the expense of killing the adult Indians. Buy whiskey and such other goods as may be necessary for the Indians and I will order vouchers given to cover the amount expended. Leave nothing undone to insure success, and have a sufficient number of men around to allow no Indian to escape.
>
> *Governor John Baylor*

"That's our orders," said Jack, "from his majesty the governor."

Sensing Jack's distress, Roque and Dan went to him. Jack was still muttering. "Invite them in to parlay then kill 'em sneaky-like and make their women and kids into slaves. Sounds un-American to me. I want no part of it."

"Nor do we," Dan told him. "We're leaving tonight."

"I'm going with you and maybe some of the other Union men, too."

That night they deserted. They took a short route north across the mountains toward Fort Craig.

Dan rode close to his friend. "I'm not taking a chance of getting drafted into another army or getting shot as sesech. I'm not going near that fort."

Separating from the others, Dan and Roque rode east to the Rio Grande and turned north along the west bank avoiding the *Jornada del Muerte*. Cooke's Route was dangerous and difficult for wagons, but the wagon train had been headed that way. On their fifth day out, they were spotted by a Union patrol headed south.

The two companions soon found themselves in the presence of Captain Paddy Graydon in command of the Company of Spies and Guides of the Regiment of New Mexico Volunteers. Before they could speak, Paddy was on them. "Well, here you be. That was naughty of you to go absent without proper leave, but I'm after letting bygones be bygones and forgiving you. You know, Private Gonzales and Private Martinez, that desertion is a crime punished by a firing squad, but since it was just this morning that you took off, we don't need to do anything drastic. Fall in with the others."

"Now wait a second, Paddy," Dan started, "you know we're not Gonzales and Martinez."

"Ah, then you were deserting, and it's the firing squad for you. And don't be familiar with your commanding officer. You must call me Sir.

He continued, "First Sergeant, mark them as present on the morning report. Our lost lambs have returned to us."

Having deserted the Texas Army, they now found themselves conscripted into the New Mexico Volunteers, nominally an all-volunteer force. What's more, they were headed back south towards Mesilla.

Several nights later, Graydon's Spies and Guides stopped a few miles north of Mesilla in a densely wooded area out of sight of the river and Camino Real. Paddy called for Gonzales, Martinez, and Ortiz. "Private Ortiz's brother is the *padre* in Mesilla. He will ride into town and gather what information he may from his brother who tends toward the Union. Gonzalez," he said looking at Dan…"

"Sorry," Dan replied, "I thought I was Martinez."

"Gonzales," Paddy said still looking at Dan, "you and Martinez circle around town to the south and get me a count of the number of troops at Fort Fillmore, or whatever they're calling it now, and Mesilla."

"You do realize, sir," Dan said, "that if we are apprehended, we will be shot as deserters."

"Good point," said the man who had so recently been the proprietor of the Boundary Hotel on Sonoita Creek. "So don't get caught. That's an order. Should add spice to your adventure." He cackled at his own humor. "Besides, you're not much good to me if the Texians shoot you."

Dan and Roque spent the night circling far to the west of Mesilla and then riding south until they had passed by Fort Fillmore. Finally, they turned east to the Camino Real. The friends approached Fort Fillmore in daylight from the south, hoping that the sesech would not be expecting anything untoward from that direction. The 2nd Texas wasn't much on discipline and didn't seem to be expecting trouble from anywhere. They weren't watching the road. The two friends moved up easily and then disappeared into an arroyo at the foot of the mountains to the east. They found a broad spot with a little water and good grass hidden by a bend of the arroyo where they could hobble their stock and the stock could feed and water themselves.

"Up there, Roque," said Dan pointing to the ridge above the *arroyo*. Dan started toward his chosen position.

"Sí, amigo, it will be a good spot to observe Fort Fillmore." Roque worked his way further north until he was near Mesilla.

They spent a long hard day lying still, occasionally dozing, and watching the activity at the fort and town.

Until early afternoon with the sun behind him, Dan felt safe scanning with his small telescope. In the afternoon he didn't want to take a chance that the sun would reflect off its glass and attract attention.

The fort had adobe walls with barracks built right up against them. Barracks' roofs provided a parapet for soldiers. There were two bastions facing the *Camino Real* and each held two cannon. Able to distinguish guidons and flags, Dan learned that only two companies of the 2nd Texas Mounted Rifles occupied the fort. At dusk, they conducted retreat. All of the soldiers lined up in neat columns and files to salute the flag one last time as it came down for the day. Dan made out two hundred and fifty men even without his glass.

As soon as it was full dark, Dan headed north along the *Camino Real* as Roque and he had planned. He worried that if he was approached, his Out East accent, although buried by twelve years in the New Mexico, might give him away. Fortunately, Dan encountered no one. Roque was waiting, concealed by brush for Dan's approach.

"Halt! Who goes there?" queried a voice from the roadside.

"A poor blind candidate...Knock it off, Roque! It isn't funny."

They followed the river road north for three miles and then headed west toward Graydon's hiding place.

"Danito, why we don't just keep riding and go about our business without seeing Paddy Graydon no more."

Dan thought about this for a moment. A woman and fulfilling his promise to Topper lay in the direction Roque indicated. "Because we're headed into Union territory and it would be just like Paddy Graydon to report us as deserters."

"Danito," pleaded Roque. The Mexican, descendant of conquistadors, could think of no more to say. He knew Dan's explanation wasn't what his friend was really thinking. Dan was avoiding both Sebriana and all mention of the Ark.

Dan reported for Roque and himself. "Privates Gonzales and Martinez, he's Gonzales, beg to report no more than two hundred and fifty men of the 2nd Texas at Fort Fillmore and fifty more, give or take, in Mesilla as gubernatorial guard. We know that the governor also has at his disposal Captain Tevis' Rangers, about fifty, Rey Frijoles' Forty Thieves, about twenty-five..."

"Wait a second!" snarled Graydon. "Rey Frijoles? How can forty be twenty-five?"

"King Frijoles," Dan replied, "is what the Mexicans are calling Roy Bean and forty thieves is a name from a story, the one about Ali Baba, I believe. In any event, it is a unit of only twenty or twenty-five."

"And that's it? That's all Baylor has?" Graydon roared with laughter.

Dan scowled. "That's all, sir, by actual count. He may have more in Franklin."

Ortiz returned a short time later and gave his report.

"Capitan Graydon, Baylor has three thousand men between Mesilla and the *Presidio*. There are many, many more at Franklin, maybe five regiments. All are very well supplied. They will begin a campaign to take Santa Fe within the week."

"We'd better make haste to get word to Colonel Canby at Fort Craig," replied Graydon.

"Paddy," Dan interjected. "Didn't you hear what Roque and I told you?"

"Yes," he smiled. "Obviously you miscounted. We've got to get this news to the Colonel. We leave in thirty minutes. First Sergeant, get the men ready."

Fort Craig, many miles south of Socorro, was a rarity among western forts most of which had no walls or defensive works. Fort Craig, standing above one of the principal Rio Grande fords, had bastions, walls, and gun emplacements to dominate the *Camino Real*. The fort was also within sight, if not gunshot, of the crossing at Val Verde so it was well placed to defend them both. Within the fort were adobe barracks for a large force of soldiers. The fort was crowded with infantry consolidated from towns up and down the river and dragoons pulled from posts further west. The men who had abandoned Fort Fillmore without a fight crowded in side by side with the newly raised New Mexico Volunteers.

Entering the post, Captain Graydon was of a mind to deliver his report immediately to Colonel Canby. "You two, Gonzales, Martinez, come along with me to headquarters."

There they found Colonel Canby studying a map and going over his plans with some of his officers. Among them, Dan recognized Kit Carson in the uniform of a colonel and Lieutenant George Bascom of the 7th Infantry, whom they had met at Fort Buchanan. Kit nodded to them. Graydon saluted smartly. "Sir, I've come from Mesilla with a report of conditions there."

"Please, Captain Graydon, bring us up to date."

Graydon cleared his throat and began. "The enemy has over three thousand troops at Fillmore and Mesilla. Three thousand more are coming up soon from Franklin bringing twenty cannon. One of my men is brother to the padre in town. The padre's been takin' confessions and listenin' to all that is said by the secesh officers. Colonel Baylor, who has pronounced himself governor of Arizona, plans to attack to take Santa Fe as soon as the troops from Franklin come up." Dan noticed something: Paddy Graydon lost his Irish brogue when speaking to Canby.

Kit saw the look on Dan's face and indicated he should keep silent. Graydon must have thought Roque and Dan would be intimidated by all the officers in the room.

"Gentlemen," said Canby, "it is exactly as I feared. They've built up their forces faster than anyone else predicted. We must make our defenses ready. They will be forced to attack us here as we stand astride the *Camino Real* and defend its principle ford."

"Pardon me, Colonel." It was Kit Carson speaking quietly and politely as always. At a nod from Canby, who seemed to respect him, Kit went on. "The valley of the Rio Grande is broad and the river has many fords. They can easily bypass this fort."

"That is correct, Colonel Carson," Canby replied. "But we also stand astride his lines of communication and supply. The enemy cannot bypass us without worrying that we will cut him off."

Hearing him speak, Dan began to understand some of the problems the commanders in New Mexico faced.

They were waiting for orders and unwilling to make any move lest it be the wrong one. There were questions of the southern states right to withdraw from the Union as well as questions concerning the Texas's claim to New Mexico, for Santa Anna had ceded it to them at San Jacinto. Washington had vacillated by giving instructions that weren't clear. If a battle was won, it might be one the government didn't want to win and might provoke unforeseen problems. The generals had been ordering more and more troops to be sent east. If any were lost in battle, the commander might be blamed.

As the meeting broke up, Kit turned to Graydon. "Would you mind, Captain, bringing these two men and following me to my quarters?"

Graydon could hardly refuse a superior officer.

Once there Dan said, "Colonel, Privates Gonzales and Martinez beg to report?"

"Gonzales and Martinez, is it?"

"Aye, Colonel." Paddy was backpedaling fast. "A little misunderstanding over the terms of their enlistment. I'd be after correcting it directly."

"Private Gonzales," said Kit, "please continue your report."

"I'm Martinez," Dan said. "He's Gonzales. Sir, we crawled up to within a few hundred yards of Fort Fillmore and Mesilla, respectively, and watched all day. I counted two hundred and fifty men during retreat at Fillmore. Roque counted fifty more in Mesilla. They do not appear ready to advance. They had the four cannon left behind by Union forces. We know they have another forty or fifty men in the field fighting Indians."

"Captain Graydon," said Kit, Dan was sure Carson would castigate him for his false report, "would you be so kind as to transfer Gonzales and Martinez to my command?"

"Yes, sir, at once. Consider it done." Dismissed Graydon saluted, turned, and departed.

"So, Señor Kit," said Roque, "do we tell Canby the truth?"

"No. Graydon is popular with his men and with the commander. The report he gave was the one Colonel Canby wanted to hear. It suits his intentions."

"But, Kit," Dan said, "Canby could easily take Mesilla with all the men I see here. Mesilla is the gateway to California. The Texians can attack toward Santa Fe or San Diego. If the Union held Mesilla, they would have to attack there. That way there would be only one place to defend, not two."

Kit looked at Dan his eyes soft and sympathetic. "Colonel Canby won't listen. You'll be wasting your breath. Now tell me how you came to be Martinez and Gonzales."

They explained about being deserters from the Army of Texas and the circumstances of their enlistment with Graydon,

Kit shook his head. "Paddy was a good sergeant, but he doesn't belong in command."

Dan realized Kit was right. "He wasn't really a leader. He did the company books."

Roque grunted. "He lacks the honor and honesty that guides most officers."

As a company clerk, Dan thought, he had learned to please his superiors and to write reports that cast his commander and unit in the best light. "Yet he's hard to dislike. He looks after and truly cares for his men, perhaps better than any commander in New Mexico. They love him for it and will follow him anywhere."

Kit smiled. "Unfortunately, he has no idea where he is going."

Dan didn't blame Ortiz or his brother, the padre, for their report on the situation. They were untrained and didn't know what they were looking at. That's a dangerous quality in a scout. Men who think five men are a battalion and ten a regiment will always file false reports.

"Well then," said Colonel Carson, "I think the solution is easy. Rest and feed yourselves for a few days as my guests at Army expense, and then Gonzales and Martinez can desert."

"I wouldn't want to get them in trouble," said Roque thoughtfully.

Kit looked at him. "They've already deserted, and you've given them several weeks head start. And," he smiled, "the Army won't be looking for you."

"Kit," Dan blurted, "have you seen Sebriana?" In that instant, he realized that she was more important to him than his friends Rojo and Verde. He should have asked about all three.

"Yes," Colonel Carson replied, "she passed by here six weeks ago headed for Santa Fe with Peregrino Rojo and Rodado Verde."

Dan longed for Sebriana but knew she could never be his wife. He had a quest to continue. He'd played Jonah long enough. Providence had brought the two friends to Colonel Carson and the opportunity to return to their mission. For now, New Mexico was safe from Texans.

Chapter 13

Back to Chaco Canyon

"Amigo, cheer up," said Roque for the tenth time that day. Dan had been sullen and aloof on the trip from Fort Craig. "There are many women, and we are headed for Santa Fe where you can find most of them. Do not let the loss of just one trouble you."

Apparently, he had recovered from the loss of Great Western. A heart easily broken must easily mend, Dan thought, yet Dan believed Roque's love for Sarah Bowman had been genuine.

As he rode, Dan's thoughts turned to Sebriana. The New Englander did not know what he would find in Santa Fe. She might have been taken by her former in-laws. She might still be angry over some accidental slight he'd given her or even be angry because she worried over Dan's months-long absence. She might think him dead and have taken another lover to console her. Dan had known women so insecure that they would be certain that the absence meant he'd taken another lover. For Dan, their long affair had been casual, little more than two old friends having a good time. He was sure at the start it had been so for her as well though he couldn't be sure. Perhaps she cast a deeper net than he had suspected and had thought to snare him from the first. He had been a boy of nineteen, unfamiliar with the ways of women, fresh off the Santa Fe Trail, and still confined to English alone. She was already twice a widow known as Doña Loca.

He rode in trepidation, unsure of the greeting he would receive, even more uncertain of what greeting he wished to receive and certainly unprepared for the one he got. As Roque and Dan walked, leading their stock through the narrow streets and approaching their casa west of the great plaza, Dan caught a glimpse of a green top hat. It scurried away disappearing into a doorway. Verde was here, and Dan wasn't expecting what happened next.

Doña Loca burst from their doorway into the street and raced toward them shrieking like the Sea Hag herself, brandishing a butcher knife. Three paces from Dan, she leapt into the air. Colliding, she nearly knocked him over as she wrapped her legs about his middle; her arms went to his neck. She hugged him tight, bathing his head and neck in warm, soft kisses. She smelled of lavender, piñon, and spices.

"O, Pobrecito, I am so glad to see you," she whispered between caresses. "We were so worried the Apaches had gotten you. No word came. I feared I would never see you again. I missed the warmth of your body next to mine. I needed you to wash my back."

Santa Fe, a town where anything went, was thoroughly scandalized.

"We heard you were coming," she went on. "Come in. I have a special dinner for you."

The dinner contained no pork. Chicken prepared in a hot molé sauce was served with rice cooked with chili and onions, peas were sautéed with piñon nuts, the last of the summer squash steamed with tomatoes, chili, onions, and garlic. She served chili rellenos stuffed with shredded beef and cheese. Along with the lavish dinner she served tortillas, coffee ground with piñon nuts, and hot chocolate made with cinnamon and spice.

When Roque and Dan had eaten their fill and more, Sebriana hiked up her skirts and nestled herself into Dan's lap as deeply as she could, pulling his head down between her breasts. Like most of her Mexican sisters, she wore no undergarments of any kind, a fact of which Dan was soon painfully aware.

Verde, the devil incarnate, always there when least wanted, called them back from heaven. "Sebriana, my dear, if you can contain your passions for just a wee bit longer, there are matters we should discuss. I've been going over Topper's papers." When they split up months before, the pack animals and thus the journal, had stayed with the three friends, Verde, Rojo, and Sebriana, who had taken the road north to Santa Fe.

To Dan it was clear now that his separation from Topper's journal had been a blessing, for the precious papers weren't lost, nor were the notes from their own inquiries.

"The season grows late," Verde went on. "The snow will soon fly in the high country. I'm after recovering the treasure yet this year. We know it must be in the San Juan Mountains, but I think our best course is to return there through Chaco."

"Why Chaco?" asked Roque.

"Because last time you were there, you didn't think in terms of the Masonic Ritual and the Templars. You were still thinkin' only in terms o' the ancient Hebrew. And ye didn't have me with you providing my deep Templar insight."

"I agree," Dan said. "We'll send for Rojo in the

morning. Is there anything else? Otherwise, I need to get to bed. All that food has made me very tired." Dan took Sebriana by the hand.

Behind him Dan heard Verde saying to Roque, "Bed maybe, but I doubt it's sleep that lad will be gettin'."

It didn't take them long to put an outfit together for the expedition.

"Verde," Dan told the man in the green top hat, "I'm sure we are observed."

Verde agreed. "We'll tell the others and then let us follow the Jemez River out as far as we can, passing Cochiti, Zia, and Jemez Pueblos."

They continued west passing Jemez following ancient trails.

Rojo had spent time with his people asking pointed questions to the point of being rude. Father Nighthawk and Doña Luna enjoyed having a bright student and told him much of what they knew.

On the long ride, Rojo spoke of ancient wonders." Long ago on this very trail, there were traders who brought salt from the Colorado to villages near Santa Fe in exchange for buffalo hides and turquoise. From the south came people with parrots, colorful feathers, and copper bells."

"I have never heard of this," challenged Roque.

"No, you haven't" said Rojo calmly. "Ancient trade vanished with the coming of the Mexicans."

Dan thought about how the Spanish had upset ancient patterns. "It is difficult to believe that such extensive networks ever existed only to vanish so thoroughly."

Verde chortled. "Oh, they existed, boyo, they existed."

"And yet," said Rojo looking at Dan, "you have seen the evidence at Chaco, and here we follow an ancient trail that leads to no living town or village."

The third day from Jemez, they came upon a ruined torreon, a tower, standing on a promontory. Around its base, they found signs of ancient warfare. Here and there skulls grinned up at them, some with an arrowhead protruding or buried among ribs. The merest touch would turn these things to dust. They had lain there a very long time indeed. The beams and pilasters of subterranean houses were blackened to charcoal where they could be seen indicating they had been burned. Walls of houses and torreon, defensive towers, were red in places.

Lifting his hat, Dan scratched his head. "I think I recall a note in Topper's book. He mentioned that the walls of ruins that had burned were often red."

"Father Nighthawk told us of these people," said Rojo. "They are ancestors of the Jicarilla slaughtered long ago by the Jemez. They built towers that could see all over the country and each tower could be seen by others so they could pass messages swiftly. I have seen many of these towers north of here. That the people were killed suddenly in warfare is always obvious. The Jemez say they had reason. Father Nighthawk says the Jemez were jealous and greedy. The torreon people had better luck with crops.

"The Jemez surprised them. The Jemez were a numerous people, striking everywhere at once so the people of the torreons, the Gallina people, couldn't warn each other. Women and children were taken to Jemez as slaves. Those who escaped were taken in by the Jicarilla and became Ollero clans, the people of the Moon, the Jicarilla band who dwell in the mountains along the Rio Grande."

Verde and Roque became interested in the torreon, convinced that it was the work of men who knew how to build castles. They puttered around and eventually managed to climb to the top. Rojo would not enter the places of the dead.

Sebriana came to Dan quietly with questions. "What do you know about the Jicarilla Apache?"

"Jicarilla stories say they have lived here forever," he told her. "There are two bands, as I think you know, the Ollero and Llanero. The Llanero live on the llano, the plains, and hunt buffalo. The Ollero live in the mountains where Rojo says the Gallina, who made the torreons lived. They farm a little, make pottery, and make baskets with a peculiar weave that looks like Pueblo work. The quality of the baskets is much better than anything the Pueblo make. Their one great ceremony, Go jii ya, is about the division between the two bands and the balance between plants and animal food."

Before she could ask more, Roque and Verde emerged from the tower, running towards them.

"We're followed," cried Roque.

"As certain as the dawn, I'm after believin' it's those Penitente devils," chirped Verde. "In the telly-scoop, Roque saw the gleam of armor and lance points."

Rojo nodded. "We must conceal our trail by each going from here in a different direction. We will meet tonight by that rock." He pointed with his lower lip to a pinnacle near the horizon, ten miles away.

"Wait a moment," Dan said. "Let's think about this. It's a good plan for throwing them off unless they know where we are going. Do you suppose they do? There have been Mexican expeditions against the Navajo that went through Chaco."

Rojo agreed. "So the Dineh, the Navajo, have told us."

Dan thought for a minute. "Can we safely assume

these Penitentes, the heirs of the Conquistadors, after three centuries of occupation haven't tumbled to Coronado's error?"

Roque shook his great ursine head. "We have a fierce enemy, and we don't know the state of his knowledge or his intentions. They've had three centuries to search for the prize."

Dan nodded. "They might have learned a lot in that time. I want to talk to their leader."

"That is very dangerous," said Roque.

"Let's figure out a way to make it less so," said Sebriana.

Rojo thought for a minute. "Chaco is west toward the setting sun. If we turn south and meet at that peak this evening, we will learn if they are following us or simply assuming we are headed to Chaco." He pointed to the peak with his lower lip. "Where we stand, here by this torreon, is a crossroads for ancient trading trails. It is a good place to change direction without arousing suspicion. Near that southern peak, the trail leads through a little cañon where we can set an ambush."

The companions scattered, Rojo riding northwest, Roque southeast, Verde west, and Sebriana and Dan together heading south. They changed direction often, sometimes crossing each other's trails. The trail they left was confusing. They had each taken one of the ancient paths, followed it a few miles, then cut cross country, and joined another ancient way for a while. Anyone following would have to be serious about wanting to find them.

"If they continue west to Chaco," said Dan to Sebriana, "then they know about its mysteries and think we are going there. If they manage to follow our trails, it will be confirmation they were following our party and don't know where we are going."

At dusk, Dan heard Roque's voice in the dark. "We meet according to appointment."

Behind him Verde's voice drifted from a place of concealment. "Quoting from the ritual, boyo? Are ye a Fellowcraft and a brother from Tyre then, a right villain?" He cackled in the dark.

They met near a peak that bore a surprising resemblance to an oriental pagoda. Rojo urged them on into the dark, up the cañon he had spoken of. They dismounted a mile from the entrance and in a narrow defile rearranged some of the smaller boulders and rolled more down from the walls ensuring that coming further would be like entering the gate to a maze. Anyone following them would be forced to turn this way and that and go around obstacles.

They rode three miles farther to the first place where they could scramble up the walls to the mesa above and then doubled back until they were above the obstacles they'd arranged. Unless the Penitentes knew another way up, the companions had made sure there would be six miles between themselves and those following them. The path Rojo had chosen was so hidden that there was a good chance they would go much farther in trying to reach the mesa top.

In a small hollow, they camped and made their dinner where their fire could not be seen. It was after midnight on a cool, early fall evening before they rolled into their warm buffalo robes.

The next morning, Dan awoke to the smell of piñon smoke and coffee. Sebriana was up and making their breakfast, so he pitched in and assisted with bacon, warm tortillas, refritos, and cornmeal mush. Dan feared their smoke might endanger the position, but Rojo assured him they were safe.

"She thinks like a Jicarilla," said Rojo. "She chooses wood that is very dry and does not smoke. Even if it is seen, the way we came is the only way they can approach."

Rojo had another surprise for their guests. "Pile stones on the mesa rim fifty feet above the cañon floor, two hundred yards up cañon from our previous obstacle. Once they ride in, they will have difficulty getting out."

"Aye, we've seen this work before, haven't we now, lad?" asked Verde. "Out on the llano with Chief Chacón fighting Comanche."

"Verde," Dan said. "I've got to ask you something. Sebriana practices the Hebrew faith as best she can. Roque was raised Catholic, but veered away seeing corruption and joined the Freemasons. I was raised as a West Country Dissenter, a Methodist. Rojo worships the Creator. What about you?"

"So do we all, lad," he replied. "We all worship the Great Architect of the Universe."

"Are you telling me that your religion is Freemason?"

Verde cocked his head and took stock of Dan as if he were a stupid child. "You know better than that, boyo. Freemason is not a religion. I'm only after telling you that I worship the One God in my own way.

"My antecedents," he went on, "were Knights of the Temple, as you know. Their brethren were betrayed and tortured at the Pope's command. The Templars had been the great defenders of the Catholic faith, and the leaders of that faith turned on them. They could hardly continue to follow the Pope, nor could they put their faith in other human religious leaders. They became the Freemasons upholding the right of all men to worship in their own way. Freemasons traveled the world, hiding from persecution and protecting others, too. Knowledge of the existence of the Royal Society became public in 1660, but its scientists had already been under our protection for centuries and the Wycliffe people, too."

Verde let this Masonic history sink in. "Don't you know that it was the Masons among the Founding Fathers of our great nation that insisted that Congress would make no law establishing one particular doctrine over another, that all men could practice their religion in freedom? Of course, you do."

The day warmed dry and dusty. They waited in scrub woodland of juniper and piñon that retained little of its rich summer aroma. The fall sky was clear, lacking even playful clouds. In the late forenoon, their adversary appeared, groups of riders assembled at the mouth of the cañon from myriad directions, having followed diverse trails left by the companions. Entering the cañon, they were slow in passing the first obstacle. Blocking each other as they passed around rocks they ran into each other and were forced to proceed one and two at a time.

Dan counted seventy-six mounted men followed by a baggage train. They had taken the field it seemed and were prepared to campaign as long as need be. Arrayed in a motley collection of patched and rusted armor they carried lances and crossbows and a few ancient muskets. One stood out, his armor a little more complete and shiny than the others and in better repair.

The friends tilted their pile of stone into the gorge and watched it fall well ahead of the riders. Horses stamped and pirouetted, reared and whinnied causing confusion in the ranks as riders lost their seats.

Dan stepped to the rim and addressed the one he took for their leader. "Señor Conquistador." The man seemed to accept the title, "I would speak with you."

A crossbow bolt shot through the leg of Dan's

trousers at thigh level gouging his limb deeply. Blood oozed. Although it hurt, Dan did not want the conquistador aware of his vulnerability and refused to give any sign of his pain.

"Your trap has failed," the conquistador replied. "Your avalanche has done us no harm."

"I did not intend it to harm you, only to slow you down so we could talk. Do I need to have my men fire on you for you to know how few of yours would emerge from this trap if I so wished it?" Without waiting for a response, Dan went on. "Why do you follow us?"

Dan thought the man in armor might try to deny his intent, but he was arrogant. "We have been charged by the Pope himself to protect the holy places you have defiled with your presence. For three hundred years we have been sentinels on the path to Cebolla."

"Cebolla?" Dan said. "Am I indeed on the road to Cebolla? Where is it?"

Waving his arm, the man brushed aside Dan's questions. "You desecrated the place of the Lord's Commandments." That would be Los Lunas. "Then you went to Zuñi in search of the Pope's Treasure."

Dan nodded. "So, it is the Pope's Treasure. How did the Holy Father come to hide it in New Mexico?"

The conquistador glared. "The Knights Templar were commissioned to bring the treasure from the Holy Land, but seeing its value, they snatched it from the Holy Father's grasp and took it beyond his reach."

Dan cocked his head. "I did not know there was such a place, beyond the reach of the Bishop of Rome. I thought he was given power over all things in this world so that what he bound here would be bound in heaven, and what was loosed on earth would be loosed in heaven."

Dan felt a little ashamed of that comment. He didn't intend to make light of the man's religion though he certainly had a different understanding of Christianity, one that he hoped was more historically accurate. Dan did, however, want to make him angry hoping rage would get him to reveal things he might not talk about otherwise. Dan was surprised the conquistador let him ask so many questions. The interrogator is the one in control of the conversation. Arrogance and insecurity are an interesting mix. Insecure over the knowledge that he lacked, his arrogance led him to bluff.

"You went to Zuñi in search of treasure," the man accused. "You cannot deny it!"

"I see, Zuñi, so that is Cebolla. You know where the treasure is to protect it. Why do you not recover it and take it to the Pope?"

The armored man pointed his sword at Dan. Even at this distance Dan could see the man's veins protruding and his helmet-shaded face turning red. "As you well know, the Zuñi are an obstinate people descended from stiff-necked Jews whose people murdered Our Lord. Acting with assistance from Templar warriors hidden in their ranks, they fought Coronado and continue to impede what is proper."

Dan did his best to look puzzled. "Templars? Jews? I have no idea what you are talking about. What treasure?"

The conquistador rose in his stirrups waving his sword. "The treasury of Solomon's Temple taken by the people of Dan before Jerusalem fell to the Babylonians and the treasury of Herod's temple buried before Jerusalem fell to Rome and discovered by the Templar Knights. More gold than you can imagine. Gold enough for seven cities of seven Templar bishops! And you thieves think to steal it from us. We've watched you and have seen you search.

"Enough of your questions!" he went on. "Now you will answer mine. Where have the Zuñi concealed the treasure?"

"I don't think they have," Dan replied truthfully. "It sounds like you're pursuing wraiths and ancient legends with no more substance than mist."

This final insult was all the Penitente could take. With a wave of his arm, he signaled his crossbowmen to fire. Fortunately, Rojo had shown Dan how Apache boys learn from an early age to dodge slow moving arrows. It also helped that Rojo hit Dan behind the knees and knocked him down.

Not to be outdone, Verde leaned over the cañon rim and shot a bowman. "Damn, shot went high. I was aiming for his horse."

Roque and Sebriana fired as Verde reloaded. Recovering, Rojo and Dan followed suit. They fired three times each disappearing from the enemies' sight to reload and concentrating on riders trying to escape through their obstacles. Below the companions all was pandemonium.

With lancers having no weapons lethal at long range, the bowman and musketeers were the only ones able to return fire. Their horses reared and bucked giving their riders a choice between escape and dismounting to return fire.

"Let's get out of here," Dan called to his friends. The carnage they'd created would slow the Penitentes as they dealt with wounded and the loss of horses. The dead an army can bury and be done with. The wounded have to be cared for pulling additional men from the ranks.

The five companions resumed their course for Chaco without attempt to conceal their trail. Tomorrow would be soon enough to make tracks for Zuñi. Toward dusk as they approached a spring to water their stock, Dan began to feel light-headed and fell from his mule.

The last thing he recalled as he went down was Verde saying, "I think he means for us to camp here."

The situation was not serious, and Dan was well in the morning Sebriana having stitched and bandaged his leg. Dan had forgotten about it and had leaked a fair amount of blood while riding.

Rojo went to his friend. "Deception is an interesting game. It always works best when you're trying to convince someone of what they already believe."

They rode northwest in a body leaving a plain trail away from Zuñi. The day after Dan's collapse, the friends split up Apache-like and headed southwest toward Zuñi. The first day's ride made it look like they were attempting to conceal their true destination. The third day they joined a well-used trail for Zuñi.

At midday, Rojo signaled them to move off the trail. "Here hard ground and slip rock will make our departure less than obvious."

Two days later, they arrived at Chaco. They saw no dust along their back trail.

Roque chuckled. "Perhaps the Penitentes rode all the way to Zuñi before they realized we'd turned off. They will search that neighborhood very hard looking for our hiding place."

Chaco was much as they'd left it the previous spring. They camped in the ruin by the arroyo, for it seemed to them defensible and central. The local Navajo took note of their presence.

Sebriana noticed before the others. "They don't seem as warm and friendly as before." Nonetheless, she was able to hire a few to assist in camp. She chose people with knowledge of the area.

Rojo spent time with the local people as they tended flocks and brought in crops from their fields. He soon learned why they were less than cordial.

Around a piñon fire with deep darkness beyond, the friends digested a meal of beef, chili, and beans prepared by Sebriana. Smoking their pipes and passing a small bottle Verde had brought, they were content until they heard Rojo's news.

"The Navajo who tends our horses," Rojo said, "was very nervous around me. After much talk, I learned the Mormons returned here with gifts for the people. Last summer, they built a trading post near the mouth of the cañon saying they would return again each summer. Navajo men watch for our return so they can send word and receive more gifts. The Danites have a company no more than a week away."

They were alarmed by the news. Dan spoke for them. "We haven't much time then."

"Perhaps the Navajo, with proper incentive, will work for us, too." Roque suggested the idea, but all were thinking it.

Rojo agreed. "I'll ask the Navajo to watch our back trail for Mexicans."

Sebriana shook her head. "We need to be away from here in a day, two at the most, and we should leave an obvious trail in the wrong direction."

Roque scratched his head. "What direction will we go?"

"North" said Verde, "you pea-wit. We're about goin' to the River of Saint John and his fine mountains, too. Lad, ye have seen the map carved in stone down in the country of the Chiricahua."

"Then what are we doing here?" snarled Roque ready to knock some manners into Verde.

"We are here," said Sebriana sweetly, "so that you gentlemen may reinterpret what you see in light of your Masonic ritual and, thereby, limit our search of the otherwise vast wilderness."

Dan thought for a moment. "We considered the first degree before, and I suggest that everything we learned from it had to do with where the treasure originally came from and where it first went. The first degree brought us to the cañon of the Colorado and eventually here to the second resting place of the Ark. If the purpose of the first degree was to lead us to the first resting place, the second must take us along the next stage."

"Can it be so simple?" retorted Roque. "Hebrew Danites taking the Ark to the big cañon made trail markers on stone to show where they'd gone after leaving their intended course. But they were unable to get a complete message back to their people waiting at Roslyn. Centuries passed, and they came to Chaco without leaving a trail, perhaps despairing of those they left behind."

"Topper found evidence of the journey at Roslyn," Dan replied, "enough to make him sure the Ark had arrived safe in its new Holy of Holies."

"But," Roque continued, "Templars who came later disappeared and never returned to Verde's people with news of the third lair. None of them survived." He folded his arms across his chest, certain of his status as an intellectual giant.

Sebriana winked. "Some always survive."

Verde jumped to his feet. "Sure and the lass's mind is as lively as the fire, just as Roque's is as busy as the piper's little finger." He looked at Roque. "Someone left a message on rock in the Chiricahua country, lad."

Roque massaged his head and made a gesture with his hands suggesting the playing of the pipes. "I don't use my little finger when I play the pipes."

"Someone made it to Scotland," Dan insisted. "Topper found evidence. And that someone knew enough to bury clues in the ritual just as the Masons were being formed from the ruin of the Templar Order. That took talent, effort, and knowledge, so they must have followed a route that bypassed Verde's people.

Dan shook his head from side to side clearing cobwebs, and then he stood bolt upright. "By the lord Harry, the second line at Newport Tower, it must point to the San Juans. Topper said it ran a little north of Taos. Someone at Newport knew where the Ark lay. There were survivors!"

The morning dawned with a rime of frost and a promise of a hard winter in the high country. Such mornings mute odors until the coffee begins to perk. Green chili stew with tortillas made a fine start to the day. It filled the air with the clean, crisp, sharp scent of chili and the warm aroma of meat and piñon.

They each went to their own tasks or interests. Rojo went in search of art on stone hoping with the help of a Navajo guide to find something akin to the map. Roque searched for roads and stairs. Sebriana and Dan walked through the clustered ruins and climbed to the cañon rims both north and south. Verde followed them at a distance.

Trails leading to the mesa above were not uncommon though often hidden. Here and there, the walls were broken by cañons and clefts where ancient steps had been cut. The largest and most impressive ruins stood within a few feet of sheer rock walls that rose one hundred feet and were clustered within a half mile of each other. From the rim, Sebriana, Verde, and Dan looked straight down into them.

Sebriana was puzzled. "There's not enough stone, not

enough blocks of stone to rebuild the walls, and many vigas are missing."

Dan thought about the structural elements that were absent. "The vigas, the great beams that support the roofs, are only wood. They could have rotted away. When the roof starts to fail, they get wet and rot sets in."

Sebriana stamped her foot. "Look more closely. They're only missing where the stones are missing, too." She was right. There were plenty of places where roofs had collapsed. They could see where the vigas had failed and took the top courses of stone with them. The walls retained most of their height, and the full height could be accounted for in scattered stones. Some part of the vigas always remained.

As Dan looked more closely, he became certain that where the vigas were completely missing, there was not enough stone to erect the walls again. "What? But why?"

She smiled at him. "It looks like they knocked rooms down intentionally and carried away vigas and stone to build elsewhere."

They stood on the north rim looking down into two of the largest ruins. Verde came closer.

"Verde," Dan said, "this place existed long before the Templars came, didn't it?"

"So it did, lad. What's on ye'r mind?"

"It's been six hundred years," Dan replied. "The message in the buildings has had time to degrade. They couldn't move whole buildings very well, but they did do some remodeling. That should make anything we can tell is new the more important."

As dusk approached, they gathered in camp unable to distinguish any message from remodeling where they could identify it.

Roque was the last to arrive, coming into camp in a

cloud of dust on a lathered horse. "Quick, get your mules! Come with me! You must see what I've found! Andalé! Arriba!"

They mounted and followed Roque down a side cañon, and at its end he pointed upward. "There! Don't you see? It is a flight of winding stairs consisting of three, five, and seven steps, just like in the ritual!"

And there they were. The steps began at the top of a talus slope out of reach of even the tallest man and led to the cliff top.

Verde looked up in awe. "They're as high as the gables on a house and upside down, too."

"Think," Dan said. "What does the second degree say? 'Keep a tongue of good report. Maintain secrecy.' Don't you see? Having them in reverse, seven-five-three, is a way to maintain secrecy."

Sebriana perked up. "It's why the signs pointed south, when we were supposed to go north!"

"Help me up." Dan rode his mule to the top of the talus and stood precariously in the saddle. Roque rode in close and made a fist, which he braced against the wall for Dan to stand on. By these measures Dan reached the bottom steps and began inching his way up.

"Good thing," said Rojo, "you got so much practice at this in the big cañon."

"Those steps are as old as the mist," chimed Verde, "and about as solid."

Midway up the seven steps Dan's foot slipped, and he slid back to the first step. He felt as though his fingernails must come loose before he slowed himself to a stop. At the top of the seven came the five set at a new angle with space between. Shifting his body and extending the proper limb proved a challenge. He slipped and caught himself by fingertips, hanging there until he could extend a leg upward above his head and catch a grip with the toe of his boot. The transition to the last three steps was equally difficult though he didn't slip.

Then he saw them: three pots, well-sealed and tucked under a ledge.

"You've got to see this!" Dan yelled to those below. "Come up and bring a rope."

He had a long wait as his friends backtracked down the cañon until they found a place where they could ascend.

When they had all arrived he opened the first pot. "What is that?"

"Corn," said Rojo. "It's corn."

The remaining pots were tarred with pitch to tightly seal them. Dan opened one. The bottom of the pot was full of something thick and gummy.

"It's oil, I think," said Sebriana. "I've seen old cooking oil get like this. It smells like oil."

He opened the last pot. It contained only moist residue and a smell.

"Oof, vinegar," Roque grimaced.

"Yes, vinegar!" Dan was elated.

"What's got into you, lad?" demanded Verde.

"It's vinegar!" He cried. "It was wine when it went in. Now it's vinegar. Don't you see? It completes the set. Here we have corn, wine, and oil. What are the wages of a Fellowcraft , a second degree Mason?"

"Corn, wine, and oil," replied Roque looking puzzled.

"And how," Dan asked, "does a Fellow Craft receive them?"

Rojo answered. "He goes between the two great pillars set up at the entrance to Solomon's Temple, Jachin and Boaz, through a long aisle or portico, and up a flight of winding steps consisting of three, five and seven steps to a place representing the inner chamber of the temple."

Roque still looked confused and Verde even worse. Unfamiliar with the ritual, Sebriana listened intently.

Dan went on. "The two big pueblos we passed between are the pillars, the cañon is the portico. These clearly are the steps. And this," he pointed to the covered ledge, "represents the inner chamber of the temple. We have received our wages!"

Dan glanced up and saw Rojo's eyes growing large. He rarely showed emotion or surprise. His arms rose pointing like one in a trance.

That's odd, Dan thought. He always points with his lip.

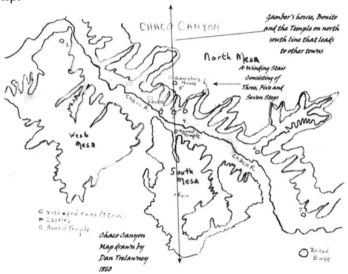

Dan turned to look where Rojo was gazing. As the sun retreated in the west, it cast long shadows making visible a road outlined with low hummocks and stone. At any other time of day, it would have been invisible. For those fleeting moments at sunset, it was there and plain disappearing into the distance north of northeast.

As always anticipating such a need, Dan had brought his compass and sextant from Santa Fe. They'd been with him since Greenport, Long Island, long unused until this, Topper's quest, began. Now he had need and took the bearing of the road.

"Let's get back to camp," Dan said. "We've much to do. We're leaving tomorrow."

In camp, Sebriana and her Navajo help prepared supper while Dan outlined his plan.

"Tomorrow morning at sunrise, Roque, and Verde, would you be pleased to ride east following the cañon for half the day taking all of the stock and equipment with you? At noon, turn north and find a way up onto the mesa concealing your trail if you can. Double back and meet us at the Gambler's house about sundown."

Continuing Dan said, "Sebriana, Rojo, and I will stay here and take some measurements and draw a map. Roque's line, the one we followed south, goes north through the Gambler's house. I think at dusk we will find another road. We've signs of it before. The road we just found goes east of north. If we draw these roads, stairs and villages on a map and include Topper's Newport line, I think we'll find a convergence along a river north of the San Juan in the mountains of the same name."

Dan had been taking readings on locations they visited and recording them in Topper's book. A watch was no ship's chronometer, but a good one helped to mark the meridian.

"Then why not go directly there?" asked Verde. "Why go north?"

Rojo answered. "He thinks we'll find other clues if we follow the road north. Whoever left these signs wanted us to go north."

Chapter 14

Pursued

On the mesa top near the Gambler's House, they drew their map using Dan's notes, the compass, and sextant. Topper had recorded the longitude of the Newport Tower and of Jerusalem. Knotting string around rope at intervals representing degrees, they measured out a huge map on the mesa top stretching a line three times the length of Dan's forearm for each of the one hundred and forty-three degrees of longitude between Chaco Cañon and Jerusalem. Topper's notes showed Roslyn at 55°51'20"N by 3°09'38"W and Jerusalem at 31°46'41"N by 35°14'08"E. Dan's own measurements put Chaco at 36°03'36"N by 107°57'27"W. They formed a square and measured north from the latitude of Chaco to Roslyn and south to Jerusalem. Having time, they added Newport Tower and Casas Grandes.

A north-south line from Chaco passed from Casas Grandes on through the heart of Chaco Cañon and continued north through Gambler's House. They erected stone monuments to represent important points. Rojo, familiar with maps, was able to fill in some of the regional geography laying pebbles to approximate the course of the San Juan River and large stones for important or distinctive mountains. Holding his compass,

Dan stood above the stone that represented Solomon's Temple in Jerusalem and had his friends stretch the rope along the bearing of the second line at Newport Tower until it crossed their north-south Chaco meridian. It passed about one hundred miles north of where they stood, perhaps ten miles north of the San Juan. They did the same running the bearing from Newport Tower and from Roslyn, but the lines passed far to the north and held no significance for them as they'd expected. They added a line representing the road from Roque's stairs to the north. It crossed the line from Jerusalem about fifty miles east of the Casas Grandes-Chaco meridian or north road.

Rojo cocked his head, and then looked surprised. "There is a rock formation above the San Juan where the line of Roque's stairs crosses the Jerusalem line. All the tribes know it. Some think it sacred, calling its two columns the Hero Twins."

"Brother Elder and Brother Younger from the stories?" Dan asked.

"Exactly."

"I know these stories from the Pueblos and the Navajo," Dan continued. "There is mention of them in Topper's notes. I thought it strange that he included them. I couldn't see their importance. The Jicarilla have these stories, too?"

"We do," Rojo responded, "and the Utahs as well. The brothers stand where Utah and Jicarilla ranges overlap."

"I think we're onto something," said Sebriana.

They transferred their map to a deerskin, the largest portable surface they had. Verde and Roque joined them as the sun set, and they all watched in wonder as the lengthening shadows proved the existence of what they now considered the Great North Road. One moment there was nothing; then suddenly the road stretched away clearly visible even on distant hills continuing straight as an arrow's flight.

North the road ran through a barren wilderness of stone and sand. Conical hills riven by dry water courses stood out like Joseph's coat of many colors of black, yellow, red, orange, and gray, a petit four layer cake of sterility. Elsewhere the north *llano* sprouted sparse grass, sage, and scrub juniper. Ruins along the road proved to be way stations where water could be found. The road never curved but continued over and through obstacles; a cañon cut their path. Rojo and Dan descended the carefully cut staircases to its depths. The others, leading their stock, searched long for routes down and back up on the far side.

At sundown each day, they paused to watch the shadows cast by a setting sun revealing the road before them. Selecting a distant hill, they'd make it the next day's goal. They never lost the road. It ran true north toward the polar star as they confirmed each night. By day, the compass led them. Sundown on the third day found them on a bluff overlooking the San Juan River and examining the large ruin on its north bank.

"It looks like Templar work," said Sebriana, "though I also see Hebrew elements."

"Something they built together," Dan said, "as we've been led to suspect."

They watered and grazed their stock. As they cooled themselves in the river, their weapons never far from their hands, Rojo spotted a deer come to drink. It ended up providing them with fresh meat. Camping by the ruin that night, they took the opportunity to cook a more complete meal than usual.

The next day was a lesson in frustration. Try as they might, they could find no relationship between the architecture of the ruin and the ritual. A large kiva stood in a central plaza while many smaller ones lay interspersed among houses. The great apartment of well laid stone reached three and four stories in height. It gave the appearance of a castle as the Templar works did while lacking the symmetry and harmony that the Hebrew dwellings showed with the landscape. These were all things they'd learned to expect at Chaco. Nothing else stood out. At the noon meal, they sat conversing.

"Columns Doric, Ionic, Corinthian, Tuscan, and composite," mumbled Roque, "but the Tuscan and composite offer nothing that is new or distinct, so there are really only three. There's some relationship to directions and to beauty."

"I don't see anything that looks like a column," said Verde.

"The seven steps were grammar, rhetoric, logic, arithmetic, geometry, music, and astronomy," said Rojo. "We've used logic, arithmetic, geometry, and astronomy to get this far. It seems like we need to use one more at least, maybe music. Perhaps Roque could favor us with a tune on his bagpipes." There was no suggestion of jest in his tone.

"I'm not at all sure his playing counts as music," said Verde. "Perhaps the darlin' lass could sing for us."

Dan's frustration became obvious. "This is getting us nowhere."

"Pack up. There still time this afternoon," said Rojo. "The Jerusalem line passed ten miles north of here."

"He's right," said Sebriana, and they broke camp.

At the tenth mile, a clear, rushing, mountain stream flowing southwest toward the San Juan cut across their path. On its far bank stood two large D-shaped pueblos, each with a large central kiva of the kind Dan thought of as a temple.

Dan considered the layout. "I think we are seeing the pillar motif again. Here are the two great kivas, representing pillars at the entrance to Solomon's Temple." With his compass he took a bearing, touching the southern edge of one and the northern edge of the other. The bearing ran northeast miles above the Jerusalem line. Dan was confused.

It was Verde who spoke up first. "Maintain secrecy! I have an idea. In the morning, let's go back to the ruin on the San Juan."

"I don't know, Verde," Dan said. "Maybe I've got the alignment wrong. Maybe I'm supposed to use other features. Or maybe it's correct, and the next stage is not where we think."

"Now, lad, I'm after believin' you used the so called pillars as you've done before," he replied. "And that is how we should do it again."

"Trust him," said Sebriana.

Dan did, and in the morning they rode back to the San Juan. There Dan stood in the center of the largest kiva and took a bearing. The line crossed the Jerusalem line above the San Juan River exactly where Rojo said the brothers stood. That was confirmation enough.

They followed the San Juan to the northeast. After many miles, cañon walls rose to enclose them. As they made their evening camp, Rojo borrowed Dan's telescope and rode out to the top of a southern promontory. In the clear, dry western air, it was no trick to see mountains over one hundred miles away. Light glinting off ornaments and equipment could be seen from afar as well.

Returning, he had news. "Dust rises to the south," said Rojo pointing with his lip. "Many riders are coming from Chaco."

Verde stood. "Aye, laddie, that can't be good."

Roque was concerned. "How far away are they?"

"More than a day's ride, maybe two," replied Rojo.

"Away from this river," Dan said, "the countryside to the north is barren and offers little water or forage for our stock. If we stay with the river, our course will be obvious."

"As we go east, the country becomes higher," said Rojo. "Cañons and hills will provide water and forage for those who know where to look. I know this country well. There are three cañons that join the San Juan. The first two are dry, but the third carries a fine river. The first leads south almost to the torreon the ancient tower, where we first spotted the Penitentes who dog us so determinedly. The second tends north and comes close to the cañon of the fine river, which will lead us back almost to the Hero Twins, the Two brothers.

"I suggest," he continued, "we head south down the first cañon, double back, go cross country over the mesa tops to the second and finally find our way to the river that flows west to the San Juan."

Roque seemed puzzled. "Are you suggesting that as they follow us down this first and most southern-tending cañon, they might lose our trail and continue south to the *torreon*?"

Rojo smiled a twisted Apache grin. They all agreed, and Rojo selected a prominent rocky feature miles ahead. Following different paths, they rode north of the river and joined again where Rojo had indicated. Thereafter, the terrain worked to confine them to the cañon bottom. At the end of the second day, they came to Rojo's first cañon and began their wide swing back to their original course.

By Dan's reckoning, they were riding close to the Great Continental Divide which, he thought, made understanding the terrain even more difficult than it would normally have been. The Divide was subtle, not pronounced, high ground surrounded by much higher ground. Seeming to avoid the great ridges, meandering across the countryside through gently sloping meadows, it often followed a low hill or hummock hardly noticeable among the mountain giants all around. On one side, water flowed to the Pacific and on the other to the Atlantic, making the Divide a place of origins. A person could step into a cañon tending southeast and find it joined another turning west, then north, and finally northwest. Another led northwest to join a western flowing stream that joined another going south, then northeast, or southeast to the Rio Grande. Pick the wrong cañon to follow, and they would soon be far from their goal.

Among the small party, only Rojo knew which cañons would carry them to their destination.

In this land of twisted canons, grassy bottoms, home to springs and marshes, supported the occasional stand of cottonwood. Hillsides adorned with oak give way to juniper and piñon, which in turn yielded to pine and aspen. Steep slopes were crowned by crenulated bastions of sheer sandstone. The hilltops above the cliffs were as rounded as a bald pate above a coronet. The view from each hilltop showed a world of pine covered hills riven by endless twisting cañons surrounded in the purple distance by high peaks in the north and east and south.

They hunted turkey, deer, and mountain sheep as they went. An elk, part of a herd retreating from the snowy high country, fell to Roque's marksmanship. Eating well, they enjoyed the abundance of upland beauty.

Five days ride brought them to a marshy valley tending north.

Rojo stood in his stirrups sniffing the air. "We are near the river I spoke of that runs back to the San Juan.

The sweet spring where Escalante camped is just ahead where cañon walls close in. Someone camps there even now. I smell the smoke of their cooking."

The late afternoon breeze brought them the odor of pine and moist meadow mixed with piñon smoke and the smell of roasting meat. Approaching cautiously, they found two tepees and several brush shelters standing in a little cove around the spring. In the center of all, Doña Luna stood beside the fire, wrapped in ecstasy and seeming insensible to their approach.

Beside her, Father Nighthawk rose to his feet even before they could hail the camp. "Welcome, my friends. We expected you today. The old woman told us five days since of your coming. We must hasten. There is much to tell you and little time, for you are pursued. Rojo's plan worked well, but still they come."

Dismounting Rojo asked, "Who follows us Father?"

Hosteen Béézh, Navajo *hataali*, and Aa'ku of Acoma, the Sky City, emerged from the brush shelters.

"Two tribes follow you. One is the Children of the Conquistadors, and the other is a tribe of *Mangani* from the west, a people I do not know." *Mangani*, Anglos from the west had to be the Mormon Danites. "One has found your trail already, and the other will find it soon."

Dan could think of no way he could know these things. The frontiersman thought the elderly Jicarilla might have had Jicarilla spying for him, or maybe it was Doña Luna's *Power*.

Father Nighthawk spoke again. "After you have cared for your animals and eaten, we will talk long into the night. Tomorrow you will start your journey to the Hero Twins."

Hosteen Béézh embraced Verde. "Rodado Verde, my friend, I see that you are well and unchanged. It has been many years."

Aa'ku thumped Verde's back as well. "Soon you may find the lost trail of your ancestors." Standing with the two of them, Verde for once looked young.

Roque dug out their remaining coffee and began to prepare it with water from the spring.

As the aroma spread, Hosteen Béézh spoke. "Good, good, that sweet water will make excellent coffee. It is magical, you know, giving a man strength and an alert mind."

"We will bless you this evening," said Father Nighthawk, "with herbs, purifying smoke and our prayers. It is good that you will have coffee, too, especially coffee made with water from this spring that the Mexicans call *dulce*."

Roast elk, Dan had expected it. They could smell it cooking at half a mile. Doña Luna had cooked lamb with chili, wild berries, and onions and cattail root in place of potato. Dan wondered whose herd was short a sheep. Sebriana made tortillas. The seasoning came from the four elders out of pouches and bags, bits of root, bark, berries, and leaves as well as powders. Some of these were pleasant, many bitter and queer smelling and tasting.

Doña Luna added herbs to the food. "Each imparts to you its *Power* and protection."

When they had eaten and drunk their fill, Aa'ku packed the bowl of a finely decorated pipe. Puffing smoke to the four directions, he had each of the others do the same. Dan realized the smell and taste were not those of tobacco; they came from something else. By the time he blew smoke to the north, his head was swimming.

Rising the elders pulled the five friends away from the fire and had them sit in a circle shoulder to shoulder facing outward. Taking positions at the cardinal directions, the four shamans began to circle them, going counterclockwise and stopping at each direction to sprinkle them with pollen and intone prayers of blessing.

Dan heard Father Nighthawk's blessings. "From the east comes wisdom; listen to its lessons. From the south comes beauty; let her heal you. From the west comes strength; let it empower you. The north is darkness; seek the light but do not fear the dark. We cannot see the north. It is dark, but there we must seek knowledge. Only by minutely analyzing the works of the creator can we be fulfilled."

Roque poked Dan. "The words, they are the same as in the Masonic ritual. The south is beauty, the north is darkness, the west is strength, and the east is wisdom."

Dan realized that he was right. The wording wasn't quite the same, but the themes were.

"Rise, come back to the fire," said Father Nighthawk who had the leading role in these proceedings. The fire had died down to embers. Doña Luna covered them with the smoke of sweet grass, sage, and juniper bark. There were more scents that Dan didn't recognize raising a thick steamy smoke that was not choking.

"With your left hand, take the right hand of the person on your right," the Jicarilla shaman said, and thus the shamans and the companions together formed a circle bathed in smoke. They stood thus in a mystic circle until the smoke dissipated.

Seated again, the shamans built up the fire and passed the pipe and a single cup of coffee much sweetened by Doña Luna.

Aa'ku rose first and produced a square of buckskin. On it was drawn what appeared to be the square and compasses of the Masons. He held it to each of them so that the fire shone through the skin. The legs of square and compass were joined by additional lines.

As he came to Sebriana, he showed her first the square and compasses which she knew to be a symbol of the Masons. As he held it up before the light, she gasped. "It is the Star of David, the symbol of the Temple." Aa'ku sat.

Hosteen Béézh began a story.

"When the Gambler had been subdued by Young Warrior, their two peoples joined as one and went north to the San Juan River and to other rivers in that country. They built many towns, some of them quite large on the banks of the river, and lived there for generations. The world was still in drought, but the rivers yet flowed.

"They searched for a place to hide their treasure, something precious and sacred to them. They found the place in the mountains, but the drought had deepened, and the rivers ran low. Only a small band stayed in their village near the Hero Twins. The rest went far to the south beyond the mountains, and there they built a new city by a river.

"The ancestors of the *Dineh* watched the remnant of the Young Warrior's people who dwelt among the people of the Gambler. One season they disappeared, and the *Dineh* knew not what had happened to them."

Hosteen Béézh had finished speaking.

Verde's excitement increased visibly. "That sounds like the story I was told. I'm after believing it provides us nothing new, only confirmation of what we know."

"And what do we know?" asked Sebriana. "The

treasure is hidden in the San Juan Mountains near the headwaters of the river. The map may show a symbol for a waterfall. Signs have led us to the Hero Twins, who are north of the San Juan River and many miles west of the headwaters. Something at the Hero Twins village must get us closer to our goal."

"In the Third Degree," Roque muttered, "we learn that the Master's body was buried three times."

Rojo, Verde, and Dan looked at him dumbly. Then Dan had an epiphany. "The Ark has been buried three times, once in the great cañon of the Colorado, once at Chaco in the Temple, and finally it was hidden in the mountains. Whatever we learn at the Two brothers by applying the Ritual of the Second Degree, I think it will be the last knowledge we derive from that degree. Thereafter, it will be time to start applying the lessons of the Third."

Each of the shamans pronounced a blessing in their own tongue, satisfied that the companions were thinking clearly and had gained wisdom. Dan had summarized what Rojo, Roque and Verde were thinking; they had all contributed to the conclusion.

Dan noticed that Doña Luna did not speak Jicarilla in her incantations and blessings. Her words at times sounded almost like Latin but mixed with other things he couldn't identify. Perhaps, he thought, it was just his imagination.

Without preamble, Father Nighthawk began a story.

"Long ago, it happened here by the Sweet Spring and in the Valley of the Wild Turkeys. When the men from Hero Twins Village had hidden their treasure, they made their way from the mountains to Turkey Valley. Not wanting to call attention to themselves, they left their metal tools in the mountains and armed themselves with bows, arrows, and spears. They intended to continue south to join those who had preceded them.

"Along the way, they were welcomed by the people of Turkey Valley, a deceitful race, who lived in houses half underground like kivas and farmed the mesa tops and valleys. They stored their grain in little houses in caves high up the cliffs. Turkey Valley people made a big feast for the men of Hero Twin Village. They ate until they were full and drank *tizwin,* corn beer, and slept deeply. In the morning when they woke, the men of Hero Twin Village learned they were prisoners and slaves.

"The Turkey Valley people knew the strangers built strong villages and put them to work building towers and fortifications. Soon, a warrior standing on top of a tower could see at least two others, and in this way the Turkey Valley people could be warned of the approach of enemies. Their villages grew and prospered.

"Some years later, the Jemez were migrating from the west and passed through Turkey Valley. They were a numerous and warlike people, both poor and jealous of others. When they saw the wealth of Turkey Valley, they contrived to have it. Pretending to be friends, they came among the Turkey Valley people, trading precious stones and game for corn. They came often and the Turkey Valley people came to know them and trust them and were not alarmed by their arrival.

"One day, they came all at once to every village and struck suddenly, killing all the men. The Turkey Valley people had no time to warn other villages or to retreat to their towers. They were taken by surprise. Towers and homes were burned, often with people in them. Women and children were taken away to be slaves.

"They are there to this day among the Jemez. The Jemez know, but they will not tell you. They still hide their crime.

"A few of the people escaped to the campfires of the Jicarilla. They are among the ancestors of the *Ollero* Jicarilla, the White clans. That is why *Ollero* farm and make baskets and pottery unlike the *Llanero*, Red clans, who roam the *Llano Estacado* hunting buffalo."

The companions sat for a moment taking in this link between ancient peoples and the Jicarilla. The pipe with its special mix that wasn't tobacco went round again. Doña Luna took Sebriana away from the fire. The two left arm in arm to discuss things of special interest to women or so Dan believed. Sebriana never told him what was said or done though later she had herbs and potions she must have gotten from the shaman.

"Father Nighthawk," Rojo asked, "do you have anything more for us?"

"No, Rojo," the aged shaman replied, "only our blessings."

"So the Master's word is lost," said Verde, "until future generations may discover it anew."

"Perhaps not, my old friend," said Aa'ku. "These young people have come further and discovered more than anyone else in many generations."

Roque blushed. "We haven't done anything so special."

Dan spoke up. "We've had help from all of you and from Topper. We could not have succeeded alone. I'm still not sure we have. We have a long way to go, and we are pursued."

Dan paused to think and for breath, his mind addled by herbs and wonder. "Who has led us thus far?"

"He Who Casts His Shadow Beyond the Rainbow," said Hosteen Béézh. Dan had never heard any *Dineh*, Navajo, use this name before. Nor it seemed had Rojo or

Roque. "The Creator casts His shadow where he will," the hosteen clarified.

Father Nighthawk added, "The Creator who made First Man and First Woman."

"The Great Architect of the Universe," said Aa'ku with a sly smile.

Dan was overwhelmed. "Why would He choose us? Who are we? What have we done to deserve this?"

Verde grinned and spoke. "Who was Moses, lad? A murderer who fled to the desert, that's who. He was a man who lacked the silver tongue of the Irish and needed another to speak for him."

"I'm no Moses," Dan said. "Are you?"

"Who was David?" asked Sebriana returning to the firelight. "He was a boy with a stone who went where God bid him to go despite the odds. He was a man who sinned often. David even had a loyal soldier killed so he could steal the man's wife."

"I'm no King David," Dan replied. "I'm uncomfortable with the mere suggestion."

Sebriana persisted. "But you've been asked to quest for God's treasures, and you're doing it despite the danger. We all are."

Roque frowned. "Topper made us promise to go, not God."

"Why us? Why now?" Dan asked.

There was silence for a long time, finally broken by Sebriana. "Because evil is afoot in the land. You've seen the attraction of the Secessionist cause and the evil behind it that wants to swallow Mexican territory as well as Yankee territories that want no part of them. You know that at least some of the Texians seek the treasure. Maybe this is why Texas invades us." Sebriana paused for thought.

She continued. "West of here, the men of Deseret grabbed the new territories of the United States while her attention was still turned south to Mexico. Capable of murdering their neighbors in cold blood, as they did at Mountain Meadows, they now seek the treasure.

"Both of these groups have knowledge, much of it gained from Topper, knowledge that no one has assembled or used for hundreds of years. They are behind us, but they are close. Do you want them to have it?" She didn't wait for an answer. "Then you must keep it from them."

There was silence again for a long time. Dan spoke. "Those who hid the treasure were men of God. Not perfect, but trying to do His will. The Masons, look how many of the founders were Freemasons, birthed a nation as they thought God willed, a nation of God given rights. Now it's threatened by sesech, Mormons, and perhaps a Catholic church that doesn't believe in freedom of religion. It's been threatened before, but this time the treasure is in reach."

There were murmurs of assent and then silence. Embers sparked, smoke rose, the stars sped through the heavens in their course.

Dan cleared his throat. "If we find the treasure," he began, "what do we do with it?"

"Live like kings for the rest of our lives!" exclaimed Roque.

Verde rose to his feet and danced a little jig. "Sounds good to me."

"Is that why," Dan asked, "the Great Architect of the Universe is devoting His august attention toward directing us? So we can live like kings? And how will we keep these other forces from taking it away from us once we find it? We have to find it so that the evil forces following us don't, but the act of searching directs them to it."

Doña Luna cackled. "That is the way of things."

Dan spoke again. "Let me put it another way. Who does the treasure belong to besides God?"

Sebriana looked at him. "The Hebrew Nation."

"How do we find them to return it?" Roque asked.

"You don't," she said. "They don't have a nation right now, but the Bible says they will again someday."

"We take it to the Union," said Rojo.

Dan nodded slowly. "The Union? Since when has the Union treated your people fairly?"

Rojo rose to his feet. "Never. The Union has not dealt with Jicarilla fairly. When the Union broke with England, they expressed many fine sentiments in the Declaration of Independence and the Constitution. Those sentiments shame your people into trying to do better. I know of no other people who feel ashamed."

"The Union," said Roque. Dan didn't dare remind him of the wrongs done his people by the Union. His temper would run very hot. "Anyone but the Texians!" New Mexican, mothers frightened their children with threats the Texians would get them, large, hairy, uncivilized brutes, covered in the half-cured skins of cattle, armed with big knives and guns. "The Yankees have not treated New Mexicans fairly, but they treat us better than Mexico City did, and they do not treat us as a conquered people. What other country can say that?"

"The Union," said Verde not sounding convinced, "but we keep a huge finder's fee."

"The Union," said Sebriana firmly. "The Union claims that God has made it evident that all men are created equal. The people of the Union are the only people I know of who claim to guarantee their citizens rights of life, liberty, and the pursuit of happiness. The

Union claims to have been founded on principles that God made. Woe betide the Union if its government should ever depart from those principles. The treasure has brought great misfortune on all that held it that did not stand in awe of the One God. The Union can hold the treasure in trust for the People of Israel until such time as it can be turned over.

"Of course, we'll keep a small finder's fee," she concluded with a smile.

Their journey started again in the morning of a late October day with snow already glistening on the peaks and a crisp chill in the air. They rode north to a westward tending river and followed it to the San Juan. A short journey downstream on that river brought them to the cañon they sought, one that took them north to the Hero Twins.

Going around a bend, Dan saw the Twins for the first time. A ridge divided the valley and rose to a sharp peak topped by two stone towers, the Twins.

Dan commented to Rojo. "Brother Elder is a good deal larger than Brother Younger."

Rojo scowled.

Roque pointed. "It is a *huerfano*, no? An orphan."

Dan saw something different. "It looks like two chimneys from a house that has burned."

Sebriana squinted. "When a house burns, the roof collapses and leaves the adobe walls standing. I don't see it."

"*Mija*, a frame house like we build Out East."

The ridge was a lone mountain. Beyond the twins, it fell away again to valley. The valleys there were meadows thick with grass. The hills were strewn with pine, all except the Hero Twins. The eastern end of the ridge was so steep that even scrub plants found it difficult to grow, so it remained stark and bare. On the west, the ridge was wooded and offered an approach. Below the twins was a talus slope of disintegrating shale which breaks into tiny pieces of stone as slippery as the mud from which it formed.

"When I was young," said Roque, "I used to play on slopes like those. Run as hard as you can and leap far out into the air. You come down 30, 50 100 feet below, sink in, and slide as far as you want."

Climbing through pine forest on the western end rising high above the valley floor, they rode passed ruins of those who had dwelt there long ago. As they emerged from the forest, they saw the Twins across a span as narrow as a footbridge and half a mile long. The drop of one thousand feet on either side was not sheer, but it might as well have been, men or beasts falling would not stop until they reached the bottom. Single file they led their surefooted stock, not daring to ride along this precarious rim to where it broadened slightly at a hummock overlooking the Twins at the level of the base of the rock towers.

A ruin of fourteen rooms stood there, its center dominated by a large kiva open to the sky. A *banco* ran round the clean interior, there being no debris of roof remains as there had been everywhere else they had been. The rooms surrounding the kiva were smaller than most living quarters they had encountered.

Sebriana, standing on the upper wall of the kiva, looked down. "I think it's a temple. The whole complex is a temple."

An amazing vista confronted them. To the east and north, the high peaks of the San Juan Mountains topped with snow enclosed them; to the south and west hills heavy with pine completed the encirclement. As they looked back down the river toward the San Juan, their view took in the desert as far as Chaco.

"I didn't expect that," said Rojo. "If we camp here, our fires will be visible far away."

"Water is a problem," added Roque. "There's none up here, nor any grazing."

"Danger will approach from the south following our trail," said Sebriana. "Look north and east for a spot our stock can graze hidden on the far side of this ridge."

Following her advice, they looked for a place where there was water and grass and where the terrain would help corral their animals. "There," Dan said. "How does that look?" He pointed to a meadow in the valley north of the ridge near the edge of the pine forest.

"If the way we came is the only way," said Verde, "that's going to be a long ride."

They found a way down on the northwest side, but the ride back to camp was still long. Each day, they took turns as herdsman for their stock, leaving half the riding animals and all of the pack animals to graze and fatten while they could. They were in Utah country, and while those Indians were generally friendly with *gavachos* and Jicarilla, they were not above taking horses and mules from the unwary.

Each day they rode to the temple taking food, their weapons, and plenty of water.

Verde surveyed the temple as if it were a fortification. "Templars had a hand in building it. It's sure to be defensive."

The narrow trail leading up to the temple could be covered by fire, rifle or arrow, from many of the temple's rooms, lending credence to Verde's assertion. Only one side needed protection. The other sides were too steep for an assault to succeed.

With their camping arrangements made, they turned their attention to learning what the last citadel of the Templar-Hebrews had to tell them.

"Well," said Roque, "we have two pillars and a long valley, that is, an aisle or portico, leading to the mountains, an upper room. This is a pattern we've seen before."

The head of the valley at their feet to the south led over a low saddle to another river valley.

"Rojo," Dan asked, "is that the San Juan River sparkling between us and the mountains in the east."

"It is," he said. "We are looking right along its valley. From where we stand, it is south of us just beyond those hills, but it cuts across them to be east of us."

Three days went by, and they learned nothing new. It snowed once, accumulating six inches, but it melted by noon the next day. Dan was glad to see it go and glad he had Sebriana to warm his robe.

It was Sebriana who spotted an odd projection above the rim of the kiva. Dan had thought it a chimney of sorts and it did hide one.

Sebriana pointed. "One side is flat. Everything else follows the curve of the kiva wall, but this one side is flat. See this ridge built in the stone? It slopes downward toward the notch between the brothers. If I stand just here, looking along the side, the two brothers are so close together I can barely see between them. It is like a gun sight in reverse."

Dan looked, then got his telescope, laid it on the stony ridge, and sighted along the wall. A rock face in the mountains appeared in the glass.

"Roque, Rojo," he called. Verde was minding the camp and stock. "Come and see!" As they approached, he gave the telescope to Sebriana. In time, she handed it to

Rojo and then to Roque.

"This definitely points to one spot," said Roque. "I think this place is not more than a half mile on a side."

"I think I know the rocks we see," said Rojo, "but I can't be sure."

"Sebriana, *mija*," Dan inquired, "how many mirrors did you bring with you?"

"Two."

"A fine start," he said. "What else have we got that will flash the sun?"

"I have two small, round mirrors," said Rojo. Roque looked at him oddly. "I keep them for pretty girls," he explained.

"Armies and navies in Europe have used mirrors for signaling," Dan told them. "We need to work out a code, three flashes for "go north," five for "go south," seven for "go higher on the mountain." Nine flashes will mean "you are there!" Two flashes means "understood," four means "repeat," six means "come to me." Do we need anything more?"

"Why do we need four mirrors?" asked Roque.

"Two at each end. If we only had one up here, we would only be able to signal when the sun is in the east. With a second mirror, we can reflect the sun into the first, no matter where it stands."

Verde agreed to tend the camp. They did a quick test of their signaling system from the first low pass Roque and Rojo came to. It worked well enough, and their project began.

Matters proceeded well at first. It took them a day to get to the rock face Rojo thought he recognized. It was then that they realized their uncomplicated system of light signals was not complicated enough. Roque and Rojo began by sending Dan and Sebriana four flashes waiting a minute and sending it again until Dan and his *mija* noticed. And again. It took a while for the pair to notice. The flashes from Rojo and Roque were barely visible without the telescope. Dan wondered how the two men without a telescope managed to see the response.

"Rojo has sharp eyes," Dan said aloud.

Dan's return signal said to "go up" and "go to the south." It took the two men a little while, but they did and their very next signal flashed from the right spot. Dan flashed twice, which meant understood, waited, and repeated the signal, hoping they'd understand. They did and repeated the signal back to Sebriana and Dan. They'd gotten their two friends very close to the final point on their quest, but hadn't given them a signal for "search continues."

They were close to their target, but almost five hundred years had passed hiding evidence of those who had gone before. Templars had come, settled, and finally hidden the treasure. On Friday the 13th in 1307, Jacques de Molay had been arrested, and the knights began their diaspora.

Absorbed in watching for signals, Dan and Sebriana failed to watch their back trail. Their enemies were almost on them when a clumsy foot dislodged a stone starting a small avalanche. Sebriana and Dan heard the rocks tumbling down the hillside and suspected they were followed. Looking back down the causeway ridge, they saw the enemy approaching. Without a word, they dashed across the tops of walls to the most advantageous fighting positions in the west end rooms. For the moment, the enemy was forced to come on single file, scrambling on their hands and knees. If they got to the point where the ridge broadened and could attack more than one at a time, Dan and his *mija* would be in trouble. Leading the attackers was Porter Brannan, the Danite from Deseret.

A shot rang out, and one of the Danites behind Porter screamed and fell. He went on screaming for a very long time as he tumbled down the southern slope. He spun through the air, hit, bounced, slid, and screamed until finally he hit his head on something and stopped screaming.

"Hold! That's not what I want," yelled Brannan standing up and exposing himself.

"The man is brave, I'll say that. Good shooting, Sebriana," Dan said.

"No, it wasn't," she replied. "I was aiming for Porter's head, and I hit that poor man in the leg."

"We just want to talk to you," said Brannan. "We'd like a little information."

"So talk," Dan said. "We've haven't any plans for the immediate future."

"We know what you seek," he said. "We are its rightful owners. Deseret is the new Zion, and Brigham Young has erected a new Temple. What you seek belongs in the Temple of a theodemocracy, such as we have created in the desert. We are the true Children of Israel, blood descendants of the Hebrews of old. Joseph Smith learned of these treasures from the profane Freemasons and sent us out to make a home and a temple for them. Give us your information. No one else has the right!"

"You lost your right at Mountain Meadows," Dan called back. He turned to Sebriana. "I could argue with him, but his mind is closed, his ignorance profound."

"It was necessary and just," Porter replied. "They mocked the Prophet." He showed no shame at what the Danites had done. "Who better than the Prophet and his Apostles to receive God's treasury? We need it to build God's kingdom. Let us come up, and we can talk."

"Thanks all the same," Dan said. "I don't care to have my brain cooked like you tried to do to Roque."

"Where are your other friends?" Brannan asked.

Dan resisted the temptation to look down in the valley to see how Verde faired. "They're near with their weapons aimed at your heart!"

"Did you have a falling-out over the gold?" Brannan went on. "Unholy men fight over gold."

Sebriana fired her weapon. This time there was no cry, the man just fell, hit, tumbled, and fell some more. She turned to Dan to explain. "He was trying to come around on our side. I got him through the forehead."

"I think that ends our discussion, Porter Brannan," Dan said. "You've tried to use this truce to outflank us. My next shot goes through your heart. You have ten seconds to get out of range."

Brannan scrambled for cover. Four or five of his people, Dan couldn't be sure, were in concealed positions waiting to fire on Dan and Sebriana, and as Porter took cover, they did. Stone has disadvantages for defense. Bullets glancing off stone can buzz around an enclosed space like an angry wasp. Bullets striking stone sparked off chips sharp as razors that fly with almost as much force as a bullet. It wasn't long before Sebriana and Dan found their faces and arms running with blood from tiny cuts. It wouldn't be long before one of them lost an eye.

Dan took a chance, rising above the wall so he could move between rooms to Sebriana's position. He looked at her. "We have food and water for a day or two and plenty of lead and powder. We can hold out for a while, three or four days."

Lifting his head high enough to see over the wall, Dan gazed toward the valley and their camp. The stock was disappearing into a grove of pine where it would be out of sight. The campsite, too, had been picked clean of equipment. He didn't see any Danites down that way, so he guessed Verde had heard the commotion and was making these moves.

Dan wondered why the Mormons hadn't tried a shot at him. They probably really do want us alive for information, he thought.

Sebriana looked toward the mountains in the east. "How long before Roque and Rojo return?"

"I don't know," he told her honestly. "They may be searching for the treasure. They could spend days doing that. They don't know we're in trouble. Even if they were here, what help would two more guns be against thirty? And they might walk into a trap. We've no way to warn them."

Dan had rarely seen her worry. She looked into his eyes. "We have to sleep sooner or later. With five, we could hold this place forever against any enemy."

He worried over her safety. An unworthy thought came unbidden. If they were captured, they'd torture her to get him to talk. He pushed it away. She was his companion and partner, not a burden.

"With five," Dan said gently, "we would run out of water very fast. We'll have to make do with two. What do we have that we can use?"

"A buffalo robe," she said, "one hundred feet of rope, our rifles and pistols and knives, water, powder, ball, telescope, mirrors, and food."

They'd tethered their mules down slope beyond the narrow causeway where they could graze among the trees. They were in Danite hands now and there was naught Dan could do about it.

The buffalo robe was good protection from flying shards of rock and bits of lead. They kept vigil in shifts and fired when they had a clear target. At different times, they watched three Danites being dragged away writhing in pain when their bullets found a home. One tried snaking his way forward to get close to their position. Dan let him come as his approach path was in the open. When he was near, Dan shot him, the bullet entering the shoulder. Blood spurted four times like water from a pump; then, he lay still and bled no more. He'd been close enough to their position that Dan could smell the coppery scent of his gore.

Sebriana spat. "He'll stink before long. Shoot when they are farther away."

"I'm shocked," said Dan. "Don't you know they claim to be saints? And the Catholics say that saints don't rot or putrefy."

She giggled. He'd succeeded in raising her spirits a little.

They saw Porter Brannan rise and make his way back downhill off the causeway. Dan guessed he was headed back to see how he might deploy the rest of his troops. Sebriana didn't stop to think about what he might be doing. At over two hundred yards, she fired taking away most of Porter's ear. Thereafter when they saw him, he had a great bandage around his head.

She spat. "I forgot to ask the Saint's blessing before I fired." Dan wasn't sure she was joking until she smiled.

The long hours crept by and the sun set, painting the sky in crimson rivulets. They ate jerky and *pinolé*, the one tough and stringy, the other like wet sand, and waited. Below them, the Danites lighted cook fires, and the smell of burning juniper and roasting meat drifted up to Dan and Sebriana high above. They could see the Danites walking back and forth, but they were out of range. Nonetheless, Dan aimed high above the firelight and squeezed off a shot. The fire kicked sparks delightfully as his bullet struck a log. Among the Danites, there was no response. They must have thought the explosion in the fire was caused by a naturally popping log. Grabbing his second rifle, Dan fired again off to one side. The bullet made a lovely sound as it bounced off rock. Far below, the Danites scattered like quail. Good, Dan thought, they wouldn't dare take comfort or warmth from the fire. Now, they'd rest less easy and less comfortably.

"*Pobrecito*," whispered Sebriana, "don't waste your bullets. Even if you hit one at this range, it won't go through him."

"No, but it will loosen his bowels."

The night dragged on. Leaning against Dan under the robe, Sebriana slept, breathing softly, warm against his side. Dan watched Orion lead the hunt across the sky in pursuit of Taurus. Cassiopeia lounged on her couch, and the stars whirled. His eyes became heavy, and he woke Sebriana to take the watch. When Dan awoke, the sun was well up.

Brannan surprised them by coming up under a white flag of truce. He must be having a hard time finding a flank to assault, Dan thought.

"Sorry," Dan called. "We can't accept your surrender."

"May I come up to talk?" Porter pleaded.

"Sure," Dan replied. Sebriana gave him an evil look. "Sure you can, but if any of your men make a move, you'll die before they do." She smiled sweetly. "You've come far enough. Talk!"

Porter Brannon cleared his throat and winced, the act making his ear throb. "We can wait you out, you know. You'll run out of food and water soon."

"It will snow on you soon," Dan replied. "Will you

survive here in the mountains?"

Brannon tried a different tack. "There's only one way you can get out of here alive, that's if I let you. I don't want you dead. I only need information, and you can go."

"What if I don't have the information you want?" Dan asked. "Will you believe me or roast me over a small fire 'till you're sure?

"Sebriana, don't!" Dan yelled grabbing her barrel. "Porter, you'd better get out of sight while I can still control her."

"We'll talk again when you're thirsty." Brannan sneered and retreated down the causeway.

The day wore on, and the sun set in blazing, bloody crimson on a dreary world. Sebriana and her *pobrecito* were low on jerky and water.

Sebriana was concerned. "They'll last the night."

The stars whirled in their fixed dance, moving but not promising change. Low twelve, midnight, passed and the stars continued their cold, quiet waltz spinning 'round familiar paths.

The world below them erupted. Flames stabbed the night as rifles fired. The two companions heard shouts and the beating of hooves. The men on the causeway ran toward the Danite camp. More shots came from below.

"Now's our chance," Dan said to Sebriana. "I've got an idea, but you need to trust me."

They wrapped up everything including their rifles in the buffalo robe and went over the wall and headed toward the causeway.

Dan pointed. "There, see the trees? That's where we can get down to our camp in the valley."

Juniper trees grew on the steep ground on the north side of the ridge. The slope was too steep to climb, and below the ridge, too steep for trees to grow. It was slick shale scree all the way to the valley.

"With luck, we might make it." Dan tied a large knot in one end of their rope. "We wrap the rope around a rock or tree like this," Dan said, "so that it passes over itself near the knot. Our weight on the rope keeps the knot from slipping under. Now I pass the rope from my left shoulder down under my leg, up along my back, and down the right side of my body where I control it with my hand. This is going to hurt, but go slow, and at least it won't burn. I'll slide down a few feet. Then you come so you can learn how."

"You've gone *loco*, no?" asked Sebriana, her eyes large with fear.

"Watch." Dan slid down a few feet and stood with his feet on a tree trunk that stuck out at right angles to the hillside. "Your turn." Dan thought, Sebriana has guts.

She did it and slid down to his position. He flicked the rope, which lifted off the knot, and fell toward them. He looped it around the trunk of their tree and slid down the full length of the rope.

Looking up at her, he smiled. "The French call it rappelling."

"Do you trust anything the French do?" came her frosty retort. "They eat snails."

She joined him, and they rappelled down twice more before they faced a problem. No tree grew directly below them. One did grow some distance out of line. Dan explained to her what he planned to do, then rappelled down, and walked away from the tree allowing himself to swing back. Like a pendulum he swung back and forth not daring to go too far or too fast for fear the knot would slip from under the rope, and he would fall. On the fourth swing, he gained the tree, and it was her turn.

The hillside was not a rock face but a very steep

scree-slope of sand and bits of shale almost as fine.
Boulders stuck out here and there. Whether they were the
roots of the mountain or just fallen from the top and lying
loose was not clear. It was too steep and too loose to
climb but not to walk vertical. They walked backward on
the rope, their feet on the ground, not hanging in the air.

From the last tree, they spied some rocks and made
for them. As Dan's foot touched the first one, it came
loose and rolled down to the valley still hundreds of feet
below. The others held, and they wrapped their rope
around them.

Dan shook his head. "I hope this will support my
weight." They made their way down to another boulder.

Dan looked down helplessly. They were more than
two thirds of the way down, and there was nothing more
to tie onto beyond the rock on which they stood. The
slope below them was loose shale and perhaps more
gentle than before.

Dan held Sebriana close for a moment. "We've got to
try something dangerous."

She cocked her head, looking at him like he was a
two-headed calf she was seeing for the first time. Dan
unpacked their bundle. They slung rifles and the rest from
their shoulders until the buffalo robe was empty.

"You're going to sit behind me with your legs
wrapped around my middle. Be alert. When I lean over,
lean with me."

Sitting on the robe, Dan extended his legs straight out
and pulled its forward edge back toward him making a
crude bow.

Together they pushed off and slid down the slope
gaining speed at an alarming rate. Chilly night air rushed
by as they descended. Dan leaned over hard to his left,
and Sebriana came with him. The robe-toboggan turned,

and they were soon moving at an angle to the slope going a little slower. Children scream on sled rides. They dared not for fear of alerting the Danites above them though the noise in that camp would probably have drowned out any sound Dan and Sebriana made. They had a chance as long as the Danites thought the pair was still in the ruin.

Dan could feel stones passing beneath him but the heavy robe protected them from cuts if not bruises. The robe beneath them hissed or growled with changes in the surface it slid over. A boulder loomed in their path and Dan leaned hard over to the right with Sebriana following his lead. Dan thought she must be terrified. The robe turned, and they were headed straight down and gaining speed. Dan brought them around, and they were headed across the slope again. The night was dark. Obstacles did not appear until the last second.

Dan was terrified. He knew that one sharp rock the size of his head or larger passing under the robe would rend their nether regions asunder. It was not a pretty prospect. But if he could keep them from going straight down, they would go slower and stood a chance. They slid on, dodging obstacles along the way, occasionally bruised by those they could not avoid. Dan's fingers ached from clenching the edge of the robe.

A boulder the size of a house loomed. Dan saw it too late. He couldn't turn. There were more like it everywhere Dan looked. They arrived at the boulder and mercifully they slid to a stop. Dan and Sebriana had made it to the bottom where the big boulders stopped rolling. And they'd made it alive.

Aching Dan stood and undid his clenched fingers. He reached down and helped his *mija* to rise. She looked up at him with astonished eyes. "Can we do that again?"

Gathering themselves in the predawn light, they

started across the valley to their former campsite. Verde's voice called to them from the wood line where they found him mounted and the mules packed. He presented the pair with their two favorite mules: Dan's Appaloosa and Sebriana's pinto, Deborah, saddled and ready.

Dan shook his head astonished. "We'd thought we lost them to the Danites."

"Climb aboard," Verde said. "We need to make haste out of here."

"But how?" Dan asked. He'd thought never to see those beasts again.

"Later. Let's go. *Vamanos*."

They rode to the east, and Verde stopped them at the first saddle, a low spot between hills. Picketing the stock, still saddled and packed and on the east slope out of sight of their enemies. They crawled back to look at the valley behind them.

Dan was worried. "We can't head toward the treasure. The Danites are hot on our trail."

"Don't worry," Verde said. "They're afoot and won't be following us."

Dan looked at him for explanation. "Some young Utah bucks stopped by painted for war and headed for the Rio Grande to fill the winter larder with mutton. They were about wanting me mules, a toll for bein' in dere land. I argued with them. It being that the lack of me mules would put me afoot with winter coming and offered them a gift of horses instead. Knowing me for an honest man and a great trader, they agreed and together we liberated the Danites horses, every last one. The Utahs are quite happy now.

"Now bide here a time," Verde continued. "The Danites are no longer a danger to us."

At midmorning pandemonium fell upon the Danite

camp on the ridge. Dan and his two friends observed from a distance, unsure of exactly what was happening. Shots were followed by screams. The storm abated a little only to start again. Smoke rose from weapons on the western end of the ridge where it was less steep. Through the telescope Dan could see men on horseback with lances riding down on men afoot.

"The Penitentes have caught up with us," Dan told the others, handing the spyglass to Sebriana.

"So they have, too," said Verde. "The Utahs told me of their coming sure as the dawn."

"But why would they attack the Danites?" asked Sebriana.

"O, and they've both been after following us for quite some time now," said Verde. "I'm sure they were aware of each other and guessed they were both after the same prize...us. I'm after guessing the Utahs talked to the Penitentes and told them the Danites had you pinned down up there. That would have been enough, I'm thinkin'."

The fight proceeded down the hill and out onto the valley floor. Danites fell to lances, but their weapons were taking a toll among the mounted men. Dan saw Brannan, trying to rally his men and clearly discernible by the bandage around his head, turn and shoot the leader of the Penitentes from his horse only to be skewered by a lance that lifted him from the ground. Both sides backed off to tend their leaders.

"Have no fear," said Verde. "The Utahs have promised to escort the survivors from their land."

Roque and Rojo arrived at sundown. "When you didn't return our signal," Roque said, "we feared the worst and returned right away. We would have come anyway. I think we've found what we sought."

The night was chilly, and Dan's buffalo robe worn very thin. He was doubly glad Sebriana was with him. She had her own robe, and they shared.

The five friends, reunited, headed east after a cold sunrise under a sky like blue ice. October was almost over, and it was time to be out of the high country. Coming to the San Juan, they followed it back towards it source in the mountains.

"Here!" said Rojo pointing to a waterfall.

Roque couldn't contain his excitement. "See that rock formation? Just like a column, broken like it says in the third degree ritual. And see the falls? See how they twine? It is like a maiden undoing the locks of her hair. And there, up high, behind the falls, a cave! The opening is like the entrance to a beehive. It is all in the third degree. And up there, we found stairs! There we will find our upper room and receive our wages."

Beside the waterfall, unnoticed by Roque and Rojo, were two symbols cut in the rock. One was a star with wavy points, the Masonic symbol for the Great Architect of the Universe. Beside it was the square and compasses with points faintly joined forming the Star of David.

Sebriana spotted the glyphs. "Look there. I think I see the Star of David."

They made their way up to the top of the falls by a long circumambulation that included gentler slopes and watercourses that could be climbed by mule and man. Up above the falls, they gazed down into the streambed that fed it and began the search for the top of the stairs Roque had seen.

Roque soon found them. "Here they are, stairs leading down to the cave."

Sebriana looked. "They were well hidden by folds in the rock."

"And lass and laddies, after six hundred years very worn. Sections have fallen away."

Dan frowned. "Worse than that, mist from the falls blows across the stairs making them wet and moss covered."

Roque was still euphoric. Yes, yes, but just look. The first three flights were three, five, and seven steps."

Sebriana shook her head slowly and doubtfully. "There's a few more steps after that, and they wind down steeply."

Vertigo seized Dan. "They fall away sheer for hundreds of feet. One missed step and you're an eagle." Nothing guarded the outer edge. That side fell away to nothing.

Rojo, their best climber, volunteered to go down first. Dan was glad he did. It was he who insisted the Jicarilla be roped off, and after a few steps, both men were glad he had. The stair Rojo stood on broke and fell away, spinning toward the valley. Rojo hung from the rope. He scrambled up and continued slipping now and again, sometimes knocking a step free. He clung to the rope, and it saved him.

They had equipped him with a bullet lantern. He disappeared inside the cave to light it and the rope went slack. He was gone a long time before Dan heard Rojo's voice calling to him from below. "Danny, come down and tell me what I'm seeing."

They pulled up the rope, and Dan slipped into it and started carefully down the stairs. Rojo had knocked away the loose stones so all Dan had to contend with were gaps and slippery moss. By the time he arrived at the cave, his thighs and buttocks were well bruised. Dan lit his lamp from Rojo's, and together they illuminated a wonder.

The cave was a crystal palace decorated with icicles

of rock that hung from the ceiling and grew from the floor. Rock tapestries hung from the walls, and where a small stream flowed, there was a layered wedding cake of dams holding back glistening water. Any cave, looking like this, would be deemed a wonder in white limestone with faint shades of coloring. In this cave, minerals covered the limestone. Dan thought he recognized crystals of azurite, calcite, carnalite, chrysoberyl, wulfenite, smithsonite, and malachite, but there were more he could not identify in shades of red, purple, blue, yellow, green, and turquoise. Stunned to silence, Dan stood there mouth agape.

Rojo shook him. "Come. This way." He led Dan deeper into the cave to drier passages.

Stacked neatly beside the passage were bars of silver and gold and bags lumpy as if with coin. Dan lifted one, and the bag disintegrated spilling gold coins. He picked up a coin and looked into the visage of an ancient pharaoh.

"This is it!" Dan breathed. "The treasure Moses buried recovered from Egypt by the Templars."

"There's more," Rojo said, leading him through a stone arch to the chamber beyond where on a golden table the Menorah stood, flanked by two silver trumpets.

"Rojo, that is the Table of the Presence on which the priests laid out the show bread, the Menorah that lighted the sanctum and the Trumpets of Truth."

They stood silent willing their hearts not to beat and disturb the silence of this awesome, holy place. Dan's breathing stopped and he stood still until blackness began to close in around the edges of his vision. He swayed. Rojo whispered one word, "*Power.*"

Slipping to his knees, Dan found himself in prayer and discovered Rojo in like condition. How long they remained like this they could never say, but Sebriana and Roque claimed they were gone for hours and changed men when they returned.

Slowly regaining his senses, Dan pointed to an opening beyond almost hidden by stone draperies and started toward it. He held out a hand. "Wait. For safety, take off your moccasins and kneel and say a prayer before we go further." Not entering the room, they only looked in and saw what only the High Priest was supposed to see, a golden chest topped by winged creatures facing away from each other, their wingtips touching behind.

The world went dark. Dan never knew if he was blind for a time or if he had simply closed his eyes. When breath returned, he spoke."That fits the description of the Ark of the Covenant."

Beside him Rojo intoned a prayer. Dan saw the Indian's eyes were closed. Senses reeled. Time stopped.

When it started again, Rojo seemed concerned. "You have told me about it from your Bible. Can we touch or even see it and not die?"

Dan slowly shook his head from side to side. "I don't know, Rojo. We've been led all this way. I guess we've been permitted to see it since I think we're still alive."

One at a time, they brought the others down to see.

Sebriana was practical. "How will we get it all up here?" she asked.

Dan thought about it. "It will take an engineering miracle. I know some tricks that sailors taught Out East. They could sway a heavy mast up high with block and tackle. We'll need a lot of rope." He whistled and frowned deep in thought.

Rojo considered the engineering marvels of nautical science. "There is no way we can have everything done before the snow becomes very deep."

Verde's eyes glowed amber. "We should take a few things with us. Say a pound or three of gold."

Dan mumbled. "We'll need pack animals and a wagon and poles to lift the Ark." He began calculating and ticking off on his fingers.

"What shall we take right now?" asked Sebriana.

Roque answered. "The Trumpets of Truth and some gold."

They spent a day concealing signs of their presence and started south for Santa Fe where they could obtain supplies

.

Chapter 15

Defeat at Bloody Valverde

Genesis 49

[16] "Dan shall judge his people
As one of the tribes of Israel.
[17] Dan shall be a serpent by the way,
A viper by the path,
That bites the horse's heels
So that its rider shall fall backward.
[18] I have waited for your salvation, O LORD!

They rode west along the San Juan River searching for a gap that would lead them south. Not too far off, Dan knew, the headwaters of the Chama flowed south and east to the Rio Grande. That would be their course home. The Old Spanish Trail followed the Chama, a path for stock and pack animals, crossing the Great Divide by several routes. Where they were on the San Juan, everything flowed west to the distant Colorado. A few miles ahead of them, steam rose from hot springs near the river. Before they reached the springs, they found a promising stream that ran from the south.

Sebriana insisted she needed a hot bath. "It is a lady's right to bathe. It's in the Constitution somewhere, I'm sure. Besides, I can smell the rest of you from far away."

Rojo cocked an eyebrow. "My people come here to sit in the hot water and heal their wounds and aches. Drinking the stinking water cleans out your insides after a winter of too much dried meat."

They stopped to try the springs, their great quest brought to a standstill by a woman's whim. Another reason I don't need a wife, thought Dan.

The season had been kind to the companions so far. There had been light snows that had melted away everywhere except in the shadows, but there had been no heavy snowfall. A thousand feet above them, the snow already thickly capped the peaks. They were in high country, higher than the peaks of what in the East were termed mountains. Elk and mountain sheep had already descended to the grasses still bright green in valleys edged with pine and aspen, gold with the season though holding their leaves while waiting a winter storm.

Surrounded by beauty in vales thick with grass, Dan bathed in hot water with Sebriana. They soothed each other's bruises and hurts, while she worked the stiffness from his body. Far away across the steaming lake thick with its own fog, they could hear the voices of their companions as they splashed and frolicked.

"I shan't be bathin' in this noxious brew!" Verde howled loud enough to be heard across the lake. "Jist smell the awful stuff, boyos. That might melt off something important."

"Your crusty body needs it!" The pronouncement came in Roque's voice, followed by a loud splash.

"Don't be drowning one of the little people now, the wee leprechaun." The voice was Rojo's, but the accent was a perfect impression of Verde.

The following day riding south along the valley they hoped would lead them to the Chama and enjoying the crisp fall air, Dan thought about what a great place this would be for ranch. The grass was thick and good. There was plenty of water.

A few miles on, they ran out of valley and crossed a low ridge into the cañon of a stream running west.

Dan loved the country. "You could hide a house, barn, and corral down there, snug and out of the wind," he told Sebriana.

Plenty of timber for building and for firewood was available, and game abounded in the hills: elk, bear, mule deer, and mountain sheep. Then Dan remembered the winters at this elevation were bitter cold and the good grass was watered by deep snows. If the stock didn't freeze, it would starve trying to paw through the snow. A man could die here trying to find his way home through a storm. It was beautiful country but cruel. There were no towns nearby where stock could be sold. This was the country where Jicarilla and Ute hunted even they didn't camp here in the winter. The growing season was too short for crops.

"Roque," Dan asked, "can we pull a wagon over these hills?"

Roque thought a moment then nodded. "I think so. We'll need to pull them with oxen. They are slow, but we'll need their strength up these hills."

They crossed five valleys and forded a cold river. Rojo looked around closely. "I know this place. Not far to the west is the place where we met with Father Nighthawk and the others."

He led them east up a long, gently sloping rise and they crossed over into the Chama valley under the high peaks of the San Juan Mountains. As they went, they scouted for a path for wagons. The mountains north of Piedre Lumbre would be tough. They'd have to leave the

Chama's narrow cañon and find another way down.

As they passed upslope to the tree line, men with drawn bows emerged from the wood. Behind the armed men, the game trail the companions had been following disappeared into the dark forest sharp with the smell of pine. The late-afternoon fall sun shone with orange light casting long shadows.

Verde howled, "I thought we had an Injun with us so this kind of thing couldn't happen! And here we are taken flatfooted without even a wee chance to draw our weapons."

Seven warriors clad in buckskin and wool stood before them.

Rojo looked at Verde. "I knew they were there. They've been following us for two days and only rode up here to wait for us a short time ago." He waved an arm in greeting and the warriors lowered their bows. "These are my people, a hunting party." He dismounted, and the warriors gathered round him glad to see him. They talked and then squatted to the ground sketching figures in the dust.

As they talked, Dan watched their agitation grow, gesturing as excitedly as only Jicarilla can and pointing only with their lips. All of them were pointing toward the friends' back trail.

Rojo looked up. "We're being followed. The description matches the Danites."

Verde snarled. "I thought the Utes killed them for us."

Thinking, Rojo shook his head slowly. "Maybe they escaped or paid the Utes off. From what these warriors say, some are wounded. They might be survivors of the original group and some reinforcements."

Dan sighed. "Persistent, aren't they?"

Roque smiled. "We'll have to kill them, of course."

"How many?" asked Sebriana. Dan thought his mija was always practical.

Rojo conferred with the hunters. "They have seen twenty-two."

"Wait a second," Dan said. "What if they are only seeking to return to civilization? They'd have to come this way, wouldn't they?"

"It is not so," said Rojo. "My cousins have been watching them. The Danites follow us. And my cousins insist on helping us."

Dan shook his head. "I don't want to involve them in our troubles through some false sense of obligation or honor. This is our fight."

Rojo stood grinning. "These are Jicarilla lands. They have graciously invited you to join their hunt."

"How shall we do it?" asked Roque. "They are many, and they are skilled in war. Some of us are sure to die."

He's so cheerful, Dan thought, he must be looking forward to battle and a glorious death.

Rojo asked the hunters and then smiled. "They want to conceal themselves in these woods among the litter on the forest floor and let the enemy pass. As they go by, one of the warriors will shoot the last Danite in the neck with his bow. With luck, many will fall before they realize they are under attack. They will think they are attacked by ghosts. We will go to the other end of the wood and await them. We will kill them and drive them back as they emerge from the trees. We will have them between two fires."

"Sounds good to me!" growled Verde, checking the loads in his weapons.

Dan shook his head sadly. "We can't. We have to talk to them...tell them to go back to Utah. These are men. We can't kill them as if we were butchering animals."

"Why not?" asked Verde. "Soldiers ambush their enemies all the time."

Roque frowned and protested. "They have attacked us before. They would not hesitate to ambush us."

Rojo looked into Dan's eyes. "These hunters won't like it. My cousins think of this as their ambush. You may participate or not. But do not interfere."

Dan looked back. "They can do as they like. I have to do what I feel is right. I will await them on the far side of the wood and confront them there, giving them a chance to return to Brigham Young."

"And if that don't work," snarled Verde, "we'll send 'em to Joseph Smith!"

Roque scratched his head. "I thought he was dead."

Verde cocked his head. "He is, you dumb Mexican, and in Hell by now!"

"Oh." Roque smiled. "I understand."

Rojo talked to the Jicarilla. "They agree to this plan. I will stand beside you."

Dan nodded gravely. "I ask no one to risk their life doing what only I think is right."

"I stand with you," said Verde and Roque together. Sebriana nodded her head.

"No, Sebriana," Dan pleaded. "You must seek safety away from the fight."

She smiled sweetly. "Pobrecito, I've been in every fight beside you up till now. Why should this one be different?"

Dan knew he couldn't win. Angrily he thought, I only want to protect her. This is another reason never to marry a mule-stubborn woman.

Leaving the Jicarilla behind, the five companions trotted their stock through the wood to an open meadow half a mile uphill. Fallen timbers from a long ago fire offered means for blocking the path. They securely tethered their stock, riding mounts, pack animals, and remounts out of sight. Rojo and Verde took up positions to Dan's right where they had some cover while Sebriana and her primo, Roque, took cover to Dan's left. Dan stood in the open where the path emerged from the woods behind their newly-made barricade. If they could keep the fight in among the trees, the enemy's horses would be cramped and get in each other's way. They might get by with facing only one or two Danites at a time. They didn't have long to wait as they nervously checked their weapons one last time.

At least, Dan thought them as nervous as he. It was hard to tell. Rojo sang a war song under his breath. Verde warbled a Gaelic ballad about a minstrel boy while Sebriana hummed a lullaby. Roque sharpened his knives.

No weapons fired or raised voices alerted the friends to the arrival of the Danites. Lying undetected in the forest, the Apaches were having great success with their hunt. Killing without warning was their business. They had cause enough.

Dan thought one last time, what the Jicarilla do is their business, but I must offer these Danites the chance to save their lives without giving away the presence of the Apache.

The Danites, closed in by the wood, approached single file. Given time, they could ride through to Dan's position, but getting there would be slow going. They'd do better on foot. A bend in the trail concealed them until the last. Suddenly, Porter Brannan appeared barely twenty-five yards from Dan.

Dan stood up. "That's far enough, Brannan. It's time for you to head back to Utah."

Brannan kept coming. He had sand. His eyes cast

about right and left looking for concealed riflemen, sure he must be riding into an ambush. He stopped at Dan's barricade so close Dan could smell his breath. His men crowded up behind him, making it impossible for Brannan to back his horse. With a few yards to gather speed, his horse might have leapt the logs they'd piled, but he didn't have those yards.

He snarled. "I think not. I'll head for Utah when I have what I came for."

Dan glared at him. "What would that be?"

"Professor Pendarvis' book," Porter replied. "The Prophet will know everything we need to once he has seen that book. Hand it over, and you can go. I don't need you anymore, nor do I need whatever information you think you might have. If you've been anywhere interesting, I can follow your back trail."

Dan interrupted. "You can't have it. The Professor gave it to me."

Porter growled. "Don't presume I won't kill you because I need information from you. I don't anymore. Your only chance is to leave the book and run." Behind him his men were bunched up. Most were still in the forest hemmed in by trees.

Dan smiled. "Winter's comin.' That's why we're headed for Santa Fe. Snows have probably wiped out our trail already."

Porter smiled and his hand moved like lightning to his Colt. "Get 'em, Danites!"

Behind Porter, two guns crashed in the hands of the Danites who could see Dan. Further back, horses reared and screamed as branches cracked. Men were trying to get to where they could see. Even as they did, Dan and his friends responded with gunfire. Dan took out one of the Danites with his rifle. Then dropping it, he drew his first pistol and fired at a shadow as the world disappeared in a cloud of white gun smoke. As the fog thickened, it began to glow orange. Lightning flames stabbed through it like a hellish thundercloud. Dan moved and fired when he could find a target, conscious of his friends to left and right doing the same.

Dan searched for Porter Brannan. The part of Dan's mind not involved in the fight reproved him for not killing Brannon first. Seeing Porter, Dan unthinking leapt the barricade and collided with one of the Danite riders still in the saddle. The collision knocked Dan down and caused the horse to rear, throwing the Mormon to the ground. Scrambling to his feet, Dan saw the rider still on the ground and bringing his pistol to bear. Dan, his pistol already raised, was quicker and shot him through the heart.

Firing at a fleeting shadow, the hammer fell on an empty cylinder. Pulling his second pistol, Dan leapt back over the barricade.

The friends had known the Danites would try to flank them and that they would have to pull back from the wood line to "refuse" their flanks. Sound and shadow flitting in the thick white fog told Dan that he was the apex of a V, like a flight of swans facing the woods; his friends having already pulled back. Firing had dulled Dan's ears to the screams of men and horses. The stench of black powder filled his nostrils and burned his eyes. There were other smells of blood and the contents of bellies now released upon the ground.

The smoke swirled, and Dan glimpsed Roque with a Danite almost on him, his rifle leveled at the Mexican's breast. A crash sounded as flame and smoke tore the scene away. Dan holstered his second pistol, pulling 'hawk and Bowie. Dan's comrades had discharged their projectile weapons. All fire now came from the Danites' side.

Brannan broke out of the wood line, running toward Dan from his right, the Mormon's Colt extended toward Dan. A yard away, he fired. Flame bit into Dan's face. Opening his eyes, Dan saw Porter standing looking confused. In this momentary check, Dan slashed him across the belly with his Bowie drawing blood the entire length. From the feel, Dan thought, he'd hit Porter deep into the belly, but Brannon was tough. Brannon's pistol crashed into the side of Dan's head, awaking stars and pain so sharp Dan froze. Porter's left caught Dan under the chin knocking him off his feet and a yard back. Porter aimed his pistol. The hammer must have fallen on an empty cylinder for he tossed the weapon away. He closed, kicking Dan in the side. A rib cracked loud enough for even Dan's dull ears to hear. Dan sprang up, butting Porter in the stomach and blinding himself with Porter's blood. Unthought of, Dan's 'hawk struck Brannon behind the knee knocking him off his feet. Head still clearing, Dan could not press his advantage and Brannon rose slowly, drawing a knife almost as big as Dan's.

With his left hand, grabbing from his belt, Porter loosed a coiled bullwhip, snapping it with amazing speed so that it cut Dan's cheek below his eye to the bone. Porter Brannon smiled. Dan was sure he had aimed for the eye, but he wasn't letting on. A second whip crack cut Dan's upper arm, stunning the limb for a moment. There was only one thing for it. With the next strike, Dan stepped in close, and dropping his 'hawk, he grabbed the whip. It stung his hand, but Dan held on.

It was now a tethered knife fight, and Brannon was fast, faster than anyone Dan had ever seen, even faster than Kit. A flick and the forearm holding the business end of his whip was cut deeply by the knife. Dan maneuvered but couldn't gain advantage. A flick of Porter's knife opened a cut above Dan's belt, bloody, painful, but not deep, praise God. Brannon laughed enjoying himself.

He wasn't watching the hand holding his whip, out of play he must have thought. He was using the whip to jerk Dan off balance and to pull Dan in to him. Dan swung his blade across Porter's chest wildly, missing. Porter saw the opening and lunged. Releasing the whip, Dan grabbed his wrist even as the knife pierced his chest near his right shoulder. With all his remaining strength, Dan brought his Bowie down backhanded, striking with the blade across Porter Brannon's throat. The heavy knife was razor sharp. Brannan's head fell back opening the ghastly wound, blood spurting. His eyes stared, surprised, and then the lights went out. He fell heavily to his back, head under his body.

Dan stood, staggered, and reloaded his pistols, searching for enemies in the clearing fog. Sebriana knelt over a fallen Danite administering the "last rights" with her misericorde. Gut wounded, her enemy would have died, painfully, taking days. He screamed as he saw death coming; she slid the thin blade up his nose. He knew pain for only a second. Wiping the blade on his shirt, she stood and looked around in the thinning haze, stopping when she saw Dan. Running she embraced him as he hugged her to him. Then she began bandaging his wounds even as he stood, looking for more enemies. In the wood, the Jicarilla were making sure of the Danites. Dan counted seven warriors but saw no Mormons.

And then Dan saw Roque alive, but batting at a smoking vest. His hand struck a watch pocket. He looked surprised as he lifted a bullet from it. The center of the burn in his vest was over his heart just above his pocket.

Rojo appeared and looked quizzically into Dan's face. "You are powder burned, my friend, as if a weapon was fired in your face. There is a small, white spot in the middle of your forehead between your eyes that is not burned." He shook his head slowly. "I saw that one," he indicated Brannan, "shoot you in the face."

The Apache hunters emerged from the woods, happy with the booty they had captured and talking excitedly. Rojo conversed with them.

He translated, "They say a glowing, orange cloud descended between you and the Danites repulsing their shots and protecting you. It roiled like the thundercloud and within it were flashes of flame like lightnings. They say the gods came down to protect you! Power walks with you!"

"Rojo," Dan said, "look at the orange sun setting. Surely it was only the long red light of a fall sunset shining through the smoke of gunfire. See. We were between them and the sun. The Danites were at a disadvantage looking into the sun."

Dan knew the Jicarilla word for Power, naawo, and heard them say it over and over, naawo, nodding to each other. Power is a living thing with them that comes to a man and helps him if he obeys its rules and dictates. It lives in the world and is part of all things.

Rojo looked at Dan again, up and down. "There is a scratch across your throat. Why didn't the blade cut deeper? Who thinks, who is fast enough, who is strong enough to grasp the wrist of the hand holding the blade piercing his chest? Not I. Power is with you."

"Where's the leprechaun?" asked Roque. "He's never disappeared from a fight before."

The corpse of a very large Danite lying face down began to rock back and forth making hideous noises. The

Apache, his eyes wide, jumped back from it.

"Quick," Dan called. "Get him out from under there before he decides to butcher his way to the surface."

Roque rolled the corpse over revealing an angry Verde. "Never call me leprechaun, ya daft Mexican!"

They gathered their horses. Dan turned to see Verde standing over Brannan urinating. He looked at Dan and said, "That's for Mountain Meadows."

"You were there?" Dan asked.

"With Carleton in '59."

Night was gathering fast around them. No one wanted to camp on this ground. Bidding farewell to the Jicarilla, they left the Danites' bones to bleach, fit food for vultures and coyotes. They didn't ride far, through the next pine woods to the next clearing where they stopped on the cliffs overlooking the Piedre Lumbre. No one was hungry but coffee and the fire were welcome. They fed the fire all night keeping demons at bay. Sebriana and Dan huddled under a blanket by its warmth, leaning on each other, sleeping off and on. They broke one of Kit's rules staring into the fire, abandoning their night vision. The group set no watch but hobbled their stock and let it graze. The butter soft smell of piñon eased their fears and hurts.

Dan arose with the sun, his body stiff and sore. The sounds emerging from his companions indicated they felt much the same. The descent into the Piedre Lumbre was beautiful. The rocks blazed red, yellow, ochre, and white. The day after the battle, the descent was a nightmare. Each jolt on the downhill ride awoke pain anew. Beyond the Rocks on Fire, Redwall Canyon led down to Abiquiu. It, too, was a painful ride.

It may have been the pain that made Dan maudlin. He missed Topper. His thoughts ran to those who pursued his little party. The Pope himself was among them, he thought, or at least men doing his bidding. Dan wondered if the Pope was really aware of them so far away in Rome. There had been time for a message to reach him, but his warriors in New Mexico had been acting on orders three hundred years old. Had they been wiped out? It seemed likely the troop that had pursued Dan and his friends was no more, but there were plenty more Penitentes in Rio Arriba. If they were alerted, Dan would soon have trouble again. Brannan's Danites were gone, but there were more in Utah, and they would surely come when the Prophet learned Porter Brannon and his company were no longer following Dan and his companions. Ambition and malice came together in the Mormon Prophet. Dan shuddered to think what might happen if he ever got hold of the treasure.

Albert Pike was another man of ambition who sought to take Mexican lands and spread slavery. If he ever took the treasure, the United States would be permanently split, and Mexico would become very small indeed. His men were still out there unaccounted for and dangerous.

Dan pondered the future. Presuming he and his friends could bring the treasure down without arousing suspicion, how would they get it to President Lincoln? Kansas and Missouri were war torn and bleeding but Dan could see no way around them. The way to California and the ocean was blocked at Mesilla by Confederates. The ocean route was slow and too many people would want to know their business. That left the plains as the only route, the Santa Fe Trail, and that led through Kansas to Missouri and the bosom of Quantrill's Raiders and Bloody Bill Anderson. If Dan traveled with too small a party, Indians would attack, aware that the dragoons were no longer guarding caravans. If he traveled with too large an escort, they would attract unwanted attention. Dan intended to keep their cargo a secret. No one should know what they were carrying beyond the five friends. Perhaps they could hire some Jicarilla for drovers. They would guard and respect secrets.

Santa Fe looked wonderful as they descended the last ridge into town thinking of hot food and warm beds. It smelled of piñon fires and roasting meat heavy with spice, which this time of year drowned out the stench of people and animals. Friends cried out to them as they rode in.

Dan thought, I may be happy to see them, but this isn't good. I didn't want to attract this much attention.

The last caravans were in for the season, so parties of travelers raised a stir. The town buzzed with excitement and fear anyway, as Dan soon learned. General Sibley's brigade had begun to arrive in Mesilla. They crossed west Texas in small parties so as not to strain water and other resources. It would be more than a month before the brigade could assemble. Many of their friends had gone south to serve as volunteers under men like Kit Carson. There was justifiable fear there might still be traitors among the citizens. Most of the Santa Fe traders were from Missouri and many were Southern sympathizers. There were men of questionable loyalty, though traitors might be the wrong word. Perhaps they were patriots of their home states, Dan thought. Or perhaps they were just ambitious, hoping for rank and position in the new governments forming.

They arrived in Santa Fe in time for the monthly meeting of the Montezuma Masonic Lodge, Free and Accepted Masons, Grand Lodge of Missouri. Rojo, Roque, Verde, and Dan attended lodge while Sebriana went to find a rabbi. Dan was pleased she was seeking a teacher, not a priest: what she had to confess might shock a priest into unconsciousness and afterwards he might pass it along to the Pope.

The Lodge was a different matter. There were brothers on both sides of the War. Secesh kept their feelings quiet, but they were prepared to help Sibley obtain supplies and Union depots. Feelings ran high but in the Lodge, no one would discuss politics so as not to disrupt the harmony of the brotherhood. After they "met upon the level," they were prepared to "part upon the square." Many of the brothers who approached Dan and Roque for news were from the south and sought news of Mesilla. Others came with requests that they take messages to Kit. They made arrangements to meet in coming days at La Fonda on the Plaza.

General Sibley was leading the rebels. Dan knew him as Captain Sibley from the dragoons at Fort Union. Soldiers who served under Sibley idealized him, and most thought him a great warrior. He and Colonel Canby had been close friends sharing campaigns in the Mormon War and against the Navajo. Their meeting in war might prove interesting.

La Fonda, the inn, stood across from the Palace of the Governors where the Santa Fe Trail arrived at the plaza. Its herringboned latilla ceilings supported by huge vigas were low and blackened by soot. The floor was dirt and the rooms long and narrow with beehive hornos in the corners that provided both heat and light. The food was the best in town, and it was the only place Dan knew of that had plates and silverware. Everywhere else the tortilla served as spoon and plate. A variety of liquors from the States were available, but Dan and his friends stuck to the local wine. Beer was slow in coming to New Mexico. It did not transport well, and no one as yet was brewing it locally. The La Fonda was also a place to gather information.

Lucien Maxwell found Roque and Dan there one evening. He boomed. "And there's the two of you! Did the governor declare a Christmas pardon 'cause the jails was too full? Have you heard the news?" Then he answered his question not waiting for them to speak. "Magoffin's sons, Joseph and Samuel, are officers in Sibley's Brigade. Samuel's a major."

Lucien was powerful and tall with a great drooping mustache. He wore black city clothes and knee-high riding boots. Bulges under his long coat concealed hidden knives and guns. He owned a land grant handed down from his father-in-law and built up by himself that covered the northeast quarter of New Mexico. He'd been a mountain man with Kit who came to Taos and married a vecina girl.

They knew Magoffin as one of the most prosperous traders on the Santa Fe Trail. His rancho, Magoffinville, near Franklin, Texas, was leased to the army as a fort.

Lucien continued. "I'm surprised Magoffin was fool enough to let them."

Dan stopped him. "What's so foolish? Officer status will translate into power and position in Confederate Texas."

Lucien countered. "You think New Mexico will become a Confederate territory? These people round here, the Mexicans and the mountain men, will never stand for it. All of Sibley's friends and acquaintances may have talked like they were Secesh till he thought everyone was, but he's forgot the people; they hate Texians with passion."

"Well," Dan replied, "could be. But Sibley's a fine officer who's won lots of battles. He's dangerous."

"Bah," Lucien answered. "He's lost the campaign already."

"How's that?" asked Roque.

"Started wrong time of the year," Maxwell replied. "He's got to send his men across from San Antonio in small groups to allow the grass to grow back and the waterholes to refill. Only it's fall, and the grass won't grow. There is nothing to supply his men with food and feed until they get to Franklin, and there's damned little between there and Mesilla. After that, he faces the Jornada. And it's the wrong time of year. Grass don't grow in winter."

Dan thought about Confederate prospects. "So it will take him a couple of months to reassemble and recruit his command between Franklin and Mesilla."

Lucien grinned pleased with his own clever analysis. "They'll be hungry and their stock almost dead before they arrive."

Roque gave his opinion. "Maybe they got a big wagon train with food and feed."

"Bravo," said Lucien. "Maybe they do. But they've still got a problem. What's the distance from San Antonio to Mesilla?"

Dan figured for a moment. "'Bout a thousand miles."

Lucien nodded. "So we load up a wagon with feed and hitch four mules to it. How long does it take them to make the crossing?"

"I don't know," said Roque rubbing his temples. "Fifteen or twenty miles per day. That's…maybe forty-five days. Maybe longer."

"Bravo!" said Lucien. "How much feed do four mules eat each day?"

"They eat a lot," Dan said understanding. "Why, they'd eat everything in the wagon before they got to Mesilla!"

"Aye, they would." Lucien grinned again.

Roque struggled with the puzzle. "They could go half way and turn around for another load."

"Good thinking, Roque." Lucien smiled. "And they'd finish the last of it just as they got home to San Antonio. They'd be better off to go two hundred fifty miles, a quarter of the way, unload half of the original load, make a supply depot, and return for more. Then they could go another two hundred and fifty miles and establish another depot. And so on. That would take a long time and a lot of supplies. The Texian Secesh aren't rich or overly well supplied. No, Sibley is trying to make it in one go."

Dan nodded slowly. "His men and stock will be exhausted when they arrive."

"So they will," replied Lucien. "Sibley is out of his depth, good in a fight, but no strategist. And he's got Baylor to contend with."

"Baylor?" asked Roque.

Lucien replied. "The new self-appointed governor of Confederate Arizona."

Roque growled low in his throat. "Oh, him. He's the hombre that ordered us drafted into the Confederate army. I thought he was on Sibley's side."

"With friends like him," Lucien said, "Sibley don't need any enemies. Baylor's offended everybody."

The Christmas season soon arrived in Santa Fe with a mix of Gavacho and Hispanic customs. Luminarias or farolitos lighted path ways and the roof lines of buildings. Special breads and foods were prepared. Sebriana made bizcochitos with hot chocolate and posole. She was planning a Christmas dinner that included venison and wild turkey as well as empañaditas, little pockets of bread containing meats and sweets. There would also be natillas, milk puddings, and sopapillas. At Epiphany, there would be Rosca de los Reyes, Three Kings Bread.

Dan thought that it was good to be home with Sebriana warm in their adobe casa.

Late in the night, she made Dan warmer still. She was a wild creature, Dan thought, who would never submit to a man. A lover might gentle her for a time, but that was all. He doubted anyone was strong enough to gentle her for a lifetime. With five husbands buried on the trail behind her, Dan wondered that she hadn't had any children. Perhaps one of them had injured her.

Chill winter winds blew through Santa Fe, but the drafts were good; they swept away the smoke of a thousand fires. Returning from La Fonda, Dan entered their casa. The warmth from the horno enveloped him. Then he was overwhelmed by another heat.

"Pobrecito! You are home!" she cried.

Running across the room, Sebriana threw her arms about his neck and leaping wrapped her legs about his middle drowning his face in wet kisses. Dinner would have to wait. It was a long time before Dan's head cleared. The dinner they shared, when they finally recalled that food was heating, was the best he'd ever had.

"It will not be necessary to dress for dinner," Doña Loca said. Later, Dan couldn't recall what they ate. The world was soft and warm, and the long winter night lasted long beyond dawn.

In January, while crossing the plaza, Roque, Rojo, and Dan ran into Colonel Paul and his adjutant, a young lieutenant whose name Dan promptly forgot. Drinks at La Fonda seemed in order. Paul was a big man, so tall his head poked through his hair. He had been a professional soldier but now was a colonel of New Mexico volunteers in charge of Fort Union on the llano beyond Las Vegas. Bayonet straight in a properly fitted uniform, he looked a proper commander.

"Colonel Canby is calling most of the volunteers and militia to him at Fort Craig," Paul said. "The way along the river is narrow at Craig, but Sibley might still bypass the fort. Canby will have to take his force out to meet them."

Dan was puzzled. "He still hasn't gathered everyone?"

The eager young adjutant jumped in with both feet in his mouth. "Colonel Canby has got it all figured out. There are three ways the Texians can come. They most likely will come up the Rio Grande as that way has the most water and supplies. But they could come up the Pecos. They'll find water, but no supplies, and he'll have Apache to contend with."

Colonel Paul glanced around the room to see who might be listening. In a quiet voice, he picked up the story. "Sibley is having trouble with Apaches. His small parties of Texans aren't setting proper guard, and the Apache are helping themselves to his livestock." He glanced around again. "There are supplies and men at Belen to delay him if he comes that way. The last way is up the Canadian across the Llano Estacado. They've tried that before without much success, but I'm waiting at Fort Union, if they do."

"The Secesh don't stand a chance!" the adjutant said loudly. "There are regiments raising in Colorado and a whole brigade in California under Colonel Carleton. Colorado and California won't rise for the South any more than the Mormons in Utah will throw in with them. If they can't capture supplies at Fort Craig or Fort Union, they're done for."

Roque nodded. "Sage words. It is good that Colonel Canby has you to advise him."

The lieutenant may have had it all figured out, but Colonel Paul didn't look so certain. "We don't know how many men Sibley's bringing or how many columns there will be. There could be brigades coming up the Pecos and over the Canadian even now. Look at how they took Fort Fillmore and all its supplies. It could happen again. All of the supplies and munitions of our army in Texas fell to them. There are people in Colorado and California who would rise for them. The Prophet Brigham Young will go whichever way he thinks he sees the most advantage."

In early February, a letter came from Kit, now a Colonel of New Mexico Volunteers, written by some helper in his command. The letter said, "Get down here quick. I need your help. Fun's about to begin. Sibley's full brigade is at Mesilla, and they're starting north along the river."

The five companions discussed Kit's appeal over a fine dinner prepared by Sebriana. They all owed much to Kit Carson. If he called them, the summons must be important.

"I guess he means Roque and me," Dan said. "The rest of you can stay here and guard our find, if that's okay." They didn't refer to what they'd found by name lest anyone overhear. It was safer that way and a good habit.

Verde's voice rose. "Devil I will! Fight this big you can bet I'm going to be there. You can't keep me out."

Rojo smiled that evil Apache grin. "I would like to see how you Mangani fight each other. I might pick up something useful."

Dan protested. "We can't leave Sebriana here alone with the things we found."

She smiled sweetly. "You don't have to worry about that, I'm coming with you."

Dan tried to sound reasonable. "There's going to be a big battle. It will be dangerous."

"When hasn't it been so?" she smiled.

"You can't come!" Dan said firmly.

"You can't stop me!"

Dan warned. "Really, it's too dangerous. You can't come."

She flushed with anger. "When did you start giving me orders?"

"So we'll compromise," said Roque, "and she'll come with us. But we'll need a place to hide things. I don't think Topper's cupboard will work if we're gone a long time."

"That's right, Roque," Dan said. "We'll have to hide the Professor's book, too."

Roque massaged his head. "We could take them to the Cathedral and ask the Bishop to keep them for us."

"I don't think that's a good idea," said Sebriana. "The Pope may have alerted him to be looking for us."

"I don't know," Dan said. "I get the feeling the Penitentes' lines of communication to the Pope were severed a long time ago.

"I read a book by Edgar A. Poe, a very strange writer. He says things can be hidden best in plain sight where nothing calls attention to them."

Verde said merrily, "So we'll be about leavin' the book and things, on the bench in the Plaza as foolish as the cow's calf."

Dan thought for a moment. "No, they have to be where'll they'll fit in and not look out of place, and it should be someplace controlled where strangers can't just pick them up."

"Good," said Roque. "Let's take them to the governor's palace and leave them there."

Verde shook his head violently. "I wouldn't be about leaving anything where a politician, wise as a serpent, can get his hands on it. It's certain as the dawn that politico crew will steal them, even if they've no use for them. Treacherous as an Englishman, they rob the common folk as often as there's fingers on your hand."

Sebriana spoke quietly, uncertain of the course they should take. "Danito, we could take them to Solomon Speigleberg's store. He has a big safe. We'll ask him to hold them in pawn for us."

"The Speigleberg brother's store then!" Dan exclaimed. "Solomon's a brother in the Lodge and sworn to keep the secrets of a brother Master Mason!"

A few days later, they rode south for Fort Craig. Arriving on February 20, they found the fort at the center of a huge tent city, a hive of soldierly activity. Here and there, squads and companies drilled and marched. The regulars were housed inside the fort, and outside were the volunteers and militia. As they passed, Dan noted that the militia looked like what they were, dazed and confused, unused to their weapons. New Mexico had no tradition of drilling on the plaza on Sunday afternoon. The militia was called, for they were in the States to defend their homes, but in New Mexico they brought their own weapons, mostly spears and bows. They had been issued muskets and clearly were still learning to use them.

Roque shook his head. "They don't look like confident soldiers."

The volunteers had signed up for a year of soldiering. There were many gavachos among them. Some were mountain men they recognized from Taos, and others were brothers from Montezuma Masonic Lodge in Santa Fe. The fighting quality of the men varied from unit to unit. Men followed colonels and captains they respected. That was how recruiting was handled. Kit Carson had a very salty regiment. Dan didn't know if they'd stand and fight in lines of battle or charge with the bayonet, but with rifle, tomahawk, and Bowie knife, they had no peers anywhere. The Mexicans in Kit's ranks were Indian traders, trappers, and cibolleros, buffalo hunters. All were men who knew guns and survival. Colonel Miguel Piño's 2nd New Mexico Volunteer Regiment looked uncertain of themselves and almost as green as the militia. It would take time to turn that regiment into a fighting command. An outfit like the 2nd would make anyone, except the enemy, glad there were regulars about.

"Look there," said Roque. "He's spotted us." He was Paddy Graydon, commander of the Spies and Guides Company. "See the devil's light in his eyes. He's up to no good and wants us in it."

Verde smiled. "A man after me own heart."

Usually taciturn, Kit greeted them warmly. "I'm glad you're here. There's a big battle brewing. Colonel Canby has gathered almost four thousand men, and General Sibley has at least as many. I've never been through anything like this huge, coming battle. I was always in small fights with just a few men on each side. I want men I can trust as aides to run messages for me."

"That let's Verde out," said Roque. "Nobody can trust him."

Verde sniggered. "Roque Vigil, you're wicked as an Englishman."

"Sebriana," continued Kit taking no notice, "they're sure to want your help at the hospital if you're willing." She nodded her assent.

Paddy Graydon burst in. "I see you've found my deserters, Colonel Carson. Be kind enough to hand them over."

"Paddy, we've been over this before," said Kit mildly. Only Kit could put so much menace into something said so politely.

Seeing how matters stood, Graydon took a new course. "Well, then Colonel, how about you let me borrow these four tonight on a special mission, and I'll forget about the deserters and return the lot to you tomorrow?"

The four friends never enlisted or volunteered but found themselves in the thick of preparation for the battle. Soon they found themselves participants. Kit called them "civilian contractors," and no one questioned him. Paddy Graydon had them roped into a plan so crazy Verde might have come up with it.

Paddy explained the situation to them. "On the 16th Sibley and his Texans camped just two miles south of the fort on this side of the river. He looked the fort over good, and we think he's decided it's too strong for him to assault. He's scared of those Quaker cannon Colonel Canby made from wooden vigas. He's been backing down south again, probably looking for a way to swing around Mesa del Contadero to the east and come down on the Valverde fords north of us crossing back to the west bank there.

"I know where his supply wagons are parked. The Texians' camp is now at Paraje de Fra Cristobal on the far side of the river."

Long after dark, they packed two old, worn-out mules with all the gunpowder they could carry and set a one minute fuse to it.

"See now," said Paddy, "we'll ford the river and lead the mules up near the wagons, light the fuse, slap their backsides, and run. Nothin' to it."

Dan frowned. "Seems a cruel way to retire an old mule, Paddy."

Paddy grinned. "It'll be over in a second, and they

won't feel the pains of old age."

They forded a very cold river with water up to the mules' bellies and slowly made their way within one hundred yards of the wagons. They could clearly see the Texans around their campfires. They heard the Secesh talking and joking and their livestock bawling their distress. The animals hadn't been watered all day. Union forces were on the river, preventing the Texans from getting close.

Paddy slapped the mules' rumps and signaled his squad to run. They ran for the river pursued by urgent hoof beats.

Roque looked behind them. "Your mules must like you very much, Paddy. They are coming after you!" Two scared old mules didn't want to join that thirsty herd of animals. They were following Paddy's squad.

Dan had been told that a man can out run a mule over a half mile course. After that night, he believed it was so. He'd done it. But after that half mile even an old mule loaded with gunpowder starts to gain. They were right behind Paddy's squad when his men dove into the river. Above the water all was roiling flame as the mules exploded.

Pandemonium broke out in the rebel camp. Shots were fired. Men shouted. Paddy's men heard the crashing of six hundred hooves and thought that it must be the rebel cavalry coming after them. They splashed and swam across the freezing river to the far bank where a small Union force awaited them. As they crawled out, Dan looked behind them to see hundreds of Texas mules watering themselves. The livestock figured they'd had just about enough, and in the noisy commotion, they broke free of the picket line and had followed the leading Union mules.

Grasping the situation more quickly than Dan would have thought likely, Paddy shouted, "Gather 'em in, boys. Those mules have deserted and come over to the Union!"

One hundred and fifty long-eared, Texas "deserters" joined the Union that night. At midday on the 21st, Major Wesche, after running off a small force of Texans, found unattended wagons in the rebel camp and burned them along with the supplies they contained. Without mules to pull them, the Texans had been forced to leave the wagons behind.

Colonel Canby, unaware of the difficulty the loss of mules had caused his foe, was concerned that the slow withdrawal to the south might be a ruse. At first light on the 21st, he ordered Colonel Carson and the 1st New Mexico Volunteers to a position south of the fort near the ford. Major Wesche took the 2nd New Mexico Militia across the river and set up there. Captain Seldon and the regular infantry were already in position below Wesche. A short time later, Dan heard cannon fire to the north toward Valverde.

Shortly after 8:00 a.m., Kit sent Dan up to have a look. He forded the river behind a cavalry unit that headed east toward a thick stand of cottonwoods. Looking for the man in charge, Dan located Major Tom Duncan, a regular cavalry officer, who had with him a battalion of cavalry regulars and a battalion of Valdez's New Mexico Volunteer Cavalry. All were armed with rifled muskets.

"See 'em hurryin' down through that arroyo, coming off the mesa," said Major Duncan, pointing to a spot five hundred yards away. "There's two regiments here already and more coming all the time. Tell that to Colonel Roberts at the ford. He's got infantry and cannon. We need infantry to hold them off. The Texian Sesech are bringing up cannon now!"

As he spoke, two canister rounds exploded in the air forward of the Union position. Duncan frowned. "If they get the range, how am I to defend against that?"

With a whoop and a yell, a regiment of Texas cavalry with their sabers held level and forward, reins in teeth, and colt pistols in their left hands thundered down on the New Mexicans. The "fourth men," holding the horses for Duncan's cavalry looked nervous. They had to depend on the other three to protect them. Fortunately, the Union men were armed with rifled muskets loaded with "buck and ball." Paper cartridges contained a minié ball backed by four buckshot. The buckshot spread out and was sure to hit something. It might not kill, but it would leave someone hurtin'. With longer range accuracy than the Texans, the Union soldiers started firing when the enemy was still three hundred yards away. Unable to return fire, the Texan Cavalry broke off the attack. The cannon started firing again wounding and killing some of the Union cavalry. It was harder to face than the Texans' charge, for the soldiers had no way to defend themselves or fire back.

"Fortunately, they're only a couple of light cannon," said Duncan. "But tell Roberts I need artillery to support me!"

Dan rode back across the river and delivered the message to Colonel Roberts. "Duncan needs to flank the enemy," the colonel said. "He needs to get moving. Don't worry," he continued looking at Dan. "I'll send my adjutant to tell him. He'll have a bit more authority."

Dan headed back south to Kit and filled him in. "We'll be heading north soon," Kit said.

About 10 a.m., they saw Captain Selden and regular infantry head north toward the fort. A short time later, a rider reined in his mule by Kit to deliver orders from

Colonel Canby. "Your unit is ordered to report to Colonel Roberts at the lower Valverde ford just north of Fort Craig." Canby was now as sure as a commander could be that General Sibley was bypassing Fort Craig, so he was committing most of his remaining force to the battle in the north behind Fort Craig.

Kit sent Dan ahead to scout out the situation. He reported to Colonel Roberts. "Kit sent me to find out where you want his regiment."

Roberts explained, "I'm senior officer on the scene. Major Duncan is across the river working his way to the right to flank the enemy. We can't see most of the ground because of these cottonwoods to our front. That's going to make it hard to defend from this side. We need to be forward in the trees. The artillery will cross as soon as we have enough troops over there to support them. See the dust? The Texians are coming down that arroyo into an old, abandoned river bed. It gives them cover and concealment. They can move back and forth in it and there isn't much we can do about it. They can shift to mass their regiments on either ford. I'm going to send Kit forward to reinforce Duncan's cavalry. Go on across the river and talk to Duncan and then get back to Colonel Carson. Can you remember all that?" Dan nodded. "Good. Get going."

Dan forded the river and turned south back toward Mesa de Contadero at the point where the old bed joined the new. The valley bottom was shaped like a spearhead. The river ran down the left side under steep banks ten feet high. On the other side was the abandoned bed running from tip to tail with banks five feet high. Uneven ground between the two was parceled between meadows and a band of cottonwood trees. The stand of trees was no more than one hundred yards in depth. In between and throughout the meadow, grass covered old snags.

"Roberts wants me to mount up and charge the Rebs," Duncan told Dan. "They have cannons, and I don't. They have a covered position and a force larger than my own. I've been extending my line to the right, moving around their flank, while I wait for reinforcements. We've finally got some artillery." He pointed to a battery of twenty-four pounders that were tearing up the Texans' flank.

Dan headed back to the lower ford and saw Colonel Roberts and his staff galloping toward the upper ford that Selden and the regular infantry were defending. The left wing had artillery support, too, and McRae's battery was setting up in the middle between Duncan and Selden. There was a big gap between the two. Crossing at the lower ford Dan found Colonel Canby and his staff where Roberts had been across the river behind Duncan. Kit was with him.

"Danny," said Kit, "we've been ordered to form the reserve behind Selden on this side of the river at the upper ford. Colonel Piño is being sent to the lower ford as reserve on the right."

Dan marched with Kit's regiment toward the upper ford. A little snow fell on the soldiers as they marched. Dan was cold and wet from crossing the river, soaked to the waist and glad he wasn't infantry, for he would have been completely wet. The air was full of the acrid smell of gunpowder. Their ears rang with the double bang of artillery. So far attacks from both Union and Texan armies hadn't accomplished much. Units moved forward tentatively and were driven back with a volley or two. The Texans, equipped with a collection of civilian weapons, squirrel guns, pistols and shotguns hadn't done the Union much damage. The New Mexicans had stung the Texans hard a couple of times, but most of the damage was being wrought by artillery.

"Roque," Kit called, "cross over and let Captain Selden know we're here. Rojo! Verde! Go to Colonel Roberts and stay with him in case he has messages for us." They splashed their way across the river, riding to the sound of the guns.

The sound of gunfire was increasing from Selden's position. He was attacking. Dan and Kit heard occasional cheers but couldn't tell if they came from Union men or the Texans. Roque was gone so long Dan began to fear for him. There was more cheering and more firing. Selden's men fell back through the cottonwoods to the river's banks just across from Kit's regiment. There was Roque riding high, a pistol in one hand. He fired until it was empty and swapped it for his second one. The Texans did not follow up immediately. The Union soldiers seemed to be in good order. Waving to Kit, Dan crossed the ford. Roque pointed to something off to their left.

Within the Texan lines cavalry was forming up for a charge. They were armed with lances, each decorated by a red pennant. They looked gay and deadly. Hooves thundered as the charge began. They bore down on the Union's most exposed unit, the Pike's Peakers from Colorado. Spear points, glinting in the sun, were brought level on command, pennants flapping like dripping blood. The charge of the lancers was heroic, exciting, and threatening. Dan thought they looked like crusaders, the knights of old. The Coloradans fired a volley that seemed to tear half the riders from their saddles. Another volley followed. Surviving Texans fell back to their own lines, while their leaders brought up cannon to work on the Union left.

Roque and Dan crossed back to Kit's unit. "Danito, you should have seen it," Roque, wild-eyed, his hat gone, and hair standing out like a mass of dark thunderclouds told Dan. "Selden advanced from cover to cover until we were almost on top of the Texians. The rebels were armed with squirrel guns, pistols, and shotguns. I think I even saw one with a pitchfork. Their fire didn't have much effect on us until we got close and were tearing them to pieces. We were almost into their position when another regiment rode up to confront us. Then they were more than twice our strength, and we had to fall back. But Selden's men did it in good order. It was no rout.

"Danito, you never heard so many guns firing at the same time. The noise was unbelievable. You can't hear the man next to you. The smoke burns your eyes, and suddenly you feel alone. You can hear the bullets buzz by close to your ears like a million bees. Smoke and flame, only now and then can you see a man. The inferno can't be much worse than this."

The battle quieted for a time as they watched Colonel Canby come up with the ammunition train and take personal control of the battle. Orders soon came for the regiment to cross the lower ford and join Duncan. The center had been strengthened with McRae's battery, which was engaging the Texans' right wing. Duncan was to move astride their left flank after which Kit's regiment would swing to its left like a door closing and roll up the Confederate force.

Dan turned to Roque. "It is a good plan, but I'm told no plan survives contact with the enemy."

Duncan's force with Kit's regiment in train moved to the right. Later Dan realized that this movement had opened a gap between the regiment and McRae's battery in the center, a big gap, almost half a mile. As Kit's men formed to attack, the Texans, sensing the move coming, attacked the regiment with cavalry. They looked superb until they came in range of Kit's rifles. Volley fire left many saddles empty. Two volleys and Kit's force was smoke-blind waiting for enemy sabers and pistols to beat it down. But the smoke cleared and instead of sabers, they saw horses' tails as the Texans veered off.

The Texans, seeing the weakness in the Union center and how exposed McRae's flank was, attacked between the Kit's regiment and the battery. They set up in the cottonwoods and fired their rifles at the artillery gunners. Artillery was supposed to be able to handle its own defense with canister and grape. Both were like great shotgun charges, but a canister goes farther and explodes over the enemy. For the artillery to defend against infantry, it was just a matter of turning the guns and loading grape, firing the great shotguns into the enemy's faces. McRae couldn't. The cottonwoods ringed him in too close to turn the guns. Soon his guns would go silent for want of gunners.

Not waiting for orders, Kit shouted, "Danny, take your friends and get over there to assist them! Tell them we're coming!" It would take a few minutes to get the regiment moving. Dan, Verde, Rojo, and Roque galloped off to save McRae.

Canby recognized the problem before Dan got to the battery, and his staff rider passed Dan on his way to tell Kit to close the gap, confirming with orders what Kit was already about. Others were rushing to the center as well. Canby ordered Colonel Piño to take his regiment across the river, but they were slow in starting. The rebels also saw what was happening, and with McRae no longer firing on their right wing, they advanced toward the center.

As Dan approached the silent battery, he saw the gunners fighting hand to hand with the Texans. His friend, Lieutenant Bascom, appeared through the smoke only to take a ball through the head. The four riders fought their way to McRae with 'hawk and pistol, but arrived too late to give him the news as he'd already gone down. His eyes burning and his ears ringing, Dan looked for someone to report to but could find no one.

"We've got to fall back," Dan shouted. Roque nodded, but Dan didn't think the others heard. Rojo looked at once fascinated and horrified as he plied his weapons. Verde had dismounted and was grappling with a Texan. "Get him!" Dan called to Roque as he went after Rojo.

Off to Dan's right, a gunner climbed atop an ammunition limber, pointed his pistol downward, and fired. The blast knocked down two dozen nearby men, mostly Texans. He might have shouted, "Death before dishonor!" as he fired, but Dan couldn't hear him. Never one to let a bad idea pass him by, Verde climbed up on an open limber full of canister rounds and drew his pistol. A Texan knocked him a dozen feet with an artillery swab, and Roque raised the unconscious little man across his saddle. Rojo saw Dan's gesture and followed him back toward Kit.

As they arrived at the ford, Piño's regiment, starting to cross to the side where the fight was on the east bank, ran into men retreating from the mêlée over the guns. Texans began firing into the ford. With these two pressures pushing them back, Piño's regiment balked and refused to cross.

Beside Dan, Rojo shook his head. "You white men are insane. You don't care how many you lose as long as you win. Crazy. T'keesh! If my people fought like this, soon all my brothers and cousins would be dead. T'keesh!"

Seeing them approach, Kit stopped his men and took

up a position on the flank of the ford. The Texans would not cross.

A while later, realizing the Texans were as spent as his own force, Colonel Canby sent a delegation under a flag of truce to the Texans proposing a two-day truce to bury the dead and gather the wounded. The Texans agreed. The Battle of Valverde was over.

That night, the four friends sat with Kit and Colonel Canby, smoking their pipes and Roque his cigarito of tobacco rolled in corn husk.

Kit spoke. "Your attack would have worked right fine, Colonel. Shame."

"Yes," Canby replied. "We could have rolled them up and finished it right here."

Verde, his wits only partially recovered, said, "I guess God wasn't on our side. Looking down on such fine Christians on both sides, He decided to leave the decision of the battle to purely tactical factors."

"No," responded Canby, "He was on our side. Sibley is finished. He may yet surrender if he has any sense."

"How's that?" asked Kit.

"He didn't take the fort and the supplies he desperately needs," Canby said. "The little stunt with the mules ended up costing Sibley livestock and, perhaps you don't yet know, his supply train. He didn't have the stock to haul it. We burned his wagons. Half of his cavalry is on foot. He's done. He's weakened, and he'll end up leaving his wounded behind."

"How 'bout that?" smirked Verde. "Two mules that ran the wrong way have doomed the Confederate cause. Sibley will fail, Colorado, Utah, and California stay in the Union, and Jeff Davis doesn't get the gold he needs to win the war!"

"Do not make fun, mosco," growled Roque. "I swat

flies like you. Many good men died here."

"If he tries to continue north," Dan asked, "will you pursue?"

"No," Canby said. "Sibley's done, and I need to be here to protect our supplies and to cut his lines of communication. He won't get any reinforcements or supplies while I'm here.

"I'll send the militia home and some of the volunteers north to harass the Texans. We haven't enough stores to continue feeding them."

"That was some fight," said Roque.

"Worse than you know," replied Canby. "Between dead, wounded, and missing, we've lost almost one man in five. Two hundred and fifty good Union men lie dead out there. This was the bloodiest fight I've ever been in."

Most of the blood had been shed over McRae's guns. The Texans had them now but with very little ammunition for them. Both sides had converged on the center. The heaviest losses fell to the Company of Pike's Peakers and to the artillery. Those few minutes of furious fighting had taken more lives than all the other fighting that day.

Later Roque pulled Dan aside. "I saw him you know. When I picked up Verde, there he was that guero Texian, Tiler Guillermo Caine. I'm pretty sure he saw me, too, and I think he fired at you."

"Hell of a thing for a one brother to do to another. One ball did pass close by my head," Dan replied. "It could have come from anywhere though."

"And Rheingold, I think," said Roque, "was there, too, maybe leading the company that attacked the guns."

"We'll let the others know tomorrow," Dan said. "I guess they could still be hunting us."

Dan paused in thought. "Roque, there was something about this fight that bothers me. We were called here to learn how horrible the battles are in the East where the armies are 100 times larger. Rheingold firing on me frees us of our Masonic obligation to him. And I think Colonel Canby is wrong. Sibley isn't done. There is still fight in his army and he might capture Colorado and the West, if he can capture undefended supplies at Fort Union or if frightened Mexicans rise and join him."

"Sí, amigo," replied Roque. "Colonel Canby uses wishful thinking. There are no supplies coming from Texas for him to intercept. The army does nothing here, but is too weak to follow the Texians."

Dan nodded. "There is something we're supposed to do. Something that will effect New Mexico and the country. Do you remember the stories of the Ark of the Covenant?"

"Sí, when the Ark went before the Israelites, their armies could not lose in battle."

Verde found a bottle somewhere and undertook to "doctor the pain in me head by drinkin' it all." It wasn't long before he was asleep and snoring loudly. Rojo sat by himself withdrawn and moody. All Dan could get out of him was "t'keesh Mangani." Crazy white men.

Even more taciturn than usual, especially where his feelings were concerned, Rojo spoke to Dan on the second day after the fight. "This is madness. No Apache would kill like this. Ussen, God, would refuse his aid to men who kill so wantonly. Daniel, you must do something to stop it."

Dan thought about this. The God of the Old Testament could seem horrible, a Hairy Thunderer, someone had once said, and bloody minded, too. Yet, the psalmist always spoke of God's love and protection. Did the Ark going before their armies ensure that the Israelites would slaughter their enemies or only that they would decisively defend themselves from the wicked? Their enemies were wicked. Topper had told him how the Phillistines sacrificed babies to their idols. And that wasn't just Israelite propaganda. Topper had seen the altars. The Confederates might talk about preserving the Constitution, but they wickedly kept slaves, conscripted men into their armies and wished to seize land from neighboring countries. They should be stopped, not slaughtered, but stopped with less bloodshed than Dan had seen at Valverde.

Two days after the battle, the Texans slipped away to the north, fording the river near Socorro. "Kit," Dan said, "We've got to get to Santa Fe before the Texians do."

"Thanks for being here, Danny," Kit said. "You and your friends. Go when you're ready."

Five more days passed before they were ready to leave. On the fourth day after the battle, Sebriana appeared by the tent they all were sharing.

She was covered in blood, none of it hers. Exhausted, she staggered toward Dan. "Pobrecito, it was horrible, awful. The doctors cut off arms and legs while I held men down. I saw men with their eyes gone and lower jaw shot away. The worst were those with belly wounds. They screamed, and there was nothing we could do for them. They had so much pain as they swelled up and died. I watched wounded legs and arms turn black and stink even as their owners screamed. There was blood, so much blood."

Then she toppled over asleep. Dan caught her and laid her down on her bedroll. She hadn't slept since the battle. She now slept deeply, but cried out in her sleep, the horrible screams of a woman seeing hell.

The next day Dan borrowed Colonel Canby's quarters. It was his turn to give her a bath though he thought he might have enjoyed it more than she. She kept dozing off, still recovering from her ordeal. They rode north for Santa Fe the next day already days behind the Texans.

Chapter 16

Victory at Glorieta

Most of New Mexico's towns were on the east bank of the Rio Grande. Socorro was the exception.

"Take care. The Texians may be there in Socorro ahead of us," said Dan. "We have to be careful to avoid them."

Roque laughed. "They are beaten."

Verde scowled at him. "Boyo, there's still 2,000 of them, and they have guns even if they're moving slow since we took their mules."

Rojo spoke. "They may recognize us from the battle."

Dan nodded. "Or, more likely, they'll just consider us suspect. Texian soldiers would want to know what five riders are doing heading north."

Dan realized that the Texians would see his group as five riders who had been approved to pass the Union blockade at Ft. Craig and acceptance by the troops in blue would announce them as Union spies. Avoiding towns was no easy matter. Roads run through towns and there was water in towns, sometimes the only water available for miles. Riding cross-country was more difficult than it sounds.

Stones and brush tugged and delayed, injuring horses and slowing them. Trails follow the easiest ground. At times, they were confronted with a precipice or other impassable terrain. Backtracking where water was scarce could be deadly. Even worse, if the Confederates had caught them going cross-country, they were sure to hang as spies.

Roque came to a conclusion. "We could travel at night."

Verde smiled agreeing. "Aye, boyo, we could, but if detected, the Texians wouldn't wait long to hang us."

"If we can get past Socorro," said Rojo, "we can head for the Rio Puerco and follow it up to Laguna Pueblo or Acoma and ask the Pueblos to hide us and show us the way to Jemez. From Jemez we can cross the mountain to San Ildefanso and come back to Santa Fe from the north."

"That might work," Dan said. "The towns are all Pueblo people and remote from the Camino Real."

Roque laughed. "Tejanos, Texians, don't have enough men to occupy the Pueblo towns."

Verde nodded. "They'll stick to the big towns and to places where they can capture government stores. Aye, it's as good a plan as any."

Nonetheless, the friends decided to continue north on the road to Socorro, taking their chances until nightfall when they would bypass the town. On the road, they unexpectedly met one of Colonel Piño's men.

Roque was the first to recognize him. "It's Captain Juan Gallegos of Colonel Piño's regiment. Perhaps he'll have news."

"Señores, Señorina, buenos dias," said Gallegos.

"What are you doing here, señor?" asked Roque. "Isn't Piño making war on the Tejanos?"

"Not anymore," Juan replied. "He surrendered honorably in Socorro. We were very much outnumbered, and they gave us honorable terms. We lay down our guns and ammunition, and they let us go home."

Dan turned to Roque and said, "Colonel Canby isn't going to be happy about this."

"It is well, señor," said Juan. "The Tejanos did not stay in Socorro. They left their wounded and a few men to care for them and went north. They took the powder and shot but could not carry the guns. They are still in the pueblo."

"Juan," Dan said, "will you carry this word to Coronel Cristobal Carson? He will reward you as a hero if you tell him the guns are safe."

Juan Gallegos said he would and continued south while the five companions went north.

Sebriana looked up at Dan. "I think we should ride right into Socorro. I don't think the hospital attendants will bother us."

Verde was fuming, but before he spoke, he'd made sure he was beyond Roque's reach. "That damn Piño! Gives a bad name to Mexicans and militia!"

Dan saw Roque start to draw a pistol. "Roque, no! Choke him to death if you must, but don't waste a bullet and make so much noise this close to town.

Dan turned to Verde. "At the ford, Piño had green troops who had scarcely any training. Fording the river under fire with your own men retreating into your formation would have been tough even for regular troops."

Verde glared. "The whole battle got fought by regulars and those Pike's Peakers. Even Kit's regiment didn't really get a chance to engage the Texians."

Roque calmed visibly. "After the battle, Canby sent Colonel Piño away in disgrace. Piño and his men would have seen Canby's action that way. They wouldn't have understood Canby had given them a new mission to which they might be better suited. Piño was disgraced in front of his men, and his men were disgraced. Confronted with a larger enemy force at Socorro, they regained their honor. They accepted an honorable surrender."

Dan looked surprised. "I understand, but I think I'd have to look all the way back to King Arthur's Court to find knights who would have thought Piño's actions honorable. To a Yankee boy raised in a little whaling village, it looks a lot like treason and putting the knife in Canby's back. Our peoples are far apart in how they see such things."

"Damn right!" said Verde.

"T'keesh!" said Rojo. "Nakaiyeh or Mangani, Mexican or Yankee, you are all crazy."

Dan thought about the news he'd just heard. "I think it's safe for us to ride into Socorro without danger from the Texians." So they did, announcing that they were scouts for a larger Union force following not far behind.

"What will they do with us?" asked a sergeant, a hospital attendant.

"Parole you, I expect," Dan replied. "I'd take your parole right now, but I'm not senior enough to have the authority. But I'm sure the colonel will, seeing as how you are taking such fine care of yourselves. There's plenty of wounded at Fort Craig, and he don't need the extra burden."

The sergeant looked relieved. He wouldn't be a prisoner of war. He'd just have to find his own rations and rations for those in his care and then find a way to get them all back to Texas safe and out of the war. That would be a tall order, but to his way of thinking, getting the wounded in his charge back to Texas and not being made a prisoner was a good thing. He wouldn't be shot as a traitor to the United States or shipped to a prison camp.

There were rumors about prison camps already, though this early in the war, most prisoners were still being paroled, released to go home on their promise not to take up arms again during the conflict. It was a shooting offense to break parole. There were also stories from the War of 1812 and the Revolution about prison hulks, old rotting ships, where prisoners were confined to rot, starve, and die in filth and darkness locked away from the light of the sun. Parole was a better way to handle captured soldiers, but armies that relied on forced conscription, like the French, thought of parole as a kind of desertion.

Sebriana made them stay the night in Socorro. She had wounded to attend.

They traveled in daylight, kept their wits and were constantly on guard as they rode up the Camino Real, watching for dust that would indicate Texan patrols. The Texans, though, were already far to the north. The day they left Socorro, March 2, 1862, the Texans occupied Albuquerque. They heard about the Duke City's fall from friends in Los Lunas before they started west on the Rio Puerco and knew the Texans would arrive in Santa Fe before them. The five were high in the Jemez Mountains descending toward San Ildefanso on March 10, when the capitol was taken.

The Jemez Mountains were beautiful but cold. Crystalline streams ran through dark pine forests with groves of aspen just starting to bud. Elk and deer grazed in vast meadows within the ancient volcanic caldera while snow lingered in the shadows. Dan found the trail surprisingly easy to travel. They forded the Rio Grande with less ease. The river was up and icy with melting snow. It was mid-March when they reached friends at Chimayo twenty miles north of Santa Fe.

Chimayo had been Sebriana's home when Dan first

met her in 1849 during his first months in New Mexico. Dan remembered now how they had danced the cuna during the fandango for the wedding of Pedro Martinez's hermana. Long before he could understand Sebriana's language, she talked to him with her eyes as she led Dan away into the dark night. Kit Carson and a brawl ended that adventure. When Dan learned she was Roque's prima and had already buried several husbands, he thought he had been saved from the dangerous Doña Loca. Now Dan wasn't so sure. She had become a reliable companion and friend, and he sensed her deep wisdom. A wise Latina never tells a man directly that she is wise, Dan laughed to himself.

The Plaza del Cerro in Chimayo was an enclosed plaza, a fort, with a bell to warn of Indians and a torreon, a tower, for defense.

Spying an old friend, Roque called out. "Pedro Martinez, is that you? Amazing! They still have not hanged you." Both men smiled broadly, obviously delighted the hangman hadn't gotten around to either of them.

"Bienvenidos, mi amigos!" said Pedro. "You are safe here." In a few words he had told them what they most needed to know: the hunt for Sebriana was over. The Texians were not searching for them, so the friends could use Chimayo as a base.

"Pete, are you a Penitente?" Dan asked rudely but with a grin.

Pedro grinned back. "If I were, could I tell you?"

This too was reassurance. He might be, Dan thought, but if he were, they were not currently hunting for Dan and his companions. Dan did not know how certain the Penitentes were of his or his friends' identities away from the context of their search. If they were hunted, Pedro would have known. He was the kind of man who made it his business to know what was up. His life often depended on a scrap of intelligence.

Chimayo grew the finest chilis in New Mexico, if not the world. Pedro found them rooms, and his wife prepared dinner. The enchilada of Chimayo was unsurpassed. Corn tortillas cooked in oil were dipped in chili sauce and covered with onion or cheese. Another and another are laid on top with more cheese and onion. Lettuce is added and the whole topped with a fried egg. Señora Martinez served their dinner with refritos, peas with piñon nuts, and roasted corn salsa. She made a hot chocolate with cinnamon and spiked it with Taos Lightning, serving the steaming mugs, jicarillas, as they talked of how best to enter Santa Fe.

"The Tejanos," Pedro informed them, "keep guards posted at night on all of the roads into Santa Fe. They run patrols around town to keep their own men under control and out of trouble in the cantinas and gambling salas. There are lots of them all around town all night long."

Roque frowned. "Even if we enter in the daytime, they will want to know our business, and we might be recognized."

Pedro nodded. "Even in the daytime every road is watched and every traveler questioned."

Sebriana smiled. "They would trust a woman bringing food or produce to the market. I could make contact with Señor Speigleberg so he can open his doors to us at night."

"How do the rest of us get in?" asked Verde, acknowledging her ability to go unnoticed.

"Separately," Dan said, "towards dusk when we will be harder to recognize."

"I can go in any time," said Rojo grinning. "As long

as we are not together, they will not suspect an Indio. I'll sit with the peddler's at the Governor's Palace and listen to the gossip."

"And I will go in the daytime," said Roque. "I will dress down so I look like a simple shepherd." This concept was difficult for Dan to imagine. The proud Roque would be hard pressed to resemble a humble shepherd.

"Then," said Verde, "only Danny and I will have to enter with the dusk."

"Perhaps we should not take you," said Roque. "You would look suspicious even dressed as a priest, maybe especially as a priest. Could you disguise yourself as a burro now? That might look natural."

Pedro told them of the events leading up to the occupation of Santa Fe. "The Governor lifted up his skirts and with his officials and the legislature fled out to Fort Union where there is an army to protect him. The quartermaster was brave. He took all the supplies that had poured in from Albuquerque and hid them north of town."

"Do you know where they are?" Dan asked, scarcely believing the quartermaster's secret was out.

"I think so," said Pedro.

"How many others know?" Dan asked.

Pedro thought a minute. "The quartermaster and his soldiers, who are now gone to Fort Union, Mrs. Canby, the colonel's lady, and me. I make it my business to know these things." A grin showed white on his dark face shaded by a huge, drooping black mustache.

For Dan, the reality of Roque's masquerade was as difficult to imagine as it is to describe. Somewhere there must be shepherds who dressed in ruffled silk shirt and fine pantaloons topped by brocade vests. Somewhere there must be, Dan thought, but he'd never seen one in

New Mexico. Frayed cotton trousers and shirts topped by wool-on sheepskin vests were what Dan had observed worn with moccasins on feet, not the tall, tooled boots that Roque wore. Undoubtedly, his attire would confuse the Texans.

Keeping with their roles, the others walked into town. Verde and Dan rode.

Dan held the reins of his Appaloosa mule tight in his hand as he stood beside the Texan sergeant answering his questions. "I've come down from my rancho at Arroyo Hondo, that's near Taos, to see if you Texians will pay a good price for mules."

The sergeant's eyes opened wide. They had lost stock to Indians and the trail, exhaustion, and lack of water and feed. What they had left was ready to turn keel upward. "I'll take you directly to the quartermaster, sir."

Dan pursed his lips, cocked his head, and squinted an eye. "You've got money then?"

"I don't know, sir," was the reply, "but I must take you to him."

"In the morning," Dan replied. A mule trader doesn't want to seem too anxious. "It's late. I've been in the saddle for two days, and I want food, whiskey and a bed. Tomorrow will be soon enough."

He accepted Dan's claims, and Dan entered town, taking the Appaloosa mule to a good corral where he paid a boy to find him alfalfa and corn and to curry him. Walking across the plaza, Dan saw that his friends were already in place. Sebriana was doing a lively business selling tamales from a basket. Rojo dozed in the shade, indolent, but Dan knew he was alert and listening. Roque stumbled from cantina to sala looking the rustic shepherd dressed in his outlandish best come to town with his pockets full of coin. Dan made his way to the zaguan of

Solomon Speigelberg's store. Solomon was a German Jew who in 1862 ran the store with his brothers, Willi and Levi. There were more brothers later, perhaps as many as seven, all good upstanding men. Levi had a beautiful wife, Betty. They said she was only the fifth white woman to come to Santa Fe and by far the prettiest. The store was a covered passage big enough to admit a wagon, leading to an interior courtyard and closed on the street end by a wagon gate with a man-sized portal, the kind where you have to step up and duck at the same time while shifting your shoulders to squeeze through.

"I'm closing soon," said Solomon pushing the big gates shut. "Doña Loca has already been here. Step into the back where you won't be seen." He indicated his storeroom-office off to one side. The covered way was crowded with stacked goods packed in wooden boxes, straw, and sawdust. Solomon had pots and pans, china, spices, canned goods, cloth of all kinds and tools to sell. Willi and Levi stepped from the shadows. Both were armed, which was rare for them.

Solomon saw Dan's puzzlement. "Levi's wife is very beautiful," he said. "Last week some Rebel soldiers saw her on the street and remarked on her beauty. They said they would kidnap her and do what they would with her. We have kept her hidden ever since, and we sleep with guns in the zaguan."

Night descended, and one by one at lengthy intervals Dan's friends were let into the darkened store through the portal in the gates. "Quietly now," said Solomon each time as he led them to the back room.

Solomon opened the safe and took out the trumpets heavily wrapped to disguise their shape. One package was a yard long. The other was the leather pouch that contained Topper's journal. Dan wanted to open the package and look at the trumpets, making sure they were safe, but Solomon was there and didn't know what was in the package

"I sure wish I knew what I been guarding already," said Solomon. "I am a Masonic brother after all, sworn to keep your secrets."

Dan looked at Solomon sympathetically. "Solomon, I'd really like to tell you. I know you'd keep the secret but you're better off not knowing and I think you wouldn't believe me anyway."

"Try me!" he said.

Dan looked around at the others. They nodded their assent. A dozen thoughts went through Dan's head. The only true secret is known to only one person. On the other hand, the Masons had done a pretty good job of keeping their secrets for a long time. Still, Dan wondered if there any purpose to showing Solomon. Was it fair to expect his help, perhaps at the risk of his life without showing him?

Dan started unwrapping the package. "Solomon, these are very old. They were stolen by a foreign army while the Apostles were still alive and disappeared thirteen hundred years ago."

Solomon looked at Dan without comprehension. On his desk in front of Dan the trumpets lay revealed. They were as long as an extended arm with a bell at one end as big around as a man's face made of beaten and worked silver.

"What are they?" asked Solomon.

Dan looked into his eyes. "The Bible says in Numbers 10:

And the LORD spoke to Moses, saying: "Make two silver trumpets for yourself; you shall make them of hammered work; you shall use them for calling the congregation and for directing the movement of the camps. When you go to war in your land against the enemy who oppresses you, then you shall sound an alarm with the trumpets, and you will be remembered before the LORD your God, and you will be saved from your enemies."

Solomon was profoundly amazed and confused. "The trumpets from Solomon's Temple? Like in Torah? Impossible. They were lost so long ago. In New Mexico? Are you crazy already? You're having me on, aren't you?"

Dan carefully wrapped them up again. "You haven't been through what we've been through to get these. You haven't seen what we've seen. I told you that you wouldn't believe me."

Solomon's eyes were big and round. He mumbled. "The Trumpets of Truth? Touched by the hands of Moses and Aaron and Solomon..." His hand went out toward them.

"Probably not Solomon," Dan said. "He was a king, not a priest."

Their reverie was cut short when the small door in the zaguan shattered and men dressed in black, their heads covered in sacks with eye and mouth holes, poured in.

"To the courtyard," yelled Verde. "There isn't room for a fight in here."

Dan grabbed an axe handle and the others armed themselves similarly. He burst into the covered way shouldering the first man back into the others as they emerged from the cramped portal. Dan received a knife cut to the forearm for his kindness in not shooting the man. Crates and boxes tumbled as things shattered and crockery tinkled its death knell. Dan backhanded the man with the axe handle, putting him out of the fight and causing further confusion in the ranks. Behind him Roque and the others emerged into the courtyard.

They formed a phalanx, waiting the enemy with poles and handles, Verde with a crowbar. That would draw blood and shatter heads. Instinctively, Dan's friends knew they didn't want the noise of guns that would draw the Confederate night watch. Their enemies, armed with knives, seemed to have the same idea in mind.

"My china!" howled Solomon.

"That's the spirit," howled Verde. "Throw it at them!"

"It's breaking," said Solomon tearfully. "Everything is breaking."

Verde glanced at him. "Don't worry, peddler. We'll help you pick their pockets after we're finished killing them."

Then the fight was on in earnest. The attackers spread out, knives extended foremost, trying to turn the flanks of the defenders. Dan and his friends stepped in, denying their motion, using their weapons to break arms and heads and, striking from below, causing great pain. Verde's crowbar came down on a man's head to below his eyeholes spattering Dan with blood. Using both hands, Rojo struck a man with an axe handle embedding the man's head-cover an inch or more into whatever was beneath. The man fell like a dropped sack of flour. Striking hard, Dan brought his handle out straight into a sack between eye and mouth openings. His opponent fell backward into the man behind him and continued his slide to the ground. Dan did not see him rise again. Roque struck high and low, efficiently paced and professional like a lumberjack taking down a forest, needing only to strike once at each tree.

The fight was amazingly quiet. Thumps, grunts, and groans were accompanied by a few low screams deadened by the surrounding adobe. The attackers seemed as intent as the defenders on not attracting the attention of the night watch, though how they hoped to manage this trick with so many men crowding the street outside, Dan couldn't imagine. They used knives and didn't call out. Guns would have brought more likelihood of success, but the sound would have attracted the Texans. As the fight progressed, the enemy reached for staves and handles.

"Who are they?" demanded Solomon staring down at a bloodied hood.

"By process of elimination," Dan said, "knowing which of our enemies they can't be, I'd say they were Danite Mormons."

"But why?" Solomon stammered.

"You saw a moment ago," Dan replied.

"Then it's real!"

The fight went for Dan and his friends. They achieved tactical surprise early on. That is to say, the enemy found itself in a compromised position from which it could not respond effectively. They had to approach one at a time through the small door in the gate. Dan wondered when they'd think of opening the gate. Soon, he thought. Even worse they might try finding another route to the inner courtyard, over the roof two stories above or through another house. Attackers coming from two directions would be a challenge. Then a pistol crashed, and Verde fell.

Sebriana, fast to respond, was next to fire, felling the man coming through the gate with a single shot through the center of his forehead. Rojo downed the man who tried to climb over the dead one. Their bodies blocked the opening. A pistol was extended through the hole, and Roque and Dan, dropping their axe handles, both fired drawing a welcome scream in return for their efforts. The four of them peppered the zaguan, the gate, with fire expecting splinters to have as much effect as bullets on the far side. Solomon, Levi, and Willi were firing as well. There were enough yelps and groans to suggest some success.

"Quick," yelled Solomon, pointing to a stairway up to his balcony.

Dan grabbed the package containing the precious trumpets. The friends followed Levi and Solomon, Roque lifting Verde over his powerful shoulder. As they passed by Levi's wife, Betty, stepped onto the balcony.

Levi kissed her. "I've been in Taos for several days on business, and I'm not expected back for a few more. The hooded men downstairs must be robbers who broke in. Some of our neighbors and my brothers must have stopped them. You heard the noise and came to look. Do you understand? They will ask."

She smiled sweetly, and Dan's heart fluttered. She was a merchant's wife and no fool and beautiful as well. Perhaps the most beautiful woman in all Santa Fe, Dan thought, a town noted for its beauties. No wonder the Texans had been attracted to her.

Solomon looked at Dan and pointed to a low viga. "Now swing up to the roof."

Climbing up on the railing, one by one the friends clambered to the roof by grasping the protruding beam, Roque handing Verde and Sebriana up to Dan. Solomon was thinking fast and well. The night watch had been alerted. The companions could hear the sounds of running feet and calls of men in the dark. They were converging. Below, Danites were fading into the dark as quickly as they could, leaving their dead behind.

The parapet concealed the five from the street. Verde was alive and conscious, his leg only grazed by the bullet.

Roque bound a kerchief around the wound.

"See!" chortled Verde, "I knew you cared."

Roque pulled the bandage extra tight. "I don't want you to leave a blood trail that can be followed."

"Follow me," whispered Solomon.

He led them across rooftops to narrow Burro Alley. There he showed them a plank he'd left there intentionally. They extended it across the six-foot wide street below. Watching, lest they be observed, they made their way one at a time across the chasm. Verde was limping, unlikely to balance his way across. The beam didn't seem strong enough to carry both Verde and Roque. Without warning Roque grabbed Verde at belt and collar, tossed him to Dan, and then hurried across himself, pulling the plank in behind him. Dan wondered at Solomon's foresight in having this escape route ready. Making their way from flat roof to flat roof, they came ever closer to the edge of town. They dropped down into a courtyard belonging to one of their Masonic brothers.

"Solomon," Dan asked, "why did you have all this prepared?"

He smiled. "One day shortly after I was 'raised' in the Lodge, Professor Pendarvis came to my store." He paused. "You remember the Professor, don't you? He was murdered some time ago." Dan nodded. "He gave me a long explanation of why I needed an escape route. I don't remember the details now, but it seemed very wise then and didn't cost much to prepare."

"Didn't cost much," frugality would appeal to a merchant, Dan thought.

Solomon continued speaking. "The noise will have drawn all the watchers to my store. We should be able to slip out of town unnoticed. There is an arroyo here that will provide cover. Quick! Duck down into the wash."

They slipped out, one of them every few minutes. They could hear the hubbub a few blocks away of a military camp roused like a hive of bees. It was a long walk in the night until they found the place where they'd left Roque's horse and some of their mules.

"I will leave you now," said Solomon. "If the guard sees me, I can make some excuse."

"Take care," responded Dan. "And thank you." Solomon's face darkened. He'd risked his life and lost merchandise, not to mention, a door. More than any of these losses hanging heavy between them, Dan was sure the merchant still thought he'd been the butt of some strange joke.

Dan hated to lose the Appaloosa. He realized the Texans would find him and take him for sure.

He mumbled. "I should have ridden an old mule into town."

The Texans were in need of livestock. Already one of their Mounted Regiments was on foot. There was no way to go back and get the Appaloosa. Dan rode double with Sebriana, and Verde rode with Roque who kept accidentally poking Verde's wound. Solomon took Verde's mount.

In the dawn, Dan felt Chimayo was a welcome sight.

Flour tortillas, eggs poached in chili, refritos, panfried potatoes with chili and onion, and good coffee thick with sugar was their breakfast. Afterward sleep was welcome. Pedro found boys to care for their stock. Dan awoke in the afternoon to find Sebriana binding wounds he didn't know he had. He soon learned there were bruises, too. Afterward, it was his turn to search her body for wounds.

Pedro's wife served posole, hominy stewed with pork, and ground red chili, for dinner in wooden bowls. Tortillas were their spoons. Afterwards they discussed their options.

Rojo frowned. "I must talk over what I have learned with my father, Chief Vicenti. He may have left his winter camp already, and it may take time to find him. I will return in ten days or fifteen or a month. I will return when I have done what I must."

"Verde can't ride," Sebriana insisted. His wound was looking worse, probably all that poking Roque had done.

"Aye, lads," said Verde. "I'm gravely wounded and require the attentions of a beautiful young lady." He leered at Sebriana. Dan thought him an old wretch.

Roque looked thoughtful. "It is spring. In the mountains, the shepherds are sheering the lambs and collecting the mountain oysters, cajones, from the young rams. What a meal the oysters are! How delicious. Sebriana, mi prima, would you feel safer if we collect the oysters from this old cabrón before we left?"

"No," she smiled. "I'll be safe enough around el viejo, the ancient one. I have a sharp knife and can collect my own oysters, if needed."

"Roque," Dan said, "I think you and I should take the package and head for Fort Union. It's what Kit would want us to do. If the Texians take Fort Union, they'll have New Mexico and Colorado, too."

Roque nodded. "Can't go through Santa Fe. It'll be a long, cold ride through the mountains, through Truchas and Trampas to Picuris, over the Sangre de Cristo, and then down the valley of the Mora to the llano. It's Penitente country. Some say they are like the Freemasons for Catholics who lack priests. They are the Pope's enforcers as much as the Masons are his prey."

"We could take the River Road to Taos and cross the mountains from there," Dan suggested.

"Almost as bad and a lot longer," Roque said. "We'll

have to try avoiding the towns. Sebriana can pack lots of food for us so we have no reason to approach anyone."

It was a long, cold ride through icy pine forests and freezing streams full of the spring melt. They seldom dared a fire for fear of being noticed and remained wet from the streams and cold until nature dried them. They arrived at Fort Union on March 26, 1862. The post was in an uproar with news of the Pike's Peakers who had gone to Glorieta Pass.

Dan and Roque found Colonel Paul, the commander, at his office fuming about volunteers. "Colonel Slough and his Pike's Peakers made an amazing march over the Raton Pass all the way from Denver in thirteen days. Amazing! They heard Captain Dodd's company had been wiped out at Valverde and came running. Astounding!"

"Dodd was in the thick of it," Dan said. "He took more losses than any other volunteer unit, but he didn't come close to being wiped out."

"Colonel Canby ordered us," Paul continued, "to stay here and defend the depot against the Texans. Colonel Slough marched in here with Coloradans, claimed he out-ranked me—insane!—and took off with almost all of our combined regiments on a reconnaissance in force. Says he can do that under Canby's orders. Incredible! He's up in Apache Canyon near Glorieta Pass spoiling for a fight."

Word came at midday on the 27th of March, that Colonel Slough, commander of the Pike's Peakers, had made contact with a large Rebel force headed for Fort Union.

"Colonel," Dan said, "thanks for your hospitality. I think we better head up there."

"Hurry back and let me know if things go sour," said the colonel.

They rode at noon and arrived in Apache Cañon near

the ruins of Pecos Pueblo at dusk. There was firing in the cañon, canon and rifle. The sound of battle drew closer as they searched for Colonel Slough. They found his headquarters at Pigeon's Rancho not far away.

"Colonel," Dan said, "we've come from Colonel Paul. He wants to know how the battle is going."

"How do you think?" he replied. "I'm being driven back. Only this wild terrain keeps the Texans from turning my flank. I'm sending that Methodist preacher, Chivington, out in the morning to the mesa south of the pass with a third of my force. He'll hit them in the flank at midday."

The following day Slough was driven back even further. Midday came and went.

Colonel Slough was enraged. "What's become of that idiot Methodist street preacher? He was supposed to hit them in flank as soon he heard the sound of battle. Where is he? I'll tell you. He's disappeared with a third of my force, over four hundred men! Go! Find Chivington, if you want to know how the battle is going!"

Dan and Roque were given directions to where Major Chivington had begun his ride to glory...or perdition. It was hard to tell which at this point. They found the spot.

"Roque," Dan asked, "do you think you can follow their tracks?"

"Do I get a blindfold?" Roque replied grinning. Four hundred men leave quite a trail, and the trail left by four hundred horses is only slightly less clear than a paved road even through rough country. They made much better time than those ahead of them. The distance was about eight miles. Dan and Roque caught up with Major Chivington at about half-past two in the afternoon. A soldier pointed out the chubby, bearded major who sat on a rock staring down the steep hillside into the valley below where a hundred wagons were parked. There was livestock, too, and one little canon pointed down the valley toward the sounds of battle. Men milled about below.

Dan looked at the valley and then turned to Roque. "Those look like teamsters. This must be the Texians wagon park. Only a few look like organized combat soldiers."

It was the Texans' wagon park, their supply train.

Major Chivington was a contradiction in every sense, standing well over six foot tall, maybe six foot three, and weighing at least 250 pounds. He should have looked big and powerful. Maybe he did standing in the pulpit. Sitting on a New Mexico rock, he looked chubby. Rising, he greeted Dan with a Masonic sign no one but a brother Mason would know. Dan learned later that Chivington was Grand Master of Colorado. Brother or no, Dan took a dislike to him. He was pompous and overbearing while indecisive.

A red-faced Captain W.H. Lewis turned on his heel and stalked away from the major. Dan had met Bill Lewis, and his current state of rage was as angry as Dan had ever seen the officer get.

"Bill," Dan said, "what's wrong?"

Captain Lewis snarled. "The damned-fool doesn't want to follow his orders!" Lewis was a regular officer leading the contingent of regulars from Fort Union. "When we heard firing this morning, he couldn't hear it."

A lieutenant hurried to the officer's side. "Captain Lewis, be careful what you say. He has command."

"Lieutenant Sanford," Lewis said, "this is Danny Trelawney and the handsome fellow is Roque. They're friends of Colonel Carson and useful guys to have around.

"About the major, he has dithered for two hours

looking down from that rock where he sits. First, he didn't want to attack because he couldn't see Colonel Slough's force. He thought the attack might not have started yet, and he'd get in the way or have to face the entire enemy force alone. Then, he thought Colonel Slough might have been forced to withdraw."

Another officer joined them. "Captain Wynkoop," Lewis said, "how can I help you?"

"If we attack," Wynkoop answered, "I'm sure my Colorado sharpshooters can handle the artillery by taking out the gunners."

Captain John Bonham, a regular, joined them. Dan and Roque had met him before at Cantonment Burgwin. Dan thought him a competent officer. He acknowledged Dan but said nothing. Too angry to speak Dan thought.

Rarely did Dan to have to look up at anyone, but he did now. Wynkoop was even taller than Chivington, but strongly built, broad of shoulder, and narrow of hip. He wore fringed buckskins and carried a Bowie knife almost as large as Dan's. It looked small in his big hands.

"I don't think there's much danger of that," Lewis replied disgusted. "Now the major is worried that we'll get attacked by Confederate reinforcements coming over Glorieta Pass."

"Bill," Dan said, "excuse us a moment." He motioned to Roque, and they stepped aside. "I think I know why we've ended up on this hilltop."

Roque understood instantly. "Let's blow the trumpets and see what happens. Do you know how to play one?"

"No," Dan replied. "Do you?" Roque shook his head as he unwrapped the package. "I guess you just blow."

"Which end?" Roque asked looking at the trumpet in his hands.

"The little one, I think," Dan replied.

They blew. Dan found himself unable to stop. The music came out in a pattern Dan had heard before, Charge. They blew and blew. Lewis, Wynkoop, and Sanford rallied and swiftly organized their men. Mounted troops all, they left their horses behind. The hill was far too steep for horses. They would roll on ground like that, killing themselves and their riders. Like a flood over a waterfall, they poured over the lip of the cañon, descending on ropes and leather straps, helping each other down, and sliding.

Wynkoop stopped his men above the valley floor and poured fire into the team of gunners struggling to turn their gun to face this new threat. One volley ended their resistance. As Major Chivington continued to watch from his rock, far below him, his men rounded up the Confederate force as a few escaped up and down the cañon.

Dan rebundled the package of trumpets. "Roque, the music sounded like Charge to me. Were you playing bugle calls? I don't know how to play."

Roque shook his head. "Neither do I."

Far below, Dan saw one Texan trying to escape on a fine Appaloosa mule. He hid in the river bed where Captain Lewis and his men were unaware of him.

"Roque, look!" Dan yelled. "That's my mule." Without thinking, he handed the package to Roque and took off running, jumping and sliding down the hillside. Unaware of Dan above him, the Texan started his escape riding upstream. Dan angled his assault to intercept the soldier. Nearing the bottom, Dan leapt across the stream, colliding with the Texan and knocking him out of the saddle, unconscious on the ground. The wind knocked out of him, Dan lay on the ground beside the soldier looking upward. Ground-broken, the mule, his reins touching the ground, stood fast.

Above him, Dan saw a wonderful and horrible sight. Roque was descending mounted on his fine grullo. The horse leapt and reared, slid, changed direction, found footing, and kept on coming. There on top was Roque high in the saddle, his hat firmly on his head, shifting his weight with his charger's movements, the package high in one hand held aloft. On he came like an avenging archangel. The sun seemed to shine on Roque alone, lighting him as if on fire.

Now at Dan's side, Roque said, "Leave the Texian and get your mule."

They joined Lewis. Bill ordered the wagons pushed together so he could burn them more easily. "I would love to take this stuff back," he said, "but the hillside is too steep. We'd never get it to the top. We'll have to shoot the livestock, too." Killing horses and mules didn't sit well with anyone, but there was no way to take the animals up the hill.

Roque looked at Dan. "You've got your mule. Now what are you going to do with him? Can't go to Santa Fe. Confederates are over that way and reinforcements coming. Can't go back the way we came. Mountains are that way, and that way," he pointed down cañon, "is the main Texian army. What are you going to do?"

Captain Bill Lewis looked up at them and said, "Chivington has ordered us to burn the trains. Then we're climbing back up to our horses on the mesa. Can your beasts make it up the hill?"

Roque shook his head. "My grullo is the best horse in the world, but I don't think he can climb that hill."

"I've got an idea," Dan said. "Bill, good show. Take care. Roque, follow me."

He kicked the mule and took off down the cañon

towards the sound of battle.

"Are you loco?" called Roque.

"Hey, you're headed toward the enemy!" yelled Captain Lewis.

Dan said nothing. Soon they came to a group of Texan soldiers. "Message for the colonel!" Dan yelled. They pointed down cañon as Dan and Roque passed. To the next group, he yelled, "Dispatch riders coming through! Dispatch for the colonel." The cry of dispatch sounded more official and military. They rode hard not sparing themselves or their animals. Between Dan's legs, great lungs heaved and muscles rippled. The smell of hot, sweaty mule rose with the dust of their passage and mixed with the sulfurous stink of cannon and musket fire. Ahead, men stood in formation facing each other no more than two hundred yards apart. A cannon thundered. Bayonets clicked into place as they were fixed. Infantry prepared for another charge or lay waiting to receive one. These westerners used the terrain for cover and concealment, forming uneven lines, men who aimed before they fired. Dan and Roque had come to the battle. Now, if one side didn't shoot them in the back, the other was sure to shoot the front. The distance was only a few yards, and there was cover only part of the way.

No time to think, Dan yelled. "Where's the colonel? Dispatch for the colonel. Dispatch rider coming through!" His voice was growing hoarse with effort. They rode into the stream bed as they passed a Texan unit. Pointing frantically to the other wing of the army, the soldiers attempted to steer the pair toward their colonel.

Halfway between the Texans and the Union force, both sides looking on with mouths agape in wonder, Dan called back, "Wrong colonel. Dispatch riders coming through. Dispatch for Colonel Slough!" It's amazing that no one fired on them. They were taken in hand by an alert sergeant who had them disarmed and then led them under guard to Colonel Slough.

"Danito," said Roque, "I saw that big Tejano, Rheingold. He told his men not to fire. Pennington didn't want to listen, so Rheingold slugged him and took his gun away. That fancy man, Tiler Caine, drew on his commander. I saw them!"

Escorted to Colonel Slough, Dan reported. "Sir, we found Major Chivington. He has attacked and burned the enemy's trains. That's the smoke you see." About this time, the Confederates broke off their attack. The battle was over. It took Chivington until midnight to find his way back.

The battle at Glorieta Pass was the end of the Texan conquest of New Mexico. Given no choice but to retreat, the Texans had difficulty even doing that. Often burying their weapons, they tried to avoid Union forces, going to great lengths to do so. Worn out, starving, and out of supply they staggered and withdrew. With little to eat and no blankets or tents, they stumbled back to Texas by any road that wasn't blocked. They had ridden into New Mexico, the lords of imperial Texas, but now most of them were walking: the Army of Texas limped back home. The Battle for Glorieta Pass wasn't much of a battle. The forces engaged were small, and the bloodletting wasn't great. Texas almost won. Slough was on the ropes at Pigeon's Rancho when Dan and Roque saw him. A loose cannon of a major missing with a third of Colonel Slough's force almost cost the Union the battle.

"They had a plan," Dan told Roque, "a vision of a Confederacy stretching from sea to sea and rich with Colorado and California gold."

"Sí, but I don't think they have a plan now. Their General Lee wants to defend a South blockaded from the sea. How they going to win a war like that, no? Colonel Sibley had a vision that might have won the war."

Dan nodded. "And it died here at Glorieta, a close run thing."

Roque shivered. "Major Chivington hesitated and almost lost the battle. Something wonderful happened to change that."

Weeks later, Dan was reading the newspaper. Chivington was taking credit for destroying the Texans' trains and winning, not just the battle, but the campaign. Dan looked at Roque. "Damn! That chubby weasel of a major, that fat street preacher, is giving himself credit for winning the battle. Captain Lewis and Ned Wynkoop deserve the glory. He talks like they weren't there."

Had the attack on the trains not happened when it did, Slough might have lost. Nothing would have stood between the Texans and the supply depot at Fort Union. Renewed with supplies, there was no force to stand between the Confederates and Colorado. With Colorado's mineral wealth in hand, the Confederacy might have won the war. Had Major Chivington conducted a defense on the good ground he held in the area of the Confederate trains, the entire Texas regiment might have been captured. Colonel Scurry, the Confederate commander, and his men were caught between two strong Union forces without ammunition or supplies. They'd have had no choice but to quit. Chivington, for inexplicable reasons of his own, retreated the way he had come back up onto the mesa, and the Texans got away to make more mischief in New Mexico.

The Texans began their long retreat at Glorieta. First, they pulled back to Santa Fe where starving, wounded, and ragged, the proud conquering army found itself without clothing, food, or medical supplies and surviving on the charity of New Mexicans. Mrs. Canby showed Colonel Scurry the location where Union stores had been hidden. Union blankets, clothing, and medicine saved Confederate soldiers who left New Mexico in Union uniforms. The survivors, in later years, were effusive in their praise of their "angel," Mrs. Canby.

Chapter 17

On the Road Again

Searching for the treasure had stirred up interest in unwelcome places. Albert Pike was a brother Mason but on the wrong side in this war, or so Dan thought. Pike's side had some nasty attributes, slavery together with a tendency to conquest and empire. Handing him wealth and power to pursue an unjust war didn't seem right. Dan didn't like to think of the Mormons coming into possession of military power and incredible wealth. They'd terrorized their neighbors everywhere they had gone, and then cast themselves as the victims. Being convinced that you were a persecuted victim while being certain that you had the one, true religious truth was a bad combination. When the people at the top were corrupt and evil men, manipulating the weak-minded for their own gain, it was even worse. The sense of being persecuted led to events like the massacre of innocents at Mountain Meadows where robbery was the only plausible prime motive. The Penitentes had their own version of truth and were equally fanatic. From somewhere in the Rio Arriba, New Mexico north of Santa Fe, a shadowy figure known as the Padre directed the Holy Brotherhood, operating on ancient instructions from the Pope himself.

Dan sighed. "My friends," he said to the Roque,

Verde, and Sebriana, "moving the treasure is apt to be even more dangerous than anything we've done so far. Our moves are likely to be detected."

Sebriana spoke up. "We will contact Rojo, and he will hire Jicarilla as teamsters to drive our wagons while we protect them. They will keep our secrets and fight hard if asked."

"It's true," said Roque. "They'll be fearless as men can be, unlikely to find anyone to talk to other than Jicarillas and untempted by the kind of treasure we will be moving."

Dan spoke again. "We'll want to be a long way from Santa Fe before anyone notices we've gone. We have to pass by Abiquiu unnoticed and somehow get our wagons to the top of the cliffs at Redwall Canyon."

Weeks later and having notified Rojo, they gathered at Pedro's table in Chimayo. Rojo had a suggestion. "We could set the Governor's Palace on fire. If we got a big enough fire going, no one would notice us leaving town."

Dan blurted. "Good Lord, he's serious."

Verde looked at him. "Well, of course he is. This is a serious discussion, boyo." Verde smiled. "Burning government houses appeals to me."

Dan looked on wide-eyed. "You're serious, too."

"Perhaps we could leave from Chimayo," offered the wise Sebriana. "Is there anything we need in Santa Fe?"

"No," Dan replied, "but we probably have to pass through Santa Fe on our way east."

"We could cross the mountains from Taos to Cimarron," said Roque. "We could ask protection from our friends, Ceran St. Vrain and Lucien Maxwell."

"Doesn't seem fair to them," Dan said. "And we might call too much attention to ourselves. That could become a problem when we're alone on the Llano

Estacado. Once we get beyond the reach of their protection, we'll be fair game."

They sipped their hot chocolate spiked with Taos Lightning and sucked on their clay pipes while Sebriana smoked cigaritos. Time passed. The fire burned down, but still the horno warmed the room. Its heated adobe bricks would stay warm all night. Verde and Roque competed with each other blowing rings of smoke. Rojo frowned and blew smoke to the four directions asking forbearance from the gods against the barbaric behavior of his friends in the way they handled the sacred tobacco. Pedro's wife poured more hot chocolate and aguardiente. Sebriana cuddled against Dan's side.

Pedro asked, "What if you used pack mules?"

Roque liked the idea. "That would simplify everything." Dan sighed. "I wanted to use a wagon to carry the Ark and conceal its shape."

"Is there any other way to carry it?" asked Pedro.

Roque looked thoughtful. "It would be very heavy for a mule."

Dan thought a moment. "In the Bible, it says four men carried it on poles. It isn't very heavy. I think a wooden box, gold leaf, two stone tablets, and manna bread. The whole thing might come to as little as one hundred pounds.

"The problem," Dan went on, "is that the Bible tells of men dying just from touching the Ark. That's why they used the poles."

"I can show you," said Rojo, "trails that only my people use, hidden trails across the mountains. Perhaps we don't need wagons before we get to Cimarron."

Sebriana nudged Dan. "That might work."

Verde looked disappointed. "Does this mean we won't be burnin' down the Governor's Palace?"

"Sorry," said Sebriana smiling sweetly.

A year went by. It was difficult staying away from the treasure. It was late summer before all the Texans had managed to remove themselves from New Mexico. Dan and his friends laid low. There was too much chance that their purchases would be noticed in Santa Fe and word of their activities reaching the Texans, Rheingold, or Pike. So they waited through summer and into fall. By late fall with winter coming, they had to wait for spring snowmelt 1863. Returning to their find would have beaten a trail for others to follow.

"What we need to do," said Dan, "we must do quickly, all in one trip."

Honored by the Union for his success against Sibley, Colonel Canby, now a general, departed for the East. Sibley was in east Texas or Arkansas with Sterling Price and Albert Pike, now also a general accused of some terrible and vicious acts. General Carleton had arrived in the summer of 1862 with his California Column too late to fight the Confederates in more than token actions. He did what he knew best, fought Indians. He also continued martial law on the theory that the Confederates might return. There were still many local sympathizers.

Finally, weather and circumstances made it possible for the five to head north in the early spring of 1863.

Dan found Verde on a spring day in early 1863, sitting in the shade, cackling as he read the Santa Fe Republican. "What's so funny?" Dan asked.

"Listen to this," Verde chortled:

'Behold him! His martial cloak thrown gracefully around him like a Roman toga, his military cap worn precisely six inches from the extreme tip of his nose, his chin drawn gracefully in, his teeth set firm, his Jove-like front, his eyes like Mars, that threaten and command as with slow and measured tread, each step exactly twenty-eight inches, he rules the land.'

Don't that just sound like our old friend?"

Dan thought that it did indeed sound like their old friend Major, now General, Carleton.

Dan and Roque arranged for pack mules and for new wagons to meet the five friends in Cimarron with mules broken to harness. Lucien Maxwell would hold the equipment and stock for them until they arrived. It would take Lucien's authority and skill to keep them out of army hands.

Some of their most pressing needs were difficult to come by. They needed block and tackle gear and lots of heavy rope. This was stuff common enough in a seaport, but not readily available in Santa Fe. Lariats of rawhide might have done, but none were made long enough. Dan solved the problem by placing his order with Speigleberg in time for it to come out during the shipping season of 1862. By the time the chandler's gear, rope, block and tackle had arrived, early winter storms had closed the high country.

When the shipment came in, Dan and Roque went to Solomon Speigleberg's store. "All the time you're asking favors already. You should order something so special like this, and it has to be a secret. And what do you give me? Mess and breakage and my life threatened."

Dan hesitated. "Solomon, we sure appreciate your help. The breakage was really caused by those Mormons who were after us."

Speigleberg smiled. "Do you want I should come with you or something already? You might need me to say a prayer or two in Hebrew to keep you safe."

Dan thought about the need for Hebrew prayers and a high priest. "I think your absence from Santa Fe would draw attention."

Solomon shook his head. "Your purchases draw attention already! This is Santa Fe. What else they got to gossip about? I tell people you're reopening an old mine, and I scoff already at our chances of finding anything. Don't want we should start a gold rush."

Roque laughed as the merchant continued. "All this secrecy and skulking about might lead people to think you've got something to hide, like the location of a gold mine or treasure. Already that fellow with the bushy red beard, Tom Jeffords, has headed for the San Juan country."

Solomon nodded. "Peoples has seen Solomon gathering what you needed."

Finally, they slipped out of Santa Fe.

"I don't think," said Dan, "that anyone saw our special equipment leave Santa Fe."

Rojo disappeared for a while checking their back trail. "I don't see anyone following."

In Chimayo, gathering mules and packing equipment made their presence too public.

Dan looked at his friends. "We need a cover story."

Nothing seemed to fit. "What can a man do in this country?" asked Roque. "Only so many things. Clearly we are not preparing to go hunting or trapping. We are not working for the army or ranching. These are not trade goods for the Indios."

Sebriana summed up their conclusion. "It might attract prospectors, like Jeffords, but it's the best we can come up with."

Roque nodded. "A while back there were prospectors

who said they found 'color' up by Angelfire, you know, that big valley between the two ridges of the Sangre de Cristo southeast of Taos on the way to Cimarron."

Dan agreed. "We could head that way. Angelfire is a great starting point for legends." Dan remembered watching the setting sun glow off spindrift snow along the ridges, making them look as if on fire.

The Jicarilla, Utahs, and Mexicans all had stories. It would be easy to turn the glowing, burning mountain into a mountain of gold. The difficult part would be in not making the strike sound too good. The story they passed was of searching for an old, played out mine that might still provide some ore.

The night before they left, Pedro, who hadn't been formally introduced to the quest, told them a story as they sat with their pipes and hot chocolate.

"A long time ago when Rio Arriba was still part of Spain, Frenchmen went to the San Juan Mountains in search of gold. The French were always snooping around our borders. We fought them, you know. We crossed the *llano* and defeated them near the villages of the Indians who live in great, round earthen houses by a big river, so it is no surprise that the French came snooping. These French were an army unit hunting gold, almost three hundred men. They found an exposed ledge thick with *oro* up above the *Rio Lobos*, the Wolf Creek. Soon they had a treasure box full of gold worth more than five hundred thousand Mexican silver dollars. A high waterfall comes down from the mountain near there, and, when they heard our soldiers were searching for them they hid their wealth nearby. That is why it is called Treasure Falls. The French fought among themselves, died of the cold and Indian attacks. When Spanish soldiers came, only a few were left. There was a battle, and all but five were killed. These escaped back to the French settlements far across the *llano* in Louisiana. Searching for treasure, the French continued coming to New Mexico often disguised as trappers and mountain men. They've never found the hidden horde of gold."

He paused and Dan asked, "Do you think that's what we are looking for?"

"Maybe," said Pedro. "I will not pry. There are Indian stories of a much older treasure. This treasure is *Power*. The Penitente believe in such a treasure, too. They say Coronado left it for them. I think you may be looking for Coronado's treasure. I have never seen Treasure Falls, but I think it must be near that place."

"Pedro," said Roque, "you know too much already. For your safety, I will not tell you more, but I think my friends will agree that if we find anything, you should have something from it." He looked around at Sebriana, Dan, Verde, and Rojo. They nodded agreement. Pedro had been a true friend.

Pedro glanced around the room. "I do not ask for anything, my friends. I help my friends and share with them willingly."

"We know that," Dan said, "but you should have something. You have helped us, and you have taken great risk for us. If not for yourself, for your *niños*."

Before they set out, Roque insisted that they visit the Santuario de Chimayo where cripples came to be healed by *Cristo* and leave their crutches behind. Sebriana insisted that they go to ask His support for their endeavor.

"Sebriana, why would you want to pray at the Santuario de Chimayo?" Dan asked. "It's a Catholic shrine. You're Jewish."

"I am Jewish," she said, "but my family has prayed in Catholic churches for hundreds of years."

"We should go to the Santuario," said Roque. "It is only a short walk from here, and we are beginning a long and dangerous journey."

"Si," said Pedro. "You must go and seek the *bendición*, the blessing."

The Santuario was close to Pedro's home. They had to walk only a few steps and wade the cold river. The shrine was called the Lourdes of North America. People went there crippled and walked away whole. At Easter, people from Santa Fe and even Albuquerque made pilgrimages walking day and night to reach the shrine. The friends walked under mighty cottonwoods and sycamore grown up to shade the adobe ranchos, blending with the color of the earth, their protruding *vigas* festooned with chilis. It was a pleasant walk. Only Verde refused to come.

"Papish nonsense," he had growled. Roque, Sebriana, Rojo, and Dan followed Pedro and his *esposa*, his wife, down the dusty road and across cold, though only knee deep, Rio Santa Cruz. The Santuario was an adobe pilgrimage shrine with two bell towers connected by a *mirador*, a recessed balcony. Crowded with crosses leaning in all directions, the graveyard stood in front of the chapel surrounded by an adobe wall.

Pointing, Roque said, "See how close the crosses are."

Dan had seen graveyards like this one before, the crosses all jumbled up in no discernible order. He'd thought they marked something other than graves. "I see. They must be buried on top of each other."

Roque shook his head. "Mixed together. When they dig a new grave they break through old ones. The bones get all mixed up."

"Sí," said Pedro smiling. "The families are all mixed together. They never get lonesome."

Dan glanced at Rojo. His eyes were wide, but he said nothing. Apaches do not like to be near the dead. There is danger from the spirits.

They entered the chapel grounds and made the proper signs. Dan bowed as Sebriana had taught him, walked forward, and knelt near the altar. The *retablo* beyond it stretched to the *vigas* painted in bold primary colors showing scenes from the Bible and lives of the saints lighted by windows high above. There was more, symbols associated only with the Penitentes. There were no pews, as was the Mexican custom: people knelt to pray.

Pedro hurried off to find a priest to pronounce the *bendición* on the adventurers. The ladies, Sebriana and Pedro's wife, disappeared into a side chamber. Dan peered in as Sebriana and Pedro's wife knelt by a circular opening in the floor. The room around it was full of abandoned crutches. The hole in the floor was full of clean, white clay. Sebriana was digging into it and filling a small buckskin bag.

She caught Dan watching. "This is for later, in case we get hurt. It is the *Tierra Bendita*, the holy earth. You mix it with your food, and it will cure you. That's what Pedro's wife says. I have heard of its power before." She continued filling her bag.

Pedro came back shaking his head. The priest was away. When the ladies returned the entire party walked to the altar rail and knelt. Beside Dan, Sebriana prayed in a whisper just loud enough for him to hear, asking blessings on their project and for a clear sign that they were doing the right thing. Roque and Pedro mumbled their prayers aloud as well. Rojo knelt and looked toward the ceiling, an unaccustomed barricade between himself and the creator.

Their prayers at an end, they rose and walked back toward the handsomely carved door. A dark figure emerged from the shadows of the baptistery and blocked their path. An alabaster oval face and high forehead, framed in dark hair, briefly caught the light as it glinted off ebony eyes in deep, dark craters. The mouth frowned. Padre Antonio Martinez, Master of the Penitente Brotherhood, had found them. Dan spun about looking for men approaching from behind.

Roque saw Dan's move. "No, they will not desecrate the church by attacking us here. They will wait until we have stepped outside and are blinded coming from the dark chapel into the noonday sun. Then they will skewer us on their long lances."

Dan said, "Then we should stay here, but we have no way to escape."

Roque nodded. "Yes, we will ask sanctuary, and the church will grant it."

"My children," the dark figure said, "I wish to speak to you."

He was foolish to enter alone.

Dan spoke. "Perhaps I'll pin your arms and use you as our shield. Sebriana, follow my lead."

"Peace, my son," he said gently. "I have come to bless you and your project."

"What deceit is this?" Dan roared.

Roque, stunned to silence, finally found words. "It is he! This Padre is Master of the Holy Brotherhood."

Pedro and his *esposa* stared aghast. Rojo's blade was already in his hand.

"No deceit," the priest replied. "I have seen what you have done. The brotherhood tells me of your preparations. The brethren are everywhere, watching. I know what you plan, and it is good. We have seen the Texians and know they would destroy that which they say they would protect. The Constitution is a light to the world. The Union must be preserved. Take what you have found to Mr. Lincoln and save our country."

Dan was stunned. "Your brotherhood has searched for hundreds of years..."

"So has yours," he replied.

Dan thought, if he could smile, I think he would. His mouth looks pained.

Dan was aghast. "The Pope will be wanting his prize. He will surely punish you."

Padre Antonio Jose Martinez nodded. "It was never the Pope's property. Who will tell him it has been found? I won't. Will you?"

Dan was stunned. So was Sebriana who was never at a loss for words.

It was Roque who broke the silence. "I have heard that you have been punished by the church for keeping *paisano* art in the *nichos* and on the *retablos* and for leading the Penitentes. I have heard you baptized children whose parents had not paid the tithe and were excommunicated for this."

"It is so," the priest replied.

Roque was puzzled. "If you are not the pope's man, why do you send your Penitentes against us?"

"I am not and did not," the priest replied calmly. "I am God's man. They acted on very old orders. Now that I know what they have done, they will bother you no more.

"Kneel that I may bless you."

"Do it!" pronounced Sebriana. "He is sincere."

They knelt and received his blessing on themselves and their project. The whole time they knelt, Dan kept thinking of a story about a would-be governor of New Mexico Martinez had blessed. He'd blessed him so Governor Manuel Armijo could have him shot. The priest made the sign of the cross and had them kiss his crucifix, a bejeweled silver cross as large as Dan's hand. Then he held his hand over them palm downward and said:

> "'The Lord bless you and keep you;
> The Lord make His face shine upon you,
> And be gracious unto you;
> The Lord lift up His countenance upon you,
> And give you peace.'
> Go with God, my children. *Vaya con Dios.*"

Sebriana kissed the Padre's hand and rose to her feet, cheerful as a schoolgirl. She gave the old man a hug. The priest seemed to like it.

Roque saw Dan looking. "He likes the girls. Rumor has it he has five children."

They emerged into the light, Sebriana skipping at Dan's side as his eyes darted right and left searching for hidden lancers. Dan noticed that Rojo's blade was still in his hand.

Sebriana grinned like a Jack-o'-lantern. "That was our sign."

Dan was stunned when Padre Martinez confronted them, but after a while he came to understand. The padre was a complex man who backed his beliefs with action. He was a churchman but also a liberal who believed in the promise of the Constitution. He defended New Mexico's people and their customs and what he saw as their rights. Once he understood that Dan and his friends weren't

Templars or treasure hunters, he was able to look past his duty to the Pope.

The next day, they received another blessing, of a sort, from Kit Carson. A rider came from Santa Fe and gave a packet to Pedro who passed its contents to Dan.

Dan told his friends, "Kit doesn't write very well, but he has had his friend General Carleton write us letters of introduction. There were two of them. One is directed at all military commanders we might meet along the way instructing them to give us their trust and assistance. The other is directed to brother Masons, mentioning both himself and Kit, and asking for all the assistance they might provide to their brothers."

Roque smiled. "These may prove useful if we run afoul of the military or if we can't get government officials to give us an audience."

The mountains were beautiful in early spring flowers and budding aspens. The five companions rode the long ridge to where the town of Truchas stood like a castle and turned north reaching Trampas the next day, letting themselves be seen. They left a clear trail toward Angelfire and the wealth of the Sangre de Cristo Mountains. Beyond Picuris, they turned west and disappeared into the Embudo Mountains on trails known only to the Jicarillas. The next day they reached and crossed the Rio Grande at a hidden ford and began their climb up into the San Juans. Their destination lay on the western slope where rivers drained toward the Pacific.

Sebriana snuggled close to Dan. "These high country nights are cold even in spring. Come closer, *mija*."

Perhaps it was something in the spring air. It had been a long time since Dan had thoughts for anything but the quest. Now her warm body was close to his. They had been together a long time, almost three years he recalled.

He couldn't keep leading her on unless there was some hope he would marry her.

Discomfited by these thoughts, Dan found sleep eluded him. He began to mull other problems, rethinking what he had learned about rope, block, and tackle. Some teachers you never appreciate, and perhaps they deserve no appreciation. Others you only come to appreciate later. The best teachers you appreciate right away, knowing they are teaching something special you will never forget. Shaddrick Nelson was one such teacher. He taught Dan mathematics, engineering, geometry, and trigonometry. Frail and sickly, he had never been to sea, but respected the sailormen and observed their ways. He took Dan to the docks to study the practical application of his lessons.

"A ship is a great machine and an engineering marvel," Nelson said. "Everything moves and has to be adjusted and balanced to get the best performance. The shape of hull and sail effect the way the ship will deal with wind and water. Cargo must be balanced to lift or push down the bow for better sailing.

"You and I can make calculations that will confirm these dynamics of sail." He taught Dan how to do the necessary math, always demonstrating with some part of the ship or its equipment. Dan learned to calculate longitude and latitude and to see the marvel of simplicity in the sextant. "The sextant is the navigator's tool and he must know some trigonometry to use it well, but the bosons have tools as well, and very few of them have knowledge of mathematics or reading. They have tools they can manipulate manually to arrive at very accurate answers." He showed Dan the mathematical proofs of how the tools worked.

"The ship is often broken by storms or enemies," Nelson told his student. "The sailormen must repair it using things at hand, often lifting heavy loads." He showed Dan how block and tackle worked. "Each block, or pulley, has a number of sheaves. Tie off to a fixed object, like a mast or tree, with a block near the mast and another near an object you want to move. Now run your line through one sheave in each block and pull. If you pull in ten feet of rope, the two blocks come five feet closer together. The interesting part is that a five foot move takes only half the force that would have been required if you'd try to pull the object directly. Get two blocks with three sheaves each so that when you pull in nine feet of rope, the object moves only three feet closer, and you'll find the force needed is only a third of what would have been required otherwise, a mechanical advantage. It's called a threefold purchase. Say you can lift a hundred pounds of cargo by yourself and no more. With the right blocks, you can lift three hundred pounds."

Nelson also showed Dan knots and made him learn how to tie them. "Each knot has a purpose. Each puts strain on different parts of a rope. Ropes break, and knots spill, and they change shape from one knot to another, a holding knot becoming a slip knot, and collapse when used improperly. Their properties can be discovered with geometry, but the sailormen understand without it."

On their trip through the mountains, Dan spent the evenings knotting and splicing. He made longer ropes that were smooth and didn't show a great lump where they were joined. These would pass easily though a sheave and have the strength to carry as much weight as the original ropes. He knotted two cargo nets. These would be the safest and surest way to lift heavy objects. On paper, he designed the lifting boom they would need to create in order to swing in loads atop the cliff. Even more difficult was the beam needed inside the passage to lift and slide loads out the entrance.

Dan demonstrated to Roque what they needed, and with a knife Roque carved the final pieces of their engine.

"That's it, Danito," Roque said as the final pieces of their hoist went into place. "I'm glad we don't have to bring anything up those stairs." The stairs that led down under the waterfall were wet, slippery, and crumbling. Falling one thousand feet or more would not be pleasant even with an armload of gold and silver.

"The view is wonderful," said Sebriana stepping to the edge of the cliff. "I can see forty miles."

"That is a problem," said Rojo. "Anything we do up here can be seen from forty miles away."

"I think we've hidden the hoist rather well," Dan said, "and our fires."

"I will ride down to the valley and across the way," said Rojo. "In the morning, I will try to find your machine."

Fire was a problem. Anything they could see from near the fire could see their fire from afar. Hiding the fire and smoke might give them away in the daytime. Putting the fire back among trees would break up the smoke, making it hard to see. At night though, the light reflected from the trees could give them away.

Dan shook his head. "Up here atop the cliff, as we are, anyone detecting our fire is sure to have their interest pricked and come and see."

Sebriana agreed. "It is spring. There is still snow on the ground, and all the wood for the fire is wet and makes smoke."

"Who is looking for us?" asked Roque. "Not the Penitentes anymore. The Texians have been driven out of New Mexico. We killed the Mormons' best man and most of his Danites. Who is left?"

"More Mormons," said Dan. "And don't think a handful of Texians couldn't be about."

"Bah," said Roque turning back to the work. "Your hoist works well."

In the cave, Dan and Roque packaged the treasure and moved the packages toward the entrance.

Dan looked sad. "It's a shame about these silks and robes."

"Yes," said Roque. "They will turn to dust if you just breathe on them. But be happy. Everything else seems to have survived the long journey from the past."

As they worked, Dan learned about caves. They seemed to be cut by underground streams in much the same way as streams above ground cut canyons. Above ground, streams occasionally abandoned their old beds, and these beds became dry. Protected from the elements, the dry streambeds underground were drier than any place Dan had ever known. The dry air preserved wood, cloth, and iron. The cloth, unfortunately, crumbled to dust when touched. It had hung, cool and dry, for millennia without a breeze to disturb it. Elsewhere, the ceiling dripped water soaking in from above. In these places, the cave grew teeth and rock draperies and made dams that held pools of clear water.

They filled cargo net after cargo net with the treasure. They brought up the Table of the Showbread and the Menorah. All that remained was the Ark, and it was going to be a challenge.

The hardest part was that they didn't dare touch it or even brush up against it. The night before their attempt, they talked about the meaning of the Ark.

"Why is the Ark so important?" asked Rojo. "What is it?"

"It's a wooden box made three thousand years ago,"

Dan said, "covered with gold leaf inside and out. Inside it, Moses placed the stones of the Ten Commandments written by the Hand of God and a bit of the manna, the bread from heaven with which God fed the Israelites in the wilderness."

"So," said Rojo, "it is like the Jicarilla's Medicine Bundle, a very great source of *Power*."

"I suppose it is," Dan replied.

"Why are you afraid to move it?" the Apache asked. "Is it because gold is very heavy?"

Dan replied, "It's covered in gold leaf. That's gold hammered very thin and attached with an adhesive. The gold and the wood, which is very dry, don't account for much of the weight. Most of it is in the stone tablets of the 10 Commandments."

"That doesn't sound very heavy," said the Jicarilla. "What is the problem?"

"Well," Dan started, "the Bible talks about several occasions when the Ark was moved. One time God was punishing the Israelites by letting the Philistines defeat them. Somebody got the idea of bringing out the Ark because in the past when the Ark was marched before the people, they won battles. So the Ark was brought out, and the Israelites cheered until they shook the ground and frightened the Philistines. Then they went to battle, and the Israelites lost, and a whole lot of them were killed."

"Yes," added Sebriana, "you can't use God. You have to be right with Him."

"Ah," said Rojo nodding, "it is so with *Power*. Work with *Power* and wonderful things happen. Try to use it, and it leaves usually playing a nasty trick on the way."

"That's right," Dan said.

Verde and Roque were goggle-eyed and open-mouthed listening. Dan thought their surprise was odd after all they had experienced together. Verde should have heard all about *Power* before, but he really liked the stories.

Dan continued. "After the Philistines captured the Ark, they had bad crops, lost battles, suffered plagues and all sorts of bad luck, so much so that they returned the Ark to Israel and begged the Israelites to take it."

"Trying to use someone else's *Power* is very dangerous," said Rojo.

"King David was in favor with God," Dan said. "*Power* was right with him, so he wanted to bring the Ark up to his city. Here's what the Bible says happened." Dan opened his Bible and started reading.

"2 Samuel 6:

[6]And when they came to Nachon's threshing floor, Uzzah put out *his hand* to the ark of God and took hold of it, for the oxen stumbled.

[7]Then the anger of the Lord was aroused against Uzzah, and God struck him there for *his* error; and he died there by the ark of God."

Dan stopped for a moment and closed the Bible. "King David became afraid of the Ark and wouldn't move it any further. He left it in keeping with a family near the place of Uzzah's death. The family had wonderful good fortune the whole time it was there.

"So, I guess you can see why we're afraid to touch it or move it. It represents very great *Power,* and we might be doing wrong. If we touch it, we might be dead."

The Apache nodded and sucked on his pipe, blowing exotic smoke rings each time he exhaled. Deep in thought, he sat no longer seeing or reacting to his friends. Dan guessed he was reviewing everything he knew or had been told about *Power*. Eventually, Rojo opened his eyes and asked a question. "How can you be sure it is right to move it now?"

Dan didn't have a ready answer.

Sebriana spoke up. "We have been protected and led to this place. It wasn't any genius on our part that got us here."

Roque spoke next. "What happened at Glorieta Pass should have told us God was pleased with us."

"Tha's all we've got to go on, laddie," concluded Verde.

"So it is with *Power*," said Rojo. "We will move the Ark."

That left only the "how" to work out. The box was large, and the passage small. It would be difficult to move around it without touching it.

They laid out the cargo net on the floor of the passage near the entrance, and after inserting poles, they carried the Ark to the net and set it down on top. They set up two bipods with a beam on top and rigged it so the cargo net could be lifted with the system of pulleys on top of the cliff. The package needed to lift, slide down the beam, and swing out of the entrance with force provided from far above. Rojo and Roque were behind the Ark, Verde and Dan in front nearer the entrance. Only Sebriana was left above to pull on the rope and belay the line, making it secure, after each pull.

To help her, they lifted the Ark as high as they could and felt her take up the slack. Roque pulled the pin, and the Ark slid toward the entrance, pushing Verde and Dan before it.

Dan grabbed both poles. "Go!" he shouted to Verde who scampered up the stairs. It was Dan's turn. He had to move before the Ark pushed him over the edge. He leapt out of the entrance into space, hoping to connect with the stairs before the Ark connected with his back. Dan landed on the stairs and felt some of the slippery, moss covered steps collapsing beneath him. He ran and did not stop until he reached the top. Below him the Ark swung out into space. Dan's system held together.

Dan grasped the rope alongside Verde, telling Sebriana to belay the line behind them each time they pulled. If they lost their grip, Dan did not want the Ark slowly descending until it reached the end of the rope and then falling faster and faster. Each gain had to be checked so that it could not be undone by a stumble or tired muscles. It was too dangerous for Rojo and Roque to try to ascend while Dan, Verde, and Sebriana were hauling the Ark up. Finally, it was done.

Rojo leapt from the entrance and gained the stairs. He moved nimbly, like water flowing uphill. Behind him, Roque, by far the larger man, jumped, but as he gained the stairs they crumbled under him. He jumped from a disappearing step and found a good one. The one above that one disintegrated. As he ran, it seemed the stairs evaporated behind him. Dust and gravel fell to the valley floor far below.

That night they disassembled their engines and burned most of the equipment. As Dan worked, Sebriana inventoried the hoard. She was fascinated with a set of armor and coat of mail made of hard, white metal. The dimensions and forms were female, the workmanship exquisite. She picked up the only garment that had survived.

Dan looked at her. "When we found that silk gown, it was with the armor. See. It is still a vibrant royal blue, cut to fit under the armor. I'm amazed. It is the one piece of cloth that did not fall to dust. It is a wonder that the silk is still in one piece after all these years. It must have belonged to Princess Tea Tephi."

Sebriana held the silk gown up to herself. "My size," she said smiling sweetly and spinning as she held it to herself as women do.

In the morning, they packed the mules and covered the Ark with Rio Grande blankets. Sebriana rode ahead leading a long pack train. Rojo, Verde, Roque, and Dan manned the four poles and lifted. The Ark was heavy but never too heavy. Three days of walking brought them to the Chama River. There they were met the four Jicarilla helpers Rojo had arranged. He explained the nature of the Ark's *Power* to them. They would respect it. Thereafter, the trip was easier as they shared the load. They disappeared on Jicarilla trails into the high San Juans. A few days later, they crossed the Rio Grande just at dusk.

After hiding the Ark and their mule train up a side cañon, they made camp.

Sebriana addressed the others. "I wonder if we should gather up twelve stones and make an altar."

"Huh?" said Roque.

"Joshua did when Israel crossed the Jordan," she said.

And so they did marking the spot as special. They were near Embudo. The altar may still be there.

During the next days, they crossed the Embudo Mountains near Picuris south of Taos and then the towering Sangre de Cristo Range, stopping at Dan and Roque's rancho near Rayado. They divided shares including one for Pedro and buried them together, trusting each other as none of them, including Verde, seemed to be afflicted with the gold fever that caused friends to turn on one another. If anything happened to any of them, the others would have his share. Dan did not see the white gold armor and mail of the Jewish Princess Tea Tephi. It must have been there somewhere, he thought. With everything concealed, Roque, Sebriana, Verde, and Dan went north to Cimarron to gather wagons and teams while Rojo and the Jicarilla awaited their return.

Lucien Maxwell met them. He was a big man, tall and broad shouldered with a huge black mustache dressed in a dusty, black frock coat, high boots, and a wide-brimmed felt hat. He'd been a mountain man and Dan thought he was still a pirate though good and trustworthy with his friends.

"Young lady," he said to Sebriana, "I got the things you ordered: Rio Grande blankets, fine dressed deer and elk hides, buffalo robes."

Dan looked at her in wonder. She'd thought of a shipment of such would look like it belonged on the Santa Fe Trail and turn aside queries. They'd look almost normal.

"Dan," Lucien Maxwell continued, "I've got your stuff, too: four wagons, eight teams, and packing crates plus the gear you'll need for the trail, food, blankets, cookpots. Want to tell me about what you're up to?"

"Luke," Dan said, "I better not. It might prove trouble for you." Lucien was a Masonic brother and could be trusted, but he really was better off not knowing.

He nodded. "What do you want me to tell people? Have I seen you?"

"Sure," Dan said. "No need to lie. Tell them we saw a chance to make a profit with the war disrupting the trail. With Rojo along and a few trade goods, we ought to be safe from everything but Comanches and Kiowa Apaches."

Dan thought about what they'd done. During the stop at their rancho south of Rayado, they'd buried ten percent of the gold and silver, their share. It would be enough to make them each individually the wealthiest men in New Mexico alongside Lucien Maxwell.

They'd packed their Conestoga wagons carefully. The treasure was crated and packed along the bottom. On top of it, they placed their supplies, Rio Grande blankets, hides, and skins. It would take hours to find anything a trader wouldn't normally have.

The trip was uneventful. There were few travelers and no Indians bothered them. The war had closed the trail.Their journey went well out past Point of Rocks and through the Cimarron Crossing. The Jicarillas drove their four wagons while Roque, Rojo, Verde, Sebriana, and Dan rode as guards and scouts.

"Another day," said Roque, "and no travelers. Amigo, I am tired to the bones. We ride all day scouting for water and grass, and we spend all night on guard."

Dan agreed. "I'm bone weary myself. And I have to gather buffalo wood for Sebriana to cook over. If we had more men, we could spread the work out."

Roque shook his head. "Curry the stock. Feed them. Guard the *ramuda*. Guard the camp. Guard duty for one hour, sleep for three."

Rojo instructed them not to look at the fire. "You will lose your night vision. Stand guard far out from the camp where they don't expect you."

Roque questioned the wisdom of placing guards so far from camp where they could not support one another and could be approached from all sides. "What if the leprechaun falls asleep on guard? We might never know. We might not even find him in the morning. Hey wait, maybe this is a good idea."

Rojo continued. "Never present a silhouette against sky or fire. Too many times guards have been taken as a prelude to an attack. On the *llano,* it is important to shelter the fire. On even a low hill the fire will be seen from far away."

"We'll finish cooking by dusk and let the fire burn out," said Sebriana.

Rojo agreed. "Cook most of what you need in the morning twilight before your smoke can be seen and when the light of the fire does not show."

When Sebriana went on watch, Roque signaled that he wanted to talk to Dan quietly. "What do you think of my *prima*, heh?"

Dan shrugged. "She very nice. Trim figure, very smart, deadly."

"She is not getting any younger," Roque said.

"None of us are," Dan replied, knowing where this conversation was headed.

Roque's features scrunched into a frown. "Danito, you are not getting any younger yourself. Someday you must marry."

"You, too, Roque." Dan smiled. "Got anyone in mind? Or are all your lady friends already married?"

As he drew on his pipe, its coal glowing like a furnace, Roque huffed smoke from his nose and mouth, and possibly his ears, like an angry locomotive.

"Danito, I am serious. You must think about this."

Dan took a puff on his pipe, playing for time. He knew Roque didn't want to tell him directly to marry her. "Why I think about it all the time. It would be nice to have a wife and a few *niños*, but you know how it is. We're on the move all the time. That's no life for a woman."

Dan thought Roque might chew the end off his pipe or burn a hole through its clay bowl. Roque turned and walked off into the night. Dan heard him sigh. He's frustrated, Dan thought. Left with his own thoughts Dan wondered if Roque believed he was as dense as he was pretending. There are times when Dan really failed to get the point. This wasn't one of them.

Dan knew he wasn't being fair to Sebriana. Over the course of ten years, he and Sebriana had seen each intimately other now and then when she was between husbands. They had been constantly together on this treasure hunt for three years. It wasn't fair of him not to take her seriously after all this time. She was a good friend and companion and was skilled in other ways and good with horses, knives, and guns. But she was Mexican, and he was an Out Easter, a New Englander. Dan knew he couldn't tell Roque that he couldn't marry Sebriana because she was Mexican or Jewish.

He laughed to himself as he thought about how many of her husbands had died, some of them smiling.

What should a man look for in a woman he wants to marry? Some looked for wealth and position or for a woman who could push their career along with her connections. Some, Dan supposed, with enough wealth of their own, looked for an ornament, beautiful with little weight of mind. Sebriana was not afraid to speak her mind and more often than not had important knowledge and conclusions to contribute. Moreover she was never an embarrassment either from saying something stupid or from holding her man up to ridicule. Some married because they think they are in love when all they are is in lust. That faded pretty fast, leaving everyone unhappy. Dan supposed a man should look for a woman to be "a help mete to him," that is, someone whose skills, desires, and ways are a compliment to his own, someone who will help him to the kind of success he wants to achieve. The problem with finding a help-mete, Dan thought, was that a man had to know what he wanted.

He glanced up from his reverie to find Roque returning from the dark. It was hard to see a man approaching from total darkness even if he was smoking a clay pipe, but Roque's nose warmer was glowing red just above the base which had turned black. "Darn it, Danito, what are your intentions toward *mi prima*?"

"Intentions? Why, I intend to be a kind friend to her," Dan said smiling and doing his best to look confused, oblivious to Roque's meaning.

"She's not getting any younger!" He stormed. "She needs a husband."

"I'm flattered," Dan said, "but I'm not ready to move my bedroll."

"I'm sure," he said, "she would be willing to move out to the rancho."

"No, no, no." Dan replied. "I meant I was not ready to move to the graveyard. She has buried five husbands already. I am not brave enough for such a challenge."

Roque growled. "She will not kill you, and you know she is no *bruja* with a curse."

"She might be a *bruja*, though," Dan replied. "She's pretty handy with herbal medicine and healing arts." The Mexicans suspect anyone who works with herbs and healing of being a witch even if all they do is good.

"She...is not...a *bruja*," Roque said with finality. "What are your intentions?"

"Well," Dan said, "I guess I'll tell her about your concerns."

"You wouldn't dare!" He drew his big knife. They were interrupted by female laughter coming from beyond the circle of firelight. Out in the dark, an alert female sentry had been listening. Roque put away his knife, flushing so violently Dan could see red face by firelight.

Dan went on thinking. It had been a pretty nice three

years, and neither of them needed to worry about money.

Between the Cimarron and the Arkansas, water was scarce and grass poor. On the day they forded the Arkansas, they heard firing behind them. Rojo and Dan, who were scouting, rode back to take a look.

Rojo stopped them short and signaled they should secure the horses and crawl forward to the top of a low hill. The *llano* isn't flat. It undulates like waves on a sea. Beyond the hill, perhaps two hundred yards away, a small group of men was pinned down in a buffalo wallow. In the open between them a man lay dead. Dan recognized twitchy Jim Pennington even in death, even dressed as a feathered porcupine decorated with twenty or more arrows, Dan knew him. Further out, beyond the range of the men in the wallow, Indians wearing only breechclouts and moccasins taunted the survivors. These naked men were skilled riders. Dan counted sixteen of them.

"Comanche," Rojo whispered, but Dan already knew. Three of them charged to within a few yards of the men in the wallow, swinging down under their horses' necks and firing arrows. As they rode off out of range, one of the men in the wallow stood up and made a strange gesture with his arms. Did he hope one of the Indians was a Freemason? He did it again. It was a sign Masons use to signal other Masons that they are in extreme distress. There are stories of brothers rescued from the firing squad and prison when they gave this sign. Any Mason who saw it was supposed to give help. Joseph Smith used it when accosted by an angry mob, but by then he had been expelled from the fraternity. Did they hope that some wandering brother would happen by? Or was this sign to remind Rojo and Dan of their responsibilities? Did the Texians think Dan's party was nearby?

Dan realized that they might know how near he and

his comrades were if they were following his group.

"Rojo," Dan whispered, "we've got to help them." The Jicarilla shook his head violently.

The Comanche charged down in a bunch using the same technique Dan had seen before. As they came close, one of the Texans rose up abruptly to his feet, Tiler Caine. He had pistols in each hand. He fired once, twice, and killed a warrior. Then his hammers struck on empty chambers. Dan watched him cock and aim over and over, but no smoke, bang, or flash followed. He stood defiant in his fancy clothes, guns in hands, cocking and firing. Then a Comanche rode close and slammed a lance through his chest. It emerged bloody from his back. He stood looking at it, his face contorted in confusion.

Dan didn't stand. He shot the Comanche from his horse and heard the thunder of Rojo's weapon beside him. Dan ran to his horse and charged over the hill along with Rojo screaming like a banshee. They drew their pistols and closing rapidly dropped two more. The Comanche scattered like quail. They'd be back, Dan thought, but we've bought a few minutes.

Dan looked at Caine, still standing. "Caine, I can't do anything for you. If I remove that thing you'll either die of the pain or the bleeding."

"I know," Caine said. "Reload my pistols. I'll take a few with me and save the last for myself." Dan nodded, and Rojo and he set to the task.

"Captain Rheingold," Dan said, "mount up and come away from here. You can't stay with us. Understand? You either head north away from the Comanche or back to Texas. I don't care, but if I ever see you again dogging my trail, I'll kill you myself, Masonic brother or not. Got it?"

"Yes, thank you," Rheingold replied. He and his two

remaining men mounted.

Finished with reloading, Rojo and Dan mounted too. Tiler still stood, defiant, though listing from side to side in the prairie wind. If he went down, that lance was going to do a lot of damage, might even kill him. Tiler, Dan wondered if it were his name or title. In the Lodge, a tiler is the armed guard by the door.

"I don't see any way to get the tiler on a horse," Dan said to Ranger Captain Rheingold who shook his head.

"Good luck, Tiler," he said as they all rode off.

A few moments later they heard the rhythmic firing of a six-shooter. Dan counted the shots…one, two…eleven and twelve. He'd fired them all. Dan hoped he'd saved the last for himself. The Comanche could be very cruel with a live captive.

Dan and Rojo rode hard, fearing they might be leading the Comanche back to their caravan. How many? Dan wondered. Had they seen them all? Was it just a small raiding party? As they rode, Dan could see how worn the Texans' stock was. They'd been chased across the *Llano Estacado* riding without rest for a long time.

"We're out of powder and caps," said Rheingold as they crossed the last hill before the Arkansas. He held up his horses. Across the river, Dan could see that his caravan had been joined by a troop of Union cavalry, pennants fluttering. "I can't go any further."

That he dared not cross the river was certain. He'd be arrested as a spy and hanged. Dan and Rojo gave the Texans all the powder and caps they had on them and some lead as well. It wasn't much.

"Good luck, Captain," Dan said. "You'll need it."

At their caravan, Dan found their friend Captain John Bonham headed east with a troop of cavalry no longer needed in New Mexico now that the California Column had arrived. They had come by Raton Pass and Bent's Fort.

"We heard firing," said Lewis.

"Comanche," Dan said.

"I saw men with you on the hill," Bonham said expecting an explanation.

"Texians," Dan replied. "They thought they preferred taking their chances with the Comanche to being hung as spies."

"Saves me the trouble," replied Bonham wisely. Some officers would have chased them down for the sport of hanging them.

Bonham's troop rode with them across most of Kansas. "Dan," Bonham said one night, "I've looked in your wagons. You've got the usual stuff, blankets and hides."

"Don't forget the mules," Dan said. "Mules are bringing a high price these days, what with the war and all. We thought the rest might, too, with trade so reduced."

Bonham cocked an eyebrow. "You know the real money always came from much further south where they've got gold and silver to buy things. This lot is barely worth the trip. That's why no one is taking the risk."

"I guess Roque and I figured wrong..." Dan said.

John Bonham tilted his head at Dan's seeming admission of a miscalculation. "You and he seldom figure wrong in my experience. But your reasons are your own, and I won't press further. Besides, it's nice having a woman to entertain us after dinner though if you let Verde get drunk and start singing again, we may have to part company."

"Thanks, Captain," Dan said.

Weeks later, they went their separate ways at Council Grove where Bonham and his troop went north to Fort Leavenworth, and Dan's caravan continued east bound for Independence. There they would have to decide whether to book passage by riverboat or continue on to Saint Louis by wagon. If they went by river, they would lose privacy and their cargo might be seen, but Kansas and Missouri were alive with renegade militias, making the roads unsafe. Union or Confederate either could prove a problem for the small caravan. Dan would be glad when he could put their cargo on a train. No train had ever been robbed.

The hills now were green with tall grass, the countryside hospitable and welcoming. When you've been where the tribes run wild, Dan thought, constantly on guard against them, nearing civilization naturally causes you to relax. Your guard comes down. You know you're safe from Indians and Texians.

"Civilization," he told Sebriana, "you can't see it yet, but we're close."

"Yes," she agreed, "the country is not so *cimarron*."

Dan couldn't help but express himself. "You're surrounded by civilized people. Aid and assistance are at hand."

"*Socorro*." Sebriana smiled. "That's what the Spanish called it on the *Camino Real*."

Whatever Dan might have thought, eastern Kansas and western Missouri in 1863 were not civilization. They only resembled it. What was happening there was more dangerous even than Indians who'd figured out the army was busy elsewhere. The hills were full of fanatics, both pro- and anti-slavery. They'd moved there because they had a grudge one way or the other.

A philosopher once said that no man thinks himself

bad. Men with grudges were dangerous because they believed they have a right to even the score any way they could. In carrying out their depredations, they created more like themselves, men who'd had their homes burned and families slain. These men would commit unthinkable crimes to make the world right again. God and justice were on their side.

Dan had once explained to Roque and Sebriana how men who counted themselves victims were treacherous. "What makes the Mormons dangerous is that they think themselves victims out righting wrongs done to them. Their religion may say some brutal things about what should be done to gentiles, but what drives their people is the sense that they are victims. I've got to question the philosopher. I'm not sure all men think themselves good. Most do, but there are men, who must know themselves to be evil and revel in it. Porter Brannan thought he was doing God's work, so the really evil ones, I think, are rare."

What Dan didn't realize, even though he knew about the Mormon expulsion from Missouri and Bleeding Kansas, was that all the fanatics, whether they thought themselves good or evil, had come to the Kansas-Missouri border. Men banded together into irregular units along the border. Some joined the irregulars because their grudges didn't extend to the larger war. Others did not want to join regular units and be moved away where they couldn't defend their families. Many didn't want the discipline and wanted to come and go as they pleased to tend farms, businesses, or families. Still others realized that there was no local law enforcement that could handle so many, and thus they were free to rape, murder, pillage, and burn.

Roque looked around at the new landscape. "This is a

different kind of country, softer, greener, closer, than any I have seen before. It makes me feel watched by things I cannot see."

Rojo agreed. "As a young man, I learned to mount hills and scan the horizon for sign. Here the hills are thickly wooded. When I was young, we watched waterholes for sign. Here there is water everywhere."

Roque shook his head. "All our skills were blunted by this green, wooded terrain."

Only Sebriana seemed happy and comfortable in the green land.

Crossing a little valley thick with early spring flowers surrounded by groves of trees, Dan was lost in thought about what to do about Sebriana. He mused, "In spring a young man's fancy turns to thoughts of love." He snorted. Sebriana and Roque looked at him for explanation.

Thus distracted, they didn't notice a man emerging from the trees until he was upon them. The stranger rode his horse into Dan's, stopping him cold. Sebriana and Roque rode up beside Dan. At the same time, thirty-one of the man's followers emerged from the wood, forming a semicircle around the front of the small caravan. The Jicarilla drivers instinctively turned their mules to face the assailants before stopping, forming a sort of herringbone in the road that would make it possible to continue ahead or perhaps turn and flee. The Apaches disappeared into their wagon boxes, and rifle barrels emerged. Rojo and Verde rushed forward, dismounted, and kneeled on opposite sides of the lead wagon. Their sizable *remuda* of mules, the herd of remounts and spares, after all these long miles, was good at following the wagons and staying close. No drover rode among them.

"What you got here?" asked the leader leaning almost into Dan's face. He wore dirty buckskin and sported a tangled beard, his hair greasy and long. His grey eyes were piercing, exposing the strength of will that made him leader where hygiene and intelligence were lacking. Three pistols and a Bowie knife were tucked in his belt, a saber hung at his side, and a musket rested across his pommel in front of him. The musket was rusty and crusted with black powder residue. Dan noticed that the man carried a musket, not a rifle. It was cheaper and lacked the accuracy of a hunting weapon. Dan thought this Border Ruffian didn't seem to be a frontiersman reliant for survival on the quality and care of his weapons. The apparent lack of discipline and maintenance raised a question in Dan's mind. Was this a group of Pro-slavery Missouri Border Ruffians or Anti-slavery Kansas Jayhawkers? Both were dangerous.

"What business is that of yours?" Dan responded. The man's followers, uncouth as he, took up no particular formation or state of readiness. They hoped to overawe by numbers alone. Dan wondered what sort of fights they had ever been in, maybe none, but Missourians were known as tough fighters.

The filthy man sneered. "I'm the local commandant. Now what you got in the wagons?"

Dan hesitated deciding how to handle this man. "Just a few trade goods come up from Santa Fe, hides, buffalo robes, Rio Grande blankets."

"We're confiscating your mules," the commandant said.

Roque enflamed with rage blustered. "Confiscating?!? Confiscating? What army you with? US Constitution doesn't let you confiscate! We haven't broken any laws."

"You broken our law," said the greasy leader. "You've come into our area without our permission, with no passport or import license."

One of his men moved his horse alongside the leader. "Bill," he said quietly, "I think these might be the ones Anderson and General Albert Pike told us to be lookin' for."

Bill, the leader, nodded and smiled, showing dark gaps and brown stains. Dan smelled putrefaction on his breath even at a distance. It would have assaulted his senses if he'd been closer. Dan didn't know what the man's followers called him, but thought he must be the terrorist known as Greasy Bill.

"Perhaps we can make it right," Dan said, "by making you a gift of a few mules and blankets."

Dan was thinking fast and worrying about what Albert Pike might have told them. Very soon, he would reach the Missouri River at Independence and would no longer need the *ramuda*. For the moment, he had to pretend he didn't understand what the mention of Pike implied. This negotiation wasn't going at all well, but Dan was at a terrible disadvantage. He was out numbered 32 to 9.

He who asks the questions is in control, Dan thought, as he threw out a question. "Which army are you with? I don't want to pay to the side that isn't in control. I'd end up paying twice." Without drawing attention, Dan slipped off the leather thongs that held down his pistols. He noticed Roque doing the same.

"It don't matter none at all who I's with," the guerilla leader said. "I's in control, and I takes what I wants. If you's co-op'ative, I might let you live. I recon I'll fetch me that whore, too. She might be fun in camp tonight." When he leaned forward to reach for her, Sebriana spat in his face.

"*Cabron!*" she roared lashing out and nicking the tip of Greasy Bill's nose with her *misericorde. "Tu madre es puta grande! Madre de puta!"* She didn't get a chance to favor him with a translation. His musket swung around, and he fired into her chest. The shot, buck and ball, tore her small body from the saddle and threw it crashing to the ground a dozen yards behind Dan.

Dan suddenly felt it. He was larger, more powerful, and swifter than he had ever been. He felt superhuman. He'd heard stories of Kit Carson's deeds at moments when numbers and odds seemed all against the great scout. He'd seen little Kit beat a giant Apache warrior senseless with his fists. A fighting anger descended, the spirit of a fighting archangel Roque might claim, and time stopped.

Roque's horse reared, and an iron shod hoof crushed the side of the guerilla leader's head even as Dan's pistol ball pierced his heart and lungs. A saber slashed Dan's side as his pistol swung round and blew the owner's nose out the back of his head.

Behind him, Dan heard Rojo call out to Verde, "Cover them. Shoot anyone who aims at them or approaches from behind."

What Rojo said didn't register with Dan until much later. Rojo repeated the message in Apache, and riders began to fall. The range was close. Dan and Roque worked with a pistol in each hand while Verde, Rojo and the Apaches supported them. They fired at targets so near, their clothing caught fire. Weapons roared and flamed within a fog of gun smoke. Dan's pistols couldn't miss. Twelve shots left twelve men dead with balls through heart or head. They'd taken the Border Ruffians by surprise, unready. The guerrillas didn't expect an attack. They expected submission. A saber cut Dan's back as a ball burned his face. The saber holder flew from his saddle a rifle ball in his chest as an Apache marksman grinned. Pistols empty, 'hawk and Bowie leapt into Dan's hands, 'hawk cleaving an arm from a shoulder, while Bowie buried itself in a neck nearly severing the head. 'Hawk bit into the bridge of a nose, penetrating both eyes, sticking so tight in the skull the falling body nearly dragged Dan from the saddle. Through the fog, Dan saw one man remaining in the saddle and charged at him and he at Dan. In the last instant, Roque and Dan recognized each other. Their horses collided throwing the four of them to the ground. Rising Roque and Dan cast about for more guerillas but found only Jicarillas methodically slicing the throats of any who yet lived.

Beside Dan, glancing around, Roque spat in Greasy Bill's dead face and said,

*"Un coyote huyaba
Deseando ser lobo.*

The lowly coyote has tried by his howling to be a wolf."

Dan heard one of Rojo's men grumble in Apache words he understood *"Ch'eekéé na'isii."* "Woman's work," the Apache said, slicing a throat.

Rojo was already kneeling beside Sebriana. Roque and Dan rushed to her side. Verde lay on the ground groaning, a pool of blood growing around his leg.

"She yet lives," said Rojo softly. "I don't know how much longer."

"What's this?" demanded Roque pulling Sebriana's shirt aside.

"It's Princess Tea Tephi's armor!" Dan shouted. "So that's where it went. But look! It didn't help. The musket ball went right through though the buckshot bounced off and blood is coming from the hole. It's right over her heart."

Roque nodded grimly. "We've got to get her to a doctor."

"There's one in Independence. Not far," Dan said without enthusiasm. "The trip alone might kill her."

Rojo scowled at the pair. "We're not going anywhere until you and Roque have been sewn back together and Verde, too."

One of the Jicarilla was already working on Verde. Another approached Roque while Rojo began sewing up Dan's saber cuts, adding a soothing, healing herb right in the cut. It healed rapidly over the course of the coming weeks with no infection and little pain. Roque's experience, Dan learned, was similar. But at that moment they were still bleeding profusely until the stitches staunched some of the flow.

It was a difficult journey to Independence reeling in the saddle from loss of blood and from some soporific Rojo had ordered Dan to drink, a thick, bitter brew that made his head swim. The Jicarilla lifted Sebriana and Verde into a wagon. She had not regained consciousness, and Rojo had knocked Verde out with more of the soporific. They all thought he might lose his leg. The bone seemed broken and the ball deep, but Dan, Roque, and Rojo lacked the skill to retrieve it. The leg would have to wait for Independence and the doctor.

Roque viewed the scene of the recent battle. Horses roamed and grazed amidst 32 dead bodies. "What do we do with them?"

Rojo smiled darkly. "Leave them. Buzzards and coyotes got to eat, too. You two fools should ride in the wagons."

As they set out Dan could imagine the jolt of the wagon and the rubbing of his cut side and back against hard boxes. He agonized over what Sebriana must be enduring.

"I'll ride, thanks," Dan replied.

"*Bueno*," said Roque. "We might get attacked again. It wouldn't do to have your best fighters riding in a wagon."

In Independence, the doctor examined Verde and Sebriana. He refused to speak with Dan and Roque until he had operated on both. "I pulled the ball from your friend's leg. The bone was broken, but I don't think shattered. I've set it. I think he'll lose the leg, but we'll see. The next few days are crucial.

"The young lady is a strange case. Under the armor, she had on chain mail. I've never seen the like. The bullet went through that too, but it was stopped by what was under the mail, a silk gown. The silk stopped the bullet. It made a dent in her that was bleeding, and it did some damage. She hit her head hard when she fell. She might never come back fully to her senses. Or, more likely, she'll die. Head cases are like that. We'll have to wait and see."

Dan searched among her possessions for a small leather bag. "Doctor, she made me promise if she was ever hurt, I was to see this mixed with her food and fed to her. Promise you will feed this to her." Dan handed him the *tierra bendita*, the holy earth of Chimayo.

Rojo and his Jicarilla braves agreed to watch over Sebriana and Verde, while waiting for Dan and Roque to return from the Capital to Independence. Rojo had seen the town before and was content. His braves were somewhat overwhelmed, but Dan was sure they'd inspect the town on their own, secretly. It would be a bad couple of nights for toughs confronting strangers in the shadows.

Independence was a ghost town. Trade was way off. The military had taken control of the river trade, and no boat sailed without military say so. Worse, the Missouri River was a border of a sort between North and South. River pirates ran rampant. They were almost impossible to catch. They didn't use big boats with cannons. Rather they approached in hordes of rowboats and sailboats, bringing enough men to overwhelm a ship's crew. The channel of the Missouri meandered from side to side in some places, running so close a steamboat brushed the trees on the bank.

Roque and Dan had planned to travel with the cargo, and they wanted to leave quickly before word of the fight got out. Rivermen lounging on the docks waiting for the next ship to sail, if ever, told them just how bad the situation was. "Time was you could take a riverboat all the way to Pittsburgh and a train from there to anywhere on the eastern seaboard, but not now. Damned army has shut us down. Won't let the boats run." He spat a long stream of tobacco juice.

"Roque," Dan said, "we'd have been within Union lines the whole way."

"Sí," his friend replied, "but right on the edge of the Confederacy, too. There have been Confederate raids into Ohio and a big fight in Maryland. The Baltimore and Ohio Railroad, the B&O, runs through southern Ohio along the river to western Virginia and then to Harper's Ferry at the head of the Shenandoah Valley."

Dan nodded. "We'll be riding through the heart of the war, through land that has been, and might again be, controlled by the Confederacy. But it's got to be done. How do we get the army to let us do it?

Roque was amazed by the town of Independence, Missouri. Easterners would count it a rough frontier town on the hill overlooking the Missouri River.

He looked at the town goggle-eyed. "Everything is

built of frame and lumber. There is no adobe. And there are so many tall buildings, two and even three stories high."

In New Mexico, everything was built in adobe, and most were one story without porches or adornments, often without windows or doors. Glass cost a great deal of money; no one in New Mexico manufactured it, nor were there any lumber mills. Timber was cut and shaped by axe, adz, and knife. Metal and metal tools were scarce. A building of two-stories, where the merchant and his family lived upstairs, with glass windows to display wares, and a covered boardwalk to shelter potential customers from mud and the elements while they window-shopped seemed incredible opulence to Roque. He was amazed also by the wealth of goods on display and by the prices, much lower than in New Mexico. When they'd looked the town over, Dan with less than total enthusiasm, they headed for the riverfront.

"No," said the riverboat captain, "I can't let you have an entire hold, nor can you fit four wagon loads of goods into a stateroom. You'll be lucky if I can find space for your cargo in the general hold. Priority goes to the military right now, you know." Gray-bearded and kindly enough, he was stubborn as only a ship's captain can be. Dan considered impressing him with his nautical knowledge, but thought better of it. River sailors feel saltwater tars looked down on them. The chance of giving unintended insult was great.

The captain continued, "Besides, river transport is chancy. Boats have been shot at and taken. A ship pulls into a port only to find that, on that day anyway, the port belongs to the enemy. General Ewing has closed the river for now, and I doubt I'll be allowed to sail until he can provide some sort of escort."

"Oh there you are!" cried a voice familiar to Dan and Roque. It came from a man in the uniform of a Major. It was the man they'd known as Captain Lewis of the cavalry.

"Hello, John" said Dan. "We haven't seen you since Glorieta Pass. We were afraid you'd been killed by the Texians. What are you doing in Independence?"

John Lewis smiled. "General Thomas Ewing sent me to hunt down Greasy Bill and his gang of guerilla thieves and cutthroats. He thought my training hunting Indians might give me an edge. And why not? Greasy Bill and his Border Ruffians scalp, torture, mutilate, ravish maidens, plunder, and pillage like savages."

Roque's lips curled up slightly. "Sounds like this Greasy Bill might be a slippery *hombre*."

Lewis paused a moment not quite sure if Roque's comment was a joke. "Not that our own Kansas 7th Cavalry, Jennison's Jayhawkers, are much better. Ewing is up in arms about the uprising this spring. Wagon traffic is shut down. The railroad runs for a few days after the tracks are repaired and then trains are likely to get captured.

"So, General Ewing has given me a squadron," Major Lewis continued, "and told me to put an end to Bill, kill or capture, it don't matter. Lo and behold, when I found them, somebody had already killed them for me. You don't know anything about that, do you?"

Both Roque and Dan had visible wounds. "We did run into a little trouble," Dan replied. "Don't know the fella's name though."

Roque nodded. "We weren't formally introduced."

The riverboat captain was awed. "Did they really kill Greasy Bill?"

"Looks like," said Major Lewis, "and the rest of his

band, too."

"By themselves?" asked the astonished river captain.

"They probably had four or five helpers," Lewis responded. "Where these two go there is usually an Apache called Peregrino Rojo not far away probably leading two or three braves. I saw a Mexican girl and an old mountain man healing up at the doctor's. You take care of them, captain. They're friends of Kit Carson and the army. Shake their hands."

Dan thought Lewis must have mentioned the famous frontiersman and shaking hands intentionally. He gave the captain the Masonic grip and felt it returned as the river man looked wide-eyed at Dan. "Give them anything they need," said the soldier.

"By the way," the cavalryman said, "The river will reopen tonight. There'll be cavalry patrols on both banks. With Greasy Bill out of the way, you shouldn't have any trouble. There he was with 32 of his men lying dead and scalped, and the scalps left contemptuously on the ground. Only an Apache would do that. These two, a woman and old man wounded at the doctor's, along with Rojo and some of his braves. Makes seven, I think, against 32. Don't that beat all?"

"Boys," said the river captain, now revealed as a Masonic brother, "I want you along with me. You might come in handy if anything gits past the cavalry.

"I do have a small forward hold," the captain continued. "I think I can let you camp in there. Can you pay for all the space?"

"We can," said Roque.

"Come on up to my cabin," said the captain. "Name's John-Paul Perry, by the way. I'll get you something to drink."

In the cabin behind the pilot house far atop the

riverboat, Captain John-Paul Perry put cups of brown coffee in front of Dan and Roque and turned searching his cupboards for something. Roque sipped his; it was cold and flat.

"Captain," Roque said, "I hate to complain. I don't know the local custom, but the coffee she is a little cold."

The captain spun about and grinned. "T'ain't coffee. Missouri River water, sure enough. Water the color of coffee that scours out the bowels. Good for what ails you, though I usually take it with a little of this." He poured amber fluid into their cups. "Helps to melt the grit. We sail tonight, in the dark with skylights covered and windows shuttered. Better get your stuff aboard, as soon as you finish your water."

"Is it safe to sail in the dark?" asked Roque.

Captain John-Paul Perry grinned like a 'possum. "Why not? I got two of the best Missouri River pilots alive. They know the river, night or day, rain or shine, and could run it hoodwinked."

Dan had business away from the docks and left Roque to load their cargo. At the doctor's office, he bent to kiss the still unconscious Sebriana knowing she would never regain consciousness and that he would never see her again. She would be buried here in this strange town far from her own familiar people. There would be no one to watch over her bones nor would they ever mingle in the graveyard with the bones of her kin. It was a long, sad last kiss that left drops of dew on her face.

Returning to the dock, Dan found Roque stowing their cargo in a small forward hold. Roque listened enthralled as the mate instructed his crew. "'Here, now, start that crate back'ard! Lively, now! What're you about there! Snatch it! Snatch it clean now! Aft again! Aft! Don't you hear me? Avast heaving! Are you asleep there? Going to heave it clear astern? Where're you going with that? Aft with it 'fore I make you swallow it, you split between a tired mud-turtle and a plowboy's crippled jackass!"

"See?" asked the river captain, John-Paul Perry. He was of mixed St. Louis French and Virginia blood. "See. The hold is for my personal use. As part of my compensation, I'm allowed to transport a few trade goods for profit. That's why there is a ladder leading up to my day cabin above. Once this is full, we'll brace a few things against the bulkhead, and no one will be able to enter except through my cabin."

Just before they sailed, Major Lewis came aboard and sought Dan. "I've put a platoon of infantry aboard, what's left of a company, under First Sergeant Hawkey. It isn't much of an escort, but I think you'll be safe. There are some wounded being discharged and sent home as well."

The boat was a double side-wheeler of four decks. With the loading finished, Roque explored the boat, visiting the pilot house and making friends while Dan guarded the hatch in the captain's day cabin. He soon returned and said to Dan, "This ship, she is the most beautiful thing I have ever seen, and I have learned too much. Below us is steerage, and it is joined by a ladder to our companionway. See I am learning? This is the boiler deck. Above us is the hurricane deck and then the Texas and then finally the pilothouse. The pilots are the most important people on board, even more than the captain."

Chapter 18

Rollin' on a River

Dan paid little attention to the steamboat, one of the largest on the river. Twin wheelhouses were decorated with the name of the ship, which Dan failed to note. The boat was ornate with fretwork and adornment and tall smoke stacks. She had carried wealthy passengers in fine cabins and entertained them in a grand dining room and salon.

Lost in grief and feeling sad from deserting his friends, especially Sebriana, he told Roque and tried to convince himself, "There was no way it was safe to wait. The longer we tarry, the greater the risk. Every sign says General Albert Pike is pursuing us with the aid of General Sterling Price who is expected to invade Missouri at any moment."

The Confederates had defeated Union general Nathaniel Lyon at the Battle of Wilson's Creek in July of 1861. For a while the Confederates had controlled the Missouri River all the way to St. Louis. The threat had to be taken seriously.

"Roque," Dan said as they left Independence, "I've been thinking."

"A Dios mio!" the Mexican exclaimed. "Not again."

Dan ignored him and went on, "At first I thought it

was anger and skill that helped us defeat Greasy Bill, but now I'm sure it wasn't. Our party had both in abundance, but it wouldn't have been enough. What we did was impossible. It has to have been our cargo that saw us through. God was on our side!"

"Danito, don't you know yet?" replied Roque. "Everything happens as God wills."

Annoyed at such a glib response to his deep painful thoughts, Dan said, "You know that boil you've been after me to lance? Live with it. It is as God wills." Turning, Dan headed back into the day cabin to think and mourn his loss.

Roque and Dan had enough cash for the trip. They'd melted down a few of the gold coins and made small, crude ingots of five ounces. If they never used more than one in any particular place, they would not, Dan thought, arouse suspicion or start a gold rush. Travelers often had small amounts of gold. They lived on the western frontier, and they were from New Mexico, which, though it was the poorest state in gold, still had deposits at Cerrillos, in the Manzano Mountains, near Angelfire, and at Santa Rita del Cobre and Piños Altos. Men had gold in forms other than U.S. coins.

The old coins they'd found would have roused a stir. Merchants would not have known their worth and would have wanted to know where they came from. Dan thought they might make up a story and tell the curious that the coins came from China, for there were many Chinese on the coast, but someone might remember Chinese coins had a square hole in the center. Worse, Dan thought, he might have said they were from Ceylon and still had some merchant accost them who was certain coins from Ceylon should have had a square hole. They sold an ingot whenever they could without arousing suspicion.

In fear of running the strange, new, inky river before moonrise, the first night out, Roque made his way to the pilothouse seeking reassurance. In the moonless dark, they passed River Bend and Liberty Bend. At dawn, they saw the steeple of the church at Missouri City and stopped for wood and water.

"This river she is much bigger than the Rio Grande," said Roque to Dan. Roque yawned in the morning after his long night in the pilothouse. "It is amazing. The pilot guides the boat by looking at the ripples in the water. He can't see the channel, but he can feel it in the dark. He let me ring the bells to signal the engineer for our landing."

The river, the piloting and the ship was like nothing Roque had ever seen before. He enjoyed the trip, dining at the captain's table, watching the leadsmen casting the line for sandbars and untangling the ship from snags. The nautical realm was all new and exciting. He wished Rojo could see it all. Dan didn't want to spoil his fun by reminding him that Rojo had, passing himself off as a Mexican don, ridden all the way to New Orleans as a riverboat gambler. Roque would have wanted to be a riverboat gambling Mexican don as well, but Dan figured they couldn't afford the visibility.

For Dan, a recluse in the captain's day cabin or betimes descending into the barricaded hold, the journey was a trip through hell. Time passed slowly, giving him ample time for introspection. He had left the woman he loved to die alone in the company of strangers. Crushed by overwhelming guilt and doubt and fearing he had wasted three years of their lives chasing another man's dream, he wrestled with his conscience.

He had doubts about their quest as well. Dan's logical mind told him these objects couldn't hold any power, especially power worth dying for. He had studied and learned about the scientific method. No thesis concerning power could be empirically stated or tested. If he asked Power for assistance, and it was not forthcoming, that was not a failure of the test. Power was either deferring a response, ignoring the request, fulfilling it in an unexpected way, or being displeased with the request. Power had its own volition. It did not respond the same way every time. Neither Power nor God resembled Newton dropping an apple, which always fell in the same way. Dan did not know what Power was, so he could not make a proper, testable scientific statement about it or about what it would do. He equated power with the Great Architect of the Universe--God. God is bigger than the universe. He was its creator.

Isaiah 44:

24 Thus says the LORD, your Redeemer,
And He who formed you from the womb:
"I am the LORD, who makes all things,
Who stretches out the heavens all alone,
Who spreads abroad the earth by Myself;

Nehemiah 9:

4 You alone are the LORD;
You have made heaven,
The heaven of heavens, with all their host,
The earth and everything on it,
The seas and all that is in them,
And You preserve them all.
The host of heaven worships You.

The *Power* Dan thought they were carrying to Washington had not just created the universe but was active in maintaining it. There is no way to imagine, and certainly not define, a *Power* than encompasses the entire universe. Saint Anselm had spoken those words a long time ago. According to the saint, God was greater than anything man could imagine; therefore, man did not imagine Him, and He must exist. God or *Power,* science could not cope with it. That's not a criticism of God or of science any more than saying a hammer can't saw wood is a criticism of a hammer. Science studies natural law, things that repeat in the same way over and over. It can't cast a lariat over anything that moves and thinks on its own.

Discovering that science cannot answer all questions is not much consolation when you're alone with your thoughts in the dark of a ship's hold passing time slowly, wishing you were back with someone you loved, while a non-corporeal duty pulled in another direction. It was agony. Had the Trumpets of Truth won the Battle of Glorieta Pass? It seemed that way, but Dan couldn't be sure. Uncertainty was agony, but certainty would be worse. If you were certain of the existence of God, He might as well start giving orders. If you were certain, the choice would be between obeying and the certainty of death if you did not, not much of a choice. The only way there can be real freewill was if you're not certain.

The ship's horn began to hoot repeatedly. Dan thought they must be in some danger and ran up the ladder to the hurricane deck, looking up at the pilothouse for some sign. What he saw was Roque, ship's wheel in hand, happily pulling the cord for the horn. The captain and pilot were laughing, the three of them having a grand time. Now, Roque would have a tale for Rojo. The captain was good to Roque.

That night at dinner as they rounded Rabbit Island, John-Paul asked them, "What have you got in the hold?"

"Captain," Dan replied, "I know you are taking a great risk, but I'd rather not tell you. For one thing, I think you're safer if you don't know. For another, everything on a ship is overheard."

"You know I'm sworn to keep your secrets," John-Paul said.

"I know, Captain," Dan said. "Cowans and eavesdroppers are everywhere, even on your ship. Because of the risk you take, I really can't refuse you, but I think it would be better if I did not tell you."

"Tell me, please," he said, smiling. "I want to share your risk. Burdens are the lighter for sharing. And you, sir, carry some heavy ones."

Dan looked to Roque who nodded. "Put plainly, Captain, you're carrying the wealth of the Pharaohs, given by the Egyptians to the Children of Israel as they left the land of captivity and the missing treasures of King Solomon."

"Don't mock me, boy," the captain growled low in his throat. The anger of a ship's captain is no casual thing to be lightly brushed aside.

Dan grew angry, too. "Do not scoff at me, sir," he replied. "You asked, and I have told you on the Square."

Since Dan offered his description of the cargo as Masonic truth, the captain's eyes grew large; he was taken visibly aback. "You can't be serious."

Dan said nothing.

He looked at Dan with one eye, eyebrow cocked, appraising. "So you've a few mummies and a Torah scroll and such. How will this help the war effort?"

It was Roque's turn to flare. "We have what Danito said we have."

"How could such things come to be in New Mexico?" asked John-Paul skeptically.

"That," Dan said, "is a very long story. Too long to tell in one evening where we might be overheard. I can tell you that they've been where we found them since they went missing centuries ago. Columbus was a late comer to the New World."

Relations were never quite so warm again, though the captain remained completely proper and helpful. For a time, he wasn't comfortable with them, uncertain whether or not they were liars and abusive of his goodwill, unable to believe what he had been told. Dan reflected that the captain's disbelief did not bode well for what they faced in Washington. John-Paul was a good Mason, and as time passed they were able, at high risk, to tell him the rest of the story.

Masons had helped Dan and Roque at every turn on their journey. Though Dan had to remember that Albert Pike and the Texas Rangers were also Masons, and Joseph Smith had been one for a time. Descending again to the dark hold and alone with his thoughts, Dan mused about the Freemasons. They had been present at the founding of the nation, birthed it, you might say. More than a third of the signers of the Declaration of Independence were known Freemasons.

The same was the case with the Constitution. Washington, Jefferson, Madison, Hamilton, Von Stueben, Lafayette, and Franklin were all Masons. They were sworn to treat each other as brothers with trust and respect. Before becoming Masons, they had to meet numerous qualifications as to character and trustworthiness. All believed in God, and Protestants, Catholic, and Jews were all welcome. Differences in theology were set aside in the Lodge, but faith in God was not.

Kit Carson was a Mason. Many said he did not believe in God because he converted to Catholicism and then turned his back on it over the abuses of a certain priest. He never stopped praying as an Indian does, welcoming the dawn with a pinch of dust and acknowledging the four directions.

Masons had birthed the nation, and now they were assisting Roque and Dan on their journey. He pondered the thought that Masons were being used by God. Of course, they were, for He uses all things.

In the cool evening before moonrise, Dan left the treasure alone for a few moments, confident that it would go nowhere as long as the boat was moving. Roque was at the wheel closely watched by the pilot. A cry came from far below and ahead, followed by a bump and loud cursing. Something bounced along the side and then the boat lifted to one side slightly.

The pilot removed his pipe from his mouth. "Be under the starboard wheel in a moment." The wheel thumped as it walked across something in the dark. "Floaters. Small craft that floats down the river. They're supposed to show a light, but they take it below to light their evening fun."

Roque was aghast. "Did I kill them?"

The pilot nodded. "Most like. There was nothing you could have done. If I'd been on the wheel, it would have been the same. Captain, do we back engines and look for survivors?"

"We should be on the lookout for pirates," said Captain Perry. "In these times we can't go back and search for bodies. I doubt any survived."

"I saw a pirate once," said Roque brightening. "He was up at the masthead of his ship."

"You've been down to New Orleans, then?" asked the captain.

"No," said Roque. "The pirate was in New Mexico."

"Hadn't heard you had any rivers big enough," replied the captain looking skeptical.

"Captain," Dan interjected, "have you heard of Captain Wind-Wagon Thomas?"

"I've met him," the captain said. "Crazy ideas, that one. Head full of nonsense. He was going to sail a wind schooner across the prairie sea."

"He did," said Roque with a finality that didn't brook questions. "I met him in New Mexico after his pirate ship wrecked on the rocks in a big thunderstorm."

"Leastways, he weren't no pirate!" exclaimed John-Paul Perry. "Pirates got row boats, and they come out in their dozens to take your ship. Just overwhelm the crew. Sometimes they set up snags to slow you. Now and then, they've got a steam launch, but mostly rowboats."

"Don't they need big boats with cannons?" asked a puzzled Roque. These small craft, river pirates were different from the stories he'd heard about that *Diablo* Francisco Draco and others like him who sailed the Spanish Main. They had big ships and plenty of cannon. Dan thought Roque expected to see a huge stern-wheel riverboat with at least two decks bristling with cannon and plenty of pirates with eye-patches, hooks for hands, peg legs, cutlasses, and parrots.

"Cannon!" Captain Perry expostulated. "Cannon! Why, they'd blow a ship all apart and start fires, burn up the cargo, and sink the ship. What would be the point of that? Pirates want to capture your cargo and your ship. They'd make a dangerous lad like you, Roque, walk the plank. Tie your hands together and over the side you'd go!" The captain's chest heaved, and he made a strange creaking noise that was probably a laugh. The pilot sniggered behind his hand.

The river was wide, but the channel was narrow and often took them close to shore. The boat chugged on, trailing smoke that could be seen for miles. The smell of burning wood was with them constantly, along with the stench of rotting river bottom churned up by the paddles. The humming, beating rhythm of the big engine and the splashing of the paddlewheels continued day and night. The decks were full of cargo, most of it military. People moved in and out between the cargo: the platoon of soldiers accompanying them as escort, wounded soldiers being shipped home and a few wartime business travelers.

The journey was stressful, lacking the comfort that was the peacetime standard. This trip had no gamblers and no entertainment. All available space was packed with cargo. Stops were more frequent than Dan would have liked, but they had to take on wood and water. When they stopped, there was bustle and hurry, but before each stop there was tension. They never knew who would be there to greet them. At each river port, they heard fresh stories of phantom invading armies, raiders, and pirates, but they had to stop. They needed wood and water.

Wood landings were hurried affairs for everyone. Water was piped aboard, but wood had to be carried. In peacetime, paying passengers got a better rate if they agreed to carry wood. In wartime, everyone worked except the captain who shouted instructions from above like the voice of God. They ran up and down the plank and dock fetching heavy armloads of cordwood. At landings, they'd occasionally catch glimpses of their cavalry escort, which was supposed to arrive ahead of the boat to make sure the landing was safe and then spread out as pickets.

"Stephen Long tried using river water in the boilers back around 1820," Captain Perry told Dan. "Tore his engines apart."

Roque continued to be fascinated by pirates, and the captain continued to worry about them.

Thinking perhaps to keep Dan company, Captain Perry descended to his day cabin. "In 1856, the border ruffians had cannons on the shore. They'd stop every ship and search it for Sharpe's rifles and Northern men. Had no choice but to stop back then. They'd sink you. Didn't care about your cargo. But now they want the cargo. Fortunately, cannons are heavy, hard to move if they're being pursued."

"So, how would pirates take a riverboat?" Dan asked.

"Rowboats, lots of rowboats," replied the captain, "like I told you before. But usually we can outrun them. The rowboats can't keep up with steam, so they have to have some trick, something to get us to slow. They run snags out in the river sometimes or time their attack to catch us at some bend of the river. If we were headed upriver, they could row out into the current ahead of us and let the river bring them alongside. But we're headed downriver, so we don't have to worry about that. They would have to come alongside, throw grappling hooks over the railing, and pull themselves in."

That night Roque and Dan stood at the forward end of the Texas deck, the upper deck below the pilothouse, watching the river with First Sergeant Drake Hawkey. The moon was full, but the sky was overcast as they smoked their pipes, sang bits of song, and recited stories and poems. Hawkey, their military escort and another Freemason, was a frontiersman and a man who could be trusted. He'd scouted on the plains for the Army before the war.

It being that sort of night, Dan recited for their benefit:

"The wind was a torrent of darkness among the gusty trees,

The moon was a ghostly galleon tossed upon cloudy seas…"

A voice rang out from the darkness above them. "There! Away to starboard. Do you see them?" The ship was rounding the bends near Epperson Island. "Now larboard as we come round!"

The pilot's cry was followed by Captain Perry's command. "Trelawney, Roque, Sergeant Hawkey, get up here quick!" The trio charged up the ladder to the pilothouse.

The captain pointed, but Dan and Roque saw nothing until the full moon obliged them by sending a spear of light through the clouds. In that moment, Dan saw about two miles off, a fleet of small sailboats beating out into the river. The boats were crowded with men, and Dan realized badly overloaded.

Captain Perry pointed. "They plan to sail out so that we'll be caught in the middle of them as we come down the chute."

Dan shook his head. "What a mess. I wonder if there are any sailors among them."

"Nary a one," said Captain Perry. "They've given us the weather gage."

Roque and Sergeant Hawkey looked confused, so Dan explained, "They're beating up wind at us. It's slow. They'll have to turn often to take the wind from a new direction. That will be a clumsy maneuver with that many boats getting in each other's way. They should have waited and come at us on the wind, timing things to reach us just as we were passing with the wind at their backs."

The captain looked surprised that a boy from New Mexico would know these things. Dan had never had occasion to tell him he'd been raised in Greenport, Out

East, amongst sailors, blue water fishermen, and whalers from Sag Harbor across the bay.

The moon momentarily cast a beam like a searchlight.

"Look at them, Captain," Dan called, excited, "as they try to gybe. They're all over the place. The wind has half of them locked in irons."

"The winds are crazy down here below the river terrace," replied the riverboat man. "They go every which way and change suddenly. It's not all their fault, but there isn't a sailor in the bunch."

"I've got an idea, captain," Dan said.

In the little time they had, Dan, Roque, crew, and soldiers pushed cargo, enough to conceal six parties of armed men, out to the railing. Each was supplied with axes to cut boarding lines.

"Load with buck and ball," Dan told Sergeant Hawkey. "Keep muskets primed. We'll fix bayonets in the final moments. Tell your men to fire right into their faces and close their eyes before they fire to save their night vision."

Roque and Dan ran forward, taking both of the Hawken rifles each of them owned as well as pistols, tomahawks, and knives.

"Roque," Dan said, "we want to fire at the lead boats just as they start to come about and kill the coxswain. Do you understand?"

"Yes," he nodded, "'come about' means change direction, but what's a coxswain?"

"The man at the tiller," Dan replied hastily.

"What's a tiller?" Roque asked.

"In the back of the boat," Dan said, "the thing that steers the boat and the guy that holds it."

"Like this?" he grinned kneeling and promptly shot the man at the tiller of the lead boat. The range was at least 200 yards. The moon provided light. The dead man's boat turned suddenly, beam on to the wind, and the boat following collided with it. Both sank. Two boats behind lost way, and the men in the water swamped them trying to climb aboard.

"Close enough," Dan replied, knelt, and fired at the man in the stern of the next boat while Roque reloaded. "Let's keep them all to starboard, if we can," Dan suggested, "and don't let any get over to larboard. We'll only have one side to defend."

Roque nodded, and as the moon sent its light down for a moment, he shot another helmsman. The distance between the rowboats and the riverboat was closing fast, and reloading took time. They could only fire when the moon shone through the clouds. Soon they'd be only a pistol shot away.

The pirate enemy returned fire, but they were using muskets in crowded boats. Blinded by the flash of their own muzzles, they jostled each other and rocked the boat. Men could be seen fighting in the small craft, presumably over powder burns and ringing ears inflicted on each other by accident and excitement. Another over-crowded boat went down.

"I think," said Roque, "when you are a pirate, it is good to have many men in the boat, but not too many." He grinned and fired at a boat only 50 yards away.

Time sped up. They fired the last charge from each of their rifles as grappling hooks came over the rail. From behind cover, one member of each of the sergeant's teams rose, pointed into the faces of the men in the boats, closed his eyes, and fired. The flash killed and wounded several and blinded them all for a moment. The first man ducked back under cover to reload as the second rose and cut the line to the grappling hook. Boats drifted away. By the time they figured out what had happened, it was usually too late to catch up to the riverboat. At least one capsized in the confusion. Others found themselves bumping down the side before the great wheel walked over them.

Dan heard Sergeant Hawkey's voice calling his men over to the starboard side. None of the pirates had made it to larboard. Things grew tense and confused as more boats hooked on. Men started to cross over the railing from the boats. Beating back the boarders was work for Roque and Dan with 'hawk and Colt. Ears rang with the roar of muskets and the screams of men. Eyes were open when weapons fired, it couldn't be helped, and vision filled with stars and lights. Smoke hung over the decks despite the wind.

For Dan, the world closed down to the space around him and the things he was in contact with. He swung, fired, connected, stabbed, pushed, tripped, hit, fired, and swung again. Pain across the ribs. A blow to the stomach. A face appeared and disappeared again in flame and blood. Two pistols, twelve shots soon gone. Then the fight continued with 'hawk and Bowie. A neck cut. Parry. A thrust under ribs. A flash followed by blow and burning pain along Dan's temple. 'Hawk descending on a neck, then on an arm. A man was thrown back onto his comrades climbing from a boat, and another was shouldered aside and overboard. Flashes of memory, northing clear or connected, heart pounding, chest heaving, vision closing to a tunnel, aware of every threat around him. Dan's ears rang, his vision nearly failed, but he continued to fight not knowing if his side was winning or losing. Sound grew less.

Strong hands grabbed him. He challenged with Bowie, raising his 'hawk as he did. The hands shook him. "Easy there. It's me," said Sergeant Hawkey. "Easy!"

Dan's vision began to clear. He saw Hawkey's face and then saw Roque with someone's ear stuck in his teeth. Roque was working with his knife to free his "trophy." The fight was over. Pirates lay dead at their feet.

"We won," said Hawkey and then called out more loudly to his men, "Sound off when I call your name." He called his men's names one by one. Two didn't answer, and two more sounded as if they were in pain.

Dan, Roque, and others tended to the soldiers first. One was hurt so badly they didn't think he'd make it through the night. One of the privates lay on the deck with a bullet hole in his forehead. The other private who didn't answer roll call was never found. All of the soldiers, Dan, and Roque had cuts and burns. They tossed the pirates, who were undoubtedly Confederate irregular raiders, overboard, but found none alive on the steamboat. Those who survived must have left with the boats.

Ascending to the pilothouse, Dan was greeted by Captain Perry, shotgun in hand; he'd been assisting from above.

"Dandiest thing I ever saw!" he exulted. "I counted more than 20 boats! And each had 10 or more men! And you handful defeated them! I've never seen nothing like it!"

"It's our cargo, Captain," Dan said quietly. "It's our cargo done it like I told you. God was on our side. We couldn't lose."

"What if...?"

"What if we weren't doing what He wanted?" Dan finished for him. "We'd have lost. The Israelites proved that often enough. Our Apache friend Rojo says that *Power* is with you as long as your actions are in accord with the nature of *Power*. That seems to sum up what *Power* is like pretty well."

"Still," he said, "that was the finest battle I ever did see!"

"Best not to talk about it," Dan said. "It would raise questions in the wrong quarters. As it is, I can't discount that those in the South who suspect our mission might have sent those raiders. I think it's best not to be too proud, either. The battle was in God's hands."

They sailed with Captain Perry all the way down the Missouri to St. Louis and then south on the Mississippi to Cairo, Illinois, where the Ohio pours into the big river. Cairo bustled with military activity. It was near the mouths of rivers like the Tennessee that led deep into the Confederacy. Captain Perry introduced them to another Mason, captain of a paddle-wheeler that plied the Ohio. He took them as far as Pittsburg where yet another brother was a rail conductor on the Baltimore and Ohio Railway. Dan and Roque got the private car they needed, designed for cargo not for comfort, and rode with their goods all the way to Washington, D.C., though not without misadventure.

The B&O, as the Baltimore and Ohio was known, ran along the edge of the Confederacy. It was raided more times than anyone could count. When Dan and Roque had put ashore in Cairo, Dan had picked up a newspaper that talked about the perils of the B&O. General Sheridan had given up on protecting it. They quoted him as saying, "There is no interest suffering here except the Baltimore and Ohio Railroad, and I will not divide my forces to protect it." Apparently, General Sheridan didn't think supplies coming into Washington from the west were important. Brigadier General John D. Imboden, CSA, and the 62nd Virginia Mounted Infantry, otherwise known as the 1st Partisan Rangers, had been on the loose burning trains and tearing up tracks all through the previous month, May 1863. Somewhere out there, too, was the Gray Ghost, Colonel John Mosby, and his raiders.

The trip went smoothly enough though being confined in a box car was no fun. Roque leapt out at stations as they passed through locating vendors who sold prepared food. They were lucky, Dan thought, that neither of them got seriously ill. Soon they were in the western part of Virginia that would shortly become a separated state, West Virginia. The people favored the Union, but the land was mountainous and favored the operation of partisan raiders. The road crossed back and forth over the Potomac, here not very wide, between Virginia and Maryland.

On the night they neared Harper's Ferry, Dan sitting perched on one of their crates, was thrown violently toward the front of the train, landing in a heap. Roque too had to pick himself up. Brakes squealed and shrieked, and the motion of the train ceased. The whistle screamed in the night. Roque threw open the door and peered ahead.

"The train has stopped for a big bonfire on the tracks," he said. "Is this some local celebration?"

"Yeah," Dan replied. "The Confederates call it Raiding the B&O! Close the door and help me open this crate."

They could hear riders in the night and men calling military commands in Southern accents. Boxcar doors slid open, one after the other. And then theirs opened and Dan and Roque stood with their rifles pointed at a man in a Confederate colonel's uniform. Dan was sure it was Mosby himself, and he was surrounded by a dozen armed men. Hammers clicked back to full cock. The pair was out-numbered and couldn't possibly survive.

"Colonel Mosby," Dan said politely, "Roque and I have got you covered. If anyone makes a fool move, we'll die, I'm sure, but I'm equally sure you'll precede us on the road to Hell."

Mosby held up a gloved hand above a gilt decorated sleeve, ordering his men to remain calm.

"Colonel," Dan continued, "there's no reason for fuss. We're taking good Rio Grande blankets to the hospitals in Washington for the wounded. I'm sure you folks have got need of blankets. You're welcome to some."

With that Dan grabbed the top five from the open crate and tossed them to the raider's men. A bugle sounded not far away, and a rider galloped up.

"Colonel Mosby, suh," said the rider, "it's them damn Yankees of the Railroad Brigade. We're too close to Harper's Ferry! We got to get out of here quick!"

The colonel nodded and ordered his men. "Mount up. Take what we've collected and let's get out of here." He turned to Dan and grinned. "Thanks for the blankets." And with those words, they rode off into the dark.

The raid was over. Union cavalry rode up and made short work of clearing the tracks. The train was soon underway again.

Roque turned to Dan. "That was lucky!"

"It wasn't luck," his friend replied. "Sebriana planned for something like this when she packed all those blankets on top in each crate." Dan felt immensely sad at having lost her and couldn't speak anymore. For a change, Roque, too, was subdued.

Chapter 19

In the Nick of Time

Exodus 25:

[31]"You shall also make a lampstand of pure gold; the lampstand shall be of hammered work. Its shaft, its branches, its bowls, its ornamental knobs, and flowers shall be of one piece. [32] And six branches shall come out of its sides: three branches of the lampstand out of one side, and three branches of the lampstand out of the other side. [33] Three bowls shall be made like almond blossoms on one branch, with an ornamental knob and a flower, and three bowls made like almond blossoms on the other branch, with an ornamental knob and a flower—and so for the six branches that come out of the lampstand. [34] On the lampstand itself four bowls shall be made like almond blossoms, each with its ornamental knob and flower. [35]And there shall be a knob under the first two branches of the same, a knob under the second two branches of the same, and a knob under the third two branches of the same, according to the six branches that extend from the lampstand. [36] Their knobs and their branches shall be of one piece; all of it shall be one hammered

piece of pure gold. [37] You shall make seven lamps for it, and they shall arrange its lamps so that they give light in front of it.

Dan and Roque arrived in Washington the next morning. The city bustled with activity; however, something was up in Virginia, which lay just across the Potomac. The enemy was moving troops and massing supplies. Everyone talked of an attempt to take the capitol. The city was ringed with forts that bristled with big guns and mortars and thronged with troops to defend them. This wasn't 1861. Washington was prepared, but still the Confederates were much too close, and they were preparing for something. Soldiers of all ranks crowded the streets doing the things soldiers did to pass the time: singing, drinking, gambling, and pursuing the numerous female camp followers.

Their B&O conductor introduced them to another Masonic brother, a businessman who worked in the city. He found them an empty warehouse that could be adequately secured. Finding an empty warehouse was a marvel in itself in a city bursting at the seams.

"Folks packed up and left two days ago," said Mr. Wigglesworth, their Masonic brother. "They were afraid of an invasion. I guess the only thing that kept them here this long was that they were more afraid of the Baltimore rabble than the Army of Northern Virginia."

Dan felt that a gift as important as the one he and Roque were delivering needed to go directly to President Lincoln. They considered ways to approach him, but in June of 1863, the war was in full fury, and the president was a busy man. They found themselves stuck guarding their warehouse from the inside, until one day a sergeant and several men appeared at their door to take up posts guarding the warehouse for them.

Talking to the sergeant, Dan learned that he was with a volunteer unit from Rhode Island under command of a colonel who had previously served as a lieutenant with the 1st Dragoons in New Mexico. The unit was assigned to the defense of Washington. Both the sergeant and his colonel were Freemasons, and a letter from Major Lewis to his friend the colonel had followed them. In the end, they had security that didn't look at all out of the way in this city. They enjoyed the benefits of secure obscurity, but they were still very much restricted in their movements. In a city at war, outsiders who traveled much to government buildings were apt to be taken as spies.

Dan and Roque had been introduced to their landlord as Masons, and they asked when the Lodge met. "You've just missed the regular meeting. Lodge doesn't meet again until July 7," he said.

Dan was disappointed. "We'd hoped to meet some of the brothers. It's a shame to wait so long."

The landlord scratched his head. "There's a 2nd Degree scheduled for the last week of the month. I could introduce you to some of the brothers then. Brother Edwin M. Stanton, Secretary of War, himself will guide the candidates up the Stairs."

Dan knew that the 2nd Degree was a ceremonial to raise junior brothers in standing, making them Fellowcrafts. The 3rd Degree was the most exciting, full of action, requiring many actors. The blindfolded candidate plays an important, if unwitting, part. The 2nd is the most intellectual and was Dan's favorite.

"There always seems to be a shortage of actors for the degrees. Would you be able to help?" their landlord asked.

"Between us," Dan said indicating him and Roque,

"we know most of the parts." Knowing all the parts wasn't exactly true. Dan knew many, and Roque knew a few including some Dan didn't know. No one, Dan knew, was more welcome in Lodge than a Traveling Man coming from West to East who knows several of the parts. A Mason could immediately find people he could trust in a strange city. He never had to be a stranger in a strange land for long.

The days of waiting were tense. J.E.B. Stuart and his cavalry were on the move north of the Potomac. Union cavalry crossed the Rappahannock to find out what General Lee and the Army of Northern Virginia were planning. They found the Army gone and headed north. The days of their waiting were long in a town too hot, too humid, too worried about the Rebels, and too full of soldiers. They had heard a lot about a battle at a place called Chancellorsville in May. The Union hadn't done well, and it was rumored that Mr. Lincoln was very unhappy with General Hooker.

Finally, the day of the 2nd Degree arrived.

The Second Degree introduces the Entered Apprentice to the arts and sciences. Brother Stanton symbolically escorted the candidate through King Solomon's Temple. It always reminded Dan of the Founders of the Nation and their intellectual attainments. Many of them had experienced this same ritual long ago.

All too soon the ceremony was over, and the Worshipful Master was asking the brothers, "How should Masons meet?"

"On the Level," came the reply.

"And part upon the Square," the Master finished.

That was Roque and Dan's cue to approach Mr. Stanton.

"Sir," Dan said, "I know you're a busy man. If you

could just take a moment for a pair of brother Masons."

Secretary Stanton's face clouded, and his brows knit together. They called him gimlet eyed, and indeed, Dan, who had stared General Carlton full in the face, found it hard to hold his gaze. Those cold hard orbs said, "No nonsense and be quick about it." He looked tired just then, but his body throbbed with energy. That, too, was his reputation, the hardest of hard workers. He was pestered by a great many office seekers and people with something to sell as well as cranks with big ideas on how to win the war. "We have letters of introduction from Kit Carson, General Canby, and General Carlton." Producing the introductory letters didn't help much.

Roque blurted, "We don't want anything. We have something to give you."

Somewhat mollified, Stanton took the letters from Dan's hand, read them, and then said, "Sounds like these fellows think a lot of you. So what do you want of me?"

"Come to our warehouse tomorrow," Dan said. "It will only take a few minutes." Dan didn't think it wise to mention that he and Roque wanted an appointment with the President.

Mr. Stanton, Secretary of War, came to their depot first thing next morning. It only took a few minutes to show him what they had. He was surprised to see that the two young men already had a military guard posted. The friends opened their crates and showed him everything.

"You say you found this," he stated, "and you want to give this to the government?"

"That's right!" Roque and Dan chimed.

"You know this solves a huge problem," the Secretary of War said. "High tariffs on imports had been paid before the war, mostly by Southern cotton producers. That provided most of the revenue to run the government.

When the South left the Union, we lost that income and we've had a devil of a time replacing it. We need more money than ever now to run the war. You can't begin to imagine how many men are under arms and how much food and supplies cost. President Jackson destroyed the Bank of the United States, making it difficult to expand the money supply and float loans. Your gift, the gold and silver alone, will help immensely.

"So what do you want?" he asked suspiciously.

Dan stood up straight and squared his shoulders. "To meet with the President for a few moments."

"Those things there are the most important," said Roque pointing to the Arc, the Table, the Trumpets of Truth, and the Menorah.

"Yes, of course," said Secretary Stanton skeptically. By weight of precious metal and quality of handicraft, they were the least valuable items in the room.

Dan and Roque took turns telling him their story, but there was no point in trying to explain their perils or the victory at Glorieta. He already had heroes enough to explain that battle. He didn't want to hear what a reluctant hero Chivington had been. But Stanton would get them an appointment so they could tell their tale to the President and hope he'd listen.

"Five minutes, maybe," said the Secretary. "He'll want to thank you for the gold."

Dan nodded. "We have to get him to listen. I don't want our country becoming another Philistine princedom in decline because we held God's treasures but not His pleasure."

"By the way," said Secretary Stanton, "you were lucky to get through. The Army of Northern Virginia has crossed the Potomac into Maryland and Pennsylvania. Washington is threatened. Harper's Ferry and the B&O

are in Confederate hands."

Dan and Roque accompanied by Secretary Stanton met with President Lincoln that same day and explained to him what they had and wanted him to have. He caught on quickly. Later, Dan was at a loss to describe the interview any more fully than by saying it was over much too quickly.

He said to Roque. "You'd think I'd remember every detail."

"Sí. I was so nervous I can't remember much either."

Dan frowned. "I remember that he said we must go to a place in Pennsylvania and see his new commander, General Meade. The President thinks Meade lacks confidence since he has just taken command."

Roque and Dan were so overwhelmed by the pomp and grandeur of meeting the president that little remained in memory beyond a sense that something wonderful had occurred. It was bright and warm and good, made up entirely of emotion with the details erased by the power of entering the great, white house and talking to the tall man from Illinois. Afterward, time went quickly. They were soon provided horses and pack mules.

Riding northwest out of Washington toward a Pennsylvania town named Gettysburg, Roque and Dan trailed the pack mules. The roads were choked with soldiers and wagons headed in the same direction. They often by-passed blocked roads by detouring through woods and open fields. They carried letters from Lincoln and Stanton.

"I don't think Mr. Lincoln believed us," said Roque.

"I don't know," Dan replied. "He asked us to carry the Menorah to his general, this new one, George Meade."

Meade had just taken command of the Army. He hadn't had time to train his men, but fortunately, prior combat had done that for him. General Lee and the Army of Northern Virginia were well trained, and legendary in their skill in battle. Lee's army was undefeated and seemed undefeatable. Robert Lee knew his subordinates and what he could expect from them; Meade did not, nor did the subordinates know and trust him.

Dan and Roque could hear the sounds of battle ahead. The din of armies challenging each other came from north and south but were greater near a prominent, wooded hill in the south.

"Sounds like battle," said Roque. "That hilltop must be where we'll find General Meade. That's where I'd be, up high where I could see and direct my whole army."

They rode to the sound of the guns, heading toward the large wooded hill on the south. Men in blue uniform were moving up the hill in droves. As Dan and Roque rode they passed some mounted officers and asked them for the officer in charge. The officers pointed up the hill.

"Little Round Top," said a lieutenant. "They call it Little Round Top."

As Dan and Roque went up, they came to see the battlefield laid out like the neck of a fiddle. The big wooded hill rising about 300 feet was the box of the fiddle. The neck, a very long neck, was a low ridge stretching north toward the town of Gettysburg and curving to end in a hill about 100 feet high, called Culp's. There was fighting up there. Green fields stretched westward for a mile to a low wooded ridge.

"Confederate cannon there," said Dan pointing. The battle in the other direction was hidden from them by Little Round Top.

"How to you know they're Confederate?" asked Roque. "They seem to be almost behind most of the Union soldiers."

"See the flags?" replied Dan.

"Oh."

When they arrived near the top of hill, they could see that the front of Little Round Top was a steep, rocky, open field ending below in woods and large boulders.

A gap toothed soldier seeing where they were looking grinned at them. "We calls that Devil's Den. We shoots right down into it, and the Rebs go straight to hell." He made a croaking noise that might have been laughter and went back to shooting Rebs.

Far below, the Confederates were trying to climb the face of Round Top.

"They're brave enough," said a soldier, "and determined."

"See their colors?" said a sergeant. "They're Hood's boys outa Texas."

Officers under a New York banner were talking when the two friends approached still leading their pack animals. "Is that ammunition?" they asked. Dan shook his head, and they went on with their conversation.

"To think," said one, "when the day started there were no Union troops on Little Round Top. The whole flank was open. Imagine what Hood could have done if he could have gotten his corps up here with cannon."

Dan gathered that the Union corps on the left had moved forward to confront the Rebels in a peach orchard north of Devil's Den. The move left the Rebels in Devil's Den behind the Union flank, and they moved to take Round Top and roll up the entire Union line. If they'd gotten men and cannon up on top, they would have enfiladed the entire Army of the Potomac.

An officer spoke. "That Maine regiment with all the troublemakers was sent here to get them out of the way. And they held, by God, they held."

"And now we got us one heck of a fight," his companion replied. "We were sent just in time."

"Danito," Roque said, "I can't believe these Rebels are trying to attack up this steep slope. How can they hope to succeed?"

"I don't know," Dan replied, "but there are men falling all around us from fire coming from those boulders."

The boulders, Devil's Den, were easily 300 yards away. The new Union and Confederate rifled muskets were taking a heavy toll on both sides.

"No one can advance against this kind of fire," said Roque flatly.

Roque, an experienced fighter, saw in minutes something the generals would need years to learn: men could not advance against accurate, long range fire. Charging muskets, barely accurate at 100 yards, with fixed bayonets was one thing. Covering 300 or 400 yards under accurate fire was impossible.

"Danito, look!" said Roque waving his arms to take in the whole battlefield four miles from end to end and a mile deep. "*Dios mio*, I have never imagined so many men."

Blue, gray, and butternut uniforms in their regimental files were set out below like so many toy soldiers. Below them were hundreds of regiments each of 1,000 men. Regiments were grouped into brigades and brigades into divisions that made up corps. There were a dozen corps on each side, 100,000 blue uniforms and 80,000 gray and butternut. Close to 200,000 men were fighting. New Mexico was said to have a population of 40,000, but they were spread across hundreds of miles between Taos and Fort Craig.

There was order and discipline in the movement of the

formations despite the attempts of enemy artillery to disrupt the lines.

"*Dios mio!*" shuddered Roque. "The whole world is here."

"Let's get back into the trees," Dan yelled over the din of battle. Men were falling around them, and Minié balls whizzed by making sounds like angry bees.

Off to their left, a unit with colors showing them to be the 20th Maine was having a hard go of it in heavy woods. The slope wasn't as steep on their ground, and the trees allowed the enemy to get in close. Dan saw the colors of an Alabama unit approach and fall back and then return edging around the 20th Maine's left flank in the forest. The 20th was the last unit on the Union's left, the left flank of the entire army. The colonel skillfully conducted a maneuver called "refusing the flank," which was to say he moved some of his companies back to his left forming his line like a fishhook. No matter how far the enemy went around his flank, they wouldn't find his rear; his men would always be facing them.

A soldier from the Maine unit ran up to the brigade commander standing with his aides in front of Dan and Roque directing his battle. "Sir," cried the soldier, "20th Maine needs cahtridges. We needs 'em bad."

It'd been a long time since Dan had heard such a distinctly New England voice. It was clear even over the din of battle. *The 20th Mine needed cahtridges.*

The officer looked at him. "I'm sorry. We haven't got any to spare. We're hard pressed here as well. I've sent a rider to the munitions park to see if we can have some brought up. They say the wagons can't make it up the hill. They're loading mules."

The Colonel looked hard into the man's eyes and continued. "Tell Colonel Chamberlain to hang on just a bit longer. He's doing a fine job."

The firing on the left picked up again. The soldier ran back to join his unit. The 20th was being pressed hard again.

Another runner arrived from the Maine unit to speak to the commander. "Sir, Colonel Chamberlain begs to report that the 20th Maine is flat out of cahtridges. If them Alabamans comes again, we've nothin' for it but to throw rocks at them."

The man's eyes were large with anger and frustration. His face set, he was bold to address the commanding general with such rage. Before the general could answer, they heard Colonel Chamberlain's clear voice call out, "Fix...bayonets! Charge!"

The fishhook end of the refused line swung around first driving the Alabamans before it until it was back in line with the regiment. Then the entire 20th Maine, without firing a shot, charged off down the hill killing and capturing Rebels at the point of their bayonets.

"Danito!" yelled Roque. "I have never imagined such a sight. So beautiful. So gallant. So bold! They are heroes all. There will be legends, songs, and poems."

And so there were. Roque later composed some of them himself during his journey home. Dan learned what a real commander does when he's out of ammunition and still faces the enemy. He yells, "Fix ... bayonets! Charge!"

The commanding general overheard Roque. "It's quite a thing for a school teacher," he said.

"Excuse me, sir," Dan said. "I don't understand."

"A school teacher," the commander replied. "Until a year ago, Colonel Chamberlain was a school teacher. By God, he's a hell of a fighter! And half the men in his under strength unit are captured deserters."

"Sir," Dan said, "I think you must be General Meade, and I have something for you." The sounds of battle were dying away.

"Me?" he said. "Goodness no; I only command this brigade. Meade's headquarters is in that white farmhouse about halfway between here at Culp's Hill." He pointed to his right, the north up the long ridge.

Dan and Roque rode to the farmhouse though not without interference and questioning by numerous officers and sentries. Fortunately, they had been provided with orders signed at the highest level.

"Lincoln?" said one sergeant who stopped them. "President Lincoln? Sure you got a letter from him. Can't you Rebs do no better'n thet? How come youse dressed like a Reb?"

Dan remained calm. "Sergeant, just take us to your officer, and he can read the letter and decide what to do with us."

The officer was skeptical. "I can't let you go."

"You'd best not hold us," said Dan. Instead, they found themselves under armed escort.

Headquarters was neat enough, surrounded by a whitewashed picket fence, though small and standing what seemed completely alone. Nearby farms were hidden by trees and the shoulder of the hill. Sentries stood out front. Dan and Roque gained admittance.

"General Meade," Dan began, "we have these instructions from President Lincoln." The general read them.

"It says you've brought me a lamp," said the general puzzled.

Roque and Dan unwrapped the Menorah and setting it on a table began to fill it with oil and light its branches against the evening dark.

As they worked Dan spoke, "General, Mr. Lincoln wanted you to have this to light your planning and deliberations. All he asks, he stressed that he did not want to interfere, is that you use it and return it when the battle is over."

The general looked at Dan quizzically. "That's all."

"That's all, sir," Dan replied.

"It looks familiar," he said. "I think I've read about something like this somewhere." He scratched his head. Dan said nothing. "Well, stick around, both of you. Keep Mr. Lincoln's candelabra lit. Have some dinner with me and watch how we plan the morrow."

After dinner, the senior commanders arrived. Dan was surprised that he recognized some of them. They'd served in the dragoons in New Mexico.

General Meade started with a strange announcement.

"Gentlemen," he said, "over the past two days we've taken a beating. We've been beaten back to this ridge and pummeled on both flanks. Our men are tired and have been sorely tried. Shall we stand here and fight again or fall back closer to Washington and try to find better ground? What do you want to do?"

Dan thought asking for his subordinates opinions and support seemed the route of a new and uncertain commander. No officer asked his subordinates what to do. A commander gave firm orders, challenging anyone to disobey him. Commanders led by the force of their iron will. They never showed uncertainty and asking his subordinates their opinion seemed to express uncertainty.

General George Meade had been in command for less than a week. He hadn't trained his army to follow his commands. There hadn't been time. He barely knew his senior commanders. It was a bad situation and showing weakness would make it a lot worse.

One after another, his senior commanders stood up and said they were fighting mad and wanted to finish off General Lee and the Army of Northern Virginia tomorrow on the ground on which they stood. Not one wanted to yield an inch. Every one of them was the soul of confidence certain that he could whip the whole Rebel army.

"Good," said General Meade with supreme confidence, "then we shall prepare to receive Robert Lee right here."

The generals had entered uncertain of their new commander and departed with confidence in him committed by their own words to supporting his plan.

"Stick around and see the show," said General Meade.

"Haven't got much choice," Roque said. "We're headed back west, and General Robert Lee is in the way. We'll have to wait until you chase him off."

The next day went slowly. Dan could see the Confederates moving cannons and men across the valley a mile away. They seemed to be massing directly across from General Meade's headquarters. In mid-afternoon, Roque and Dan took sandwiches for lunch to a shady spot in a little copse of trees near a stone fence where they could watch the Rebel preparations. They'd barely finished tucking in when all of the cannons in the Army of Northern Virginia began firing on them. Shells screamed overhead and exploded harmlessly behind the ridge.

"They must think the army reserve is back there," Roque opined.

"Maybe they just haven't got the range," Dan said.

Rebel guns did adjust their fire but still didn't do much damage considering the number of guns. The Union returned fire, and soon the air was full of sulfur reeking smoke, exploding shells, fragments, and shot. Never before had so many guns fired at each other. An avalanche of sound assaulted the two friends.

Roque covered his ears. "It is like being in a cloud during a thunderstorm. I see nothing but fog and flashes, and the thunder never stops."

Dan shouted back at his friend. "It's like we were hiding under a metal tub in a hail storm."

Here and there, a cannon was hit or a man went down, but for all the noise and smoke and flame, very few of the things flying through the air found their mark. Then the thundering cacophony was over as suddenly as it started.

They'd taken cover behind the low stone wall in the small gap between two regiments. All around them, men in blue stood up and leaned on their weapons looking out across the valley.

An officer commented, "The barrage didn't last very long."

Roque pointed. "Here they come!"

A mile away tens of thousands of men were dressing their lines and starting the long, slow march toward the Union position.

"They're all coming for us!" yelled Roque.

Dan looked and thought his friend was right. All of those units seemed to be focusing on the little copse of trees behind them. As the Rebels moved forward, the ones on the flanks moved in toward center and the front narrowed directly in front of Dan's position. Dan saw an officer on a horse. He'd be a certain target. That brave man would die, he thought. The colors of more units than Dan could count moved toward him. An enemy officer held his sword aloft with his hat pinned to the tip for his men to follow.

Dan's mind raced. What had he done? Could they

know? Were they coming for the Menorah? Did they know the location of Meade's headquarters? Were they coming for him?

Nearby two colonels talked. "Well, they've tried both flanks and didn't break us. General Lee must think we sent the reserves out and weakened our center."

"Yes," said the other, "he seems to be trying the center. I expect he's in for an ugly surprise. He'll make a lot of Southern widows this day."

Grim veterans were chasing the boys who beat on drums and played the fife from their lines. Sent to the rear, they would assist the regimental bandsmen, who even now were starting to come forward with stretchers to carry away the wounded to the rear. That was their job in combat. In the fighting lines, movements were precise and practiced. Men checked percussion caps and cartridge boxes. Here and there a man honed a bayonet, but mostly they watched, watched the jaunty Rebel colors and the symmetry of the approaching lines of men. They'd seen the *Elephant* before and were gauging the professionalism and esprit of the enemy. The intensity of the coming fight would depend on how serious the Rebels were about pushing the assault.

Half a mile to Dan's front was a tall, rail fence, six foot high at least. The first regiments tried to push it over but couldn't. Then pressed by men behind, they began to climb. As they climbed the Union artillery added its music to the affray. Grape and canister flew, and groups of men disappeared from the top rail in clouds of pink mist. Rebel artillery replied with counter-battery fire aimed at Union guns. The Rebel line surged forward and continued, thinner and more ragged than it had been. Behind the lead regiments, men were assisting their wounded friends to the rear and something else. Some men were just turning back, already knowing there was no point in going forward.

Dan learned later from a newspaper that this fight was called Pickett's Charge. Young General Pickett, about Dan's age with curly blonde locks, was out there somewhere leading his division and most of Longstreet's Corps.

When the enemy was 400 yards away, Union rifled-muskets opened fire and fired continuously thereafter. At first, they nibbled at the Confederate lines and then they took large bites. The enemy continued forward though many turned back, limping or helping injured friends; they headed back to safety away from the deadly fire. Two hundred yards away, Pickett's men began to fire, and then they ran forward to give the bayonet to soldiers in blue. They ran up the long slow slope losing momentum, tiring as they came and gasping for breath. They yelled and thrust with bayonets, no time to reload.

They came right up to the angle of the stone fence behind which Roque and Dan crouched. Union men rose to confront them in the angle, striking with rifle butts and ball. The smoke around them grew thick. The artillery fired over their heads. Men screamed and died. Then the firing became slower, less intense, and as the smoke cleared, Dan saw the Rebels' backs. They were limping back across the long mile over which they'd come, dragging comrades and themselves.

They wouldn't rally for another try. They were done. They'd done their best, more than anyone could believe. They'd come all the way to the Union line before they were driven back. A ragged cheer went up in strange harmony: part thankfulness at being alive, part gratitude at having won, and part warning to the Rebs not to come back.

The soldiers in blue knew and the Rebs knew, the Confederacy was beaten, not just the Army of Northern Virginia. There on that day with Pickett in the van, the Confederacy lost the war. Until then, the outcome was uncertain. There might have been a negotiated peace and separation into two countries, but the war dragged on. The Rebel was tough and tenacious and thought himself defending home, rights, and family, but he would never again threaten the Union as he had this day.

Before Dan, the grass was stained red with their blood. Their dead lay there and their wounded too injured to walk. They moaned and lay or tried to crawl, but many more lay still forever.

The stretcher bearers were all around Dan and Roque, carrying Union men to the hospitals. Union men would be taken first and then the Rebels.

A general, only days in command, uncertain of himself, and untrusted by his subordinates had found courage, confidence, and the faith of his men.

Chapter 20

Hard Road Home

Exodus 34:

> [34]But whenever Moses went in before the Lord to speak with Him, he would take the veil off until he came out; and he would come out and speak to the children of Israel whatever he had been commanded. [35]And whenever the children of Israel saw the face of Moses, that the skin of Moses' face shone, then Moses would put the veil on his face again, until he went in to speak with Him.

It was days before Dan and Roque could leave Gettysburg. The Army of Northern Virginia took a while to limp back through the passes to the far side of the mountains, back the way they'd come. Some people criticized General Meade for not pursuing the Confederates and making an end of them then and there. Those people had no idea how much the Union Army of the Potomac had suffered under General Lee's kind ministrations.

Meade could have pursued into those mountain passes, and the Rebel rear guard would have chewed his best formations to dust. He might have slid around the flank to Harper's Ferry with his back to the river. Dan couldn't imagine how he could have moved faster than Lee, who was half a day ahead of him, but he might have. The two armies would have found themselves in another contest like the one they'd just endured and the outcome would have been the same. The means did not yet exist to end the battle decisively. Armies couldn't maneuver fast enough, couldn't cut each other off from their base, so they just beat on each other until they tired. Whichever army took the initiative and attacked would take the greater losses. Lee attacked at Gettysburg, and he lost.

Dan turned to Roque. "I don't mean to minimize General Meade's accomplishment in any way. He made the right moves and found it in himself to inspire his men."

Roque agreed. "General Robert Lee entered the battle with a significant advantage; his generals were legendary heroes who wore plumed hats and wore their hair long and curly. *Magnifico!* Their reputation was as miracle workers who never lost. They were like the conquistadors of old, like El Cid."

The Army of Northern Virginia entered the field invincible and limped away licking terrible wounds that would never heal. They were broken, they had lost. General Meade proved that Lee could be beaten.

Dan and Roque saw no reason to return to Washington. When the way was clear, they rode west toward the setting sun. Dan grew morose again, awash in thoughts of the lost Sebriana.

As they ate and drank in a tavern, Dan imbibed too much. Roque overheard him sob. "I will never see my *Doña Loca* again. Sebriana, the wealthy widow and crypto-Jew is gone, her bones never to mix with those of her ancestors in the tiny churchyard of a small adobe chapel. She is lost to me forever. I am empty and alone."

"Amigo," said Roque, "think of what we have done. Think what she accomplished and what we have accomplished."

Dan sobbed. "I do not exult in what we have done. The cost has been too high."

Dan collapsed and Roque carried his friend to bed.

The summer countryside robed in green speckled with flowers should have been cheering. Men made sure it was not. They were stopped many times per day, by suspicious locals who thought they might be Rebel deserters, spies or, worst of all, deserters from one of the armies wanting food, plunder, and women. They were stopped by Union patrols who demanded to know their business thinking them deserters or Rebel spies.

As they entered southern Ohio and Indiana, they came to "butternut" country. Butternuts were backcountry migrants from the South whose sympathies still lay with the Confederacy. They were called "butternut" from the homemade dye they used on their homespun clothes. They hated Mr. Lincoln and were one of his disloyal headaches along with Irish immigrants and others in the North who opposed the war.

Once Dan explained the politics to Roque, the Mexican said, "We better not show our papers to these buttery nuts, I think. We show them a letter from Mr. Lincoln, I think we get killed."

Aware of Dan's mood, Roque tried to cheer him.

"Danito," he began, "we did it. We recovered the treasure no one else could find. We got the treasures to Señor Lincoln, and now he is winning the war!"

"Are you sure?" Dan asked feeling disagreeable. "Did Colonel Chamberlain yell "fix bayonets" and "charge" because we were there with the Menorah? Or did he manage on his own not even knowing we were there? Is that how it works, spreading a magic aura around itself? I could understand if men saw it there and took courage from it, but they would have to see it and know what it was."

"General Meade saw it!" Roque insisted. "And he won a great battle."

"He didn't really know what it was we'd given him," Dan replied.

"So?" Roque looked at his friend puzzled. "The thing had *Power* in itself like Rojo has been telling us."

Dan looked him in the face. "Then deriving the benefit didn't require faith? Didn't Rojo tell us you had to have faith in *Power*?"

The Mexican looked at his friend quizzically. Roque was not a philosopher. Big ideas and complex questions made his head hurt. Despite intellectual shortcomings, he had a real knack for processing them as smaller bits of knowledge and stumbling upon profound answers.

Dan mumbled. "Jesus said something about he who seeks will find. Have you found something, Roque?"

Roque's brows knit as he looked at Dan with glinting eyes. "All this time you have been telling me the treasure had saved our lives. It saved us from Greasy Bill and from the river pirates, not to mention Morgan and his railroad raiders. You were sure it was *Power* that told Colonel Chamberlain to fix bayonets and charge when he was out of cartridges."

Dan shook his head. "Don't you see, Roque? The cost is too high. Sebriana is dead."

"One woman dies," said Roque, "but the Union survives. She would have thought it a fair bargain."

Dan looked him hard in the face. "The venture has

been a bloodbath from start to finish. Verde is gone, too. Think of all the soldiers that died on the battlefield at Gettysburg. It was as if all of New Mexico had been slain. And while we're at it, let's count Greasy Bill and his minions, the river pirates, the Danites, the Penitentes and even the Knights of the Golden Circle."

"Amigo," said Roque, "they all made choices, some of them very bad and evil choices. You can't blame God for that. Greasy Bill, the Danites, the river pirates, they all needed killing. The Knights of the Golden Circle claimed high ideals but followed an evil code."

Dan challenged him. "What about the Penitentes, huh? They were very pious and flagellated themselves to prove how much God loved them and they loved Him."

"*Mijo*," said Roque, "do you really think that a man who beats himself to prove God's love for him is on the right track? I think he must be confused and following the wrong leaders. Even Padre Martinez admitted as much when he blessed us. Compadre, God answers prayer, even if sometimes the answer is no."

"Yeah," Dan replied, "and sometimes the answer is: 'Shove off! I couldn't care less.'"

"Danito," Roque went on, "your faith has always been strong, an inspiration to all of us."

A tear fell from Dan's eye. "Sebriana was my inspiration. The price is too high."

Not wanting to talk anymore, Dan spurred his horse on ahead, leaving Roque to bring the slower pack animals. Separated, they arrived at a small village in southern Indiana, little more than a dozen houses, three stores, and a church.

A man came running out. "I'm the sheriff," he said. "What's your business here?"

"Just passing through," Dan replied as Roque caught

up. Men were beginning to gather around them.

"How do I know you're not deserters?" demanded the sheriff.

"I've got these papers," Dan said, "that allow us free passage." He handed them to the sheriff.

The other citizens eyed Dan and Roque's pack animals and horses hungrily. Dan recalled that this part of Indiana had been home to another sort of river pirate. Around 1800, they ran a tavern of sorts and lured in travelers. Once in the tavern, they got the travelers drunk and then dispatched them, taking their goods. Dan couldn't recall if they'd ever been captured and punished. It seemed to him that the ships on the river had gotten bigger and were too much for these pirates to handle.

"What have you got in the packs?" demanded one of the men in the tightening circle.

"These papers," said the sheriff loudly, "say they have permission from Abraham Lincoln himself to travel anywhere they want. All Union officers are to provide all the assistance they can."

"Abraham Lincoln!" called a voice from the pressing crowd. "They must be Union spies."

"They've come to spy us out," said another voice. "Hang 'em!"

Voices chorused, "Hang 'em!"

Dan and Roque were too engaged to take much notice. In a trice, they were dragged from their saddles, knocked to the ground, and had their hands bound behind them. Their weapons were taken. The villagers were impressed by the number they carried and by the size of Dan's Bowie.

"Where's the judge?" said the sheriff. "We've got to make it legal."

"Here I am," said a white haired man. "What are they

accused of?"

"They've come to spy on us," said the sheriff. "These papers prove it."

"Have you anything to say in your defense?" asked the judge.

"Not guilty!" said Roque and Dan together.

"Guilty!" said the judge. "Carry out the sentence, sheriff."

The sheriff had them loaded back on their horses and nooses thrown over a tree limb slipped around their necks.

"Roque," Dan said, "it's been a privilege to know you. You've been a good amigo and compadre."

"You, too, Danito," said Roque. "You are the best of friends." He seemed almost cheerful.

Dan continued, "I lack the will to fight anymore. This was a ridiculous end to a ridiculous adventure that has cost Sebriana her life. It is fitting that I should die, too. It's like I said, no Divine Providence protects us. If it ever did, *Power* has departed."

"Shut up, you two," said the sheriff. "In a minute, I'll let you say your last words."

"Stop!" said a voice thundering like the voice of God. A man in black broadcloth wearing a clerical collar ran up to the sheriff. "Stop! Get them down."

"Can't do that," said the sheriff. "The judge has already passed sentence." There was a murmur of assent from the crowd.

"I am directed by a higher law," pronounced the man in black broadcloth. There was a sharp intake of breath from the crowd. "I was at my prayers when it came to me that we would be visited by two who had carried messages for the Lord."

"They don't look like angels to me," said someone in the throng.

"You should have seen how they were armed," said the sheriff. "Ain't no angel goes armed like that."

"Nonetheless," said the man in the clerical collar, "they are His and to slay them would be sacrilege and would bring destruction on our village."

Just then Roque's horse bolted and left him hanging.

Dan shook his head. "I warned him about riding too spirited a horse."

Roque gasped and swung and choked until someone had the presence of mind to cut the rope that suspended him. He got to his feet still choking from the tight noose around his neck, hands still bound behind and ready to take on all comers. Hopping on one leg he succeeded in giving swift kicks to two of their assailants and then smashed the sheriff's nose with his forehead. Blood spurted, and the sheriff howled. Roque bared his teeth.

Dan didn't want to see what was coming.

"Get him down!" yelled the man in black pointing at Dan. "Untie them. Release them." The skin of the preacher's face shone. It was unnatural and beautiful to behold, powerful. There was *Power* in his voice, as well, for the crowd obeyed him without question. "Restore their possessions. Now, be gone! Return to your homes. I wish to speak to these men."

The preacher escorted them through the village and beyond. As they went, he talked. "I am a sinful man. I have supported these people in the evil things that they do. They waylay travelers and kill them to take their goods. It's been going on a very long time. I have fooled myself by allowing them to convince me that the ones they took had committed some crime, they were thieves, raiders, deserters or spies. I knew they were taking travelers who appeared to have some wealth. I knew that was the reason.

"Today as I prayed," he continued, "something came over me. I knew I had to save you. All my prayers in the past years have been a sham..." He broke down sobbing and could not continue. Beyond the town, he waved farewell still unable to speak, still sobbing, his shining face wet with tears.

"See!" said Roque. "Didn't I tell you? I was praying, too. He watches over us, amigo."

"Roque," Dan said, turning in his saddle to make sure they weren't being followed, "I wouldn't be surprised if that town has a revival."

The rest of their journey was uneventful. Having seen that they were protected, Dan was only slightly less melancholy. It could all be happenstance. Sebriana's death was real. Did he have faith? The price was too high.

At St. Louis, they found Captain John-Paul Perry in port ready to head back up the Missouri carrying military stores. Sergeant Hawkey was with him, still serving as military escort although the danger of river pirates had greatly decreased in the past months. They greeted Dan and Roque like lost brothers with questions about their adventures. Time and again Dan and Roque told about meeting President Lincoln, about Colonel Chamberlain's bayonet charge that saved the Union Army, and about Pickett's charge that lost a war. Dan remained taciturn and morose. The telling and retelling was almost enough to make him cheerful in spite of himself. Time passed, good time, as the riverboat moved slowly up the Missouri surrounded by the green of summer. The scent of flowers drifted across the water. Captain Perry had taken on a Chinese cook, and even the food was good.

Dan watched day after day as the little Chinese taught Roque to fish. Their lines dangled over the side catching their dinner. Both cheered and slapped each other on the back when they caught something good or large. The Chinese almost got pulled overboard by one fish. Roque grabbed him in time, and the two of them fought the leviathan onboard. It was an ugly catfish as big as Roque's little friend.

"Good eat!" said the Chinaman grinning manically.

Not long after, Roque and Dan stood in the bows enjoying the cool spray as Independence hove into sight. A green gnome was fishing from the wharf. Dan rubbed his eyes in disbelief.

"Danito," said Roque pointing, "an *abuelo* is fishing from that dock."

"An *abuelo*, Roque?" Dan asked puzzled. "What is that? I don't think I've heard the word before."

"You know," he replied, "like a goblin that punishes little children when they are bad. He usually carries a whip. I didn't know they had them this far east or that they were green, or that they liked to fish."

About then, the *abuelo* saw them and started jumping about waving his green hat in the air.

As they got closer, Verde called out from the wharf, "Danny-boy, Roque, well then, aye, ye've returned to the bosom of your waiting companions. I'll drink to that."

"But, Verde," Dan interjected astounded, "you're walking and not just walking, dancing about like a happy leprechaun."

"And why shouldn't a lad dance," he replied, "who sees his boon companions return to the fold? A jig surely seems in order and a gallon or two of whiskey, at your expense, of course."

"Last time we saw you," Dan replied, "you were in bed with your leg half shot off and the doctor was saying you'd never walk and he might have to cut the thing off."

Roque grinned, "Maybe he's dancing on a fancy

wooden leg." He pulled his gun and took aim at the offending member. "I could put a few holes in it to find out."

"Hold on there, bucko," said Verde, "I can explain."

"So explain," Dan said.

"It was her dying wish," Verde said, "your sweet Sebriana. She told the doctor about the Chimayo clay, that miracle clay, in her pack but he was not inclined to listen. He wouldn't have no part of it at all. He wouldn't feed it to me until she was almost gone and made it her dying wish. Next day I was up and around, right as a new fiddle bow."

Tears ran down Dan's face, and he choked up hearing of her death.

"Sometimes, amigo, God's answer to prayer is no." Roque, ever more practical, asked, "What of the other friends we left you with?"

"Now that's a grand tale," said Verde. "Rojo now goes by Don Peregrino Rojo. The locals think he's a Spanish grandee, and they've elected him marshal, they have, sure as mushrooms grow in cow manure. They say he has two invisible deputies who are like the wee fairies of legend and go about making passed-out drunks comfortable in the night and seeing they come to no harm.

"The town had a real problem," Verde went on, "what with strangers always about and many of them rough and desperate men as well. They'd roll drunks for fun and waylay people in the evening. But, no more. The invisible deputies have made them disappear. Sometimes their bodies show up in the river, if they catch a snag, with their throats slit from ear to ear. But usually they are far downstream by the dawning."

"Invisible deputies?" said Roque quizzically.

"I would venture to guess," Verde replied, "that there

are four of them and they have Jicarilla names, but who am I to be pointing fingers?"

"Don't the local Southerners," Dan asked, "resent a Spanish grandee being marshal?"

"And so they do, too," replied Verde. "They come up from the south all the time to take out the marshal as he makes his rounds. But when the sun rises, the marshal is still here and they're not. In my opinion, it's the work of the invisible deputies."

Just then the sun shone through passing summer clouds throwing a spotlight on a woman approaching them on the street.

"But you said she was dead!" Dan exclaimed.

"Me? Never!" replied Verde, "I said t'was her dying wish to have the Chimayo clay. Doctor wouldn't give it to her until she was dying. Fixed her right up! Good as new."

Dan ran to her and she to him. She threw her arms around his neck and legs about his body. She kissed him hard and long. He wrapped arms tight about her. He held Sebriana and knew he would never want to let her go.

"Sebriana, will you marry me?"

Roque looked at Verde. "And sometimes the answer is yes."

fin

Behind and Beyond the Story

Is the *Mystery of Chaco Canyon* an historical fiction? It falls within the definition. The description of battles and events is accurate. Historical figures speak their lines in keeping with their roles and character. Even the mysteries are described accurately, though the solutions posited are novel.

Archaeologists pose numerous questions concerning the ruins at Chaco Canyon and the people who built them though many of these contradict each other. Chaco has seven large, over 400 rooms, D-shaped pueblos and many more built to another pattern. It is believed that Chaco was abandoned due to drought and that people came and settled at Chaco who had left Mesa Verde for the same reason. There are two large D-shaped pueblos at Aztec, New Mexico, near the San Juan and Mancos Rivers. They were occupied at a later time than Chaco. Pueblo Bonito, Casa Rinconada (the great kiva and Temple of the story), Aztec Ruins and Casas Grandes in Chihuahua, Mexico, all fall on one meridian. The side of the kiva at Chimney Rock in Colorado does align with the two rocks to form a sort of gun sight. Chaco is at the heart of a civilization that extends around it in all directions. Pottery from all of these outliers is found at Chaco. Vigas had to be brought 40 miles from the mountains to a spot with little water and less farmland between villages often less than a half mile apart. Most of the rooms at Chaco show little sign of occupation, no blackening of vigas from cook and heating fires. There are few graves. But there are roads, roads that run straight and climb canyon walls on stairs.

The Decalogue Stone and Tetragrammaton, the Ten Commandments and the Name of God, at Hidden Mountain near Los Lunas are real. They were presented to the world by Frank Hibben in 1933. He said that he had been shown the stone by a local who had first seen it in 1880. The inscription is in an ancient Hebrew text unknown in the 1930s but related closely to Phoenician. Hibben came to be known as "Fibbin' Hibbin" in archaeological circles. He excavated Sandia Cave near Albuquerque discovering 25,000 year-old Sandia Man. However, at that time the powerful editor of American Anthropologist believed that 12,000 year-old Clovis Man had been the first human in North America and this belief persisted into the 1990s. It has since been learned that humans were here 25,000 years ago, so Hibbin may not have been fibbin'.

Painted Cave high in the Mustang Mountains was recorded by archaeologists in 1983 who failed to notice Rough Hurech's grave with its inscription in English runes. The runes appear to be authentic but may have been drawn from Tolkien. Who can say? That archaeologists failed to notice them is not surprising. They didn't "fit," so they must be a hoax. I've been with a party recording rock art in the Chiricahua Mountains that recorded Chinese characters as Indian work. I told them I could read what they said, but still they wouldn't believe. I'm not saying they were inscribed by crewmen from Cheng Ho's seventh voyage in the early fifteenth century, but they were Chinese. There was, by the way, a Chinese Nestorian Christian church remnant of the early expansion of Christianity in Shanghai as late as 400 years ago. The description of the Senior Warden's throne with its symbol carved in the rock and the "map-stone" down below is accurate.

The Silverbell or Tucson artifacts, 31 items cast in lead, presenting dates of 790 to 900 A.D. are on display at the Arizona History Museum in Tucson. These leaden objects were uncovered in 1924. Coronado's route took him close to many of these sites in 1540 on his entrada. He went to Zuñi and never saw Chaco with its seven cities. People who built stone villages did live in the Grand Canyon and Mountain Men did report little men who spoke Welsh and hid in caves. The Utes, or Utahs, recognized these little men who dwelt in caves as holy. The rock art of the Grand Canyon depicts tall men in robes who look remarkably like the Hebrew priests described in Exodus, Leviticus and Numbers.

Roslyn, the Newport Tower, and Westford Knight are well known and I'll say no more about them. Nor about the Knights of the Golden Circle who were active in Texas in 1860 and 1861 and of whom much has been written.

Albert Pike was an important Freemason who organized the Scottish Rite and wrote much on Masonic thought. He had some very peculiar ideas. He fought for the Confederacy as a general and was accused of atrocities. *Born in Blood: the Lost Secrets of Freemasonry*, John J. Robinson, 1989, popular with Freemasons, gives an interesting account of the origins of the Masonic Order. I have provided a disjointed account of the ritual of Freemasonry. It is available in many sources. I do not feel I have revealed any secrets which include recognition symbols and the ritual itself. The ritual is secret so that when an initiate participates for the first time, the mystery may impact him fully. Joseph Smith, founder of the LDS church, was made a "Mason on Sight" by the Grand Master of the Grand Lodge of Illinois. This means that he did not need to pass through the ritual or learn the proficiencies before being Raised. He in turn began raising all his Mormon converts as Masons on Sight which is a privilege reserved to the Grand Master. He was told to stop and didn't and was ejected from the order. He took a degraded form of the Masonic Ritual and made it his Temple Ritual. Mormon holy or temple undergarments bear Masonic symbols. As to the theology of the LDS church, I take *No Man Knows My History, the Life of Joseph Smith*, Fawn Brodie, 1945, as my source. *Blood of the Prophets*, 2002, and *The Mormon Rebellion*, 2011, by Will Bagley, provide information on the Danites and the Mountain Meadows Massacre. The name Danites was not always used by the church for their enforcers of the faith and militia, but this military force always existed in some form and its excesses were the cause of expulsions in Illinois and Missouri. Brigham Young may not have been pursuing the Ark of the Covenant, but he did bring his people to Deseret (parts of California, Colorado, Wyoming, Idaho, Arizona, and New Mexico and all of Utah and Nevada) to found a new Temple and Zion with people who, he claimed, were genetically the Children of Israel. The LDS faith places Hebrew refugees of the Babylonian invasion in the New World.

The Penitentes of New Mexico are well known and their origins are as lost as those of the Freemasons. During the first half of the nineteenth century, they came to prominence providing much needed religious services in a land with very few priests. There are indications that they arrived with Coronado's entrada and returned with that of Oñate bringing medieval ceremonies and concepts.

The Mystery of the Copper Scroll of Qumran, Robert Feather, 1999, provides information on some of the treasures discussed particularly the treasure recovered by the Templars in the Land of Goshen, Egypt. *God's Gold: a Quest for the Lost Temple Treasures of Jerusalem,* 2007, Sean Kingsley, provides an account of the Menorah, Trumpets of Truth, and Table of the Showbread that extends back to the Babylonian sack of Jerusalem in 584 B.C. up to the return of the items to Jerusalem.

Henry Sibley provided the only strategic plan the Confederacy ever had for winning the Civil War. Basically, he proposed using two regiments of Texas militia to invade New Mexico in the summer of 1861, taking supplies from each of the Union forts in Texas, receiving supplies from merchants in Franklin (El Paso) and moving on to take Union supply depots at Fort Craig and Fort Union. New Mexicans hostile to the Union would rise to join him. In southern Colorado, Confederate sympathizers would rise and then Utah would fall since the Mormons hated the Union. Finally, Confederate sympathizers would help him take southern California. The Confederacy would be a continental power with supplies of specie to fight the war and harbors that could not be blockaded. In the spring of 1861, General Davy Twiggs surrendered the Union forts in Texas and they were stripped. The merchants failed to come up with supplies. Lieutenant Colonel John Baylor invaded New Mexico in the summer of 1861, giving the Union ample warning and time to organize while managing to offend North and South alike with his order to poison Indians. He also conscripted Union men and employed Roy Bean, a gangster before he was a judge. The Texas militia only existed on paper. Sibley spent months organizing two regiments and finding them arms. Some were armed only with lances. It was winter before he could proceed and that is a poor time to cross the western deserts. His men arrived at Mesilla ragged, hungry and with many of their mounts unable to continue. New Mexicans had a deeper hatred of Texans than the Union. Union forces organized in Colorado and California. Sibley had lost before he got to Valverde where he won the fords but failed to capture Fort Craig. It was a pyrrhic victory at best. Sibley is believed to have suffered from kidney stones during the campaign and to have attempted to ease the pain with alcohol. He won a reputation as a drunk. Although Sebriana may not have served as a nurse at Fort Craig, man for man the battle was the bloodiest of the Civil War.

Colonel William Scurry took what was left of the force to Glorieta Pass intending to descend on a virtually undefended Fort Union. The forced march of Colonel John Slough's volunteers, the Pike's Peakers, saved the fort and Slough went on to face the Confederates at the pass against the orders of the senior active duty officer present. The first day he was driven back. The second he gave a third of force to Major John Chivington to ascend the mesa and descend on the Confederate flank at the sound of battle. Chivington got lost and then discovered himself above the Confederate trains. He dallied for two hours until finally Captains Lewis and Wynkoop attacked and destroyed the trains. The captains wanted to place their men to block the upper end of the canyon so that the Confederate force would be caught between two Union forces. Chivington would not allow it, afraid he would be overwhelmed. The major ordered the destruction of livestock and the retreat to the mesa. Later, he billed himself as the hero of Glorieta Pass. Slough resigned his commission. Chivington was promoted to colonel and conducted the attack on friendly chief Black Kettle's camp to the just horror of a nation.

In July of 1861, the army pulled out of Arizona, which was still part of Doña Ana County, New Mexico Territory. In August, the settlers along Sonoita Creekm with no soldiers left to feed and buy their produce, pulled back to Tubac for safety just before the town was attacked by Apaches. As the Indians pulled back, the people left only to watch Mexican bandits move in and loot and burn the town. Moses Carson, Kit's elder half-brother, and Great Western Sarah Bowman were with them. Forming a caravan they retreated toward the Rio Grande only to be ambushed by Cochise and Mangas Coloradas at Cooke's Canyon. The Arizona Guards were conscripted by Colonel Baylor. Paddy Graydon, a former NCO, ran the Boundary Hotel in 1861, three miles south of Fort Buchanan providing all the services a soldier couldn't get at the sutler's store. He was made a captain during the war and ran a Spies and Guides (scout) company.

At Gettysburg, Colonel Chamberlain of the 20th Maine, conducted a bayonet charge when his men ran out of ammunition, and saved the Union army by preventing its flank from being turned. Half of his men were mutineers turned over to him to be guarded or shot as he saw fit. His action ranks as one of the greatest tales of leadership and tactics in American Army history. General George Meade had just taken command of the army and lacked the confidence of his generals. His decision to allow them to voice their opinions in counsel won them to his side.

Butternuts, Southerners living in Illinois and Indiana, posed difficulties for Abraham Lincoln. The Baltimore and Ohio Railroad was attacked by Confederate forces. From the Mexican War to the Civil War, volunteers called their first battle 'seeing the elephant.' Suffolk County, the eastern end of Long Island, New York, is culturally part of New England and is referred to by the natives as 'Out East.'

In the eighteenth century, the French invaded New Mexico seeking gold at Wolf Creek Pass near Treasure Falls within sight of Pagosa hot springs and Chimney Rock. The expedition came to grief but the accounts are muddled. In 1860, Tom Jeffords participated in a minor gold rush in this area before seeking gold in Arizona.

What became of the Ark and other Temple treasures after President Lincoln's time? Perhaps they reside in some obscure government warehouse or are enshrined in some private viewing room where only the wealthy and senior government leaders can see them like some private art collection closed to the public because many of the pieces were obtained by foul means. The United States rose from obscurity to lead the world and serve as a model constitutional republic, a beacon to all people. Men, women and children flooded to her shores passing the green lady, Liberty. The nation grew wealthy, powerful and free. And then, men who hated God slowly took over the mechanisms of government.

Praise for *Massacre at Point of Rocks*

Historian Will Gorenfeld said: Very readable and informative. Your knowledge and description of Aubrey's train, the men, the countryside is, thus far, superb as is Grier's failed attempt to rescue Mrs. White.

Author Gerald Summers said: Doug Hocking has done himself proud. His writing flows smoothly, his historical references are spot on, and his action exciting. I recently read Kit Carson's autobiography and found it to be one of the most interesting historical presentations I've ever read. And that is saying something, for I have studied western history for many years. Doug has captured much of this famous man and his exploits and deserves much credit for bringing him and his other wonderful characters to life. I thoroughly enjoyed this book.

Jicarilla Apache teacher from Dulce, NM, on the Jicarilla Reservation said: Written by a resident of the community - interesting story line. Reading parts to my Middle and High School classes in hopes to spark their reading interests.

Shar Porier of the Sierra Vista Herald said: It [reveals] an historical view of the life and times in New Mexico in the 1840s and '50s in a novel story, written just as one produced by western authors of the past. It is hard to set the book aside.

Greg Coar: Just finished your book. Saved it for the trip home. Loved it. Hope there is more to come. Great to meet you and your wife in Tombstone. Keep the history coming.

Dac Crassley of the Old West Daily Reader: As you know, I have a considerable interest in Western History and enough knowledge to make me dangerous. And I read a lot because of my research for Old West Daily Reader. This book was comfortable, like worn in buckskins or one's favorite Levis. Everything felt right. The story unfolded in a coherent and, for me, personal fashion. I truly appreciated and enjoyed your obvious care in building the historical background of the tale. Characters were fleshed out, real, believable. I could picture the landscapes. The trail dust...Ok, I really liked the book! Great accomplishment and a fine telling!

Rahm E. Sandoux, *Desert Tracks* (OCTA) reviewer: Doug Hocking's *Massacre at Point of Rocks* is a fascinating story of historic events along the Santa Fe Trail in 1849. Setting the White massacre and captivity in context, Hocking reveals to readers the ethnic side of of the frontier, showing how Indians, Mexicans, and blacks were just as much a part of that historical tapestry as the white men were. He brings characters like Kit Carson, Grier, Comancheros, and the Jicarilla Apaches to life, revealing how tough life was on the frontier for all of its inhabitants. *Massacre at Point of Rocks* will definitely be of interest to readers who want to learn more about the history of New Mexico and the Santa Fe Trail.

Doug Hocking grew up on the Jicarilla Apache Reservation in the Rio Arriba (Northern New Mexico). He attended reservation schools, an Ivy League prep school, and graduated from high school at McCurdy in Santa Cruz, New Mexico, in the Penitente heartland among *paisonos* and *Indios*. Doug enlisted in Army Intelligence and worked in Taiwan, Thailand and at the Pentagon. Returning home he studied Social Anthropology (Ethnography) and then returned to the Army as an Armored Cavalry officer (scout) completing his career by instructing Military Intelligence lieutenants in intelligence analysis and the art of war.

He earned a master's degree with honors in American History and completed field school in Historical Archaeology. Since leaving the Army, he has worked with allied officers and taught at Cochise College where he created the college's culinary arts program. He is now an independent scholar residing in southern Arizona near Tombstone with his wife, dogs, a feral cat and a friendly coyote. He is on the board of the Southern Chapter of the Arizona Historical Society and of Westerners Inter-national and is Sheriff of the Bisbee Corral of the Westerners.

Doug began writing a few years ago and has published in *Wild West, True West, Buckskin Bulletin* and *Roundup Magazine.* His photographs have appeared in the *Arizona Republic, Tucson Star* and *Sacramento Bee* as well as in numerous magazines. His short story "Marshal of Arizona" appears in La Frontera's *Outlaws and Lawmen* anthology, a second, "The Bounty," appears in *Dead or Alive,* a third, "Echo Amphitheater," in *Broken Promises.* His first novel, *Massacre at Point of Rocks*, is available from Amazon and from his website www.doughocking.com. He is working on a biography of *Tom Jeffords, Cochise's Friend.*

www.doughocking.com

https://www.facebook.com/pages/Doug-Hocking-Author-Page

https://www.youtube.com/user/DougHocking